Mary Jane Holmes

Millbank ; or Roger Irving's Ward

A Novel

Mary Jane Holmes

Millbank ; or Roger Irving's Ward
A Novel

ISBN/EAN: 9783337000684

Printed in Europe, USA, Canada, Australia, Japan

Cover: Foto ©Andreas Hilbeck / pixelio.de

More available books at **www.hansebooks.com**

OR,

ROGER IRVING'S WARD.

𝔄 𝔑𝔬𝔳𝔢𝔩.

BY

MRS. MARY J. HOLMES,

AUTHOR OF

TEMPEST AND SUNSHINE. — 'LENA RIVERS. — MARIAN GREY. — MEADOW-
BROOK. — ENGLISH ORPHANS. — COUSIN MAUDE. — HOMESTEAD.
— DORA DEANE. — DARKNESS AND DAYLIGHT. — HUGH
WORTHINGTON. — THE CAMERON PRIDE. — ROSE
MATHER. — ETHELYN'S MISTAKE. — ETC.
— ETC.

NEW YORK:

G. W. Carleton & Co., Publishers

LONDON: S. LOW, SON & CO.

M.DCCC.LXXII.

CONTENTS.

MILLBANK;

OR,

ROGER IRVING'S WARD.

CHAPTER I.

EXPECTING ROGER.

EVERY window and shutter at Millbank was closed. Knots of crape were streaming from the bell-knobs, and all around the house there was that deep hush which only the presence of death can inspire. Indoors there was a kind of twilight gloom pervading the rooms, and the servants spoke in whispers whenever they came near the chamber where the old squire lay in his handsome coffin, waiting the arrival of Roger, who had been in St. Louis when his father died, and who was expected home on the night when our story opens. Squire Irving had died suddenly in the act of writing to his boy Roger, and when found by old Aleck, his hand was grasping the pen, and his head was resting on the letter he would never finish. "Heart disease" was the verdict of the inquest, and then the electric wires carried the news of his decease to Roger, and to the widow of the squire's eldest son, who lived on Lexington avenue, New York, and who always called herself Mrs. Walter Scott Irving, fancying that in some way the united names of two so illustrious authors as Irving and Scott shed a kind of literary halo upon one who bore them.

1*

Mrs. Walter Scott Irving had been breakfasting in her back parlor when the news came to her of her father-in-law's sudden death, and to say that she was both astonished and shocked, is only to do her justice, but to insinuate that she was sorry, is quite another thing. She was not sorry, though her smooth white brow contracted into wrinkles, and she tried to speak very sadly and sorrowfully as she said to her son Frank, a boy of nine or more, —

"Frank, your grandfather is dead ; poor man, you'll never see him again."

Frank *was* sorry. The happiest days of his life had been spent at Millbank. He liked the house, and the handsome grounds, with the grand old woods in the rear, and the river beyond, where in a little sheltered nook lay moored the boat he called his own. He liked the spotted pony which he always rode. He liked the freedom from restraint which he found in the country, and he liked the old man who was so kind to him, and who petted him sometimes when Roger was not by. Roger had been absent on the occasion of Frank's last visit to Millbank, and his grandfather had taken more than usual notice of him, — had asked him many questions as to what he meant to be when he grew to manhood, and what he would do, supposing he should some day be worth a great deal of money. Would he keep it, or would he spend it as fast and as foolishly as his father had spent the portion allotted to him ?

"You'd keep it, wouldn't you, and put it at interest ? " his mother had said, laying her hand upon his hair with a motion which she meant should convey some suggestion or idea to his mind.

But Frank had few ideas of his own. He never took hints or suggestions, and boy-like he answered :

"I'd buy a lot of horses, and Roger and me would set up a circus out in the park."

It was an unlucky answer, for the love of fast horses had been the ruin of Frank's father, but the mention of Roger went far toward softening the old man. Frank had thought of

Roger at once ; he would be generous with him, let what would happen, and the frown which the mention of horses had brought to the squire's face cleared away as he said :

" Hang your horses, boy ; keep clear of them as you would shun the small-pox, but be fair and just with Roger ; poor Roger, I doubt if I did right."

This speech had been followed by the squire's going hastily out upon the terrace, where, with his hands behind him and his head bent forward, he had walked for more than an hour, while Mrs. Walter Scott peered anxiously at him from time to time, and seemed a good deal disturbed. They had returned to the city the next day, and Frank had noticed some changes in their style of living. Another servant was added to their establishment ; they had more dishes at dinner, while his mother went oftener to the opera and Stewart's. Now, his grandfather was dead, and she sat there looking at him across the table as the tears gathered in his eyes, and when he stammered out, " We shall never go to Millbank any more," she said soothingly to him, " We may live there altogether. Would you like it ? "

He did not comprehend her clearly, but the thought that his grandfather's death did not necessarily mean banishment from Millbank helped to dry his eyes, and he began to whistle merrily at the prospect of going there at once, for they were to start that very day on the three-o'clock train. " It was better to be on the ground as soon as possible," Mrs. Walter Scott reflected, and after a visit to her dressmaker, who promised that the deepest of mourning suits should follow her, she started with Frank for Millbank.

Mrs. Walter Scott Irving had never been a favorite at Millbank since her husband had taken her there as a bride, and she had given mortal offence to the two real heads of the household, Aleck and Hester Floyd, by putting on all sorts of airs, snubbing little Roger, and speaking of his mother as " that low creature, whose disgraceful conduct could never be excused." Hester Floyd, to whom this was said, could have forgiven the airs ; indeed, she rather looked upon them as belonging by right to one who was so fortunate as to marry into the Irving family. But when it came to slighting little Roger for his mother's error, and to speaking of that mother as a "low creature," Hester's hot blood was roused, and there commenced at once a quiet, unspoken warfare, which had never ceased, between herself and the offending Mrs. Walter Scott. Hester was as much a part of Millbank as the stately old trees in the park, a few of which she had helped Aleck to plant when she was a girl of eighteen and he a boy of twenty. She had lived at Millbank more than thirty years. She had come there when the first Mrs. Irving was a bride. She had carried Walter Scott to be christened. She had been his nurse, and slapped him with her shoe a dozen times. She had been married to Aleck in her mistress's dining-room. She had seen the old house torn down, and a much larger, handsomer one built in its place ; and then, just after it was completed, she had followed her mistress to the grave, and shut up the many beautiful rooms which were no longer of any use. Two years passed, and then her master electrified her one day with the news that he was about bringing a second bride to Millbank, a girl younger than his son Walter, and against whom Hester set herself fiercely as against an usurper of her rights. But when the sweet, pale-faced Jessie Morton came, with her great, sad blue eyes, and her curls of golden hair, Hester's resentment began to give way, for she could not harbor malice toward a creature so lovely, so gentle, and so sad withal : and after an interview in the bed-chamber, when poor Jessie threw herself with a passionate cry into Hester's arms, and sobbed piteously, " Be kind to me, won't you ? Be my friend. I have none in all the world, or I should not be here. I did not want to come," — she became her strongest ally, and proved that Jessie's confidence had not been misplaced. There had come a dark, dark day for Millbank since then, and Jessie's picture, painted in full dress, with pearls on her beautiful neck and arms, and in her golden hair, had been taken from the parlor-wall and banished to the garret ; and Jessie's name was never spoken by the master, either

to his servants or his little boy Roger, who had a dash of gold
in his brown hair, and a look in his dark-blue eyes, like that
which Jessie's used to wear, when, in the long evenings before
his birth, she sat with folded hands gazing into the blazing fire,
as if trying to solve the dark mystery of her life, and know
why her lot had been cast there at Millbank with the old man,
whom she did not hate, but whom she could not love. There
was a night, too, which Hester never forgot, — a night when,
with nervous agony depicted in every lineament, Jessie made
her swear that, come what might, she would never desert or
cease to love the boy Roger, sleeping so quietly in his little
crib. She was to care for him as if he were her own ; to consider his interest before that of any other, and bring him up
a good and noble man. That was what Jessie asked, and what
Hester swore to do ; and then followed swiftly terror and
darkness and disgrace, and close upon their footsteps came
retribution, and Jessie's golden head was lying far beneath the
sea off Hatteras's storm-beaten shore, and Jessie's name was
rarely heard. But Hester kept her vow, and since the dreadful
morning when Jessie did not answer to the breakfast call, and
Jessie's room was vacant, Roger had never wanted for a
mother's care. Hester had no children of her own, and she
took him instead, petting and caring for, and scolding him as
he deserved, and through all, loving him with a brooding, clinging, unselfish love, which would stop at nothing which she
could make herself believe was right for her to do in his behalf.
And so, when the young bride looked coldly upon him and
spoke slightingly of his mother, Hester declared battle at once ;
and the hatchet had never been buried, for Mrs. Walter Scott,
in her frequent visits to Millbank, had only deepened Hester's
first impressions of her.

"A proud, stuck-up person, with no kind of reason for bein'
so except that she married one of the Irvingses," was what
Hester said of her, and this opinion was warmly seconded by
Aleck, who always thought just as Hester did.

Had she been Eve, and he her Adam, he would have eaten

the forbidden fruit without a question as to his right to do so, just because she gave it to him, but, unlike Adam, he would not have charged the fault to her; he would have taken it upon himself, as if the idea and the act had been his alone.

For Frank there was more toleration at Millbank. "He was not very bright," Hester said; "but how could he be with such a mother? Little pimpin,' spindlin', white-haired critter, there wasn't half so much snap to him as there was to Roger."

In this condition of things it was hardly to be supposed that Mrs. Walter Scott's reception at Millbank was very cordial, when, on the evening after the squire's death, the village hack deposited her at the door. Mrs. Walter Scott did not like a depot hack, it brought her so much on a level with common people; and her first words to Hester were:

"Why wasn't the carriage sent for us? Weren't we expected?"

There was an added air of importance in her manner, and she spoke like one whose right it was to command there; and Hester detected it at once. But in her manner there was, if possible, less of deference than she had usually paid to the great lady.

"Aleck had the neurology, and we didn't know jestly when you'd come," was her reply, as she led the way to the chamber which Mrs. Walter Scott had been accustomed to occupy during her visits to Millbank.

"I think I'll have a fire, the night is so chilly," the lady said, with a shiver, as she glanced at the empty grate. "And, Hester, you may send my tea after the fire is made. I have a headache, and am too tired to go down."

There was in all she said a tone and air which seemed to imply that she was now the mistress; and, in truth, Mrs. Walter Scott did so consider herself, or rather, as a kind of queen-regent who, for as many years as must elapse ere Frank became of age, would reign supreme at Millbank. And after the fire was lighted in her room, and her cup of tea was brought to her, with toast, and jelly, and cold chicken, she was thinking more of the changes she would make in the old place, than of the white, motionless figure which lay, just across the hall, in a room much like her own. She had not seen this figure yet. She did not wish to carry the image of death to her pillow, and so she waited till morning, when, after breakfast was over, she went with Hester to the darkened room, and with her handkerchief ostensibly pressed to her eyes, but really held to her nose, she stood a moment by the dead, and sighed :

"Poor, dear old man! How sudden it was; and what a lesson it should teach us all of the mutability of life, for in an hour when we think not, death cometh upon us!"

Mrs. Walter Scott felt that some such speech was due from her, — something which savored of piety, and which might possibly do good to the angular, square-shouldered, flat-waisted woman at her side, who understood what *mutability* meant quite as well as she would have understood so much Hebrew. But she knew the lady was "putting on;" that, in her heart, she was glad the "poor old man" was dead; and with a jerk she drew the covering over the pinched white face, dropped the curtain which had been raised to admit the light, and then opened the door and stood waiting for the lady to pass out.

"I shall dismiss that woman the very first good opportunity. She has been here too long to come quietly under a new administration," Mrs. Walter Scott thought, as she went slowly down the stairs, and through the lower rooms, deciding, at a glance, that this piece of furniture should be banished to the garret, and that piece transferred to some more suitable place. "The old man has lived here alone so long, that everything bears the unmistakable stamp of a bachelor's hall; but I shall soon remedy that. I'll have a man from the city whose taste I can trust," she said; by which it will be seen that Mrs. Walter Scott fully expected to reign triumphant at Millbank, without a thought or consideration for Roger, the dead man's idol, who, according to all natural laws, had a far better right there than herself.

She had never fancied Roger, because she felt that through

him her husband would lose a part of his father's fortune, and as he grew older and she saw how superior he was to Frank, she disliked him more and more, though she tried to conceal her dislike from her husband, who, during his lifetime, evinced almost as much affection for his young half-brother as for his own son. Walter Scott Irving had been a spendthrift, and the fifty thousand dollars which his father gave him at his marriage had melted away like dew in the morning sun, until he had barely enough to subsist upon. Then ten thousand more had been given him, with the understanding that this was all he was ever to receive. The rest was for Roger, the father said ; and Walter acquiesced, and admitted that it was right. He had had his education with sixty thousand beside, and he could not ask for more. A few weeks after this he died suddenly of a prevailing fever, and then, softened by his son's death, the old man added to the ten thousand and bought the house on Lexington avenue, and deeded it to Mrs. Walter Scott herself. Since that time fortunate speculations had made Squire Irving a richer man than he was before the first gift to his son, and Mrs. Walter Scott had naturally thought it very hard that Frank was not to share in this increase of wealth. But no such thoughts were troubling her now, and her face wore a very satisfied look of resignation and submission as she moved languidly around the house and grounds in the morning, and then in the afternoon dressed herself in her heavy, trailing silk, and throwing around her graceful shoulders a scarlet shawl, went down to receive the calls and condolences of the rector's wife and Mrs. Colonel Johnson, who came in to see her. She did not tell them she expected to be their neighbor a portion of the year, and when they spoke of Roger, she looked very sorry, and sighed : "Poor boy, it will be a great shock to him."

Then, when the ladies suggested that he would undoubtedly have a great deal of property left to him, and wondered who his guardian would be, she said "she did not know. Lawyer Schofield, perhaps, as he had done the most of Squire Irving's business."

"But Lawyer Schofield is dead. He died three weeks ago," the ladies said; and Mrs. Walter Scott's cheek for a moment turned pale as she expressed her surprise at the news, and won-dered she had not heard of it.

Then the conversation drifted back to Roger, who was ex-pected the next night, and for whom the funeral was delayed.

"I always liked Roger," Mrs. Johnson said; "and I must say I loved his mother, in spite of her faults. She was a lovely creature, and it seems a thousand pities that she should have married so old a man as Squire Irving when she loved another so much."

Mrs. Walter Scott said it was a pity, — said she always dis-approved of unequal matches, — said she had not the honor of the lady's acquaintance, and then bowed her visitors out with her loftiest air, and went back to the parlor, and wondered what people would say when they knew what she did. She would be very kind to Roger, she thought. Her standing in Belvidere depended upon that, and he should have a home at Millbank until he was of age, when, with the legacy left to him, he could do very well for himself. She wished the servants did not think quite so much of him as they did, especially Aleck and Hester Floyd, who talked of nothing except that "Master Roger was coming to-morrow." Her mourning was coming, too; and when the next day it came, she arrayed herself in the heavy bombazine, with the white crape band at the throat and wrists, which relieved the sombreness of her attire. She was dressing for Roger, she said, thinking it better to evince some interest in an event which was occupying so much of the ser-vants' thoughts.

The day was a damp, chilly one in mid-April, and so a fire was kindled in Roger's room, and flowers were put there, and the easy-chair from the hall library; and Hester went in and out and arranged and re-arranged the furniture, and then flitted to the kitchen, where the pies and puddings which Roger loved were baking, and where Jeruah, or "Ruey," as she was called, was beating the eggs for Roger's favorite cake. He would be there about nine o'clock, she knew, for she had received a tele. gram from Albany, saying, "Shall be home at nine. Meet me at the depot without fail."

In a great flurry Hester read the dispatch, wondering why she was to meet him without fail, and finally deciding that the affectionate boy could not wait till he reached home before pouring out his tears and grief on her motherly bosom.

"Poor child! I presume he'll cry fit to bust when he sees me," she said to Mrs. Walter Scott, who looked with a kind of scorn upon the preparations for the supposed heir of Millbank.

The night set in with a driving rain, and the wind moaned dismally as it swept past the house where the dead rested so quietly, and where the living were so busy and excited. At half-past eight the carriage came round, and Aleck in his water-proof coat held the umbrella over Hester's head as she walked to the carriage, with one shawl wrapped around her and an-other on her arm. Why she took that second shawl she did not then know, but afterward, in recounting the particulars of that night's adventures, she said it was just a special Providence and nothing else which put it into her head to take an extra shawl, and that a big warm one. Half an hour passed, and then above the storm Mrs. Walter Scott heard the whistle which announced the arrival of the train. Then twenty minutes went by, and Frank, who was watching by the window, screamed out:

"They are coming, mother. I see the lights of the car-riage."

If it had not been raining, Mrs. Walter Scott would have gone to the door, but the damp air was sure to take the curl from her hair, and Mrs. Walter Scott thought a great deal of the heavy ringlets which fell about her face by day and were tightly rolled in papers at night. So she only went as far as the parlor door, where she stood holding together the scarf she had thrown around her shoulders. There seemed to be some delay at the carriage, and the voices speaking together there were low and excited.

"No, Hester; she is mine. She shall go in the front way;" Roger was heard to say; and a moment after Hester Floyd came hurriedly into the hall, holding something under her shawl which looked to Mrs. Walter Scott like a package or roll of cloth.

Following Hester was Frank, who, having no curls to spoil, had rushed out in the rain to meet his little uncle, of whom he had always been so fond.

"Oh, mother, mother!" he exclaimed. "What do you think Roger has brought home? Something which he found in the cars where a wicked woman left it. Oh, ain't it so funny, — Roger bringing a baby?" and having thus thrown the bomb-shell at his mother's feet, Frank darted after Hester, and poor Roger was left alone to make his explanations to his dreaded sister-in-law.

CHAPTER II.

ROGER'S STORY.

HESTER'S advent into the kitchen was followed by a great commotion, and Ruey forgot to pour any water upon the tea designed for Roger, but set the pot upon the hot stove, where it soon began to melt with the heat. But neither Hester nor Ruey heeded it, so absorbed were they in the little bundle which the former had laid upon the table, and which showed unmistakable signs of life and vigorous babyhood by kicking at the shawl which enveloped it, and thrusting out two little fat, dimpled fists, which beat the air as the child began to scream lustily and try to free itself from its wrappings.

"The Lord have mercy on us! what have you got?" Ruey exclaimed, while Hester, with a pale face and compressed lip, replied:

"A brat that some vile woman in the cars asked Roger to

hold while she got out at a station. Of course she didn't go
back, and so, fool-like, he brought it home, because it was
pretty, he said, and he felt so sorry for it. I always knew he
had a soft spot, but I didn't think it would show itself this
way."

It was the first time Hester had ever breathed a word of
complaint against the boy Roger, whose kindness of heart and
great fondness for children were proverbial ; and now, sorry that
she had done so, she tried to make amends by taking the struggling child from the table and freeing it from the shawl which
she had carried with her to the depot, never guessing the purpose to which it would be applied. It was a very pretty, fat-
faced baby, apparently nine or ten months old, and the hazel
eyes were bright as buttons, Ruey said, her heart warming at
once toward the little stranger, at whom Hester looked askance.
There was a heavy growth of dark brown hair upon the head,
with just enough curl in it to make it lie in rings about the forehead and neck. The clothes, though soiled by travelling, were
neatly made, and showed marks of pains and care ; while about
the neck was a fine gold chain, to which was attached a tiny
locket, with the initials "L. G." engraved upon it. These
things came out one by one as Hester and Ruey together examined the child, which did not evince the least fear of them,
but which, when Ruey stroked its cheek caressingly, looked up
in her face with a coaxing, cooing noise, and stretched its arms
toward her.

"Little darling," the motherly girl exclaimed, taking it at once
from Hester's lap and hugging it to her bosom. "I'm so glad
it is here, — the house will be as merry again with a baby in it."

"Do you think Roger will keep it ? You must be crazy,"
Hester said sharply, when Frank, who had divided his time between the parlor and kitchen, and who had just come from the
former, chimed in :

"Yes, he will, — he told mother so. He said he always
wanted a sister, and he should keep her, and mother's rowin'
him for it."

By this it will be seen that the child was the topic of conversation in the parlor as well as kitchen, Mrs. Walter Scott asking
numberless questions, and Roger explaining as far as was possible what was to himself a mystery. A young woman, carrying a baby in her arms, and looking very tired and frightened,
had come into the car at Cincinnati, he said, and asked to sit
with him. She was a pretty, dark-faced woman, with bright
black eyes, which seemed to look right through one, and which
examined him very sharply. She did not talk much to him,
but appeared to be wrapped in thoughts which must have been
very amusing, as she would occasionally laugh quietly to herself, and then relapse into an abstracted mood. Roger thought
now that she seemed a little strange, though at the time he had
no suspicions of her, and was very kind to the baby, whom
she asked him to hold. He was exceedingly fond of children,
especially little girls, and he took this one readily, and fed it
with candy, with which his pockets were always filled. In this
way they travelled until it began to grow dark and they stopped
at ——, a town fifty miles or more from Cincinnati. Here the
woman asked him to look after her baby a few moments
while she went into the next car, to see a friend.

"If she gets hungry, give her some milk," she added, taking
a bottle from the little basket which she had with her under the
seat.

Without the slightest hesitation Roger consented to play the
part of nurse to the little girl, who was sleeping at the time, and
whom the mother, if mother she were, had lain upon the unoc-
cupied seat in front. Bending close to the round, flushed face,
the woman whispered something; then, with a kiss upon the
lips, as if in benediction, she went out, and Roger saw her no
more. He did not notice whether she went into another car
or left the train entirely. He only knew that a half hour
passed and she did not return; then another half hour went
by; and some passengers claimed one of the seats occupied by
him and his charge. In lifting the child he woke her, but instead of crying, she rubbed her pretty eyes with her little fists,

and then, with a smile, laid her head confidingly against his bosom and was soon sleeping again. So long as she remained quiet, Roger felt no special uneasiness about the mother's protracted absence, which had now lengthened into nearly two hours; but when at last the child began to cry, and neither candy, nor milk, nor pounding on the car window, nor his lead pencil, nor his jack-knife, nor watch had any effect upon her, he began to grow very anxious, and to the woman in front who asked rather sharply, "what was the matter, and what he was doing with that child alone," he said, —

"I am taking care of her while her mother sees a friend in the next car. I wish she would come back. She's been gone ever so long."

The cries were screams by this time, — loud, passionate screams, which indicated great strength of lungs, and roused up the drowsy passengers, who began, some of them, to grumble, while one suggested "pitching the brat out of the window."

With his face very red, and the perspiration starting out about his mouth, Roger arose, and tried, by walking up and down the aisle, to hush the little one into quiet. Once he thought of going into the next car in quest of the missing mother, — then, thinking to himself that she surely would return ere long, he abandoned the idea, and resumed his seat with the now quiet child. And so another hour went by, and they were nearly a hundred miles from the place where the woman had left him. Had Roger been older, a suspicion of foul play would have come to him long before this; but, the soul of honor himself, he believed in everybody else, and not a doubt crossed his mind that anything was wrong until the woman who had first spoken to him began to question him again, and ask if it was his sister he was caring for so kindly. Then the story came out, and Roger felt as if smothering, when the woman exclaimed, "Why, boy, the child has been deserted. It is left on your hands. The mother will never come to claim it."

For an instant the car and everything in it turned dark to

poor Roger, who gasped, " You must be mistaken. She is in the next car, sure. Hold the baby, and I'll find her."

There was a moment's hesitancy on the part of the woman, — a fear lest she, too, might be duped; but another look at the boy's frank, ingenuous face, reassured her. There was no evil in those clear, blue eyes which met hers so imploringly, and she took the child in her arms, while he went for the missing mother, — went through the adjoining car and the next, — peering anxiously into every face, but not finding the one he sought. Then he came back, and went through the rear car, but all in vain. The dark-faced woman with the glittering eyes and strange smile, was gone! The baby was deserted and left on Roger's hands. He understood it perfectly, and the understanding seemed suddenly to add years of discretion and experience to him. Slowly he went back to the waiting woman, and without a word took the child from her, and letting his boyish face drop over it, he whispered, " Your mother has abandoned you, little one, but I will care for you."

He was adopting the poor forsaken child, — was accepting his awkward situation, and when that was done he reported his success. There was an ejaculation of horror and surprise on the woman's part; a quick rising up from her seat to "do something," or "tell somebody" of the terrible thing which had transpired before their very eyes. There was a great excitement now in the car, and the passengers crowded around the boy, who told them all he knew, and then to their suggestions as to ways and means of finding the unnatural parent, quietly replied, " I shan't try to find her. She could not be what she ought, and the baby is better without her."

" But what can you do with a baby," a chorus of voices asked; and Roger replied with the air of twenty-five rather than fourteen, "I have money. I can see that she is taken care of."

" The beginning of a very pretty little romance," one of the younger ladies said, and then, as the conductor appeared, he was pounced upon and the story told to him, and suggestions made that he should stop the train, or telegraph back, or do something.

"What shall I stop the train for, and whom shall I telegraph to?" he asked. "It is a plain case of desertion, and the mother is miles and miles away from —— by this time. There would be no such thing as tracing her. Such things are of frequent occurrence; but I will make all necessary inquiries when I go back to-morrow, and will see that the child is given to the proper authorities, who will either get it a place, or put it in the poor-house."

At the mention of the poor-house, Roger's eyes, usually so mild in their expression, flashed defiantly upon the conductor. While the crowd around him had been talking, a faint doubt as to the practicability of his taking the child had crossed his mind. His father was dead, he had his education to get, and Millbank might perhaps be shut up, or let to strangers for several years to come. And what then could be done with Baby. These were his sober-second thoughts after his first indignant burst at finding the child deserted, and had some respectable, kind-looking woman then offered to take his charge from his hands, he might have given it up. But from the poor-house arrangement he recoiled in horror, remembering a sweet-faced, blue-eyed little girl, with tangled hair and milk-white feet, whom he had seen sitting on the door of the poor-house in Belvidere. She had been found in a stable, and sent to the almshouse. Nobody cared for her, — nobody but Roger, who often fed her with apples and candy, and wished there was something better for her than life in that dark dreary house among the hills. And it was to just such a life, if not a worse one, that the cruel conductor would doom the Baby left in his care.

"If I can help it, Baby shall never go to the poor-house," Roger said; and when a lady, who admired the spirit of the boy, asked him, "Have you a mother?" he answered, "No, nor father either, but I have Hester;" and as if that settled it, he put the child on the end of the seat farthest away from the crowd, which gradually dispersed, while the conductor, after inquiring

Roger's name and address, went about his business of collecting tickets, and left him to himself.

That he ever got comfortably from Cleveland to Belvidere with his rather troublesome charge, was almost a miracle, and he would not have done so but for the many friendly hands stretched out to help him. As far as Buffalo, there were those in the car who knew of the strange incident, and who watched, and encouraged, and helped him, but after Buffalo was left behind he was wholly among strangers. Still, a boy travelling with a baby could not fail to attract attention, and many inquiries were made of him as to the whys and wherefores of his singular position. He did not think it necessary to make very lucid explanations. He said, "She is my sister; not my own, but my adopted sister, whom I am taking home;" and he blessed his good angel, which caused the child to sleep so much of the time, as he thus avoided notice and remarks which were distasteful to him. Occasionally, a thought of what Hester might say would make him a little uncomfortable. She was the only one who could possibly object, — the only one in fact who had a right to object, — for with the great shock of his father's death Roger had been made to feel that he was now the rightful master at Millbank. His prospective inheritance had been talked of at once in the family of the clergyman, who had moved from Belvidere to St. Louis, and with whom Roger was preparing for college when the news of his loss came to him.

Mr. Morrison had said to him, "You are rich, my boy. You are owner of Millbank, but do not let your wealth become a snare. Do good with your money, and remember that a tenth, at least, belongs by right to the Lord."

And amidst the keen pain which he felt at his father's death, Roger had thought how much good he would do, and how he would imitate his noble friend and teacher, Mr. Morrison, who, from his scanty income, cheerfully gave more than a tenth, and still never lacked for food or raiment. That Baby was sent direct from Heaven to test his principles, he made himself believe; and by the time the mountains of Massachusetts were reached

2

he began to feel quite composed, except on the subject of Hes.
ter. She *did* trouble him a little, and he wished the first meeting with her was over. With careful forethought he telegraphed
for her to meet him, and then when he saw her he held the child
to her at once, and hastily told her a part of his story, and felt
his heart grow heavy as lead, when he saw how she shrank from
the little one as if there had been pollution in its touch.

"I reckon Mrs. Walter Scott will ride a high hoss when she
knows what you done," Hester said, when at last they were in
the carriage and driving toward home.

At the mention of Mrs. Walter Scott, Roger grew uneasy.
He had a dread of his stylish sister-in-law, with her lofty manner and air of superiority, and he shrank nervously from what
she might say.

"O Hester!" he exclaimed. "Is Helen at Millbank; and
will she put on her *biggest ways?*"

"You needn't be afraid of *Helen Brown.* 'Tain't none of
her business if you bring a hundred young ones to Millbank,"
Hester said, and as she said it she came very near going over
to the enemy, and espousing the cause of the poor little waif in
her arms, out of sheer defiance to Mrs. Walter Scott, who was
sure to *snub* the stranger, as she had snubbed Roger before her.

Matters were in this state when the carriage finally stopped
at Millbank, and Hester insisted upon taking the child through
the kitchen door, as the way most befitting for it. But Roger
said no; and so it was up the broad stone steps, and across the
wide piazza, and into the handsome hall, that Baby was carried
upon her first entrance to Millbank.

CHAPTER III.

WHAT THEY DID AT MILLBANK.

H! Roger, this is a sorry coming home," Mrs. Walter Scott had said when Roger first appeared in view; and taking a step forward, she kissed him quite affectionately, and even ran her white fingers through his moist hair in a pitying kind of way.

She could afford to be gracious to the boy whom she had wronged, but when Frank threw the bomb-shell at her feet with regard to the mysterious bundle under Hester's shawl, she drew back quickly, and demanded of her young brother-in-law what it meant. She looked very grand, and tall, and white in her mourning robes, and Roger quaked as he had never done before in her presence, and half wished he had left the innocent baby to the tender mercies of the conductor and the poor-house. But this was only while he stood damp and uncomfortable in the chilly hall, with the cold rain beating in upon him. The moment he entered the warm parlor, where the fire was blazing in the grate and the light from the wax candles shone upon the familiar furniture, he felt a sense of comfort and reassurance creeping over him, and unconscious to himself a feeling of the *master* came with the sense of comfort, and made him less afraid of the queenly-looking woman standing by the mantel, and waiting for his story. He was at home, — his own home, — where he had a right to keep a hundred deserted children if he liked. This was what Hester had said in referring to Mrs. Walter Scott, and it recurred to Roger now with a deeper meaning than he had given it at that time. He *had* a right, and Mrs. Walter Scott, though she might properly suggest and advise, could not take that right from him. And the story which he told her was colored with this feeling of doing as he thought best; and shrewd Mrs. Walter Scott detected it at once, and her large black eyes had in them a gleam of scorn not alto·

gether free from pity as she thought how mistaken he was, and
how the morrow would materially change his views with regard
to many things.   She had not seen Roger in nearly a year and
a half, and in that time he had grown taller and stouter and
more manly than the boy of twelve, whom she remembered in
roundabouts.   He wore roundabouts still, and his collar was ·
turned down and tied with a simple black ribbon, and he was
only fourteen ; but a well-grown boy for that age, with a curve
about his lip and a look in his eyes, which told that the man
within him was beginning to develop, and warned her that she
had a stronger foe to deal with than she had anticipated ; so
she restrained herself, and was very calm and lady-like and col-
lected as she asked him what he proposed doing with the child
whom he had so unwisely brought to Millbank.

Roger had some vague idea of a nurse with a frilled cap, and
a nursery with toys scattered over the floor, and a crib with
lace curtains over it, and a baby-head making a dent in the
pillow, and a baby voice cooing him a welcome when he came
in, and a baby-cart, sent from New York, and a fancy blanket
with it.   Indeed, this pleasant picture of something he had seen
in St. Louis, in one of the handsome houses where he occasionally visited, had more than once presented itself to his mind as
forming a part of the future, but he would not for the world
have let Mrs. Walter Scott into that sanctuary.   That cold,
proud-faced woman confronting him so calmly had nothing in
common with his ideals, and so he merely replied :

"She can be taken care of without much trouble.   Hester
is not too old.   She made me a capital nurse."

It was of no use to reason with him, and Mrs. Walter Scott
did not try.   She merely said :

" It was a very foolish thing to do, and no one but you would
have done it.   You will think better of it after a little, and get
the child off your hands.   You were greatly shocked, of course,
at the dreadful news ? "

It was the very first allusion anybody had made to the cause
of Roger's being there.   The baby had absorbed every one's

attention, and the dead man upstairs had been for a time forgotten by all save Roger.   He had through all been conscious
of a heavy load of pain, a feeling of loss ; and as he drove up
to the house he had looked sadly toward the windows of the
room where he had oftenest seen his father.   He did not know
that he was there now ; he did not know where he was ; and
when Mrs. Walter Scott referred to him so abruptly, he answered with a quivering lip : " Where is father ?   Did they lay
him in his own room ? "

"Yes, you'll find him looking very natural, — almost as if he
were alive ; but I would not see him to-night. You are too tired.
You must be hungry, too.   You have had no supper.   What
can Hester be doing ? "

Mrs. Walter Scott was in a very kind mood now, and volun-
teered to go herself to the kitchen to see why Roger's supper
was not forthcoming.   But in this she was forestalled by Ruey,
who came to say that supper was waiting in the dining-room,
whither Roger went, followed by his sister-in-law, who poured
his tea and spread him slices of bread and butter, with plenty
of raspberry jam.   And Roger relished the bread and jam with
a boy's keen appetite, and thought it was nicer to be at Millbank than in the poor clergyman's box of a house at St. Louis,
and then, with a great sigh, thought of the white-haired old
man, who used to welcome him home and pat him so kindly
on his head and call him " Roger-boy."   The white-haired man
was gone forever now, and with a growing sense of loneliness
and loss, Roger finished his supper and went to the kitchen,
where Baby lay sleeping upon the settee which Hester had
drawn to the fire, while Frank sat on a little stool, keeping
watch over her.   He had indorsed the Baby from the first, and
when Hester gruffly bade him " keep out from under foot,"
he had meekly brought up the stool and seated himself demurely between the settee and the oven door, where he was
entirely out of the way.

Hester still looked very much disturbed and aggrieved, and
when she met Roger on his way to the kitchen, she passed him

without a word; but the Hester Floyd who, after a time, went
back to the kitchen, was in a very different mood from the one
who had met Roger a short time before. This change had
been wrought by a few words spoken to her by Mrs. Walter
Scott, who sat over the fire in the dining-room when Hester
entered it, and who began to talk of the baby which "that
foolish boy had brought home."

"I should suppose he would have known better; but then,
Mrs. Floyd, you must be aware of the fact that in some things
Roger is rather weak and a little like his mother, who proved
pretty effectually how vacillating she was, and how easily influenced."

Hester's straight, square back grew a trifle squarer and
straighter, and Baby's cause began to gain ground, for Hester
deemed it a religious duty to oppose whatever Mrs. Walter
Scott approved. So if the lady was for sending the Baby away
from Millbank, she was for keeping it there. Still she made
no comments, but busied herself with putting away the sugar
and cream and pot of jam, into which Roger had made such
inroads.

Seeing her auditor was not disposed to talk, Mrs. Walter
Scott continued :

"You have more influence with Roger than any one else,
and I trust you will use that influence in the right direction ; for
supposing everything were so arranged that he could keep the
child at Millbank, the trouble would fall on you, and it is too
much to ask of a woman of your age."

Hester was not sensitive on the point of age, but to have
Mrs. Walter Scott speak of her as if she were in her dotage was
more than she could bear, and she answered tartly, —

"I am only fifty-two. I reckon I am not past bringin' up a
child. I ain't quite got softenin' of the brain, and if master
Roger has a mind to keep the poor forsaken critter, it ain't for
them who isn't his betters to go agin it. The owner of Millbank can do as he has a mind, and Roger is the master now,
you know."

With this speech Hester whisked out of the room, casting a glance backward to see the effect of her parting shot on Mrs. Walter Scott. Perhaps it was the reflection of the fire or her scarlet shawl which cast such a glow on the lady's white cheek, and perhaps it was what Hester said; but aside from the rosy flush there was no change in her countenance, unless it were an expression of benevolent pity for people who were so deluded as Mrs. Floyd and Roger. "Wait till to-morrow and you may change your opinion," trembled on Mrs. Walter Scott's lips, but to say that would be to betray her knowledge of what she meant should appear as great a surprise to herself as to any one. So she wrapped her shawl more closely around her, and leaned back languidly in her chair, while Hester went up the back stairs to an old chest filled with linen, and redolent with the faint perfume of sprigs of lavender and cedar, rose-leaves and geraniums, which were scattered promiscuously among the yellow garments. That chest was a sacred place to Hester, for it held poor Jessie's linen, the dainty garments trimmed with lace, and tucks and ruffles and puffs, which the old Squire had bidden Hester put out of his sight, and which she had folded away in the big old chest, watering them with her tears, and kissing the tiny slippers which had been found just where Jessie left them. The remainder of Jessie's ward-robe was in the bureau in the Squire's own room, — the white satin dress and pearls which she wore in the picture, — the expensive veil, the orange wreath which had crowned her golden hair at the bridal, and many other costly things which the old man had heaped upon his darling, were all there under lock and key. But Hester kept the oaken chest, and under Jessie's clothes were sundry baby garments which Hester had laid away as mementos of the happy days when Roger was a baby, and his beautiful mother the pride of Millbank and the belle of Belvidere.

"If that child only stays one night, she must have a night-gown to sleep in," she said, as with a kind of awe she turned over the contents of the chest till she came to a pile of night gowns which Roger had worn.

Selecting the plainest and coarsest of them all, she closed the chest and went down stairs to the kitchen, where both the boys were bending over the settee and talking to the Baby. There was a softness in her manner now, something really motherly, as she took the little one, and began to undress it, with Roger and Frank looking curiously on.

"Dirty as the rot," was her comment, as she saw the marks of car-dust and smoke cinders on the fat neck and arms and hands. "She or'to have a bath, and she must, too. Here, Ruey, bring me some warm water, and fetch the biggest foot-tub, and a piece of castile soap, and a crash-towel, and you boys, go out of here, both of you. I'll see that the youngster is taken care of."

Roger knew from the tone of her voice that Baby was safe with her, and he left the kitchen with his spirits so much lightened that he began to hum a popular air he had heard in the streets in St. Louis.

"Oh, Roger, *singin'*, with grandpa dead," Frank exclaimed ; and then Roger remembered the white, stiffened form upstairs, and thought himself a hardened wretch that he could for a moment have so forgotten his loss as to sing a negro melody.

"I did not mean any disrespect to father," he said softly to Frank, and without going back to the parlor, he stole up to his own room, and kneeling by his bedside, said the familiar prayer commencing with "Our Father," and then cried himself to sleep with thinking of the dead father, who could never speak to him again.

CHAPTER IV.

THE MORNING OF THE FUNERAL.

F Frank Irving had been poor, instead of the grand-
son of a wealthy man, he would have made a splendid
carpenter; for all his tastes, which were not given to
horses, ran in the channel of a mechanic, and numerous were
the frames and boxes and stools which he had fashioned at
Millbank with the set of tools his grandfather had bought him.
The tools had been kept at Millbank, for Mrs. Walter Scott
would not have her house on Lexington Avenue "lumbered
up;" and with the first dawn of the morning after Roger's
return, Frank was busy in devising what he intended as a cradle
for the baby. He had thought of it the night before, when he
saw it on the settee; and, now, with the aid of a long, narrow
candle-box and a pair of rockers which he took from an old
chair, he succeeded in fashioning as uncouth a looking thing
as ever a baby was rocked in.

"It's because the sides are so rough," he said, surveying his
work with a rueful face. "I mean to paper it, and maybe the
darned thing will look better."

He knew where there were some bits of wall paper, and selecting the very gaudiest piece, with the largest pattern, he fitted it to the cradle, and then letting Ruey into his secret, coaxed
her to make some paste ard help him put it on. The cradle
had this in its favor, that it would rock as well as a better one;
and tolerably satisfied with his work, Frank took it to the
kitchen, where it was received with smothered bursts of laughter from the servants, who nevertheless commended the boy's
ingenuity; and when the baby, nicely dressed in a cotton slip
which Roger used to wear, was brought from Hester's room
and lifted into her new place, she seemed, with her bright, flashing eyes, and restless, graceful motions, to cast a kind of halo
around the candle-box and make it beautiful just because she

2*

was in it. Roger was delighted, and in his generous heart he
thought how many things he would do for Frank in return for
his kindness to the little child, crowing, and spattering its hands
in its dish of milk, and laughing aloud as the white drops fell on
Frank's face and hair. Baby evidently felt at home, and fresh
and neat in her clean dress, she looked even prettier than on
the previous night, and made a very pleasing picture in her
papered cradle, with the two boys on their knees paying her
homage, and feeling no jealousy of each other because of the
attentions the coquettish little creature lavished equally upon
them.

Our story leads us now away from the candle-box to the
dining-room, where the breakfast was served, and where Mrs.
Walter Scott presided in handsome morning-gown, with a becoming little breakfast cap, which concealed the curl-papers
not to be taken out till later in the day, for fear of damage to
the glossy curls from the still damp, rainy weather. The lady
was very gracious to Roger, and remembering the *penchant* he
had manifested for raspberry jam, she asked for the jar and
gave him a larger dish of it than she did to Frank, and told
him he was looking quite rested, and then proceeded to speak
of the arrangements for the funeral, and asked if they met his
approbation. Roger would acquiesce in whatever she thought
proper, he said ; and he swallowed his coffee and jam hastily to
force down the lumps which rose in his throat every time he
remembered what was to be that afternoon. The undertakers
came in to see that all was right while he was at breakfast, and
after they were gone Roger went to the darkened chamber for
a first look at his dead father.

Hester was with him. She was very nervous this morning,
and hardly seemed capable of anything except keeping close to
Roger. She knew she would not be in the way, even in the
presence of the dead ; and so she followed him, and uncovered
the white face, and cried herself a little when she saw how passionately Roger wept, and tried to soothe him, and told him

how much his father had talked of him the last few weeks, and how he had died in the very act of writing to him.

"'The pen was in his hand, right over the words, 'My dear Roger,' Aleck said, for he found him, you know; and on the table lay another letter, — a soiled, worn letter, which had been wet with — with — sea-water — "

Hester was speaking with a great effort now, and Roger was looking curiously at her.

"Whose letter was it?" he asked; and Hester replied:

"It was his,—your father's; and it came from — *her* — your mother."

With a low, suppressed scream, Roger bounded to Hester's side, and, grasping her shoulder, said, vehemently:

"From *mother*, Hester, — from *mother*! Is she alive, as I have sometimes dreamed? Is she? Tell me, Hester!"

The boy was greatly excited, and his eyes were like burning coals as he eagerly questioned Hester, who answered, sadly:

"No, my poor boy! Your mother is dead, and the letter was written years ago, just before the boat went down. Your father must have had it all the while, though I never knew it — till — well, not till some little while ago, when Mrs. Walter Scott was here the last time. I overheard him telling her about it, and when I found that yellow, stained paper on the table, I knew in a minute it was the letter, and I kept it for you, with the one your father had begun to write. Shall I fetch 'em now, or will you wait till the funeral is over? I guess you better wait."

This Roger could not do. He knew but little of his mother's unfortunate life. He could not remember her, and all his ideas of her had been formed from the beautiful picture in the garret, and what Hester had told him of her. Once, when a boy of eleven, he had asked his father what it was about his mother, and why her picture was hidden away in the garret, and his father had answered, sternly:

"I do not wish to talk about her, my son. She may not have been as wicked as I at first supposed, but she disgraced you, and did me a great wrong."

And that was all Roger could gather from his father; while Hester and Aleck were nearly as reticent with regard to the dark shadow which had fallen on Millbank and its proud owner

When, therefore, there was an opportunity of hearing directly from the mysterious mother herself, it was not natural for Roger to wait, even if a dozen funerals had been in progress, and he demanded that Hester should bring him the letters at once.

"Bring them into this room. I would rather read mother's letter here," he said, and Hester departed to do his bidding.

She was not absent long, and when she returned she gave into Roger's hands a fresh sheet of note-paper, which had never been folded, together with a soiled, stained letter, which looked as if some parts of it might have come in contact with the sea.

"Nobody knows I found this one but Aleck, and, perhaps, you better say nothing about it," Hester suggested, as she passed him poor Jessie's letter, and then turned to leave the room.

Roger bolted the door after her, for he would not be disturbed while he read these messages from the dead, — one from the erring woman who for years had slept far down in the ocean depths, and the other from the man who lay there in his coffin. He took his father's first, but that was a mere nothing. It only read:

"MILLBANK, April —.

"MY DEAR BOY — For many days I have had a presentiment that I had not much longer to live, and, as death begins to stare me in the face, my thoughts turn toward you, my dear Roger ——"

Here came a great blot, as if the ink had dropped from the pen or the pen had dropped from the hand; the writing ceased, and that was all there was for the boy from his father. But it showed that he had been last in the thoughts of the dead man, and his tears fell fast upon his father's farewell words. Then, reverently, carefully, gently, as if it were some seawrecked spectre he was handling, he took the other letter, experiencing a kind of chilly sensation as he opened it, and in-

haled the musty odor pervading it. The letter was mailed in
New York, and the superscription was not like the delicate
writing inside. It was a man's chirography, — a bold, dashing
hand, — and for a moment Roger sat studying the explicit direction :

> "WILLIAM H. IRVING, ESQ.,
>> "(Millbank)
>>> "BELVIDERE,
>>>> "CONN."

Whose writing was it, and how came the letter to be mailed
in New York, if, as Hester had said, it had been written on
board the ill-fated "Sea-Gull"? Roger asked himself this question, as he lingered over the unread letter, till, remembering
that the inside was the place to look for an explanation, he
turned to the first page and began to read. It was dated on
board the "Sea-Gull," off Cape Hatteras, and began as follows :

"MY HUSBAND : — It would be mockery for me to put the
word *dear* before your honored name. You would not believe
I meant it, — I, who have sinned against you so deeply, and
wounded your pride so sorely. But, oh, if you knew all which
led me to what I am, I know you would pity me, even if you
condemned, for you were always kind, — too kind by far to a
wicked girl like me. But, husband, I am not as bad as you
imagine. I have left you, I know, and left my darling boy, and
he is here with me, but by no consent of mine. I tried to
escape from him. I am not going to Europe. I am on my way
to Charleston, where Lucy lives, and when I get there I shall
mail this letter to you. Every word I write will be the truth,
and you must believe it, and teach Roger to believe it, too ; for
I have not sinned as you suppose, and Roger need not blush
for his mother, except that she deserted him —"

"Thank Heaven !" dropped from Roger's quivering lips, as
the suspected evil which, as he grew older, he began to fear and
shrink from, was thus swept away.

He had no doubts, no misgivings now, and his tears fell like rain upon poor Jessie's letter, which he kissed again and again, just as he would have kissed the dear face of the writer had it been there beside him.

"Mother, mother!" he sobbed, "I believe you; oh, mother, if you could have lived!"

Then he went back to the letter, the whole of which it is not our design to give at present. It embraced the history of Jessie's life from the days of her early girlhood up to that night when she left her husband's home, and closed with the words:

"I do not ask you to take me back. I know that can never be; but I want you to think as kindly of me as you can, and when you feel that you have fully forgiven me, show this letter to Roger, if he is old enough to understand it. Tell him to forgive me, and give him this lock of his mother's hair. Heaven bless and keep my little boy, and grant that he may be a comfort to you and grow up a good and noble man."

The lock of hair, which was enclosed in a separate bit of paper, had dropped upon the carpet, where Roger found it, his heart swelling in his throat as he opened the paper and held upon his finger the coil of golden hair. It was very long, and curled still with a persistency which Mrs. Walter Scott, with all her papers, could never hope to attain; but the softness and brightness were gone, and it clung to Roger's finger, a streaked, faded tress, but inexpressibly dear to him for the sake of her who sued so piteously for his own and his father's forgiveness.

"When you feel that you have fully forgiven me, show this letter to Roger, if he is old enough to understand it."

Roger read this sentence over again, and drew therefrom this inference. The letter had never been shown to him, therefore the writer had not been forgiven by the dead man, whose face, even in the coffin, wore the stern, inflexible look which Roger always remembered to have seen upon it. 'Squire Irving had been very reserved, and very unforgiving too. He could not easily forget an injury to himself, and that he had not forgiven Jessie's sin was proved by the fact that he had never given the letter to his son, who, for a moment, felt himself growing

hard and indignant toward one who could hold out against the
sweet, piteous pleadings in that letter from poor, unfortunate
Jessie.

"But I forgive you, mother; I believe you innocent. I
bless and revere your memory, my poor, poor, lost mother!"
Roger sobbed, as he kissed the faded curl and kissed the sea-
stained letter.

He knew now how it came to be mailed in New York,
and shuddered as he read again the postscript, written by a
stranger, who said that a few hours after Jessie's letter was finished, a fire had broken out and spread so rapidly that all communication with the life-boats was cut off, and escape seemed
impossible; that in the moment of peril Jessie had come to him
with the letter, which she asked him to take, and if he escaped
alive, to send to Millbank with the news of her death. She
also wished him to add that, so far as *he* was concerned, what
she had written was true; which he accordingly did, as he could
"not do otherwise than obey the commands of one so lovely as
Mrs. Irving."

"Curse him; curse that man!" Roger said, between his
teeth, as he read the unfeeling lines; and then, in fancy, he saw
the dreadful scene: the burning ship, the fearful agony of the
doomed passengers, while amid it all his mother's golden hair,
and white, beautiful face appeared, as she stood before her be-
trayer, and charged him to send her dying message to Millbank
if he escaped and she did not.

It was an hour from the time Roger entered the room before
he went out, and in that hour he seemed to himself to have
grown older by years than he was before he knew so much of
his mother and had read her benediction.

"She was pure and good, let others believe as they may, and
I will honor her memory and try to be what I know she would
like to have me," he said to Hester when he met her alone,
and she asked him what he had learned of his mother.

Hester had read the letter when she found it. It was not in
her nature to refrain, and she, too had fully exonerated Jessie

and cursed the man who had followed her, even to her husband's side, with his alluring words.   But she would rather that
Roger should not know of the liberty she had taken, and so
she said nothing of having read the letter first, especially as
he did not offer to show it to her.   There was a clause in what
the bad man had written which might be construed into a doubt
of some portions of Jessie's story, and Roger understood it;
and, while it only deepened his hatred of the man, instead of
shaking his confidence in his mother, he resolved that no eye
but his own should ever see the whole of that letter.   But he
showed Hester the curl of hair, and asked if it was like his
mother's; and then, drawing her into the library, questioned
her minutely with regard to the past.   And Hester told him all
she thought best of his mother's life at Millbank; — of the scene
in the bridal chamber, when she wept so piteously and said, " I
did not want to come here;" — of the deep sadness in her
beautiful face, which nothing could efface; — of her utter indifference to the homage paid her by the people of Belvidere, or
the costly presents heaped upon her by her husband.

" She was always kind and attentive to him," Hester said;
"but she kept out of his way as much as possible, and I've
seen her shiver and turn white about the mouth if he just laid
his hand on her in a kind of lovin' way, you know, as old men
will have toward their young wives.   When she was expectin'
you, it was a study to see her sittin' for hours and hours in her
own room, lookin' straight into the fire, with her hands clinched
in her lap, and her eyes so sad and cryin' like — "

" Didn't mother want me born ? " Roger asked with quivering lips; and Hester answered, —

" At first I don't think she did.   She was a young girlish
thing; but, after you came, all that passed, and she just lived
for you till that unlucky trip to Saratoga; when she was never
like herself again."

" You were with her, Hester.   Did you see *him* ? "

" I was there only a few days, and you was took sick.   The
air or something didn't agree with you, and I fetched you home.

Your father was more anxious for me to do that than she was. No, I didn't see him to know him. Your mother drew a crowd around her and he might have been in it, but I never seen him.

There was a call for Roger, and, hiding his mother's letter in a private drawer of the writing-desk, he went out to meet the gentlemen who were to take charge of his father's funeral.

CHAPTER V.

THE FUNERAL.

THERE was to be quite a display, for the 'Squire had lived in Belvidere for forty years. He was the wealthiest man in the place, — the one who gave the most to every benevolent object and approved of every public improvement. He had bought the organ and bell for the church in the little village; he had built the parsonage at his own expense, and half of the new town-house. He owned the large manufactory on the river, and the shoe-shop on the hill; and the workmen, who had ever found him a kind, considerate master, were going to follow him to the grave together with the other citizens of the town. The weather, however, was unpropitious, for the rain kept steadily falling, and by noon was driving in sheets across the river and down the winding valley. Mrs. Walter Scott's hair, though kept in papers until the early dinner, at which some of the village magnates were present, came out of curl, and she was compelled to loop it back from her face, which style added to rather than detracted from her beauty. But she did not think so, and she was not feeling very amiable when she went down to dinner and met young Mr. Schofield, the old lawyer's son, who had stepped into his father's business and had been frequently to Millbank. Marriage was not a thing which Mrs. Walter Scott contemplated. She liked her freedom too well, but she always liked to make a good impression, — to look her very best, — to be admired by gentle- men, if they were gentlemen whose admiration was worth the having.   And young Schofield was worth her while to cultivate, and in spite of her straightened hair he thought her very hand- some, and stylish, and grand, and made himself very agreeable at the table and in the parlor after the dinner was over.   He knew more of the Squire's affairs than any one in Belvidere. He was at Millbank only the day before the Squire died, and had an appointment to come again on the very evening of his death.

" He was going to change his will ; add a codicil or some- thing," he said, and Mrs. Walter Scott looked up uneasily as she replied, —

" He left a will, then ?   Do you know anything of it ? "

" No, madam.   And if I did, I could not honorably reveal my knowledge," the lawyer answered, a little stiffly ; while Mrs. Walter Scott, indignant at herself for her want of discretion, bit her lip and tapped her foot impatiently upon the carpet.

It was time now for the people to assemble, and as the bell, which the squire had given to the parish, sent forth its sum- mons, the villagers came crowding up the avenue and soon filled the lower portion of the house, their damp, steaming gar- ments making Mrs. Walter Scott very faint, and sending her often to her smelling-salts, which were her unfailing remedy for the sickening perfumes which she fancied were found only among the common people like those filling the rooms at Mill- bank, — the " factory bugs " who smelt of wool, and the " shop hands " who carried so strong an odor of leather wherever they went.   Mrs. Walter Scott did not like shoemakers nor factory hands, and she sat very stiff and dignified, and looked at them contemptuously from behind her long veil as they crowded into the hall and drawing-room, and managed, some of them, to gain access to the kitchen where the baby was.   Her story had flown like lightning through the town, and the people had discussed it, from Mrs. Johnson and her set down to Hester's married niece, who kept the little public-house by the toll-gate, and who had seen the child herself.

"It was just like Roger Irving to bring it home," the people all agreed, just as they agreed that it would be absurd for him to keep it.

That he would not do so they were sure, and the fear that it might be sent away before they had a look at it brought many a woman to the funeral that rainy, disagreeable day. Baby was Ruey's charge for that afternoon, and in a fresh white dress which Hester had brought from the chest, she sat in her candle-box, surrounded by as heterogeneous a mass of playthings as were ever conjured up to amuse a child. There was a silver-spoon, and a tin cup, and a tea-canister, and a feather duster, and Frank's ball, and Roger's tooth-brush, and some false hair which Hester used to wear as puffs and which amused the baby more than all the other articles combined. She seemed to have a fancy for tearing hair, and shook and pulled the faded wig in high glee, and won many a kiss and hug and compliment from the curious women who gathered round her.

"She was a bright, playful darling," they said, as they left her and went back to the parlors where the funeral services were being read over the cold, stiff form of Millbank's late proprietor.

Roger's face was very pale, and his eyes were fixed upon the carpet, where he saw continually one of two pictures — his mother standing on the "Sea-Gull's" deck, or sitting before the fire; as Hester had said she sat, with her eyes always upon one point, the cheerful blaze curling up the chimney's mouth.

"I'll find that man sometime. I'll make him tell why he left that doubt to torture me," he was thinking, just as the closing hymn was sung and the services were ended.

Mrs. Walter Scott did not think it advisable to go to the grave, and so Hester and Aleck went in the carriage with Roger and Frank, the only relatives in all the long procession which wound down the avenue and through the lower part of the town to where the tall Irving monument showed plainly in the Belvidere cemetery. The Squire's first wife was there in the yard; her name was on the marble, — " Adeline, beloved wife of William H. Irving;" and Walter Scott's name was there, too, though he was sleeping in Greenwood; but Jessie's name had not been added to the list, and Roger noticed it, and wondered he had never been struck by the omission as he was now, and to himself he said : " I can't bring you up from your ocean bed, dear mother, and put you here where you belong, but I can do you justice otherwise, and I will."

Slowly the long procession made the circuit of the cemetery and passed out into the street, where, with the dead behind them, the horses were put to greater speed, and those of the late Squire Irving drew up ere long before the door of Millbank. The rain was over and the April sun was breaking through the clouds, while patches of clear blue sky were spreading over the heavens. It bade fair to be a fine warm afternoon, and the windows and doors of Millbank were open to let out the atmosphere of death and to let in the cheerful sunshine. Friendly hands had been busy to make the house attractive to the mourners when they returned from the grave. There were bright flowers in the vases on the mantel and tables, the furniture was put back in its place, the drapery removed from the mirrors, and the wind blew softly through the lace curtains into the handsome rooms. And Mrs. Walter Scott, wrapped in her scarlet shawl, knew she looked a very queen as she trailed her long skirts slowly over the carpets, and thought with a feeling of intense satisfaction how pleasant it was at Millbank now, and how doubly pleasant it would be later in the season when her changes and improvements were completed. She should not fill the house with company that summer, she thought. It would not look well so soon after the Squire's death, but she would have Mrs. Chesterfield there with her sister Grace, and possibly Captain Stanhope, Grace's betrothed. That would make quite a gay party, and excite sufficiently the envy and admiration of the villagers. Mrs. Walter Scott was never happy unless she was envied or admired, and as she seemed on the high road to both these conditions, she felt very amiable, and kind, and sweet-tempered as she stood in the door waiting to receive Roger and Frank when they returned from the burial.

CHAPTER VI.

THE EVENING AFTER THE FUNERAL.

YOUNG SCHOFIELD had been asked by Mrs. Walter Scott to return to Millbank after the services at the grave were over. She had her own ideas with regard to the proper way of managing the *will* matter, and the sooner the truth was known the sooner would all parties understand the ground they stood on. She knew *her* ground. She had no fears for herself. The will, — Squire Irving's last will and testament, — was lying in his private drawer in the writing desk, where she had seen it every day since she had been at Millbank ; but she had not read it, for the envelope was *sealed,* and having a most unbounded respect for law and justice, and fancying that to break the seal would neither be just nor lawful, she had contented herself with merely taking the package in her hand, and assuring herself that it was safe against the moment when it was wanted. It had struck her that it was a little yellow and time-worn, but she had no suspicion that anything was wrong. To-day, however, while the people were at the grave, she had been slightly startled, for when for a second time she tried the drawer of the writing-desk, she found it locked and the key gone ! Had there been foul play ? and who had locked the door ? she asked herself, while, for a moment, the cold perspiration stood under her hair. Then thinking it probable that Roger, who was noted for thoughtfulness, might have turned and taken the key to his father's private drawer as a precaution against any curious ones who might be at the funeral, she dis-

missed her fears and waited calmly for the *dénoûement*, as
another individual was doing, — *Hester Floyd*, — who knew
about the sealed package just as Mrs. Walter Scott did, and who
had been deterred from opening it for the same reason which
had actuated that lady, and who had also seen and handled it
each day since the squire's death.

Hester, too, knew that the drawer was locked, and that gave
her a feeling of security, while on her way to and from the
grave, where her mind was running far more upon the *after-clap*,
as she termed it, than upon the solemn service for the dead.
Hester was very nervous, and an extra amount of green tea was
put in the steeper for her benefit, and she could have shaken
the unimpressible Aleck for seeming so composed and unconcerned when he stood, as she said, "right over a dreadful,
gapin' vertex."

And Aleck *was* unconcerned. Whatever he had lent his aid
to had been planned by his better half, in whom he had unbounded confidence. If she stood over "a gapin' vertex," she
had the ability to skirt round it or across it, and take him safely
with her. So Aleck had no fears, and ate a hearty supper and
drank his mug of beer and smoked his pipe in quiet, and heard,
without the least perturbation, the summons for the servants to
assemble in the library and hear their master's last will and
testament. This was Mrs. Walter Scott's idea, and when tea
was over she had said to young Schofield:

"You told me father left a will. Perhaps it would be well
enough for you to read it to us before you go. I will have the
servants in, as they are probably remembered in it."

Her manner was very deferential toward young Schofield and
implied confidence in his abilities, and flattered by attention from
so great a lady he expressed himself as at her service for anything. So when the daylight was gone and the wax candles
were lighted in the library, Mrs. Walter Scott repaired thither
with Frank, whom she had brought from his post by the candle-
box. It was natural that he should be present as well as Roger,
and she arranged the two boys, one on each side of her, and

motioned tne servants to seats across the room, and Lawyer Schofield to the arm-chair near the centre of the room. She was making it very formal and ceremonious, and *Englishy*, and Roger wondered what it was all for, while Frank fidgeted and longed for the candle-box, where the baby lay asleep.

"I am told Squire Irving left a will," Mrs. Walter Scott said, when her auditors were assembled, "and I thought best for Mr. Schofield to read it. Do you know where it is?" and she addressed herself to the lawyer, who replied, "I am sure I do not, unless in his private drawer where he kept his important papers."

Roger flushed a little then, for it was into that private drawer that he had put his mother's letter, and the key was in his pocket. Mrs. Walter Scott noticed the flush, but was not quite prepared to see Roger arise at once, unlock the drawer, and take from it a package, which was not the will, but which, nevertheless, excited her curiosity.

"Lawyer Schofield can examine the papers," Roger said, resuming his seat, while the young man went to the drawer and took out the sealed envelope which both Mrs. Walter Scott and Hester had had in their hands so many times within the last few days.

"WILLIAM H. IRVING'S LAST WILL AND TESTAMENT."

There was no doubt about its being the genuine article, and the lawyer waited a moment before opening it. There was perfect silence in the room, except for the clock on the mantle, which ticked so loudly and made Hester so nervous that she almost screamed aloud. The candles sputtered a little, and ran up long, black wicks, and the fire on the hearth cast weird shadows on the wall, and the silence was growing oppressive, when Frank, who could endure no longer, pulled his mother's skirts, and exclaimed, "Mother, mother, what is he going to do, and why don't he do it? I want the darned thing over so I can go out."

That broke the spell, and Lawyer Schofield began to read

Squire Irving's last will and testament. It was dated five years before, at a time when the Squire lay on his sick bed, from which he never expected to rise, and not long after his purchase of the house on Lexington Avenue for Mrs. Walter Scott. There was mention made of his deceased son having received his entire portion, but the sum of four hundred dollars was annually to be paid for Frank's education until he was of age, when he was to receive from the estate five thousand dollars to " set himself up in business, provided that business had nothing to do with *horses.*"

The old man's aversion to the rock on which his son had split was manifest even in his will, but no one paid any heed to it then. They were listening too eagerly to the reading of the document, which, after remembering Frank, and leaving a legacy to the church in Belvidere, and another to an orphan asylum in New York, and another to his servants, with the exception of Aleck and Hester, gave the whole of the Irving possessions, both real and personal, to the boy Roger, who was as far as possible from realizing that he was the richest heir for miles and miles around. He was feeling sorry that Frank had not fared better, and wondering why Aleck and Hester had not been remembered. *They* were witnesses of the will, and there was no mistaking Hester's straight up and down letters, or Aleck's back-hand.

Mrs. Walter Scott was confounded, — utterly, totally confounded, and for a moment deprived of her powers of speech. That she had not listened to the Squire's *last* will and testament,— that there was foul play somewhere, she fully believed, and she scanned the faces of those present to find the guilty one. But for the fact that Aleck and Hester were not remembered in this will, she might have suspected them ; but the omission of their names was in their favor, while the stolid, almost stupid look of Aleck's face, was another proof of his innocence. Hester, too, though slightly restless, appeared as usual. Nobody showed guilt but *Roger*, whose face had turned very red, and was very red still as he sat fidgeting in his chair and looking

hard at Frank. The locked drawer and the package taken
from it, recurred now to the lady's mind, and made her sure
that Roger had the real will in his pocket; and, in a choking
voice, she said to the lawyer, as he was about to congratulate
the boy on his brilliant fortune: "Stop, please, Mr. Schofield;
I think — yes, I know — there was another will — a later one
— in which matters were reversed — and — and Frank — was
the heir."

Her words rang through the room, and, for an instant, those
who heard them sat as if stunned. Roger's face was white now,
instead of red, but he didn't look as startled as might have been
expected. He did not realize that if what his sister said was
true, he was almost a beggar; — he only thought how much
better it was for Frank, toward whom he meant to be so generous; and he looked kindly at the little white-haired boy who
had, in a certain sense, come up as his rival. Mrs. Walter
Scott had risen from her chair and locked the door; then, going to the table where the lawyer was sitting, she stood leaning
upon it, and gazing fixedly at Roger. The lawyer, greatly
surprised at the turn matters were taking, said to her a little
sarcastically: "I fancied, from something you said, that you
did not know there was a *will* at all. Why do you think there
was a later one? Did you ever see it, and why should Squire
Irving do injustice to his only son?"

Mrs. Walter Scott detected in the lawyer's tone that he had
forsaken her, and it added to her excitement, making her so
far forget her character as a lady, that her voice was raised to
an unnatural pitch, and shook with anger as she replied, "I
never saw it, but I know there was one, and that your father
drew it. It was made some months ago, when I was visiting at
Millbank. I went to Boston for a few days, and when I came
back, Squire Irving told me what he had done."

"Who witnessed the will?" the lawyer asked.

"That I do not know. I only know there was one, and that
Frank was the heir."

"A most unnatural thing to cut off his own son for a grand-

child whose father had already received his portion," young
Schofield said; and, still more exasperated, Mrs. Walter Scott
replied, " I do not know that Roger *was* cut off. I only know
that Frank was to have Millbank, with its appurtenances, and
I'll search this room until I find the stolen paper. What was
that you took from the drawer, boy ? "

Roger was awake now to the situation. He understood that
Mrs. Walter Scott believed his father had deprived him of
Millbank, the beautiful home he loved so much, and he understood another fact, which, if possible, cut deeper than disinheritance. She suspected him of stealing the will. The Irving
blood in the boy was roused. His eyes were not like Jessie's
now, but flashed indignantly as he, too, rose to his feet, and,
confronting the angry woman, demanded what she meant.

" Show me that paper in your pocket, and tell me why that
drawer was locked this morning, and why you had the key,"
she said; and Roger replied, " You tried the drawer then, it
seems, and found it locked. Tell me, please, what business
you had with my father's private drawer and papers ? "

" I had the right of a daughter,— an older sister, whose business it was to see that matters were kept straight until some
head was appointed," Mrs. Walter Scott said, and then she
asked again for the package which Roger had taken from the
drawer.

There was a moment's hesitancy on Roger's part ; then,
remembering that she could not compel him to let her read his
mother's farewell message, he took the sea-stained letter from
his pocket and said :

" It was from my mother. She wrote it on the "Sea-Gull,"
just before it took fire. It was found on the table where father
sat writing to me when he died. I believe he was going to
send it to me. At all events it is mine now, and I shall keep
it. Hester gave it to me this morning, and I put it in the private drawer and took the key with me. I knew nothing of this
will, or any other will, except that father always talked as if I
would have Millbank, and told me of some improvements it

would be well to make in the factory and shoe-shop in the course of a few years, should he not live so long. Are you satisfied with my explanation!"

He was looking at the lawyer, who replied:

"I believe you, boy, just as I believe that Squire Irving destroyed his second will, if he ever made one, which, without any disrespect intended to the lady, I doubt, though she may have excellent reasons for believing otherwise. It would have been a most unnatural thing for a father to cast off with a legacy his only son, and knowing Squire Irving as I did, I cannot think he would do it."

The lawyer had forsaken the lady's cause entirely, and wholly forgetting herself in her wrath she burst out with —

"As to the sonship there may be a question of doubt, and if such doubt ever crept into Squire Irving's mind he was not a man to rest quietly, or to leave his money to a stranger."

Roger had not the most remote idea what the woman meant, and the lawyer only a vague one; but Hester knew, and she sprang up like a tiger from the chair where she had hitherto sat a quiet spectator of what was transpiring.

"You woman," she cried, facing Mrs. Walter Scott, with a fiery gleam in her gray eyes, "if I could have my way, I'd turn you out of doors, bag and baggage. If there was a doubt, who hatched it up but you, you sly, insinuatin' critter. I overheard you myself working upon the weak old man, and hintin' things you orto blush to speak of. There was no mention made of a will then, but I know now that was what you was up to, and if he was persuaded to the 'bominable piece of work which this gentleman, who knows law more than I do, don't believe, and then destroyed it, — as he was likely to do when he came to himself, — and you, with your snaky ways, was in New York, it has served you right, and makes me think more and more that the universal religion is true. Not that I've anything special agin' Frank, whose wust blood he got from you, but that Roger should be slighted by his own father is too great a dose to swaller, and I for one shan't stay any longer in the same room with you ; so hand me the key to the door which you locked when you thought Roger had the will in his pocket. Maybe you'd like to search the hull co-boodle of us. You are wel-come to, I'm sure."

Mrs. Walter Scott was a good deal taken aback with this tirade. She had heard some truths from which she shrank, and, glad to be rid of Hester on any terms, she mechanically held out the key to the door.

But here the lawyer interposed, and said :

"Excuse me, one moment, please. Mrs. Floyd, do you re-member signing this will which I have read in your hearing ?"

"Perfectly;" and Hester snapped her words off with an em-phasis. "The master was sick and afraid he might die, and he sent for your father, who was alone with him a spell, and then he called me and my old man in, and said we was to be wit-nesses to his will, and we was, Aleck and me."

"It was strange father did not remember you, who had lived with him so long," Roger suggested, his generosity and sense of justice overmastering all other emotions.

"If he had they could not have been witnesses," the lawyer said, while Hester rejoined :

"It ain't strange at all ; for only six weeks before, he had given us two thousand dollars to buy the tavern stand down by the toll-gate, where we've set my niece Martha up in business, who keeps as good a house as there is in Belvidere ; so you see that's explained, and he gave us good wages always, and kept raisin', too, till now we have jintly more than some ministers, with our vittles into the bargain."

Hester was exonerating her late master from any neglect of herself and Aleck, and in so doing she made the lawyer forget to ask if she had ever heard of a second will made by Squire Irving. The old lawyer Schofield would have done so, but the son was young and inexperienced, and not given to sus-pecting everybody. Besides that, he liked Roger. He knew it was right that he should be the heir, and believed he was, and that Mrs. Walter Scott was altogether mistaken in her ideas. Still he suggested that there could be no harm in searching among the squire's papers. And Mrs. Walter Scott did search, assisted by Roger, who told her of a secret drawer in the writing desk and opened it himself for her inspection, finding nothing there but a time-worn letter and a few faded flowers, — lilies of the valley, — which must have been worn in Jessie's hair, for there was a golden thread twisted in among the faded blossoms. That secret drawer was the sepulchre of all the love and romance of the old squire's later marriage, and it seemed to both Mrs. Walter Scott and Roger like a grave which they had sacrilegiously invaded. So they closed it reverently, with its withered blossoms and mementos of a past which never ought to have been. But afterward, Roger went back to the secret drawer, and took therefrom the flowers, and the letter written by Jessie to her aged suitor a few weeks before her marriage. These, with the letter written on the sea, were sacred to him, and he put them away where no curious eyes could find them. There had been a few words of consultation between Roger and Lawyer Schofield, and then, with a hint that he was always at Roger's service, the lawyer had taken his leave, remarking to Mrs. Walter Scott, as he did so : .

"I thought you would find yourself mistaken; still you might investigate a little further."

He meant to be polite, but there was a tinge of sarcasm in his tone, which the lady recognized, and inwardly resented. She had fallen in his opinion, and she knew it, and carried herself loftily until he said to Roger, —

"I had an appointment to meet your father in his library the very evening he died. He wished to make a change in his will, and I think, perhaps, he intended doing better by the young boy, Frank. At least, that is possible, and you may deem it advisable to act as if you knew that was his intention. You have an immense amount of money at your command, for your father was the richest man in the county."

Frank had long ago gone back to the kitchen and the baby.

He had no special interest in what they were talking about, nor was it needful that he should have. He was safe with Roger, who, to the lawyer's suggestion, replied :

" I shall do Frank justice, as I am sure he would have done me, had the tables been reversed."

The lawyer bowed himself out, and Roger was alone with his sister-in-law, who looked so white, and injured, and disappointed, that he felt, to say the least, very uncomfortable in her presence. He had not liked her manner at all, and had caught glimpses of a far worse disposition than he had thought she possessed, while he was morally certain that she was ready and willing to trample on all his rights, and even cast him aloof from his home if she could. Still, he would rather be on friendly terms with her, for Frank's sake, if for no other, and so he went up to her, and said :

" I know you are disappointed if you really believed father had left the most of his money to Frank."

" I don't believe. I know ; and there has been foul play somewhere. He told me he had made another will, here in this very room."

" Helen," Roger said, calling her, as he seldom did, by her Christian name, and having in his voice more of sorrow than anger — " Helen, why did father wish to serve me so, when he was always so kind ? What reason did he give ? "

Roger's eyes were full of tears, and there was a grieved look in his face as he waited his sister's answer. Squire Irving had given *her* no reason for the unjust act. She had given the reason to him, making him for a time almost a madman, but she could not give that reason to the boy, although she had in a moment of passion hinted at it, and drawn down Hester's vengeance on her head. If he had not understood her then, she would not wound him now by the cruel suspicion. Thus reasoned the better nature of the woman, while her mean, grasping spirit suggested that in case the will was not found, it would be better to stand well in Roger's good opinion. So she replied, very blandly and smoothly :

" After your father had given my husband his portion, he grew much richer than he had ever been before, and I suppose he thought it was only fair that Frank should have what would have come to his father if the estate had been equally divided. I never supposed you were cut off entirely; that *would* have been unnatural."

Roger was not satisfied with this explanation, for sharing equally with Frank, and being cut off with only a legacy, were widely different things, and her words at one time had implied that the latter was the case. He did not, however, wish to provoke her to another outburst; and so, with a few words to the effect that Frank should not suffer at his hands, he bade his sister good-night, and repaired to his own room. He had passed through a great deal, and was too tired and excited to care even for the baby that night; and, when Hester knocked at his door, he answered that he could not see her, — she must wait until to-morrow. So Hester went away, saying to herself:

" He's a right to be let alone, if he wants to be, for he is now the master of Millbank."

CHAPTER VII.

MILLBANK AFTER THE DAY OF THE FUNERAL.

MRS. WALTER SCOTT could not easily give up her belief in a later will, and after everything about the house was quiet, and the tired inmates asleep, she went from one vacant room to another, her slippered feet treading lightly and giving back no sound to betray her to any listening ear, as she glided through the lower rooms, and then ascended to the garret, where was a barrel of old receipts and letters, and papers of no earthly use whatever. These she ex-

amined minutely, but in vain.   The missing document was not
there, and she turned to Jessie's picture, and was just bending
down for a look at that, when a sudden noise startled her, and,
turning round, she saw a head, surmounted by a broad-frilled
cap, appearing up the stairway.   It was Hester's head, and
Hester herself came into full view, with a short night-gown on,
and her feet encased in a pair of Aleck's felt slippers, which,
being a deal too big, clicked with every step, and made the
noise Mrs. Walter Scott first heard.

"Oh, you're at it, be you !" Hester said, putting her tallow
candle down on the floor.   "I thought I heard somethin'
snoopin' round, and got up to see what 'twas.   I guess I'll
hunt too, if you like, for I'm afraid you might set the house
afire."

"Thank you ; I'm through with my search for to-night," was
Mrs. Walter Scott's lofty answer, as she swept down the garret
stairs past Hester Floyd and into her own room.

There was a bitter hatred existing between these two women
now, and had the will been found, Hester's tenure at Millbank
would have hung upon a very slender thread.   But the will
was not found, neither that night nor the next day, when
Mrs. Walter Scott searched openly and thoroughly with Roger
as her aid, for which Hester called him a fool, and Frank, who
was beginning to get an inkling of matters, a "spooney."
Mrs. Walter Scott was outgeneralled, and the second day after
the funeral she took her departure and went back to Lexington
Avenue, where her first act was to dismiss the extra servant
she had hired when Millbank seemed in her grasp, while her
second was to countermand her orders for so much mourning.

If Squire Irving had left her nothing, she, of course, had
nothing to expend in crape and bombazine, and when she next
appeared on Broadway, there were pretty green strings on her
straw hat, and a handsome thread-lace veil in place of the long
crape which had covered her face at the funeral.   Mrs. Walter
Scott had dropped back into her place in New York, and for a
little time our story has no more to do with her ladyship, but

keeps us at Millbank, where Roger, with Col. Johnson as his guardian, reigned the triumphant heir.

As was natural, the baby was the first object considered after the excitement of Mrs. Walter Scott's departure had subsided. What should be done with it ? Col. Johnson asked Roger this question in Hester's presence, and Roger answered at once, "I shall keep her and educate her as if she were my sister. If Hester feels that the care will be too much for her, I will get a nurse till the child is older."

"Yes; and then I'll have both nuss and baby to 'tend to," Hester exclaimed. "If it must stay, I'll see to it myself, with Rucy's help. I can't have a nuss under foot, doin' nothin'."

This was not exactly what Roger wanted. He had not yet lost sight of that picture of the French nurse in a cap, to whom Hester did not bear the slightest resemblance; but he saw that Hester's plan was better than his, and quietly gave up the French nurse and the pleasant nursery, but he ordered the crib, and the baby-wagon and the bright blanket with it, and then he said to Hester, "Baby must have a name," adding that once, when the woman in the cars was hushing it, she had called it something which sounded like Magdalen. "That you know was mother's second name," he said. "So suppose we call her 'Jessie Magdalen;'" but against that Hester arrayed herself so fiercely that he gave up "Jessie," but insisted upon "Magdalen," and added to it his own middle name, "Lennox."

There was a doubt in his mind as to whether she had ever been baptized, and thinking it better to be baptized twice than not at all, he determined to have the ceremony performed, and Mrs. Col. Johnson consented to stand as sponsor for the child, whom Hester carried to the church, performing well her part as nurse, and receiving back into her arms the little Magdalen Lennox, who had crowed, and laughed, and put her fat hand to her head, to wipe off the drops of water which fell upon her as she was "received into Christ's flock and signed with His sign" upon her brow.

During the entire summer Roger remained at Millbank,

3*

where he made a few changes, both in the grounds and in the
house, which began to wear a more modern look than during
the old squire's life. Some of the shrubbery was rooted up,
and a few of the oldest trees cut down, so that the sunshine
could find freer access to the rooms, which had rarely been used
since Jessie went away, but which Roger opened to the warmth
and sunlight of summer. On the wall, in the library, Jessie's
picture was hung. It had been retouched and brightened up
in Springfield, and the beautiful face always seemed to smile a
welcome on Roger whenever he came where it was. On the
monument in the graveyard Jessie's name was cut beneath her
husband's, and every Saturday Roger carried a bouquet of
flowers from the Millbank garden, and laid it on the grassy
mound, in memory, not so much of his father, as of the young
mother whose grave was in the sea. Thither he sometimes
brought little Magdalen, who could walk quite easily now, and
it was not an uncommon sight, on pleasant summer days, to
see the boy seated under the evergreens which overshadowed
his father's grave, while toddling among the gray head-stones
of the dead, or playing in the gravel-walks, was Magdalen, with
her blanket pinned about her neck, and her white sun-bonnet
tied beneath her chin. Thus the summer passed, and in the
autumn Roger went away to Andover, where he was to finish
preparing for college, instead of returning to his old tutor in
St. Louis. After his departure, the front rooms above and
below were closed, and Magdalen, who took more kindly to
the parlors than to the kitchen, was taught that such things
were only for her when Master Roger was at home ; and if, by
chance, she stole through an open door into the forbidden
rooms, she was brought back at once to her corner in the
kitchen. Not roughly though, for Hester Floyd was always
kind to the child, — first, for Roger's sake, and then for the
affection she herself began to feel for the little one, whose
beauty, and bright, pretty ways everybody praised.

And now, while the doors and shutters of Millbank are
closed, and only the rear portion of the building is open, we

pass, without comment, over a period of eleven years, and open the story again, on a bright day in summer, when the sky was as blue and the air as bland as was the air and sky of Italy, where Roger Irving was travelling.

CHAPTER VIII.

THE STRANGER IN BELVIDERE.

DURING the eleven years since her disappointment, Mrs. Walter Scott had never once been to Millbank. She had seen the house several times from the car window as she was whirled by on her way to Boston, and she managed to keep a kind of oversight of all that was transpiring there, but she never crossed the threshold, and had said she never would. Frank, on the contrary, was a frequent visitor there. He bore no malice to its inmates on account of the missing will. Roger had been very generous with him, allowing him more than the four hundred a year, and assisting him out of many a "deuced scrape," as Frank termed the debts he was constantly incurring, with no ostensible way of liquidating them except through his *Uncle Roger.* He called him uncle frequently for fun, and Roger always laughed good-humoredly upon his fair-haired nephew, whom he liked in spite of his many faults.

Frank was now at Yale; but he was no student, and would have left college the very first year but for Roger, who had more influence over him than any other living person. Frank believed in Roger, and listened to him as he would listen to no one else, and when at last, with his college diploma and his profession as a lawyer, won, Roger went for two or three years' travel in the old world, Frank felt as if his anchorage was swept away and he was left to float wherever the tide and his own vacillating disposition might take him. The most of his vacations were spent at Millbank, where he hunted in the grand old woods, with Magdalen trudging obediently at his side in the capacity of game carrier, or fished in the creek or river, with Magdalen to carry the worms and put them on his hook. Frank was lazy, — terribly, fearfully lazy, — and whatever ser-vice another would render him, he was ready to receive. So Magdalen, whose hands and feet never seemed to tire, minis-tered willingly to the city-bred young man, who teased her about her dark face and pulled her wavy hair, and laughed at her clothes with the Hester stamp upon them, and called her a little Gypsy, petting her one moment, and then in a moody fit sending her away " to wait somewhere within call," until he wanted her. And Magdalen, who never dreamed of rebelling from the slavery in which he held her when at Millbank, looked forward with eager delight to his coming, and cried when he went away.

Roger she held in the utmost veneration and esteem, regard-ing him as something more than mortal. She had never car-ried the game-bag for him, or put worms upon his hook, for he neither fished nor hunted ; but she used to ride with him on horseback, biting her lips and winking hard to keep down her tears and conquer her fear of the spirited animal he bade her ride. She would have walked straight into the crater of Vesuvius if Roger had told her to, and at his command she tried to overcome her mortal terror of horses, — to sit and ride, and carry her reins and whip as he taught her, until at last she grew accustomed to the big black horse, and Roger's com-mendations of her skill in managing it were a sufficient recom-pense for weary hours of riding through the lanes, and mead ows, and woods of Millbank.

So, too, when Roger gave her a Latin grammar and bade her learn its pages, she set herself at once to the task, studying day and night, and growing feverish and thin, and nervous, until Hester interfered, and said "a child of ten was no more fit to study Latin than she was to build a ship, and Roger must let her alone till she was older if he did not want to kill her."

Then Roger, who in his love for books had forgotten that children did not all possess his tastes or powers of endurance, put the grammar away and took Magdalen with him to New York to a scientific lecture, of which she did not understand a word, and during which she went fast asleep with her head on his shoulder, and her queer little straw bonnet dreadfully jammed and hanging down her back. Roger tied on her bonnet when the lecture was over, and tried to straighten the pinch in front, and never suspected that it was at all different from the other bonnets around him. The next night he took her to Niblo's, where she nearly went crazy with delight; and for weeks after, her little room at Millbank was the scene of many a pantomime, as she tried to reproduce for Bessie's benefit the wonderful things she had seen.

That was nearly two years before the summer day of which we write. She had fished and hunted with Frank since then, and told him of Niblo's as of a place he had never seen, and said good-by to Roger, who was going off to Europe, and who had enjoined upon her sundry things she was to do during his absence, one of which was always to carry the Saturday's bouquet to his father's grave. This practice Roger had kept up ever since his father died, taking the flowers himself when he was at home, and leaving orders for Hester to see that they were sent when he was away. Magdalen, who had frequently been with him to the grave-yard, knew that the Jessie whose name was on the marble was buried in the sea, for Roger had told her of the burning ship, and the beautiful woman who went down with it. And with her shrewd perceptions, Magdalen had guessed that the flowers offered weekly to the dead were more for the mother, who was not there, than for the father, who was. And after Roger went away she adopted the plan of taking with her two bouquets, one large and beautiful for Jessie, and a smaller one for the old squire, whose picture on the library-wall she did not altogether fancy.

A visit to the cemetery was always one of the duties of Saturday, and toward the middle of the afternoon, on a bright day in July, Magdalen started as usual with her basket of flowers on her arm. She liked going to that little yard where the shadows from the evergreens fell so softly upon the grass, and the white rose-bush which Roger had planted was climbing up the tall monument and shedding its sweet perfume on the air. There was an iron chair in the yard, where Magdalen sat down, and divesting herself of her shoes and stockings, cooled her bare feet on the grass and hummed snatches of songs learned from Frank, who affected to play the guitar and accompany it with his voice. And while she is sitting there we will give a pen-and-ink photograph of her as she was at twelve years of age. A straight, lithe little figure, with head set so erect upon her shoulders that it leaned back rather than forward. A full, round face, with features very regular, except the nose, which had a slight inclination upward, and which Frank teasingly called "a turn-up." Masses of dark hair, which neither curled nor lay straight upon the well-shaped head, but rippled in soft waves all over it, and was kept short in the neck by Hester, who "didn't believe much in hair," and who often deplored Magdalen's "heavy mop," until the child was old enough to attend to it herself. A clear, brown complexion, with a rich, healthful tint on cheek and lip, and a fairer, lighter coloring upon the low, wide forehead; dark, hazel eyes, which, under strong excitement, would grow black as night and flash forth fiery gleams, but which ordinarily were soft and mild and bright, as the stars to which Frank likened them. The eyes were the strongest point in Magdalen's face, and made her very handsome in spite of the outlandish dress in which Hester always arrayed her, and the rather awkward manner in which she carried her hands and elbows. Hester ignored fashions. If Magdalen was only clean and neat, that was all she thought necessary, and she put the child in clothes old

enough for herself, and Frank often ridiculed the queer-look-
ing dresses buttoned up before, and far too long for a girl of
Magdalen's age.

Except for Frank's teasing remarks, Magdalen would have
cared very little for her personal appearance, and as he was in
New Haven now she was having a nice time alone in the
cemetery, with her shoes and stockings off to cool her feet, and
her bonnet off to cool her head, round which her short, damp
hair was curling more than usual. She was thinking of Jessie,
and wondering how she happened to be on the ocean, and
where she was going, and she did not at first see the stranger
coming down the walk in the direction of the yard where
she was sitting. He was apparently between fifty and sixty,
for his hair was very gray, and there were deep-cut lines about
his eyes and mouth; but he was very fine-looking still, and a
man to be noticed and commented upon among a thousand.

He was coming directly to Squire Irving's lot, where he
stood a moment with his hand upon the iron fence before
Magdalen saw him. With a blush and a start she sprang up,
and tried, by bending her knees, to make her dress cover her
bare feet, which, nevertheless, were plainly visible, as she
modestly answered the stranger's questions.

"Good afternoon, Miss," he said, touching his hat to her
as politely as if she had been a princess, instead of a barefoot
girl. "You have chosen a novel, but very pleasant place for
an afternoon reverie. Whose yard is this, and whose little
girl are you?"

"I am Mr. Roger's little girl, and this is Squire Irving's lot.
That's his monument," Magdalen replied; and at the sound of
her voice and the lifting up of her eyes the stranger looked
curiously at her.

"What is your name, and what are you doing here?" he
asked her next; and she replied, "I came with flowers for the
grave. I bring them every Saturday, and my name is Magdalen."

This time the stranger started, and without waiting to go round to the gate, sprang over the iron fence and came te Magdalen's side.

"Magdalen whom?" he asked.   "Magdalen Rogers?"

"No, sir. Magdalen Lennox. I haven't any father nor mother, and I live up at Millbank. You can just see it through the trees. Squire Irving used to live there, but since he died it belongs to Mr. Roger, and he has gone to Europe, and told me to bring flowers every Saturday to the graves. That's his father," she continued, pointing to the squire's name, "and that," pointing to Jessie's name, "is his mother; only she is not here, you know. She died on the sea."

If the stranger had not been interested before, he was now, and he went close to the stone where Jessie's name was cut, and stood there for a moment without saying a word to the little girl at his side. His back was toward her, and she could not see his face until he turned to her again, and said, —

"And you live there at Millbank, where — where Mrs. Irving did. You certainly could not have been there when she died."

Magdalen colored scarlet, and stood staring at him with those bright, restless, eager eyes, which so puzzled and per-plexed him. She had heard from Hester some of the particu-lars of her early life, while from her young girl friends she had heard a great deal more which distressed and worried her, and sent her at last to Roger for an explanation. And Roger, thinking it was best to do so, had told her the whole truth, and given into her keeping the locket which she had worn about her neck, and the dress in which she came to Millbank. She was old enough to understand in part her true position, and she was very sensitive with regard to her early history. That there was something wrong about both her parents, she knew; but still there was a warm, tender spot in her heart for her mother, who, Roger had said, bent over her with a kiss and a few whispered words of affection, ere abandon-ing her in the cars. Magdalen could sometimes feel that kiss upon her cheek and see the restless, burning eyes which Roger described so minutely. There was a look like them in her own eyes, and she was glad of it, and glad her hair was dark and glossy, as Roger said her mother's was. She was proud to look *like* her mother; though she was not proud *of* her mother, and she never mentioned her to any one save Roger, or alluded to the time when she had been deserted. So when the stranger's words seemed to ask how long she had been at Millbank, she hesitated, and at last replied :

"Of course I was not born when Mrs. Irving died. I'm only twelve years old. I was a poor little girl, with nobody to care for me, and Mr. Roger took me to live with him. He is not very old, though. He is only twenty-six; and his nephew Frank is twenty-one in August."

The stranger smiled upon the quaint, old-fashioned little girl, whose eyes, fastened so curiously upon him, made him slightly uneasy.

"Magdalen," he said at last, but more as if speaking to himself and repeating a name which had once been familiar to him.

"What, sir?" was Magdalen's reply, which recalled him back to the present.

He must say something to her, and so he asked :

"Who gave you the name of Magdalen? It is a very pretty name."

There was a suavity and winning graciousness in his manner, which, young as she was, Magdalen felt, and it inclined her to be more familiar and communicative than she would otherwise have been to a stranger.

"It was *her* second name," she said, touching the word Jessie on the marble. "And Mr. Roger gave it to me when I went to live with him."

"Then you were named for Mrs. Irving?" and the stranger involuntarily drew a step nearer to the little girl, on whose hair his hand rested for a moment. "Do they talk much of her at Millbank?"

"No; nobody but Mr. Roger, when he is at home. Her

picture is in the library, and I think it is so lovely, with the
pearls on her neck and arms, and the flowers in her hair. She
must have been beautiful."

"Yes, very beautiful," fell mechanically from the stranger's
lips; and Magdalen asked, in some surprise: "Did you know
her, sir?"

"I judge from your description," was the reply; and then he
asked "if the flowers were for Mrs. Irving."

"The large bouquet is.   I always make a difference, because
I think Mr. Roger loved her best," Magdalen said.

Just then there came across the fields the sound of the village
clock striking the hour of five, and Magdalen started, exclaiming, "I must go now; Hester will be looking for me."

The stranger saw her anxious glance at her stockings and
shoes, and thoughtfully turned his back while she gathered them
up and thrust them into her basket.

"You'd better put them on," he said, when he saw the
disposition she had made of them.   "The gravel stones will
hurt your feet, and there may be thistles, too."

He seemed very kind indeed, and walked to another en-
closure, while Magdalen put on her stockings and shoes and
then arose to go.   She thought he would accompany her as far
as the highway, sure, and began to feel a little elated at the
prospect of being seen in company with so fine a gentleman by
old Bettie, the gate-keeper, and her granddaughter Lottie.
But he was in no hurry to leave the spot.

"This is a very pretty cemetery; I believe I will walk about
a little," he said, as he saw that the girl seemed to be waiting
for him.

Magdalen knew this was intended as a dismissal, and walked
rapidly away.   Pausing at the stile over which she passed into
the street, she looked back and saw the stranger, — not walking
about the grounds, but standing by the monument and apparently leaning his head upon it.   Had she passed that place an
hour later, she would have missed from its cup of water the
largest bouquet, the one she had brought for Mrs. Irving, and

would have missed, too, the half-open rose which hung very near Jessie's name. But she would have charged the theft to the children by the gate, who sometimes did rob the grave of flowers, and not to the splendid-looking man with the big gold chain, who had spoken so kindly to her, and of whom her head was full as she went back to Millbank, where she was met by Hester with an open letter in her hand, bearing a foreign postmark.

CHAPTER IX.

A STIR AT MILLBANK.

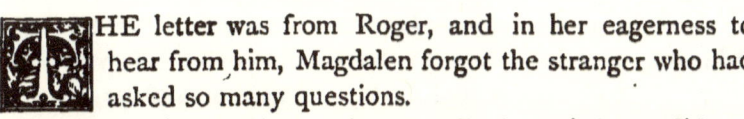HE letter was from Roger, and in her eagerness to hear from him, Magdalen forgot the stranger who had asked so many questions.

Roger was in Dresden, and very well; but his letter did not relate so much to himself and his journeyings as to matters at home. Frank, who had visited Millbank in April, had written to Roger a not very satisfactory account of Hester's management of Magdalen.

"The girl is growing up a perfect Hottentot, with no more manners or style than Dame Floyd herself; and it seems a pity, when she is so bright and capable and handsome, and might with proper training make a splendid woman. But what can you expect of her, brought up by that superannuated Hester, who keeps her in the most outlandish clothes I ever saw, and lets her go barefoot half the time, till her feet are spreading so, that after a little they will be as flat and broad as a mackerel. Besides that, I saw her trying to milk, which you know will spoil her hands sooner than anything else in creation. My advice is that you send her to school, say here to New Haven, if you like. Mrs. Dana's is a splendid school for young ladies. I would write at once to

Mrs. Floyd if I were you. And, Roger, for thunder's sake, tell her to let Mrs. Johnson or her daughter see to Maggie's wardrobe. She would be the laughing-stock of the town if she were to come here rigged out *à la Floyd.*"

This and much more Frank had written to Roger, who, in a milder form, wrote it back to Hester, telling her that Magdalen must go away, and suggesting New Haven as a proper place where to send her.

Hester was a very little indignant when she read this letter, which, without directly charging her with neglect, still implied that in some things concerning Magdalen she had been remiss, and to Bessie, the housemaid, she was freeing her mind pretty thoroughly when Magdalen came in and began to question her eagerly with regard to Roger, and to ask if the letter was for her.

"No," Hester replied, "but it's about you. I'm too old-fashioned to fetch you up any longer, and you've got to be sent away. The district school ain't good enough, and you are to go to New Haven and learn manners, and not go barefoot, nor milk, and put your feet and hands out of shape. Haven't I told you forty times, Magdalen Lennox, to put on your shoes?"

"Yes, fifty," Magdalen replied, in that peculiar winning way which she had of conciliating Hester when in one of her querulous moods. "What is it about my hands and feet, let me see?"

And coming close to Hester, she laid one hand soothingly on the old woman's shoulder, and with the other took Roger's letter, which she read through from beginning to end; then, with a passionate exclamation, she threw it from her, saying:

"It is Frank who put Mr. Roger up to this. I won't go away from Millbank to horrid old New Haven, where the girls sit, and walk, and act just so, with their elbows in and their toes out. I hate New Haven, I hate Frank, I hate everybody but you."

Magdalen's eyes were flashing, and her hand deepened its grasp on Hester, who cast upon the young girl a look which told how full of love her old heart was for the child whom she had cared for and watched over since the night she first came to Millbank. No one could live with Magdalen and not love her. Generous, outspoken, and wholly truthful, warm-hearted and playful as a kitten, she had wound herself around every fibre of Hester's heart, until the woman hardly knew which was dearer to her, — Magdalen or Roger. She would miss the former most. Millbank would be very lonely without those busy little bare feet of which Roger disapproved, and that blithe, merry voice which filled the house with melody, and it was partly a dread of the loneliness which Magdalen's absence would leave which prompted Hester to such an outburst as had followed the reading of Roger's letter ; and when Magdalen took up the theme, vehemently declaring she would never go to New Haven, Hester felt a thrill of joy and pride in the girl who preferred her to New Haven and its stylish young ladies.

Her soberer second thoughts, however, were that Roger's wishes would have to be considered, and Magdalen be obliged to yield. But Magdalen thought differently and persisted in saying she would never go to New Haven, and subject herself to the criticisms of that *Alice Grey*, about whom Frank had talked so much on his last visit to Millbank.

He had only stayed a day or two, and Magdalen had thought him changed, and, as she fancied, not for the better. He had always teased her about her grandmotherly garb, but his teasings this time were more like earnest criticisms, and he was never tired of holding up *Alice Grey* as a model for all young girls to imitate. She was very pretty, he said, with soft blue eyes and rich brown hair, which was almost a chestnut, and she had such graceful, lady-like manners, that all the college boys were more in love with her, — a little maiden of fourteen, — than with the older young ladies in Miss Dana's school.

Heretofore, when Frank had visited Millbank, Magdalen had been all in all, and she resented his frequent allusion to one whom he seemed to consider so superior to herself, and felt relieved when he went back to his Alice, with her chestnut hair, and her soft blue eyes, and wax-like complexion.

Magdalen hated her own dark skin for a little after that, and taught by Bessie, tried what frequent washings in buttermilk would do for it; but Hester's nose, which had a most remark-able knack for detecting smells even where none existed, soon ferreted out the hidden jar containing Magdalen's cosmetic, and, all hopes of a complexion like Alice Grey's were swept away with the buttermilk which the remorseless Hester threw into the pig-pen as its most fitting place. After a while the fever sub-sided, and Alice Grey ceased to trouble Magdalen until she was brought to mind by Roger's letter.

That she would not go to New Haven, Magdalen was re-solved. If Roger wanted her to try some other school she would, she said, but New Haven was not to be considered for a moment; and so Hester wrote to Roger an account of the manner with which his proposition had been received, and asked him to suggest some other school for his ward.

In her excitement Magdalen had entirely forgotten the stranger in the graveyard, nor was he recalled to her mind un-til the next day, when, with Hester Floyd, she walked demurely to the little church where she was in the habit of worshipping. It was a beautiful morning, and the air was laden with the sweet perfume of the clover blossoms and the new-mown hay, and Magdalen looked unusually bright and pretty in her light French calico and little white sack, which the village dress-maker had made, and which bore a more modern stamp than was usual to Hester's handiwork. Her shoes and stockings were all right this time, and her hands were encased in a pair of cotton gloves, which, though a deal too large, were neverthe-less gloves, and kept her hands from tanning. And Magdalen, with her prayer-book and sprig of caraway, felt very nice as she went up the aisle to Squire Irving's pew, where, in imitation of Hester she dropped on her knees and said her few words of prayer, while her thoughts were running upon the gentleman in front, the stranger of the graveyard, who turned his head as she came in with a half nod of recognition.

He seemed very devout as the services proceeded, and never had Magdalen heard any one respond so loud in the Psalter, or seen any one bow so low in the Creed as he did ; while in the chants and psalms he almost drowned the choir itself, as his head went up and back as if it were following his spirit, which, judging from his manner, was borne almost to Pisgah's top.

"He must be an awful pious man. I shouldn't wonder if he was a minister, and should preach this evening," Magdalen thought as she watched him, and, awed somewhat by his presence, she let her peppermint lozenges stay in her pocket, and only nibbled a little at the sprig of caraway when sure he would not see her.

She did not know that he had noticed her at all after the first glance of recognition, until the last chant, when her clear, sweet voice joined in the singing, making him pause a moment to listen, while a look of pleased surprise came into his face as he turned toward her.

He had not seen Hester distinctly, for she was behind him ; but Hester saw him and pronounced him some "starched-up city buck," and thought his coat too short for so old a man, and his neck too big and red.

"Jest the chap she shouldn't want to have much to do with," was her mental comment, and his loud "Good Lord, deliver us" sounded to the shrewd old woman like mockery, for she did not believe he felt it a bit.

Hester did not like the stranger's appearance, but she wondered who he was, and when church was out, and she was walking down the street with her niece who kept the public house, she spoke of him, and learned that he was stopping at the Montauk, as the little hotel was named. He came about noon the previous day, Martha said ; had called for their best room, and drank wine with his dinner, and smoked a sight of cigars, and had a brandy sling sent up to him in the evening. She did not remember his name, and she guessed he must have a great deal

of money from his appearance. He was going to New York in
the night train, and that was all she knew. Hester made no
special remark, and as they just then reached the cross-roads
where their paths diverged, she bade her niece good-day, and
walked on towards Millbank.

Meantime, Magdalen was reciting her Sunday-school lesson,
and finishing her caraway and lozenges, and telling her companions that she was going away to school by and by, as Mr. Roger
wrote she must. The school question did not seem as formi-
dable to-day as yesterday. Miss Nellie Johnson, who represented the first young lady in town, had been to Charlestown
Seminary, and so had Mr. Fullerton's daughters and Lilian
Marsh, who was an orphan and an heiress. On the whole,
Magdalen had come to think it would set her up a little to go
away, and she talked quite complacently about it, and said she
guessed it would be to Charlestown, where Miss Johnson had
been graduated ; but she made no mention of New Haven or
Alice Grey, though the latter was in her mind when she sang
the closing hymn, and went out of the church into the beautiful
sunshine. The day was so fine, and the air so clear, that Magdalen thought to prolong her walk by going round by the graveyard, as she sometimes did on a Sunday. The quiet, shaded
spot where Squire Irving was buried just suited her Sunday
moods, and she would far rather lie there on the grass, than sit
in the kitchen at Millbank, and recite her catechism to Hester
or read a sermon to Aleck, whose eyes were growing dim.

It would seem that another than herself liked the shadow of
the evergreens and the seclusion of Squire Irving's lot, for as
Magdalen drew near the gate, she saw the figure of a man reclining upon the grass, while a feathery ring which curled up
among the branches of the trees denoted that he was smoking.
Magdalen did not think it just the thing to smoke there among
the graves, and the stranger fell a little in her estimation, for it
was the stranger, and he arose at once, and bade Magdalen
good-afternoon, and called her *Miss Rogers,* as if he thought
that was her name.

" I find this place cooler than my hot room at the Montauk,"
he said ; and then he spoke of having seen her at church, and
asked who had taught her to sing.

"Mr. Roger," she replied. "He used to sing with me before
he went away. He has a splendid voice, and is a splendid
scholar, too."

And then, as that reminded her of New Haven and Alice
Grey, she continued : "We heard from Mr. Roger yesterday,
and he said I was to go to school in New Haven, but I don't
want to go there a bit."

"Why not ?" the stranger asked ; and Magdalen replied :

"Oh, because I don't. Frank is there, and he told me so
much about a Miss Alice Grey, and wants me to be like her ;
and I can't, and I don't want to know her, for she would laugh
at me, and I should be sure to hate her."

"Hate Alice ! Impossible ! " dropped involuntarily from the
stranger's lips, and turning upon him her bright eyes, Magdalen said :

"Do you know Frank's Alice Grey ?"

" I know one Alice Grey, but whether it is Frank's Alice, I
cannot tell. I should devoutly hope not," was the stranger's
answer ; and Magdalen noticed that there was a disturbed look
on his face, and that he forgot to resume his cigar, which lay
awhile smouldering in the grass, and finally went out.

He did not seem disposed to talk much after that, and Magdalen kept very quiet, wondering who he was, until her attention was suddenly diverted into another channel by noticing,
for the first time, the absence of the bouquet which she had
brought the day before and left upon the grave.

" Somebody has stole my flowers ! I'll bet it's Jim Bartlett.
He's always doing something bad," she exclaimed, and she
searched among the grass for the missing bouquet.

The stranger helped her hunt, and not finding it, said he pre
sumed some one had taken it, — that *Jim* was a bad boy to
steal, and Magdalen must talk to him and teach him the eighth
commandment. Anxious to confront and accuse the thieving

4

Jim, Magdalen left the graveyard, and was soon engaged in a hot battle with the boy, who denied all knowledge of the flowers, declaring he had not been in the yard for a week, and throwing tufts of grass and gravel-stones after her as she finally left him and walked away, wondering, if Jim did not take the flowers, who did.　She never dreamed of suspecting the stranger, or guessed that when he left Belvidere there was in one corner of his satchel the veritable bouquet which she had arranged in memory of poor Jessie, or that the sight of those faded flowers had touched a tender chord in his heart, and made him for several days kinder and gentler to a poor, worn, weary invalid, whom nothing in all the world had power to quiet or soothe.

CHAPTER X.

FRANK AT MILLBANK.

FOUR days later Magdalen received a letter from Frank, who was inconsolable.　Alice Grey had left school suddenly, without giving him a chance to say good-by.　Why she had gone or where, he did not know.　He only knew she *was* gone, and that he thought college a bore, and New Haven a stupid place, and was mighty glad that vacation was so close at hand, as he wanted to come up to Millbank and fish again in the river.

"I think he might just as well spend a part of his time at home, as to be lazin' 'round here for me to wait on," Hester said, when Magdalen communicated the news of Frank's projected visit to her.

Hester did not favor Frank's frequent visits to Millbank. They made her too much work, for what with opening the dining-room and bringing out the silver, and getting extra meals, and seeing to his sleeping room, and ironing his seven fine shirts

every week, with as many collars and pairs of socks, to say
nothing of linen coats and pants, and white vests, she had her
own and Bessie's hands quite full.

"Then, too, Magdalen was jest good for nothin' when he was
there," she said, "and made a deal more work; for, of course,
she must eat with the young gentleman instead of out in the
kitchen, as was her custom when they were alone; and it took
more time to cook for two than one."

Of Hester's opinion Frank knew nothing, and he came to
Millbank one delightful morning after a heavy shower of the
previous night, when the air was pure and sweet with the scent
of the grass just cut on the lawn, and the perfume of the flowers
blooming in such profusion in the garden. Millbank was beautiful to the tired, lazy young college student, who hated books
and tutors, and rules and early recitations, and was glad to get
away from them all and revel awhile at Millbank. He felt perfectly at home there, and always called for what he wanted, and
ordered the servants with as much assurance as if he had been
the master. He had not forgotten about the will. He understood it far better now than he had done when, a little white-
haired boy, he fidgeted at his mother's side and longed to go
back to the baby in the candle-box. He had heard every particular many a time from his mother, who still adhered to her
olden belief that there was another will which, if not destroyed,
would one day be found.

"I wish it would hurry up, then," Frank had sometimes said,
for with his expensive habits, four hundred dollars a year seemed
a very paltry sum.

In his wish that "it would hurry up," he intended no harm
to Roger. Frank was not often guilty of reasoning or thinking
very deeply about anything, and it did not occur to him how
disastrously the finding of the will which gave him Millbank
would result for Roger. He only knew that he wanted money,
and unconsciously to himself had formed a habit of occasionally wondering if the missing will ever would be found. This
was always in New York or New Haven, when he wanted some-

thing beyond his means or had some old debt to pay. At Millbank, where he was free from care, with his debts in the distance and plenty of servants and horses at his command, he did not often think of the will, though the possibility that there was one might have added a little to his assured manner, which was far more like one who had a right to command than Roger's had ever been.

Magdalen was waiting for him by the gate at the end of the avenue, on the afternoon, when, with his carpet-bag in hand, he came leisurely up the street from the depot, thinking as he came how beautiful the Millbank grounds were looking, and what a "lucky dog" Roger was to have stepped into so fair an inheritance without any exertion of his own. And with these thoughts came a remembrance of the will, and Frank began to plan what he would do if it should ever be found. He would share equally with Roger, he said. He would not stint him to four hundred a year. He would let him live at Millbank just the same, and Magdalen, too, provided his mother did not raise too many objections; and that reminded him of what his mother had said to him that morning as he sat, breakfasting with her, in the same little room where we first saw her.

Mrs. Walter Scott had not been in a very amiable mood when she came down to breakfast that morning. Eleven years of the wear and tear of fashionable life had changed her from the fair, smooth-faced woman of twenty-eight into a rather faded woman of thirty-nine, who still had some pretensions to beauty, but who found that she did not attract quite so much attention as she used to do a few years ago, when she was younger, and Frank was not so tall, and so fearful a proof that her youthful days were in the past. Her hair still fell in long limp curls about her face, but part of its brightness and luxuriance was gone, and this morning, as she arranged it in a stronger light than usual, she discovered to her horror more than one white hair showing here and there among the brown, and warning her that middle age was creeping on, while the same strong light showed her how lines were deepening across her forehead and about her eyes, effects more of dissipation and late hours than of Father Time. Mrs. Walter Scott did not like to grow old and gray and ugly and poor with all the rest, as she felt that she was doing. Her house in Lexington Avenue could only afford her a shelter. It would not feed or clothe her, or pay her bills at Saratoga or Long Branch or Newport. Neither would the interest of the ten thousand dollars given her by Squire Irving, and she had long ago begun to use the principal, and had nothing to rely on when that was gone except Roger's generosity, and the possibility of the lost will turning up at last. She was wanting to go to Long Branch this summer ; her dear friends were all going, and had urged her to join them, but her account at the bank was too low to admit of that, and yesterday she had given her final answer, and seen the last of her set depart without her. She had not hinted to them the reason for her refusal to join them. She had said she did not care for Long Branch, and when they exclaimed against her remaining in the dusty city, she had mentioned Millbank and the possibility of her going there for the month of August. She did not really mean it ; but when Frank, who had only been home from college three days, told her at the breakfast table that he was going to Millbank after pure air, and rich sweet cream, which was a weakness of his, she felt a longing to go, too, — a desire for the cool house and pleasant grounds, to say nothing of the luxuries which were to be had there in so great abundance. But since the morning of her departure from Millbank she had received no invitation to cross its threshold, and had not seen Roger over half a dozen times. He felt that she disliked him, and kept out of her way, stopping always at a hotel when in New York, instead of going to her house on Lexington Avenue. He had called there, however, and taken tea the day before he sailed for Europe, and Mrs. Walter Scott remembered with pleasure that she had been very affable on that occasion, and pressed him to spend the night. Surely, after that, she might venture to Millbank, and she hinted as much to Frank, who would rather she should stay where she was. But he was not quite unfilial enough to say so. He only suggested that an invitation from the proper authorities might be desirable before she took so bold a step.

"You used to snub Roger awfully," he said; "and if he was like anybody else, he wouldn't forget it in a hurry ; but, then, he isn't like anybody else. He's the best-hearted and most gen· erous chap I ever knew."

"Generous !" Mrs. Walter Scott repeated, with a tinge of sarcasm in her voice.

"Yes, generous," said Frank. "He has always allowed me more than the will said he must, and he's helped me out of more than forty scrapes. I say, again, he is the most generous chap I ever knew."

"I hope he will prove it in a few weeks, when you are of age, by giving you more than that five thousand named in the will," was Mrs. Walter Scott's next remark. "Frank," — and she lowered her voice lest the walls should hear and report, — "we are *poor.* This house and three thousand dollars are all we have in the world ; and unless Roger does something handsome for you, there is no alternative for us but to mortgage the house, or sell it, and acknowledge our poverty to the world. I have sold your father's watch and his diamond cross."

"Mother !" Frank exclaimed, his tone indicative of his surprise and indignation.

"I had to pay Bridget's wages, and defray the expense of that little party I gave last winter," was the lady's apology, to which Frank responded :

"Confound your party ! People as poor as we are have no business with parties. Sell father's watch ! and I was intending to claim it myself when I came of age. It's too bad ! You'll be selling me next ! I'll be hanged if it isn't deuced inconvenient to be so poor ! I mean to go to Millbank and stay. I'm seldom troubled with the blues when there."

"I wish you could get me an invitation to go there, too," Mrs. Walter Scott said. "It will look so queer to stay in the city all summer, as I am likely to do. I should suppose

Roger would want somebody besides old Hester to look after
Magdalen. She must be a large girl now."

It was the first sign of interest Mrs. Walter Scott had shown
in Magdalen, and Frank, who liked the girl, followed it up by
expatiating upon her good qualities, telling how bright and
smart she was, and how handsome she would be if only she
could be dressed decently. Then he told her of Roger's intention to send her to school, and after a few more remarks
arose from the table and began his preparations for Millbank.
Frank was usually very light-hearted and hopeful, but there was
a weight on his spirits, and his face wore a gloomy look all the
way from New York to Hartford. But it began to clear as
Millbank drew near. There was his Eldorado, and by the time
the station was reached, he had forgotten the impending mortgage, and his father's watch, and his own poverty. It all came
back, however, with a thought of the will, and he found himself
wishing most devoutly that the missing document could be
found, or else that Roger would do the handsome thing, and
come down with a few thousands on his twenty-first birthday,
now only three weeks in the distance. The sight of Magdalen,
however, in her new white ruffled apron, with her hair curling
in rings about her head, and her great round eyes dancing with
joy, diverted his mind from Roger and the will, and scattered
the blues at once.

"Oh; Mag, is that you?" he exclaimed, coming quickly to
her side. "How bright and pretty you look!"

And the tall young man bent down to kiss the little girl, who
was very glad to see him, and who told him how dull it had
been at Millbank, and how Aleck said there was good fishing
now in the creek, and a great many squirrels in the woods, though
she did not want him to kill them, and that he was going to
have the blue room instead of his old one, which was damp
from a leak around the chimney; that she had put lots of
flowers in it, and a photograph of herself, in a little frame made
of twigs. This last she had meant to keep a secret, and surprise the young man, who was sure to be so delighted. But

she had let it out, and she rattled on about it, till the house was reached, and Frank stood in the blue room, where the wonderful picture was.

"Here, Frank, this is it.   This is me;" and she directed his attention at once to the picture of herself, sitting up very stiff and prim, with mitts on her hands, and Hester's best collar pinned around her high-necked dress, and Bessie's handkerchief, trimmed with cotton lace, fastened conspicuously at her belt.

Frank laughed a loud, hearty laugh, which had more of ridicule in it than approval; and Magdalen, who knew him so well, detected the ridicule, and knew he was making fun of what she thought so nice.

"You don't like it, and I got it on purpose for you and Mr. Roger, and sold strawberries to pay for it, because Hester said a present we earned ourselves was always worth more than if we took somebody else's money to buy it," Magdalen said, her lip beginning to quiver and her eyes to fill with tears.

"The man was a bungler who took you in that stiff position," Frank replied, "and your dress is too old. I'll show you one I have of Alice Grey, and maybe take you to Springfield, where you can sit just as she does."

This did not mend the matter much, and Magdalen felt as if something had been lost from the brightness of the day, and wondered if Roger too would laugh at her photograph, which had gone to him in Hester's letter.   Frank knew he had wounded her, and was very kind and gracious to her by way of making amends, and gave her the book with colored plates which he had bought for Alice Grey just before she left New Haven so suddenly.   It happened to be in his trunk, which was brought from the station that night, and he blessed his good stars that it was there, and gave it as a peace-offering to Magdalen, whose face cleared entirely; and who next day went with him down to the old haunt by the river, and fastened to his hook the worms she dug before he was up; and told him all about the stranger in the graveyard, and about her going to school. And then she asked him about Alice Grey, and the picture which he had of her.

"Did she give it to you?" Magdalen asked; but Frank affected not to hear her, and pretended to be busy with something which hurt his foot. He did not care to tell her that he had bought the picture at the gallery where it was taken. He would rather she should think Alice gave it to him, and after a moment he took it from his pocket and handed it to Magdalen, who stood for a long time gazing at it without saying a word. It was the picture of a sweet-faced young girl, whose short, chestnut hair rippled in waves all over her head just as Magdalen's did. Her dress was a white muslin, with clusters of tucks nearly to the waist, and her little rosetted slipper showed below the hem. Her head was leaning upon one hand, and the other held a spray of flowers, while around her were pictures, and vases, and statuettes, with her straw hat lying at her feet, where she had evidently thrown it when she sat down to rest. It was a beautiful picture, and nothing could be more graceful than Alice's attitude, or afford a more striking contrast to the stiff position of poor Mag in that picture on Frank's table, in the blue room. Magdalen saw the difference at once, and ceased to wonder at Frank's non-appreciation of her photograph. It *was* a botch, compared with Alice's, and she herself was a botch, an awkward, unsightly thing in her long dress and coarse shoes, two sizes too big for her, such as she always insisted upon wearing for fear of pinching her toes. She had them on now, and a pair of stockings which wrinkled on the top of her foot, and she glanced first at them and then at the delicate slipper in the picture, and the small round waist, and pretty tucked skirt, and then, greatly to Frank's amazement, burst into a flood of tears.

"I don't wonder you like her best," she said, when Frank asked what was the matter. "I don't look like that. I can't, I haven't any slippers, nor any muslin dress; and if I had, Hester

4*

wouldn't let me have it tucked, it's such hard work to iron it. Alice has a mother, I know, — a good, kind mother, to take care of her and make her look like other little girls. Oh, I wish her mother was mine, or I had one just like her."

Alas, poor Magdalen. She little guessed the truth, or dreamed how dark a shadow lay across the pathway of pretty Alice Grey. She only thought of her as handsome and grace-ful and happy in mother and friends, and she wept on for a moment, while Frank tried to comfort her.

There was no more fishing that day, for Maggie's head began to ache, and they went back to Millbank, across the pleasant fields, in the quiet of the summer afternoon. Frank missed Magdalen's photograph from his table the next day, and had he been out by the little brook which ran through the grounds, he would have seen the fragments of it floating down the stream, with Magdalen standing by and watching them silently. They fished again after a day or two, and hunted in the woods and sat together beneath an old gnarled oak where Frank grew confidential, and told Magdalen of his moneyed troubles, and wondered if Roger would allow him more than five thousand when he came of age. And then he inadvertently alluded to the missing will, and told Magdalen about it, and said it might be well enough for her to hunt for it occasionally, as she had access to all parts of the house. And Magdalen promised that she would, without a thought of how the finding of it might affect Roger. She would not for the world have harmed one whom she esteemed and venerated as she did Roger, but he was across the sea, and Frank had her ear and her sympathy. It would be a fine thing to find the will, particularly as Frank had promised her a dress like Alice Grey's and a piano, if she succeeded.

Frank was not a scoundrel, as some reader may be ready to suppose. He had no idea that the finding of the will would ruin Roger. He had received no such impression from his mother. She had not thought best to tell him all she believed, and had only insinuated that the missing will was more in his favor than the one then in force. Frank wanted money, — a great deal of money, and his want was growing constantly, and so he casually recommended Magdalen to hunt for the will, and then for a time gave the subject no more thought. But not so with Magdalen. She dreamed of the will by night, and hunted for it by day, when Frank did not claim her attention, until at last Hester stumbled upon her turning over the identical barrel of papers which Mrs. Walter Scott had once looked through.

"In the name of the people, what are you doing?" she asked; and Magdalen, who never thought of keeping her intentions a secret, replied, "I'm looking for that will which Mrs. Walter Scott says Squire Irving made before he died."

For an instant Hester was white as a ghost, and her voice was thick with passion or fright, as she exclaimed, "A nice business, after all Roger has done for you, and a pretty pickle you'd be in, too, if such a will could be found. Don't you know you'd be hustled out of this house in less than no time? You'd be a beggar in the streets. Put up them papers quick, and don't let me catch you rummagin' again. If Frank is goin' to put such notions into your head, he'd better stay away from Millbank. Come with me, I say!"

Hester was terribly excited, and Magdalen looked at her curiously, while there flashed across her mind a thought, which yet was hardly a thought, that, if there *was* a will, Hester knew something of it. Let a woman once imagine there is a secret or a mystery in the house, and she seldom rests until she has ferreted it out. So Magdalen, though not a woman, had the instincts of one; and her interest in the lost document was doubled by Hester's excitement, but she did not look any more that day, nor for many succeeding ones.

On Frank's birthday there came letters from Roger, and the same train which brought them brought also Mrs. Walter Scott. She had found the city unendurable with all her acquaintance away, and had ventured to come unasked to Millbank. Hester was not glad to see her. Since finding Magdalen in the garret, she had suspected Frank of all manner of evil designs, and now his mother had come to help him carry them out. She had no fears of their succeeding. She knew they would not; but she did not want them there, and she spoke very short and crisp to Mrs. Walter Scott, and was barely civil to her. Mrs. Walter Scott, on the contrary, was extremely urbane and sweet. She did not feel as assured as she had done when last at Millbank. There was nothing of the mistress about her now. She was all smiles and softness, and gentleness, and called Hester " My dear Mrs. Floyd," and squeezed her hand, and told her how well and young she was looking, and petted Magdalen, and ran her white fingers through her rings of hair, and said it was partly on her account she had come to Mill-bank.

" I heard from Frank that she was to go to school in the autumn, and knowing what a bore it would be for you, Mrs. Floyd, to see to her wardrobe, with all the rest you have to do, I ventured to come, especially as I have been longing to see the old place once more. How beautiful it is looking, and how nicely you and your good husband have kept everything! How is Mr. Floyd ? "

Hester knew there was a good deal of what she called " soft-soap" in all the lady said ; but kind words go a great ways with everybody, and Hester insensibly relaxed her stiffness and went herself with Mrs. Walter Scott to her room and opened the shutters, and brought clean towels for the rack, and asked if her guest would have a lunch or wait till dinner was ready.

" Oh, I'll wait, of course. I do not mean to give you one bit of trouble," was the suave reply, and Hester departed, wondering to herself at the change, and if " Mrs. Walter Scott hadn't j'ined the church or something."

CHAPTER XI.

ROGER'S LETTERS AND THE RESULT.

HILE Mrs. Walter Scott was resting, Roger's letters were brought in. There was one for Frank, which he carried to his own room, and one for Magdalen, who broke the seal at once and screamed with delight as Roger's photograph met her view. He had had it taken for her in Dresden, and hoped it would afford her as much pleasure to receive it as hers had given him. He did not say that he thought her position stiff, and her dress too old for her, though he had thought it, and smiled at the prim, old-womanish figure, sitting so erect in the high-backed chair. But he would not willingly wound any one, much less the little girl who had picked berries in the hot sun to pay for the picture. So he thanked her for it, and inclosed his own, and gave his consent to the Charlestown arrangement, and asked again that some competent person should take charge of her wardrobe, which he wanted in every respect "to be like that of other young girls." He underscored this line, and Hester, who read the letter after Magdalen, felt her blood tingle a little, and knew that her day for dressing Magdalen was over. As for Magdalen, she was too much engrossed in Roger's picture to think much of the contents of the letter.

"Oh, isn't he splendid looking ; but I should be awfully afraid of him now," she said, as she went in quest of Frank.

She found him in his room, with a disturbed, disappointed look upon his face. Roger had *not* made him a rich man on his twenty-first birthday. He had only ordered that six thousand dollars should be paid to him instead of five, as mentioned in the will, and had said that inasmuch as Frank had another year in college the four hundred should be continued for the year and increased by an additional hundred, as seniors usually wanted a little spending money. Frank's good sense

told him that this was more than he had a right to expect, that
Roger was and always had been very generous with him; but
he knew, too, that he was owing here and there nearly a thousand dollars, while, worse than all, there was for sale in Millbank the most beautiful fast horse, which he greatly coveted
and had meant to buy, provided Roger came down hand-
somely.   Knowing that horses had been his father's ruin and
his grandfather's aversion, Frank had abstained tolerably well
from indulging his taste, which was decidedly toward the race-
course.   But he had always intended to own a horse as soon as
he was able.   According to the will, he could not use for that
purpose any of the five thousand dollars left to him.   That was
to set him up in business, though what the business would be
was more than he could tell.   He hated study too much to be
a lawyer or doctor, and had in his mind a situation in some
banking house where capital was not required, and with his
salary and the interest of what Roger was going to give him he
should do very well.   That interest had dwindled down to a
very small sum, and in his disappointment Frank was accusing
Roger of stinginess, when Magdalen came in.   She saw something was the matter, and asked what it was, at the same time
showing him Roger's picture, at which he looked attentively.

"Foreign travel is improving him," he said.   "He looks as if
he hadn't a care in the world; and why should he have, with an
income of twenty or twenty-five thousand a year?   What does
he know of poverty, or debts, or self-denials?"

Frank spoke bitterly, and Magdalen felt that he was blaming
Roger, whose blue eyes looked so kindly at him from the photograph.

"What is it, Frank?" she asked again; and then Frank told
her of his perplexities, and how much he owed, and how he had
expected more than a thousand dollars from Roger, and, as he
talked, he made himself believe that he was badly used, and
Magdalen thought so, too, though she could not quite see how
Roger was obliged to give him money, if he did not choose to
do so.

Still she was very sorry for him; and wished that she owned Millbank, so she could share it with the disconsolate Frank.

" I mean to write to Mr. Roger about it, and ask him to give you more," she said, a suggestion against which Frank uttered only a feeble protest.

As he felt then, he was willing to receive aid by almost any means, and he did not absolutely forbid Magdalen to write as she proposed ; neither, when she spoke of the will, and her intention to continue her search for it, did he offer any remonstrance. He rather encouraged that idea, and his face began to clear, and, before dinner was announced, Magdalen heard him practising on his guitar, which had been sent from New York by express, and which Hester likened to a " corn-stock fiddle."

Mrs. Walter Scott came down to dinner, very neatly dressed in a pretty muslin of a white-ground pattern, with a little lavender leaf upon it, her lace collar fastened with a coral pin, and coral ornaments in her ears. Her hair was curling better than usual, and was arranged very becomingly, while her long train swept back behind her and gave her the air of a queen, Magdalen thought, as she stood watching her. She was very gracious to Magdalen all through the dinner, and doubly, trebly so after a private conference with Frank, who told her of his disappointment, and what Magdalen had said about writing to Roger, as well as hunting for the will. Far more shrewd and cunning than her son, who, with all his faults, was too honorable to stoop to stratagem and duplicity, Mrs. Walter Scott saw at once how she could make a tool of Magdalen, and by being very kind and gracious to her, play into her own hands in more ways than one. Accompanying Roger's letter was a check for five hundred dollars, which Hester was to use for Magdalen's wardrobe, and for the payment of her bills at school as long as it lasted. When more was needed, more would be sent, Roger said ; and he asked that everything needful should be furnished to make Magdalen on an equality with other young girls of her age. Here was a chance for Mrs. Walter Scott. She had good taste. She knew what school-girls needed. She could be economical, too, if she tried, she said with her sweet, winning way ; and if Mrs. Floyd pleased, she would, while at Millbank, relieve her entirely of all care of Magdalen's dress, and see to it herself.

" Better keep family matters in the family, and not go to Mrs. Johnson, who knows but little more of such things than you do," she said to Hester, who, for once in her life, was hoodwinked, and consented to let Mrs. Walter Scott take Magdalen and the check into her own hands.

There were two or three trips to New York, and two or three milliners and dressmakers' bills paid and receipted and said nothing about. There were also bundles and bundles of dry goods forwarded to Millbank, from Stewart's, and Arnold's, and Hearne's, and one would have supposed that Magdalen was a young lady just making her *début* into fashionable society, instead of a little girl of twelve going away to school. The receipted bills of said bundles were all scrupulously sent across the water to Roger, to whom Mrs. Walter Scott wrote a very friendly letter, begging pardon for the liberty she had taken of going to his house uninvited, but expressing herself as so lonely and tired of the hot city, and so anxious to visit the haunt sacred to her for the sake of her dear husband, Roger's only brother. Then she spoke of Magdalen in the highest terms of praise, and said she had taken it upon herself to see that she was properly fitted out, and as Roger, being a bachelor, was not expected to know how much was actually required nowadays for a young miss's wardrobe, she sent him the bills that he might know what she was getting, and stop her if she was too extravagant.

This was her first letter, to which Roger returned a very gracious answer, thanking her for her interest in Magdalen, expressing himself as glad that she was at Millbank, asking her to prolong her visit as long as she found it agreeable, and saying he was not very likely to quarrel about the bills, as he had very little idea of the cost of feminine apparel.

Roger was not naturally suspicious, and it never occurred to him in glancing over the bills to wonder what a child of twelve could do with fifteen yards of blue silk or three yards of velvet. For aught he knew, blue silk and black silk and velvet were as appropriate for Magdalen as the merinos and Scotch plaids, and delaines and French calicoes, and ginghams, and little striped crimson and black silk which the lady purchased for Magdalen at reduced rates, and had made up for her according to her own good taste.

In Mrs. Walter Scott's second letter she spoke of two or three other bills which she had forgotten to enclose in her last, and which were now mislaid so that she could not readily find them. The amount was a little over one hundred dollars, and she mentioned it so that he might know just what disposition was made of his check while the money was in her hands. Then it *did* occur to Roger that Magdalen must be having a wonderful outfit, and for a moment a distrust of Mrs. Walter Scott flashed across his mind. But he quickly put it by as unworthy of him, and by way of making amends for the distrust, sent to the lady herself his check for one hundred dollars, which she was to accept for her kindness to Magdalen. Mrs. Walter Scott was in the seventh heaven of happiness, and petted Magdalen more than ever, and confirmed old Hester in her belief that "she had joined the church or met with a great change."

The will was never mentioned in Hester's presence, but to Magdalen Mrs. Walter Scott talked about it, not as anything in which she was especially interested, but as something which it was well enough to find if it really existed, and gave, as she believed it did, more money to Frank than the other one allowed him. Magdalen was completely dazzled and charmed by the great lady whom she thought so beautiful and grand, and whose long curls she stroked and admired, wondering a little why Mrs. Irving was so much afraid of her doing anything to straighten them, when her own hair, if once wet and curled and dried, could not well be combed out of place. Magdalen believed in Mrs. Walter Scott, and looked with a kind of disdain upon Mrs. Johnson and Nellie, who had once stood for her ideas of queens and princesses.   Now they were mere ciphers when compared with Mrs. Walter Scott, who took her to drive, and kept her in her own room, and kissed her affectionately when she promised of her own accord "to look for that will until it was found."

"My little pet, you make me so happy," she had said ; and Magdalen, flushed with pride and flattery, thought how delightful it would be to give the recovered document some day into the beautiful woman's hands and receive her honeyed words of thanks.

Those were very pleasant weeks for Magdalen which Frank and his mother spent at Millbank ; the pleasantest she had ever known, and she enjoyed them thoroughly.   The parlors were used every day, and Magdalen walked with quite an air through the handsome rooms, arrayed in some one of her new dresses which improved her so much, and made her, as Frank said, most as handsome as Alice Grey.   At her particular request she had a white muslin made and tucked just like Alice's in the picture, and then went with Frank to Springfield, and sat as Alice sat, with her head leaning on her hands, flowers in her lap, and her wavy hair arranged like Alice's.   It was a striking picture, prettier, if possible, than Alice's, except that in Magdalen's face there was an anxious expression, a look of newness, as if she had come suddenly into the dress and the position ; whereas Alice was easy and natural, as if tucked muslins and flowers were everyday matters with her.   Magdalen was not ashamed of her photograph this time, and she sent a copy to Roger, with the letter which she wrote him, and in which she made Frank the theme of her discourse.   There was nothing roundabout in Magdalen's character.   She came directly at what she wanted to say, and Roger was told in plain terms that Magdalen wished he would give Frank a little more money, that he had debts to pay, and had said that if he could get them off his mind he would never incur another, but would work like a dog to earn his own living when once he was through college. If Roger would do this, she, Magdalen, would study so hard at school and be so economical, that per haps she could manage to save all he chose to send to Frank Mrs. Irving had bought her more clothes than she needed, and she could make them last for two or three years, — she knew she could.

This was Magdalen's letter; and a week after Frank's return to college he was surprised by a request from Roger to send him a list of all his unpaid bills, as he wished to liquidate them. There were some bills which Frank did not care to have come under Roger's grave inspection; but as these chanced to be the largest of them all, he could not afford to lose the opportunity of having them taken off his hands; and so the list went to Roger, with a self-accusing letter full of promises of amendment. And kind, all-enduring Roger tried to believe his nephew sincere, and paid his debts, and made him a free man again, and wrote him a kind, fatherly letter, full of good advice, which Frank read with his feet on the mantel, an expensive cigar in his mouth, and a mint julep on the table beside him.

Meantime Magdalen had said good-by to Millbank, and was an inmate of Charlestown Seminary, where her bright face and frank, impulsive manner were winning her many friends among the young girls of her own age, and the quickness which she evinced for learning, and the implicit obedience she always rendered to the most trivial rule, were winning her golden laurels from her teachers, who soon came to trust Magdalen Lennox as they had seldom trusted any pupil before her.

Mrs. Walter Scott lingered at Millbank until the foliage, so fresh and green when she came, changed into scarlet and gold, and finally fell to the ground. Every day she stayed was clear gain to her, and so she waited until her friends had all returned to the city, and then took her departure and went back to New York, tolerably well satisfied with her visit at Millbank. She had made a good thing of it on the whole. She had managed.

to pay two or three little bills which were annoying her terribly, for she did not like to be in debt. She had secured herself a blue silk and a black silk, and a handsome velvet cloak, to say nothing of the hundred dollars, which Roger had sent for services rendered to Magdalen, and what was better for her peace of mind, she had made herself believe that there was nothing very wrong in the transaction. She would have shrunk from theft, had she called it by that name, almost as much as from midnight murder, but what she had done was not theft, nor yet was it dishonesty. It was simply taking a small part of what belonged to her, for she firmly believed in the will, and always would believe in it, whether it was found or not. So she sported her handsome velvet cloak on Broadway, and wore her blue-silk dress, without a qualm of conscience or a thought that they had come to her unlawfully.

CHAPTER XII.

ALICE GREY.

HILE the events we have narrated were transpiring at Millbank, the New York train bound for Albany had stopped one summer afternoon at a little station on the river, and then sped on its way, leaving a track of smoke and dust behind it. From the platform of the depot a young girl watched the cars till they passed out of sight, and then, with something like a sigh, entered the carriage waiting for her. Nobody had come to meet her but the driver, who touched his hat respectfully, and then busied himself with the baggage. The girl did not ask him any questions. She only looked up into his face with a wistful, questioning gaze, which he seemed to understand; for he shook his head sadly, and said, "Bad again, and gone."

Then an expression of deep sorrow flitted over the girl's face, and her eyes filled with tears as she stepped into the carriage. The road led several miles back from the river and up one winding hill after another, so that the twilight shadows were fading, and the night was shutting in the beautiful mountain scenery, ere the carriage passed through a broad, handsome park to the side entrance of a massive brick building, where it stopped, and the young girl sprang out, and ran hastily up the steps into the hall. There was no one there to meet her. Nothing but silence and loneliness, and the moonlight, which fell across the floor, and made the young girl shiver as she went on to the end of the hall, where a door opened suddenly, and a slight, straight woman appeared with iron-grey puffs around her forehead, diamonds in her ears, diamonds on her soft white hands, and diamonds fastening the lace ruffle, which finished the neck of her black-satin dress She was a proud-looking woman, with a stern, haughty face, which relaxed into something like a smile when she saw the young girl, who sprang forward with a cry, which might perhaps have been construed into a cry of joy, if the words which followed had been different.

"O, auntie," she said, taking the hand offered her, and putting up her lips for the kiss so gravely given — "O, auntie, *why* did father send for me to come home from the only place where I was ever happy?"

"I don't know. Your father's ways are ways of mystery to me," the lady said; and then, as if touched with something like pity for the desolate creature who had been brought from "the only place where she was ever happy," to this home where she could not be very happy, the lady drew her to a couch, and untied the blue ribbons of the hat, and unbuttoned the gray sack, doing it all with a kind of caressing tenderness which showed how dear the young girl was to her.

"But did he give you no reason, auntie? What did he say when he told you I was coming?" the girl asked vehemently, and the lady replied :

"He was away from Beechwood several days, travelling in New England, and when he came back he told me he had left orders for you to come home at once. I thought, from what he said, that he saw you in New Haven."

"I never saw or heard of him till Mr. Baldwin came, and said I was to leave school for home, and he was to be my escort. It's very strange that he should want me home now. Robert told me *she* was gone again. Did she get very bad?'"

The voice which asked this question was sad and low, like the voices of those who talk of their dead; and the voice which answered was low, too, in its tones.

"Yes, she took to rocking and singing night as well as day, and that, you know, makes your father nervous sooner than anything else."

"Did she want to go?"

"No; she begged to stay at first, but went quietly enough at the last."

"Did she ever mention *me*, auntie? Do you think she missed me and wanted me?"

"She spoke of you once. She said, 'If Allie was here, she wouldn't let me go.'"

"O, poor, poor darling! O, auntie, it's terrible, isn't it?"

Alice was sobbing now, and amid her sobs she asked:

"Was father gentle with her, and kind?"

"Yes, gentler, more patient than I have known him for years. It almost seemed as if something must have happened to him while he was gone, for he was very quiet and thoughtful when he came home, and did not order nearly as many brandy slings, though he smoked all the time."

"Not in her room!" and the girl looked quickly up.

"No, not in her room, — he spared her that; and when she first began to rock and sing, he tried his best to quiet her, but he couldn't. She was worse than usual."

"Oh, how dreadful our life is?" Alice said again, while a shiver as if she were cold ran over her. "I used to envy the girls at school who were looking forward with such delight to their vacations, when I had nothing but this for my portion. It is better than I deserve, I know, and it is wrong for me to murmur; but, auntie, nobody can ever envy me my home!"

Her white fingers were pressed to her eyes, and the tears were streaming through them, as she sat there weeping so bitterly, the fair young girl whom Magdalen Lennox had envied for her beauty, her muslin dress, her mother, her home! Alas! Magdalen, playing, and working, and eating, and living in the great kitchen at Millbank, had known more of genuine home happiness in a month than poor Alice Grey had known in her whole life. And yet Alice's home presented to the eye a most beautiful and desirable aspect. There were soft velvet carpets on all the floors, mirrors and curtains of costly lace in all the rooms, with pictures, and books, and shells, and rare ornaments from foreign lands; handsome grounds, with winding walks and terraced banks and patches of flowers, and fountains, and trees, and rustic seats, and vine-wreathed arbors, and shady nooks, suggestive of quiet, delicious repose; horses and carriages, and plenty of servants at command. This was Alice's home, and it stood upon the mountain-side, overlooking the valley of the Hudson, which could be seen at intervals winding its way to the sea.

An old Scotch servant, who had been in the family for years, came into the library where Alice was sitting, and after warmly welcoming her bonny mistress, told her tea was waiting in the little supper room, where the table was laid with the prettiest of tea-cloths, and the solid silver contrasted so brightly with the pure white china. There were luscious strawberries, fresh from the vines, and sweet, thick cream from Hannah's milk-house, and the nice hot tea-cakes which Alice loved, and her glass of water from her favorite spring under the rock, and Lucy stood and waited on her with as much deference as if she had been a queen.

Alice was very tired, and soon after tea was over she asked permission to retire, and Nannie, her own waiting-maid, went with her up the broad staircase and through the upper hall to

her room, which was over the library, and had, like that, a bay‧
window looking off into the distant valley.

Nannie was all attention, but Alice did not want her that
night. She would rather be alone ; and she dismissed the girl,
saying to her with a smile, "I had no good Nannie at school
to undress me and put up my things. We had to wait on our-
selves ; so you see I have become quite a little woman, and
shall often dispense with your services."

With her door shut on Nannie, Alice went straight to her
window, through which the moonlight was streaming, and kneeling down with her head upon the sill, she prayed earnestly for
grace to bear the loneliness and desolation weighing so heavily
on her spirits.

Although a child in years, Alice Grey had long since learned
at whose feet to lay her burdens. Her religion was a part of
her whole being, and she made it very beautiful with her loving,
consistent life. Her school companions had dubbed her the
little "Puritan," and sometimes laughed at her for what they
called her straight-laced notions; but there was not one of them
who did not love the gentle Alice Grey, or who would not have
trusted her implicitly, and stood by her against the entire
school.

Alice knew that she was apt to murmur too much at the
darkness overshadowing her home, and to forget the many
blessings which crowned her life, and she now asked forgiveness for it, and prayed for a spirit of thankfulness for all the
good Heaven had bestowed upon her. And then she asked
that, if possible, the shadow might be lifted from the life of one
who was at once a terror and an object of her deepest solicitude
and love.

Prayer with Alice was no mere form to be gone through ; it
was a real thing, — a communing with a living Presence, — and
she grew quiet and calm under its influence, and sat for a time
drinking in the beauty of the night, and looking far off across the
valley to the hills beyond, — the hills nearer to New Haven,
— where she had been so happy. Then, as she felt strong

enough to bear it, she took her lamp, and went noiselessly down the wide hall and through a green-baize door into a narrow passage which led away from the front part of the building. Before one of the doors she paused, and felt again the same heart-beat she had so many times experienced when she drew near that door and heard the peculiar sound which always made her for a moment faint and sick. But that sound was hushed now, and the room into which Alice finally entered was silent as the grave ; and the moon, which came through the windows in such broad sheets of silvery light, showed that it was empty of all human life save that of the young girl who stood looking round, her lip quivering and her eyes filling with tears as one familiar object after another met her view.

There was the cradle in the corner, just where it had stood for years, and the carpet in that spot told of the constant motion which had worn the threads away ; and there, too, was the chair by the window, where Alice had so often seen a wasted figure sit, and the bed with its snowy coverings, to which sleep was almost a stranger. Alice knelt by this bed, and with her hand upon the crib which seemed to bring the absent one so near to her, she prayed again, and her tears fell like rain upon the pillows which she kissed for the sake of the feverish, restless head which had so often lain there.

" Poor darling," she said, "do you know that Alice is here to-night in your own room ? Do you know that she is praying for you, and loving you, and pitying you so much ? "

Then as the words "if Allie was here I shouldn't have to go away," recurred to her mind, she sobbed, " No, darling, if Allie had been here you should not have gone, and now that she is here, she'll bring you back again ere long, and bear with all your fancies more patiently than she ever did before."

There was another kiss upon the pillow as if it had been a living face, and Alice's fair hands petted and caressed and smoothed the ruffled linen, and then she turned away and passed again into the passage and through the green-baize door,

5

back into the broader hall, where the air seemed purer, and she breathed free again.

The morning succeeding Alice's return to Beechwood was cool and beautiful, and the sun shone brightly through the white mist which lay on the river and curled up the mountain-side. Alice was awake early, and when Nan came to call her she found her dressed and sitting by the open window, looking out upon the grounds and the park beyond.

"You see I have stolen a march upon you, Nannie," Alice said; "but you may unlock that largest trunk, and help me put up my things."

The trunk was opened, and with Nannie's assistance Alice hung away all her pretty dresses, which were useless in this re-tired neighborhood, where they saw so few people. The tucked muslin, which Magdalen had admired in the picture, Nan folded carefully, smoothing out the rich Valenciennes lace and laying it away in a drawer, to grow yellow and limp, perhaps, ere it was worn again. Alice's chief occupation at Beechwood was to wander through the grounds or climb over the mountains and hills, with Nan or the house dog Rover as escorts; and so she seldom wore the dresses which had been the envy of her school-mates. She cared little for dress, and when at last she went down to the breakfast room to meet her stately aunt, she wore a simple blue gingham, and a white-linen apron, with dainty little pockets all ruffled and fluted and looking as fresh and pure as she looked herself, with her wavy hair, and eyes of violet blue.

Her aunt, in her iron-gray puffs, and morning-gown of silvery gray satin, was very precise and ceremonious, and kissed her graciously, and then presided at the table with as much formal-ity as if she had been giving a state dinner. There were straw-berries again, and flaky rolls, and fragrant chocolate, and a nice broiled trout from a brook among the hills, where Tom had caught it for his young lady, who, with a schoolgirl's keen appe-tite, ate far too fast to please her aunt, who, nevertheless, would not reprove her that first morning home. Breakfast being over, Alice, who was expecting her father that day, went to his room to see that it was in order. It adjoined the apart-ment where she had knelt in tears the preceding night, and there was a door between the two; but, while the other had been somewhat bare of ornament and handsome furniture, it would seem as if the master of the house had racked his brain to find rare and costly things with which to deck his own private room. There were marks of wealth and luxury visible everywhere, from the heavy tassels which looped the lace curtains of the alcove where the massive rosewood bed-stead stood, to the expensive pictures on the wall, — French pictures many of them, — showing a taste which some would call highly cultivated, and others questionable. Alice detested them, and before one, which she considered the worst, she had once hung her shawl in token of her disapprobation. She was accustomed to them now, and she merely gave them a glance, and then moved on to a pencil sketch, which she had never seen before. It was evidently a graveyard scene, for there were evergreens and shrubs, and a tall monument, and near them a little barefoot girl, with a basket of flowers, which she was laying on the grave. Alice knew it was her father's draw-ing, and she studied it intently, wondering where he got his idea, and who was the little girl, and whose the grave she was decorating with flowers. Then she turned from the picture to her father's writing-desk, and opened drawer after drawer until she came to one containing nothing but a faded bouquet of flowers, such as the girl in the picture might have been putting on the grave, and a little lock of yellow hair. Pinned about the hair was a paper, which bore the same date as did that let-ter which Roger Irving guarded with so much care.

Alice had heard of Roger Irving from Frank, who called him "uncle" when speaking of him to her. She had him in her mind as quite an elderly man, with iron-gray hair, perhaps, such as her auntie wore, and she had thought she would like to see Frank's paragon of excellence; but she had no idea how near he was brought to her by that faded bouquet and that lock of golden hair, which so excited her curiosity.

Her father had always been a mystery to her. That there was something in his past life which he wished to conceal, she felt sure, just as she was certain that he was to blame for that shattered wreck which sometimes made Beechwood a terror and a dread, but to which Alice clung with so filial devotion. There was very little in common between Alice and her father. A thorough man of the world, with no regard for anything holy and good, except as it helped to raise him in the estimation of his fellows, Mr. Grey could no more understand his gentle daughter, whose life was so pure and consistent, and so constant a rebuke to him, than she could sympathize with him in his ways of thinking and acting. There was a time when in his heart he had said there was no God, — a time when, without the slightest hesitancy, he would have trampled upon all God's divine institutions and set his laws at naught ; and the teachings of one as fascinating and agreeable as Arthur Grey had been productive of more harm than this life would ever show, for they had reached on even to the other world, where some of his deluded followers had gone before him. But as Alice grew into girlhood, with her sweet face and the example of her holy Christian life, there was a change, and people said that Arthur Grey was a better man. Outwardly he was, perhaps. He said no longer there was no God. He *knew* there was when he looked at his patient, self-denying daughter, and he knew that Grace alone had made her what she was. For Alice's sake he admitted Alice's God, and, because he knew it helped him in various ways, he paid all due deference to the forms of religion, and none were more regular in their attendance at the little church on the mountain side than he, or paid more liberally to every religious and charitable object. He believed himself that he had reformed, and he charged the reform to Alice and the memory of a golden-haired woman whom he had loved better than he had since loved a human being, save his daughter Alice. But far greater than his love for his daughter was his love of self, and because it suited him to do it he took his child from school without the shadow of an excuse to her, and was now making other arrangements for her without so much as asking how she would like them. He did not greatly care. If it suited him it must suit her ; and, as the first step toward the accomplishment of his object, he removed from Beechwood the great trial of his life, and put it where it could not trouble him, and turned a deaf ear to its entreaties to be taken back to "home" and "Allie" and the "crib" its poor arms had rocked so many weary nights. He knew the people with whom he left his charge were kind and considerate. He had tested them in that respect ; he paid them largely for what they did. "Laura" was better there than at Beechwood, he believed ; at all events he wanted her out of his way for a time, and so he had unclasped her clinging arms from his neck and kissed her flushed, tear-stained face, and put her from him, and locked the door upon her, and gone his way, thinking that when he served himself he was doing the best thing which Arthur Grey could do.

He was coming home the night after Alice's arrival, and the carriage went down to the station to meet him. There was a haze in the sky, and the moon was not as bright as on the previous night, when Allie rode up the mountain side ; but it was very pleasant and cool, and Mr. Grey enjoyed his ride, and thought how well he had managed everything, and was glad he had been so kind and gentle with Laura, and sent her that basket of fruit, and that pretty little *cradle,* which he found in New York ; and then he thought of Alice, and his heart gave a throb of pleasure when he saw the gleam of her white dress through the moonlight as she came out to meet him. There was a questioning look in her eyes, — a grieved, sorry kind ot expression, — which he saw as he led her into the hall, and he kissed her very tenderly, and, smoothing her chestnut hair, said in reply to that look :

"I knew you would hate to leave school, Allie ; but I am going to take you to Europe."

"'To Europe? Oh, father!" And Alice gave a scream of joy.

A trip to Europe had been her dream of perfect happiness, and now that the dream was to be fulfilled, it seemed too good to be true.

"Oh, auntie!" she cried, running up to that stately lady, who, in her iron-gray puffs and black satin of the previous night, was coming slowly to meet her brother, — "Auntie, we are go· ing to Europe, all of us! Isn't it splendid?"

She was very beautiful in her white dress, with her blue eyes shining so brightly, and she hung about her father in a caressing way, and played and sang his favorite songs; and then, when at last he bade her good-night, she shook her curly head, and, holding fast his hand, went with him up the stairs to his own room, which she entered with him. She felt that he did not want her there; but she stayed just the same, and, seating herself upon his knee, laid her soft, white arms across his neck, and, looking straight into his eyes, pleaded earnestly for the poor creature who had been an occupant of the adjoining room.

"Let her go with us, father. I am sure the voyage would do her good. Don't leave her there alone."

But Mr. Grey said "No," gently at first, then very firmly as Alice grew more earnest, and, finally, so sternly and decidedly, that Alice gave it up, with a great gush of tears, and only asked permission to see her once before she sailed. But to this Mr. Grey answered no, also.

"It would only excite her," he said; "and the more quiet she is kept, the better it is for her. I have seen that everything is provided for her comfort. She is better there than here, or with us across the sea. We shall be absent several years, perhaps, as I intend putting you at some good school where you will finish your education."

He intimated a wish for her to leave him then, and so she bade him good-night, and left him alone with his thoughts, which were not of the most agreeable nature. How still it was in the next room! — so still, that he trembled as he opened the door and went in, where Alice had wept so bitterly. He did not weep; he never wept; but he was conscious of a feeling of oppression and pain as he glanced around the quiet, orderly room, at the chair by the window, the bed in the corner, and the crib standing near.

"What could have put that idea into her head?" he asked himself, as, with his hand upon the cradle, he made the motion which poor Laura kept up so constantly.

Then with a sigh he went back to his own room, and stood a long time before that picture of the graveyard, which hung upon the wall. There was a softness now in his eyes and manner, — a softness which increased when he turned to his chair by the writing-desk, and took from a drawer the faded flowers and the curl of hair which Alice had found.

"Poor Jessie! I wish I had never crossed her path," he said, as he put the curl and flowers away, and thought again of Alice and the little dark-eyed girl who had designated her "Frank's Alice Grey."

"Frank's, indeed!" he said; "I trust I have effectually stopped any foolishness of that kind."

Frank Irving was evidently not a favorite with Mr. Grey, though not a word was ever said of him to Alice, who, as the days went by, began to be reconciled to her removal from school, and to interest herself in her preparations for the trip to Europe. They were to sail the last of August, and one morning, in October, Magdalen received a letter from Frank, saying that he had just heard, from one of Miss Dana's pupils, that Alice Grey had gone to Italy.

CHAPTER XIII.

A RETROSPECT.

IX years have passed away and we lift the curtain of our story in Charlestown, and, after pausing there a moment, go back across the bridge which spans the interval between the present and the past. It was the day but one before the close of the term, and those who had learned to love each other with a school-girl's warm, impetuous love, would soon part, some forever and some to meet again, but when, or where, none could tell.

"It may be for years, and it may be forever!"

sang a clear, bird-like voice in the music-room, where Magdalen Lennox was practising the song she was to sing the following night.

"Yes, it may be for years, and it may be forever! I wish there were no such thing as parting from those we love," the young girl sighed, as, with her sheet of music in her hand, she passed through the hall, and up the stairs, to the room which had been hers so long.

Magdalen had been very happy at Charlestown, where every one loved her, from the teacher, whom she never annoyed, to the smallest child, whom she so often helped and encouraged ; and she had enjoyed her vacations at Millbank, and more than once had taken two or three of her young friends there for the winter or summer holidays. And Hester had petted, and admired, and waited upon her, and scolded her for soiling so many white skirts, and then had sat up nights to iron these skirts, and had remarked, with a feeling of pride and complacency, that Hattie Johnson's dresses were not as full or as long as Magdalen's. Hester was very proud of Magdalen ; they were all proud of her at Millbank, and vied with each other in their attentions to her ; and Magdalen appreciated their kind ness, and loved her pleasant home, and thought there was no place like it in the world; but for all that she rather dreaded returning to it for good, with nothing to look forward to in the future. She understood her position now far better than when she was a child, and as she thought over the strange circumstances which had resulted in bringing her to Millbank, her cheeks had burned crimson for the mother who had so wantonly deserted her. Still she could not hate that mother, and her nightly prayers always ended with a blessing upon her, and a petition that she might sometime find her, or know, at least, who she was. She knew she had no claim on Roger Irving, and, as she grew older, she shrank from a life of dependence at Millbank, especially as *Frank* was likely to be there a good share of his time.

With all the ardor of her impulsive nature she had clung to and believed in him, until the day when he, too, said good-by, and left her for Europe. He had been graduated with tolerable credit to himself, and because of his fine oratorical ability had appeared upon the stage, and made what Magdalen had thought a "splendid speech;" for Magdalen was there in the old Centre Church, listening with wrapt attention, and a face radiant with the admiration she felt for her hero, whose graceful gestures and clear, musical voice covered a multitude of defects in his rather milk-and-watery declamation. It was Magdalen's bouquet which had fallen directly at his feet when his speech was ended, and nothing could have been prettier than his manner as he stooped to pick it up, and then bowed his thanks to the young girl, whose face flushed all over with pride, both then and afterward, when, in the evening, she leaned upon his arm at the reception given to the students and their friends. Magdalen was a little girl of thirteen-and-a-half, while Frank was twenty-two; was a graduate; was Mr. Irving, of New York; and could afford to patronize her, and at the same time be very polite and attentive to scores of young ladies whose acquaintance he had made during his college career.

After that July day in New Haven, the happiest and proud-

5*

est of Magdalen's life, he went with her to Millbank, and fished
again in the Connecticut, and hunted in the woods, and smoked
his cigars beneath the maple-trees, and teazed and tyrannized
over, and petted, and made a slave of Magdalen, just as the
fancy took him. Then there came a letter from Roger, written after the receipt of one from Magdalen, who, because she
fancied it might please her hero, had said how much Frank
would enjoy a year's travel in Europe, and how much good it
would do him, especially as he was looking worn and thin from
his recent close application to study.

Roger bit his lip when he read that letter and wondered if
the hint was Frank's suggestion, and wondered, too, if it were
best to act upon it; and then, with a genuine desire to see his
young kinsman, he wrote to Frank, inviting him to Paris, and
offering to defray his expenses for a year in Europe. Frank
was almost beside himself with joy, for, except at Millbank, he
felt that he had no home, proper, in the world. His mother
had been compelled to rent her handsome house, and board
with the people who rented it. This just supported her, and
nothing more. He would be in the way in Lexington Avenue,
and he accepted Roger's invitation eagerly; and one bright
day, in September, sailed out of the harbor at New York, while
Magdalen stood on the shore and waved her handkerchief to
him until the vessel passed from sight.

The one year abroad had grown into five; Roger was fond
of travel; he had plenty of money at his command; it was as
cheap living in Europe as at Millbank, where under efficient
superintendence everything seemed to go on as well without as
with him. He never encroached upon his principal, even after
Frank came to be his companion, and so he had lingered year
after year, sometimes in glorious Italy, sometimes climbing the
sides of Switzerland's snow-capped mountains, sometimes wandering through the Holy Land or exploring the river Nile, and
again resting for months on the vine-clad hills which overshadow the legendary Rhine. Frank was not always with him.
He did not care for pictures, or scenery, or works of art; and

when Roger stopped for months to improve himself in these, Frank went his own way to voluptuous Paris, where the gay society suited him better, or on to the beautiful island of Ischia, where all was "so still, so green, and so dreamy," and where at the little mountain inn, called the " Piccola Sentinella," and which overlooked the sea, he met again with Alice Grey.

But any hopes he might have entertained with regard to the girl whom he had admired so much in New Haven were effectually cut off by the studied coolness of Mr. Grey's manner towards him, and the obstacles constantly thrown in the way of his seeing her alone. Mr. Grey did not like Frank Irving, and soon after the arrival of the latter at the " Piccola Sentinella," he gave up his rooms at the inn, and started with his daughter for Switzerland. There was a break then in Frank's letters to Magdalen, and when at last he wrote again it was to say that he was coming home, and that Roger was coming with him.

This letter, which reached Magdalen the night preceding the examination, awoke within her a feeling of uneasiness and disquiet. She had been always more or less afraid of Roger, and she was especially so now that she had not seen him for more than eight years, and he would undoubtedly expect so much from her as a graduate and a young lady of eighteen. She almost wished he would stay in Europe, or that she had some other home than Millbank. It would not be half so pleasant with the master there, as it used to be in other days when she was a little girl fishing with Frank in the river, or hunting with him in the woods. Frank would be at Millbank, too, it was true; but the travelled Frank, who spoke French like a native, was very different from the Frank of five years ago, and Magdalen dreaded him almost as much as she dreaded Roger himself, wondering if he would tease her as he used to do, and if he would think her improved and at all like Alice Grey, whom she knew he had met again at the " Piccola Sentinella." " I wish they would stay abroad five years more," she thought, as she finished reading Frank's letter ; and her cheeks grew so hot and red, and her pulse beat so rapidly, that it was long after midnight ere she could quiet herself for the rest she would need on the morrow, when she was to act so conspicuous a part.

CHAPTER XIV.

IN THE EVENING.

AGDALEN was very beautiful in her white, fleecy dress, which swept backward with as broad and graceful a sweep as ever Mrs. Walter Scott's had done when she walked the halls at Millbank.   There were flowers on her bosom, knots of flowers on her short sleeves, and flowers in her wavy hair, which was arranged in heavy coils about her head, with one or two curls falling behind her ears.   She knew she was handsome ; she had been told that too often not to know it ; while had there been no other means of knowledge within her reach, her mirror would have set her right.   But Magdalen was not vain, and there was not the slightest tinge of self-consciousness in her manner as she went through the various parts assigned her during the day, and received the homage of the crowd.   Once her room-mate had asked if she did not wish Mr. Irving could be present in the evening, and Magdalen had answered, " No, I would not have him here for the world.   I should be sure to make a miserable failure, if I knew Mr. Irving and Frank were looking on.   But there is no danger of that.   They cannot have reached New York yet."

Later in the day, and just as it was growing dark, a young girl came into Magdalen's room, talking eagerly of "the two most splendid-looking men she had ever seen."

"They came," she said, " out of the hotel and walked before me all the way, looking hard at the seminary as they passed it. I wonder who they were.   Both were handsome, and one was perfectly splendid."

When Nellie Freeman was talking her companions usually listened to her, and they did so now, laughing at her enthusiasm, and asking several questions concerning the strangers who had interested her so much. Magdalen said nothing, and her cheek turned pale for an instant as something in Nellie's description of the younger gentleman made her wonder if the strangers could be Frank and Roger. But no: they could not have reached New York yet, and if they had, they would not come on to Charlestown without apprising her of their intentions, unless they wished to see her first without being themselves seen. The very idea of the latter possibility made Magdalen faint, and she asked if one of the gentlemen was "oldish looking?"

"No, both young, decidedly so," was Nellie's reply, which decided the matter for Magdalen.

It was not Roger Irving. She had seen no picture of him since the one sent her six years ago, and judging him by herself he must have changed a great deal since then. To girls of eighteen, thirty-two seems old ; and Roger was thirty-two, and consequently old, and very patriarchal, in Magdalen's estimation. There were some gray hairs in his head, and he began to stoop, and wear glasses when he read, if the print was fine and the light dim, she presumed. Nellie's hero was not Roger, and Magdalen arranged the flowers in her hair, and smoothed the long curls which fell upon her neck, and clasped her gold bracelets on her arms, and then, when it was time, appeared before the assembled crowd, who hailed her with acclamations of joy, and when her brilliant performance at the piano was ended, sent after her such cheers as called her back again, not to play this time, but merely to bow before the audience, which showered her with bouquets. Very gracefully she acknowledged the compliment paid to her, and then retired, her cheeks burning scarlet and her heart throbbing painfully as she thought of the face which she had seen far back among the spectators, just before she left the stage. Was it Frank who was standing on his feet and applauding her so heartily, and was that Roger beside

him? If so, she could never face that crowd again and sing
Kathleen Mavourneen. And yet she must. They were calling
for her now, and with a tremendous effort of the will she quieted
her beating heart and went again before the people. But she
did not look across the room toward the two figures in the
corner. She only knew there was a movement in that direction
as if some person or persons were going out, just as she took
her place by the piano. At first her voice trembled a little,
but gradually it grew steadier, clearer, and more bird-like in its
tones, while the people listened breathlessly, and tears rushed
to the eyes of some as she threw her whole soul into the pa-
thetic words, "It may be for years and it may be forever."
She did not think of the possible presence of Roger and Frank
then. She was thinking more of those from whom she was to
separate so soon, and she sang as she had never sung before,
so sweetly, so distinctly, that not a word was lost, and when
the song was ended there came a pause as if her listeners
were loth to stir until the last faint echo of the glorious music
had died away. Then followed a storm of applause, before
which all other cheers were as nothing, and bouquets of the
costliest kind fell in showers at her feet. Over one of these she
partly stumbled, and was stooping to pick it up when a young
man sprang to her side, and picking it up for her, said to her
in tones which thrilled her through and through, "Take my
arm, Magdalen, and come with me to Roger."

CHAPTER XV.

ROGER AND FRANK.

HE steamer in which Roger and Frank sailed for
America had reached New York three days before
Magdalen believed it due. In her tasteful parlor,
where her handsomest furniture was arranged, Mrs. Walter

Scott had received the travellers, lamenting to Roger amid her words of welcome that she could not entertain him now as she could once have done when at the head of her own household. She was a boarder still, and her income had not increased during the last five years. Her dresses were made to last longer than of old, and she always thought twice before indulging in any new vanity. Still she was in excellent spirits, induced in part by meeting her son again, and partly by a plan which she had in her mind and meant to carry out. It appeared in the course of the evening, when speaking of Magdalen, who was so soon to be graduated and return to Millbank.

"You'll be wanting some lady of experience and culture as a companion for Miss Lennox. Have you decided upon any one in particular?" she said to Roger, who looked at her in astonishment, wondering what she meant.

She explained her meaning, and made him understand that to a portion of the world at least it would seem highly improper for a young lady like Magdalen to live at Millbank without some suitable companion as a chaperone. She did not hint that she would under any circumstances fill that place. Neither did Roger then suspect her motive. He was a little disappointed and a little sorry, too, that any one should think it necessary for a second party to stand between him and Magdalen. He had met with many brilliant belles in foreign lands, high-born dames and court ladies with titles to their names, and some of these had smiled graciously upon the young American, and thought it worth their while to flatter and admire him, but not one of all the gay throng had ever made Roger's heart beat one throb the faster. Women were not to him what they were to fickle, flirting Frank, and that he would ever marry did not seem to him very probable, unless he found some one widely different from the ladies with whom he had come in contact. Of Magdalen, his baby, he always thought as he had last seen her, with her shaker-bonnet hanging down her back, and eyes brimfull of tears as she leaned over the gate watching him going down the avenue and away from Millbank. To him she was only a child, whose frolicsome ways and merry laugh, and warm-hearted, impulsive manner he liked to remember as some-thing which would still exist when he returned to Millbank. But Mrs. Walter Scott tore the veil away. Magdalen was a young lady, a girl of eighteen, and Roger began to feel a little uneasy with regard to the manner in which he would be ex-pected to treat her. As a father, or at most as her elder brother and guardian, he thought; but he could not see the necessity for that third person at Millbank just because a few of Mrs. Grundy's daughters might require it. At all events he would wait and see what Magdalen was like before he decided. He was to start next day for Millbank, whither a telegram had been sent telling of his arrival, and producing a great commo-tion among the servants.

Hester was an old woman now of nearly seventy, but her form was square and straight as ever, and life was very strong within her yet. With Aleck, whom time had touched less lightly, she still reigned supreme at Millbank. Ruey was long since married and gone, and six children played around her door. Rosy-cheeked Bessie, who had taken Ruey's place, was lying out in the graveyard not far from Squire Irving's monument, and Ruth now did her work, and came at Hester's call, after the telegram was read. The house was always kept in order, but this summer it had undergone a thorough renovation in honor of Roger's expected arrival, and so it was only needful that the rooms should be opened and aired, and fresh linen put upon the beds, and water carried to the chambers, for Frank was to accompany Roger. When all was done, the house looked very neat and cool and inviting, and to Roger, who had not seen it for eight years, it seemed, with its pleasant grounds and the scent of new-mown hay upon the lawn, like a second Eden, as he rode up the avenue to the door, where his old servants wel-comed him so warmly. Hester, who was not given to tears, cried with joy and pride as she led her boy into the house, and looked into his face and told him he had not grown old a bit, and that she thought him greatly improved, except for that hair about his mouth. "She'd cut that off, the very first thing she did, for how under the sun and moon was he ever going to *eat?*"

And Roger laughed good-humoredly, and told her his mustache was his pet, and wound his arm around her and kissed her affectionately, and said she was handsomer than any woman he'd seen since he left home.

"In the Lord's name, what kind of company must the boy have kept?" old Hester retorted, feeling flattered nevertheless, and thinking her boy the handsomest and best she had ever seen.

It was Frank who proposed going on to Charlestown to escort Magdalen home, and who suggested that they should not introduce themselves until they had first seen her, and Roger consented to the plan and went with his nephew to Charlestown, and took his seat among the spectators, feeling very anxious for Magdalen to appear, and wondering how she would look as a young lady. He could not realize the fact that she was eighteen. In his mind she was the little girl leaning over the gate with her eyes swimming in tears, while Frank remembered her standing upon the wharf, her face very red with the autumnal wind which tossed her dress so unmercifully, and showed her big feet, wrinkled stockings, and shapeless ankles. Neither of them had a programme, and they did not know when she was coming, and when at last she came; Roger did not recognize her at first.. But Frank's exclamation of something more than surprise as he suddenly rose to his feet, warned him that it was Magdalen who bore herself so like a queen as she took her seat at the piano. The little girl in the shaker, leaning over the gate, faded before this vision of beautiful girlhood, and for a moment Roger felt as a father might feel who after an absence of eight years returns to find his only child developed into a lovely woman. His surprise and admiration kept him silent, while his eyes took in the fresh, glowing beauty of Magdalen's face, and his well-trained ears drank in the glorious music she was making. Frank, on the contrary, was restless and impatient. Had it been possible, he would have gone to

Magdalen at once, and stood guard over her against the glances
of those who, he felt, had no right to look at her as they were
looking. He saw that she was the bright star, around which the
interest of the entire audience centred, and he wanted to claim
her before them all as something belonging exclusively to the
Irving family, but, wedged in as he was, he could not well effect
his egress, and he sat eagerly listening or rather looking at Magdalen. He could hardly be said to hear her, although he knew
how well she was acquitting herself. He was watching her
glowing face and noticing the glossy waves of her hair, the long
curls on her neck, and the graceful motions of her white hands
and arms, and was thinking what a regal-looking creature she
was, and how delightful it would be at Millbank, where one
could have her all to himself. He did not regard Roger as in
his way at all. Roger never cared for women as he did. Roger
was wholly given to books, and would not in the least interfere
with the long walks, and rides, and *tête-à-têtes* which Frank had
rapidly planned to enjoy with Magdalen even before she left the
stage for the first time. When she came back to sing he could
sit still no longer, but forced his way through the crowd,
and went round to her just in time to escort her from the
stage. His appearance was so sudden, and Magdalen was so
surprised, that ere she realized at all what it meant, she had
taken Frank's offered arm, and he was leading her past the
group of young girls who sent many curious glances after him,
and whispered to each other that he must be the younger Mr.
Irving.

Frank was wonderfully improved in looks, and there was in
his manner a watchful tenderness and deference toward ladies,
very gratifying to those who like to feel that they are cared for
and looked after, and their slightest wish anticipated. And
Magdalen felt it even during the moment they were walking
down the hall to the little reception room, where Frank turned
her more fully to the light, and said : "Excuse me, but I must
look at you again. Do you know how beautiful you have

grown ? As your brother, I think I might kiss you after my long absence."

Magdalen did not tell him he was not her brother, but she took a step backward, while a look flashed into her eyes, which warned Frank that his days for kissing her were over.

"Where is Mr. Irving?" she asked ; and then, seating her in a chair, and thoughtfully dropping the curtain so that the cool night air, which had in it a feeling of rain, should not blow so directly upon her uncovered neck, Frank left her and went for Roger.

Magdalen would have kissed Roger as she thought of him while sitting there waiting for him, but when he came, and stood before her, she would as soon have kissed Frank himself, as the elegant-looking young man whose dark-blue eyes and rich, brown hair with a dash of gold in it, were all that were left of the Roger who went from her eight years ago. He was entirely different from Frank, both in looks and style and manner. He could not bend over a woman with such brooding tenderness, and make her think every thought and wish were subservient to his own, but there was something about him which impressed one with the genuine goodness and honesty of the man who was worth a dozen Franks. And Magdalen felt it at once, and gave her hand trustingly to him, and did not try to draw back from him when, as a father would have kissed his child, he bent over her, and kissed her fair brow, and told her how glad he was to see her, and how much she was improved.

" I should never have recognized you but for Frank," he said. "You have changed so much from the little girl who leaned over the gate to bid me good-by. Do you remember it ?"

Magdalen did remember it, and her sorrow at parting with Roger, and could hardly realize that he had come back to her again. He was very kind, very attentive ; and she felt a thrill of pride as she walked through the halls or talked to her companions, with Roger and Frank on either side of her, Frank so absorbed in her as to pay no heed to those around him, while Roger never for a moment forgot that something was due to others as well as to Magdalen. He saw her all the time, and heard every word she said, and marked how well she said it, but he was attentive and courteous to others, and made himself so agreeable to Nellie Freeman, to whom Magdalen introduced him, that she dreamed of him that night, and went next morning to the depot on pretence of bidding Magdalen good-by a second time, but really for the sake of seeing Mr. Irving.

As Roger was anxious to return home as soon as possible, they left Charlestown on an early train and reached Millbank at two o'clock. Dinner was waiting for them, while Hester in her clean brown gingham, with her white apron tied around her waist, stood in the door, ready to welcome her young people.

Magdalen was her first object of attention, and the old lady kissed her lovingly, and then went with her to her pleasant chamber, which looked so cool and airy with its matting, and curtains of muslin looped with blue, and its snowy white bed in the corner. She could not change her dress before dinner, for her trunks had not been sent up, but she bathed her heated face, and put on a fresh pair of cuffs and a clean linen collar, and then, with her damp hair one mass of waves and little curls, she went down to the dining-room, where Roger met her at the door and led her to the head of his table, installing her as mistress, and bidding her do the honors as the young lady of the house. In spite of her gray dress, unrelieved by any color except the garnet pin which fastened her collar, Magdalen looked very handsome as she presided at Roger's table, and her white hands moved gracefully among the silver service; for there was fragrant coffee for dinner, with rich sweet cream from the morning's milk, and Hester, who cared little for fashions, had sent it up with the meats, because she knew Roger would like it best that way.

The dinner over, the party separated, Magdalen going to her room to put her things away, Frank sauntering off to the summer-house, with his box of cigars, and Roger joining Hester, who had so much to tell him of the affairs at Millbank since he went away.

CHAPTER XVI.

LIFE AT MILLBANK.

AGDALEN was very fresh and bright next morning when she went down to breakfast, in her white cambric wrapper, just short enough in front to show her small, trim foot and well-shaped ankle, which Frank saw at once. There were no wrinkles in her stockings, and the little high-heeled slippers were as unlike as possible to the big shoes which he remembered so well, wondering at the change, and never guessing that Magdalen's persisting in wearing shoes too large for her while growing, had helped to form the little feet which he admired so much as they tripped up and down the stairs or through the halls, with him always hovering near. Her bright, sprightly manner, which had in it a certain spice of recklessness and daring, just suited him, and as the days went by, and he became more and more fascinated with her, he followed her like her shadow, feeling glad that so much of Roger's attention was necessarily given to his agents and overseers, who came so often to Millbank, that he at last opened an office in the village, where he spent most of his time, thus leaving Frank free to walk and talk with Magdalen as much as he pleased. And he improved his opportunity, and was seldom absent from her side more than a few moments at a time. At first this devotion was very grati-fying to Magdalen, who still regarded Frank as the hero of her childhood, but after a few weeks of constant intercourse with him, the spell which had bound her was broken, and she began to tire a little of his attentions, and wish sometimes to be alone.

One afternoon they were sitting together by the river, on the mossy bank, beneath the large buttonwood tree, where they had spent so many pleasant hours in the years gone by, and Frank was talking of his future, and deploring his poverty as a hindrance to his ever becoming popular or even successful in anything.

" Now, if I were Roger," said he, " with his twenty-five thou· sand a year, it would make a great difference. But here I am, most twenty-seven years old, with no profession, no means of earning an honest livelihood, and only the yearly interest of six thousand dollars, which, if I were to indulge my tastes, would barely keep me in cigars and gloves and neckties. I tell you what, Magdalen, it's mighty inconvenient to be so poor."

As he delivered himself of this speech, Frank stretched him· self upon the grass and gave a lazy puff at his cigar, while his face wore a kind of martyred look as if the world had dealt very harshly with him. Magdalen was thoroughly angry, and her eye flashed indignantly, as she turned towards him. He had been at Millbank nearly four weeks, and showed no inten· tion of leaving it. "Just sponging his board out of Roger," Hester said; and the old lady's remarks had their effect on Mag dalen, who herself began to wonder if it was Frank's intention to leave the care of his support entirely to his uncle. It was her nature to say out what she thought, and turning to Frank, she said abruptly, " If you are so poor, why don't you go to work and do something for yourself? If I were a man, with as many avenues open to me as there are to men, I would not sit idly down and bemoan the fate which had given me only six thou- sand dollars. I'd make the most of that, and do something for myself. I do not advise you to go away from Millbank, if there is anything you can do here ; but, honestly, Frank, I think it would look better if you were trying to help yourself instead of depending upon Mr. Irving, who has been so kind to you. And what I say to you I mean also for myself. There is no reason why *I* should be any longer a dependent here, and as soon as I can find a situation as teacher or governess I shall accept it, and you will see I can practise what I preach. I did not mean to wound you, Frank, but it seems to me that both of us have received enough at Mr. Irving's hands, and

should now try to help ourselves. You are not angry with me,
I hope?"

She was looking at him with her great bright eyes so kindly
and trustingly that he could not be angry with her, though he
winced a little and wished that she had not been quite so plain
and outspoken with him. It was the first time any one had
put it before him in plain words that he was living on Roger,
and it hurt him cruelly that Magdalen should be the one to
rebuke him. Still he would not let her see his annoyance, and
he tried to appear natural as he answered, "I could not be
angry with you, especially when you tell me only the truth. I
ought not to live on Roger, and I don't mean to, any longer.
I'll go into his office to-morrow. I heard him say he wanted a
clerk to do some of his writing. I'll be that clerk, and work
like a dog. Will that suit you, Maggie?"

Ere Magdalen could reply, a footstep was heard, and Roger
came round a bend in the river, fanning himself with his straw
hat, and looking very much heated with his rapid walk.

"I thought I should find you here," he said. "It's a splendid place for a hot day. I wish I'd nothing to do but enjoy
this delicious shade as you two seem to be doing; but I must
disturb *you*, Frank. Your mother has just arrived, and is quite
anxious to see you."

Frank would far rather have stayed down by the river, and
mentally wishing his mother in Guinea, he rather languidly
arose and walked away, leaving Magdalen alone with Roger.
Taking the seat Frank had vacated, he laid his hat upon the
grass, and leaning his head upon his elbow began to talk very
freely and familiarly, asking Magdalen if she missed her school-
mates any, and if she did not think Millbank a much pleasanter
place than Charlestown.

Here was the very opening Magdalen desired;—here a
chance to prove that she was sincere in wishing to do something for herself, and in a few words she made her intentions
known to Roger, who quickly lifted himself from his reclining
position, and turned toward her a troubled, surprised face as

he asked why she wished to leave Millbank. "Are you not happy here, Magda?"

He had written that name once to her, but had not called her thus before in her hearing; and now as he did so his voice was so low and kind and winning, that the tears sprang to Magdalen's eyes, and she felt for a moment a pang of homesickness at the thought of leaving Millbank.

"Yes, very happy," she said; "but that is no reason why I should remain a dependent upon you, and before I left the Seminary I determined to earn my own living as soon as an opportunity presented itself. I cannot forget that I have no right to be here, no claim upon you."

"No claim up me, Magdalen! No right to be here!" Roger exclaimed. "As well might a daughter say she had no right in her father's house."

"I am not your daughter, Mr. Irving. I am nobody's daughter, so far as I know: or if I am, I ought perhaps to blush for the parents who deserted me. I have no name, no home, except what you so kindly gave me, and you *have* been kind, Mr. Irving, very, very kind, but that is no reason why I should burden you now that I am able to take care of myself. O, mother, mother! if I could only find her, or know why she treated me so cruelly."

Magdalen was sobbing now, with her face buried in her hands, and Roger could see the great tears dropping from between her fingers. He knew she was crying for the mother she had never known, and that shame, quite as much as filial affection, was the cause of her distress, and he pitied her so much, knowing just how she felt; for there had been a time when he, too, was tormented with doubts concerning his own mother, the golden-haired Jessie, who was now cherished in his memory as the purest of women. He was very sorry for Magdalen, and very uncertain as to what, under the circumstances, it was proper for him to do. The world said she was a young lady, and if Roger had seen as much of her during the last four weeks as Frank had seen, he might have thought so too. But so

absorbed had he been in his business, and so much of his time
had been taken up with looking over accounts and receipts,
and listening to what his agents had done, that he had given no
very special attention to Magdalen, further than that perfect
courtesy and politeness which he would award to any lady.
He knew that she was very bright and pretty and sprightly, and
that the tripping of her footsteps and the rustle of her white
dress, and the sound of her clear, rich voice, breaking out in
merry peals of laughter, or singing in the twilight, made Millbank very pleasant; but he thought of her still as a child, *his*
little child, whom he had held in his lap in the dusty car and
hushed to sleep in his arms. She was only eighteen, he was
thirty-two; and with that difference between them, he might
surely soothe and comfort her as if she really were his daughter. Moving so near to her that her muslin dress swept across
his feet, he laid his hand very gently upon her hair, and Magdalen, when she felt the pitying, caressing touch of that great
broad, warm hand, which seemed in some way to encircle and
shield her from all care or sorrow, bowed her head upon her
lap, and cried more bitterly than before, — cried now with a feeling of utter desolation, as she began dimly to realize what it
would be to go away from Millbank and its master.

"Poor Magda," he said, and his voice had in it all a father's
tenderness, "I am sorry to see you so much distressed. I can
guess in part at the cause of your tears. You are crying for
your mother, just as I have cried for mine many and many a
time."

"No, not as you have cried for yours," Magdalen said, lifting up her head and flashing her brilliant eyes upon him.
"Hester has told me about *your* mother. You believe her
pure and good, while mine — oh, Mr. Irving, I don't know
what I believe of mine."

"Try to believe the best, then, until you know the worst;"
and Roger laid his arm across Magdalen's shoulders and drew
her nearer to him, as he continued: "I have thought a great
deal about that woman who left you in my care. I believe she

was crazy, made so by some great sorrow, — your father's death, perhaps, — for she was dressed in black; and, if so, she was not responsible for what she did, and you need not question her motives. She had a young, innocent face, and bright, handsome eyes like yours, Magda."

Every time he spoke that name, Magdalen felt a strange thrill creep through her veins, and she grew very quiet while Roger talked to her of her mother, and the time when he found himself with a helpless child upon his hands.

"I adopted you then as my own, — my little baby," he said. "You had nothing to do with it; the bargain was of my making, and you cannot break it. I have never given up my guardianship, never mean to give it up until some one claims you who has a better right than I to my little girl. And this I am saying in answer to your proposition of going away from Millbank, because you have no right here, — no claim on me. I am sorry that you should feel so, — you *have* a claim on me, — I cannot let you go, — Millbank would be very lonely without you, Magda."

He paused a moment, and, looking off upon the hills across the river, seemed to be thinking intently. But it was not of the interpretation which many young girls of eighteen might put upon his words and manner. Nothing could be further from his mind than making love to Magdalen. He really felt as if he stood to her in the relation of a father, and that she had the same claim upon him which a child has upon a parent. Her proposition to leave Millbank disturbed him, and led him to think that perhaps *he* was in some way at fault. He had not been very attentive to her; — he had been so much absorbed in his business as to forget that any attentions were due from him as master of the house. He had left all these things to Frank, who knew so much better how to entertain young ladies than he did; but he meant to do better; and his eyes came back at last from the hills across the river, and rested very kindly on her, as he said:

"I am thinking, Magda, that possibly I may have been remiss in my attentions to you since my return. I am not a lady's man, in the common acceptation of the term; but I have never meant to neglect you; and when I have seemed the most forgetful, you have been, perhaps, the most in my mind; and the coming home at night from the business which nearly drives me crazy, has been very pleasant to me, because *you* were there at *our* home I will call it, for it is as much yours as mine, and I want you to consider it so. It is hardly probable that I shall ever marry. I have lived to be thirty-two without finding a woman whom I would care to make my wife, and, after thirty, one's chances of matrimony lessen. But, whether I marry or not, I shall provide for you, as well as Frank, who should perhaps have had more of my father's property. His mother once believed there was another will, — a later one, — which gave him Millbank, and disinherited me; but that is all passed now."

This was the first time Magdalen had ever heard the will matter put in so strong a light, and, springing to her feet, she exclaimed:

"Give Millbank to Frank, and disinherit you! I never heard that hinted before. I understood that the later will merely gave more to Frank than the five thousand dollars. I never dreamed, I did not know — when I — oh, Mr. Irving, I have been such a monster!"

She was ringing her hands, in her distress at having believed in and even hunted for a will which would take Millbank from Roger, who looked at her in astonishment, and asked what she meant.

"Have you, too, heard of the *will* trouble; who told you?" he asked. And with her eyes full of tears, which with a quick nervous motion of her fingers she dashed away, Magdalen replied:

"Frank told me first years ago, and his mother told me again, but not of the disinheritance. She said the will was better for Frank, and I — oh, Mr. Irving, forgive me, — I hunt-

ed for it ever so much, in all of the rooms, and in the garret, where Hester found me, and seemed so angry, that I remember thinking she knew something about it if there was one, and like a silly, curious girl I said to myself, I'll keep hunting till I find it; but I didn't. Oh, Mr. Irving, believe me, I didn't!"
"Don't look at me so, please," Magdalen exclaimed in a tremor of distress at the troubled, sorry look in Roger's face, — a look as if he had been wounded in his own home by his own friends. "I might have hunted more, perhaps," Magdalen went on, too truthful to keep back anything which concerned herself; "but so much happened, and I went away to school and forgot all about it. Will you forgive me for trying to turn you out of doors." She was kneeling by him now as he sat upon the bank, and her hands were clasped upon his arm, while her tear ful face was turned imploringly to his.

Unclasping her hands from his arm, and keeping them be tween his own, Roger said to her:

"You distress yourself unnecessarily about a thing which was done with no intention to injure me. I know, of course, that you would not wish me to give up the home I love so well; but, Magdalen, if there was a later will it ought to be found, and restitution made."

"You do *not* believe there was such a will, — you surely do not," Magdalen asked, excitedly; and Roger replied:

"No, I do not. If I did I would move heaven and earth to find it, for in that case I should have been living all these years on what belonged to others. Don't look so frightened, Magdalen," Roger continued, playfully touching her cheek, which had grown pale at the mere idea of his being obliged to give up Millbank. "No harm should come to you. I should take care of my little girl. I would work with my hands if necessary, and you could help me. How would you like that?"

It was rather a dangerous situation for a girl like Magdalen. Her hands were imprisoned by Roger, whose eyes rested so kindly upon her as he spoke of their working for each other and asked how she would like it.

How would she like it? She was a woman, with all a woman's impulses. And Roger Irving was a splendid-looking man, with something very winning in his voice and manner, and it is not strange if at that moment a life of toil with Roger looked more desirable to Magdalen than a life of ease at Millbank without him.

"If it ever chances that you leave Millbank, I will gladly work like a slave for you, to atone, if possible, for my meddlesome curiosity in trying to find that will," Magdalen replied; and Roger responded :

"I wish you to find it if there is one, and I give you full permission to search as much and as often as you like. You spoke of Hester's having come upon you once when you were looking; where were you then?"

"Up in the garret," Magdalen said. "There are piles of rubbish there, and an old barrel of papers. I was tumbling them over, and I remember now that Hester said something about its being worse for me if the will was found; and she was very cross for several days, and very rude to Mrs. Irving, who, she said, 'put me up.' She never liked Mrs. Irving much, although latterly she has treated her very civilly."

"And do you like my sister Helen?" Roger asked, a doubt beginning to cross his mind as to the propriety of carrying out a plan which had recently suggested itself to him. Mrs. Walter Scott, who never did anything without a motive, had petted and caressed and flattered Magdalen ever since she had fitted her out for school, and served herself so well by the means. She had called upon her twice at the seminary, had written her several affectionate letters, and it was natural that Magdalen, who was wholly unsuspicious, should like her; and she expressed her liking in such strong terms, that Roger's olden feeling of distrust, — if it could be called by so harsh a name, — gave way, and he spoke of what his sister had said to him in New York with regard to Magdalen having a companion or *chaperone* at Millbank.

"You know, perhaps," he said, "that the world has established certain codes of propriety, one of which says that a young lady like you should not live alone with an old bachelor like me. I don't see the harm myself, but sister Helen does, and she knows what is proper, of course. She has made propriety the business of her life, and it has occurred to me that it might be well for her to stay at Millbank altogether, — that is, if it would please you to have her here."

Magdalen felt that she was competent to take care of herself, but if she *must* have a companion she preferred Mrs. Irving, and assented readily to a plan which had originated wholly in Mrs. Walter Scott's fertile brain, and to the accomplishment of which all her energies had been directed for the last few years.

" It is fortunate that she is here," Roger said, " as we can talk it over together better than we could write about it. I shall be glad to assist Helen in that way, and it may prove a pleasant arrangement for all parties."

They were walking back to the house now, across the pleasant fields which were a part of Roger's inheritance, and if in the young man's heart there was a feeling that it would be hard to give up all this, it was but the natural result of his recent conversation concerning the imaginary will. That such a document existed, he did not believe, however ; and his momentary disquiet had passed before he reached the house, which looked so cool and inviting amid the dense shade of the maples and elms.

" Come this way, Magdalen," Roger said, as they entered the hall ; and Magdalen went with him into the music-room, starting with surprise, and uttering an exclamation of delight as she saw a beautiful new piano in place of the old rattling instrument which had occupied that corner in the morning.

" Oh, I am so glad ! I can now play with some satisfaction to myself and pleasure to others," she said, running her fingers rapidly over the keys, then as her eye fell upon the silver plate, with her name, " Magdalen Lennox," engraved upon it, she stopped suddenly, and her eyes filled with tears at once as she said :

" Oh, Mr. Irving, how good you are to me ! what can I do to show that I appreciate your kindness ? "

Roger had managed to have the piano brought to the house while she was away, intending it as a surprise, and he enjoyed it thoroughly, and thought how beautiful she was, with those tear-drops glittering in her great dark eyes. She was one of whom any parent might be proud, and he was proud of her, and called himself her father, and tried to believe that he felt toward her as a father would feel toward his daughter ; but somehow that little episode down by the river, when she had knelt before him, with her hands upon his arm, and her flushed, eager face so near to his, had stirred a new set of feelings in his heart and made him, for the first time in his life, averse to being addressed by her as " Mr. Irving." And when she asked him what she could do to show how glad she was, he said,

" I know you are glad, — I can see it in your eyes, and I want nothing in return, unless, indeed, you drop the formal title of Mr. Irving, and give me the more familiar one of Roger. Couldn't you do that, Magda ? "

Magdalen would as soon have thought of calling the clergyman of the parish by his first name, as to have addressed her guardian as Rogei, — and she shook her head laughingly.

" No, Mr. Irving, you can never be Roger to me, — it would bring you too much on a level with Frank, and that I should not like."

Perhaps Roger was not altogether displeased with her answer, for he smiled kindly upon her, and asked if he would have to fall very far to reach his nephew's level. " In some respects, yes," was Magdalen's reply, as she commenced a brilliant polka which brought Frank himself into the parlor, followed by his mother, who kissed Magdalen lovingly, and then stood with both her hands folded on the young girl's shoulder as she went on playing one piece after another, and making such melody as nad not been heard since the days when Jessie was queen of Millbank and played in the twilight for her gray-haired husband.

Mrs. Walter Scott was very sociable and kind and conciliatory, and lavish of her praises of Millbank, which she admired so much, saying she was half sorry she came, as it would be so hard to go back to her close, hot rooms in New York. Then she said she expected to have her house on her hands altogether, as her tenants were intending to go South in November, and how she should live without the rent she did not know.

"Perhaps I can suggest something which will meet your approval," Roger said; and then he proceeded to speak of his plan that his sister should stay at Millbank with Magdalen. Mrs. Walter Scott had never *thought* of such a thing, — she did not know that she *could* live out of New York, — and nothing but her love for Magdalen and her desire to serve Roger, who had done so much for Frank, could induce her to consider the proposition for a moment. This was what she *said;* but when five hundred dollars a year was added to her fondness for Magdalen and her desire to serve Roger, she consented to martyr herself, and accepted the situation with as much amiability and resignation as if it had not been the very object for which she had been striving ever since her first visit to Charlestown, when she foresaw what Magdalen would be, and what Roger would do for her. It was decided that Frank, too, should remain at Millbank as a clerk in Roger's office, where he pretended to study law, and where, after his writing was done, he spent his whole time in smoking cigars and following Magdalen, who sometimes teased him unmercifully, and then drove him nearly wild with her lively sallies and bewitching ways. They were very gay at Millbank that autumn; and in the sad years which followed, Magdalen often looked back upon that time as the happiest period of her life.

Roger was naturally domestic in his tastes, and would at any time have preferred a quiet evening at home with his family to the gayest assemblage; but his sister-in-law made him believe that, as the master of Millbank, he owed a great deal to society, and so he threw open his doors to his friends, who gladly availed themselves of anything which would vary the monotony of their lives. Always bright and sparkling and brilliant, Magdalen reigned triumphant as the belle on all occasions. She was a general favorite, and as the autumn advanced, the young maidens of Belvidere, — who had dreamed that to be mistress of Millbank might be an honor in store for one of them, — began to notice the soft, tender look in Roger's eyes as they followed Magdalen's movements, whether in the merry dance, of which she never tired, or at the piano, where she excelled all others in the freshness of her voice and the brilliancy of her execution. Frank, too, with his gentlemanly manners and foreign air, and Mrs. Walter Scott, with her city style and elegance, added to the attractions at Millbank, where everything wore so bright a hue, with no shadow to foretell the dark storm which was coming. The *will* seemed to be entirely forgotten, though Roger dreamed once that it had been found, — and by Magdalen, too, — and that, with an aching heart, he read that he was a beggar, made so by his father, and that he had gone out from his beautiful home penniless, but not alone, or utterly hopeless, for Magdalen was with him, — her dark eyes beamed upon him, and her hands ministered to him just as she had said they would, should he ever come to what he had.

Roger was glad this was only a dream, — glad to awake in his own pleasant chamber and hear the robins sing in the maple-tree outside, and see from his window the scarlet tints with which the autumnal frosts were beginning to touch the maples. He was strongly attached to his beautiful home, and to lose it now would be a bitter trial.

But he had no expectation of losing it. It belonged to him without a question, and all through the autumn months he went on beautifying and improving it, and studying constantly some new surprise which would add to the happiness of those he had gathered around him, and whose comfort he held far above his own. Wholly unselfish, and liberal almost to a fault, he spent his money freely, not only for those of his own household, but for the poor, who had known and loved him when a boy, and

6*

who now idolized and honored him as a man, and blessed the day which had brought him back to their midst, — the kind and considerate employer of many of them, — the friend of the destitute and needy, — the cultivated gentleman in society, and the courteous master of Millbank.

CHAPTER XVII.

LOVE-MAKING AT MILLBANK.

HE holidays were over. They had been spent in New York, where, with Mrs. Walter Scott as her *chaperone*, Magdalen had passed a few weeks, and seen what was meant by fashionable society. But she did not like it, and was glad to return to Millbank.

Roger had spent only a few days with her in New York, but Frank had been her constant attendant, and not a little proud of the beautiful girl who attracted so much attention. While there Magdalen had more than once heard mention made of Alice Grey, who had returned to America and was spending a few weeks in New York, where she would have been a belle but for her poor health, which prevented her from mingling much in fashionable society. Frank had called on her several times, and occasionally she heard him rallied upon his penchant for Miss Grey by some one of his friends, who knew them both. Frank would have denied the charge openly had Magdalen's manner towards him been different from what it was. She called him her brother, and by always treating him as such, made anything like love-making on his part almost impossible ; and so Frank thought to rouse her jealousy by allowing her to believe that there was something serious between himself and Alice Grey. But in this he was mistaken. The charm he had once possessed for Magdalen, when, as a child, she enshrined him her hero and lived upon his smiles, was broken, and though she liked him greatly and showed that she did so, she knew that any stronger feeling towards him was ut. terly impossible, and was delighted at the prospect of his trans. ferring to another some of the attentions which were becoming distasteful to her, from the fact of their being so very marked and lover-like.

Once she spoke to him herself of Alice, who was stopping at the St. Denis, and asked, "Why do you not bring her to see me or let me go to her?" and Frank had answered her, "Miss Grey is too much of an invalid to make or receive calls from strangers. She asks after you with a great deal of interest, and hopes —"

Frank hesitated a moment, and Magdalen playfully caught him up, saying,— "Hopes to know me well through you. Is that it, and is what I have heard about you true? I am so glad, for I know I shall like her, though I used to be jealous of her years ago when you talked so much of her."

Magdalen was very sincere in what she said, but foolish Frank, who set a far greater value upon himself than others set upon him, and who could not understand how any girl could be indifferent to him, was conceited enough to fancy that he detected something like pique in Magdalen's manner, and that she was *not* as much delighted with Alice Grey as she would like him to think. This suited him, and so he made no reply, except, "I am glad you are pleased with her. She is worthy of your love."

And thus was the conviction strengthened in Magdalen's mind that she might some day know Alice Grey intimately as the wife of Frank, towards whom she showed at once a greater decree of familiarity than she had done hitherto, making him think his ruse a successful one, which would in due time bear the desired fruit. Meanwhile his mother had her own darling scheme, which she was adroitly managing to carry out. Once she would have spurned the thought of accepting Magdalen as her daughter-in-law, but she had changed her mind after a conversation with Roger, who, wholly deceived by the crafty, fascinating woman, had grown very confidential, and been led on to admit that in case he never married, or even if he did, Magdalen would stand to him in the relation of a child, and share in his property. Indeed, from his conversation it would seem that, feeling impressed with the uncertainty of life, and having no foolish prejudices against making his will, he had already done so, and provided for both Magdalen and Frank.

He did not state what provision he had made for them, and his sister did not ask him. She preferred to find out in some other way, if possible, and not betray the interest she felt in the matter. So she merely thanked him for remembering Frank, for whom he had done so much, and then at once changed the conversation. She did not seem at all curious, and Roger, who liked her now much better than when he was a boy, never dreamed how the next day, while he was in his office and Magdalen was away on some errand for old Hester, the writing-desk, which still stood in the library, was visited by Mrs. Walter Scott, who knew that some of his papers were kept there, and whose curiosity was rewarded by a sight of the desired document. It was not sealed, and with a timid glance at the door she opened it nervously, but dared not stop to read the whole lest some one should surprise her. Rapidly her eye ran over the paper till it caught the name of Magdalen, coupled with one hundred thousand dollars. That was to be her marriage portion, paid on her bridal day, and Mrs. Walter Scott was about to read further when the sound of a footstep warned her that some one was coming. To put the paper back in its place was the work of a moment, and then, with a most innocent look on her face the lady turned to meet old Hester Floyd, whose gray eyes looked sharply at her, and who merely nodded in reply to her words of explanation,—

"I am looking at this silver plate over the doors of the writing-desk. How it is tarnished! One can scarcely make out the squire's name. I wish you'd set Ruth to polishing it."

The plate was polished within fifteen minutes by Hester

herself, who had caught the rustle of papers and the quick shutting of the drawer. She knew the tarnished plate was a pretence, and stood guard till Roger came. He merely laughed at her suspicions, but when a few days after Mrs. Walter Scott found an opportunity to try the drawer again, she found it locked, and all her hopes of ascertaining how Frank fared in the will were effectually cut off. But she knew about Magdalen. One hundred thousand dollars as a marriage portion was worth considering, and Mrs. Walter Scott did consider it, and it outweighed any scruples she might otherwise have had concerning Magdalen's birth, and made her doubly gracious to the young girl whom she sought as her future daughter-in-law.

That was just before they went to New York, where the favor with which Magdalen was received confirmed her in her intentions to win the hundred thousand dollars. Every opportunity for throwing the young people together was seized upon, and if by chance she heard the name of Alice Grey coupled with her son's, she smiled incredulously, and said it was a most absurd idea that Frank should wish to marry into a family where there was hereditary insanity, as she knew was the case in Miss Grey's.

After their return to Millbank she resolved to push matters a little, and so one afternoon, when she chanced to be walking with Frank from the office to the house, she broached the subject by asking how long he intended to let matters go on as they were going, and why he did not at once propose to Magdalen, and not keep her in suspense !

"*Suspense !* mother ; " and Frank looked up joyfully. "Do you think, — do you believe Magdalen really cares for me ? I have been afraid it was only a sisterly regard, such as she would feel for me were I really her brother."

"She must be a strange girl to conduct herself towards you as she does and not seriously care for you," Mrs. Walter Scott replied ; and Frank continued, "She has been different since we came from New York, I know, and has not kept me quite so much at arm's-length. Mother," and Frank spoke more energetically than before, "I am so glad you have broken the ice; so glad you like her and are willing. I did not know but you might object, you are so straight-laced about blood and birth and all that."

"I am a little particular about such things, I'll admit," Mrs. Irving replied; "but in Magdalen's case I am ready to make an exception. She is a splendid girl and created a great sensation in New York; while better than all, she is, or will be, an heiress. Roger has made his will, and on her bridal day she is to have one hundred thousand dollars dowry."

"How do you know that?" Frank asked quickly, and his mother replied: "No matter how. It is sufficient that I do know it, and with poverty staring us in the face the sooner you appropriate that hundred thousand the better for both of us."

"Mother," and Frank spoke sternly, "I wonder what you take me for! A mere mercenary wretch? Understand plainly that I am not so base as that, and I love Magdalen well enough to marry her if she was never to have a penny in the world. Much as I hate work I could work for *her*, and a life of poverty shared with her has more attractions for me than all the kingdoms in the world shared with another."

They had reached Millbank by this time, and Magdalen met them at the door. She had been out for a drive, and the exercise and clear wintry air had brought a deeper glow than usual to her cheeks and made her eyes like diamonds. She had never been more beautiful to Frank than she was that evening in her soft crimson dress, with her hair arranged in long curls, which fell about her face and neck in such profusion. Magdalen did not often curl her hair; it was too much trouble, she said, and she had only done so to-day because of something which Roger had said to her. He had been standing with her before the picture of his mother, whose golden hair covered her like a veil, and to Magdalen, who admired the flowing tresses, he had said, "Why don't you wear curls, Magda? I like so much to see them when I know they are as natural as yours would be."

That afternoon Magdalen had taken more than usual pains
with her toilet, and Celine, the French maid, whom Mrs.
Walter Scott had introduced into the house, had gone into·
ecstasies over the long, beautiful curls which fell almost to
Magdalen's waist and somewhat softened her dashing style of
beauty. Roger, too, had complimented her, when about four
o'clock he came in, saying he was going to drive out a mile or
two from Millbank, and asking her to accompany him. The
day was very cold, and with careful forethought he had seen
that she was warmly clad, — had himself put the hot soap-stone
to her feet, and wrapping the fur robes around her, had looked
into her bright face and starry eyes, and asked if she was comfortable. On their return to Millbank, he had carefully lifted
her from the sleigh and carried her up the steps into the hall,
where he set her down, calling her Mother Bunch, with all
her wraps around her, and trying to help her remove them.
Roger was a little awkward in anything pertaining to a woman's
gear, but he managed to unpin the shawl and untie the ribbons
of the ‚pretty, coquettish rigolette, which were in a knot
and troubled him somewhat, bringing his face so close to Magdalen's that her curls fell across his shoulder and he felt her
breath upon his cheek.

"Your ride has done you good, Magda. You are looking
charmingly," he said, when at last she was undone and stood
before the fire. He was obliged to go out again, and as it was
not likely he should return till late, they were not to wait
dinner for him, — he said.

Something in his manner toward her more than his words
had affected Magdalen with a sweet sense of happiness, and
her face was radiant as she met Frank in the hall, and went
with him to the dining-room, where dinner was waiting for
them. She explained that Roger would not be there, and then,
as Frank took the head of the table, rallied him upon his
awkwardness in carving and his absent-mindedness in general.
He had a bad headache, he said, and after dinner was over and
they had adjourned to the library, where their evenings were

usually passed, he lay down upon the couch and looked so pale and tired, that Magdalen's sympathy was awakened at once, and she insisted upon doing something for him. Since their return from New York she *had* been far more familiar in her intercourse with him than she would have been had she not believed there was something between him and Alice Grey which might ripen into love. With no fears for herself, she could afford to be *very* gracious, and being naturally something of a coquette, she had tormented and teased poor Frank until he had some reason for believing that his affection for her was returned, and that his suit would not be disregarded should he ever urge it upon her. With the remembrance of Roger's words and manner thrilling every nerve, she was in an un· usually soft, amiable mood to-night, and knelt at last by Frank's side and offered to bathe his aching head.

"The girls at school used to tell me there was some mesmerism in my fingers," she said, "some power to drive away pain or exorcise evil spirits. Let me try their effect on you."

Mrs. Walter Scott, who had been watching the progress of matters, found it convenient just then to leave the room, and Frank was alone with Magdalen. For a few moments her white fingers threaded his hair, brushing it back from his forehead and passing lightly over his throbbing temples until it was not in human nature to endure any longer, and rising suddenly from his reclining position, Frank clasped his arms around her, and straining her to his bosom, pressed kiss after kiss upon her lips, while he poured into her astonished ear the story of his love, telling her how long ago it began, — telling her how dear she was to him, — how for her sake he had lingered at Millbank trying to do something for himself, because she had once suggested that such a thing would be gratifying to her, — how thoughts of her were constantly in his mind, whether awake or asleep, and lastly, that his mother approved his choice and would gladly welcome her as a daughter.

As he talked, Magdalen had struggled to her feet, her cheeks burning with surprise and mortification, and sorrow too, that

Frank should have misjudged her so. She knew he was in earnest, and she pitied him so much, knowing as she did how hopeless was his suit.

"Speak to me," he said at last, "if it is only to tell me no. Anything is better than your silence."

"Oh, Frank," Magdalen began, "I am so sorry, because —"

"Don't tell me no. I will not listen to that answer," Frank burst out impetuously, forgetting what he had just said when he begged her to speak. "You do like me, or you have seemed to, and have given me some encouragement, or I should not have told you what I have. Don't you like me, Magdalen?"

"Yes, very much, but not the way you mean. I do not like you well enough to take you for my husband. And, Frank, what of Alice Grey? You say I have encouraged you, and perhaps I have. I'll admit that since I thought you loved Miss Grey, I have been less guarded in my manner towards you; but I never meant to mislead you, — never. I felt towards you as a sister might feel towards a brother, — nothing more. But you do not tell me about Miss Grey. Are *you*, then, so fickle?"

"Magdalen," Frank said, "I may as well be truthful with you now; that was all a ruse, — done for the sake of piquing you and rousing your jealousy. I did care for Alice when she was a young girl and I in college at New Haven, and when I met her again abroad, and found her the same sweet, lovely creature, I don't know what I might have done but for her father, who seemed to dislike me, and always imposed some obstacle to my seeing her alone, until at last he took her away and I saw her no more, until I met her in New York; and had learned to love you far more than I ever loved Alice Grey."

"And so to win me you stooped to play with the affections of another. A very manly thing to do," Magdalen rejoined, in a tone of bitter scorn, which made poor Frank's blood tingle as he tried to stammer out his excuses.

"It was not a manly act, I know; but, Magdalen, so far as Alice was concerned, it did no harm. I *know* she does not care

for me now, if she ever did.   Our intercourse was merely
friendly, — nothing more; and I cannot flatter myself that she
would feel one heart-throb were she to hear to-day of my marriage with another.   Forgive me, Magdalen, if in my love for
you I resorted to duplicity, and tell me that you can love me
in time, — that you will try to do so.   Will you, Magdalen?"

"No, Frank.   I can never be your wife; never.   Don't
mention it again; don't think of it again, for it cannot be."

This was Magdalen's reply, which Frank felt was final.   She
was leaving the room, and he let her go without another word.
He had lost her, and throwing himself upon the couch, he
pressed his hands together upon his aching head, and groaned
aloud with pain and bitter disappointment.

CHAPTER XVIII.

THE LOOSE BOARD IN THE GARRET.

HESTER FLOYD was sick.   Exposure to a heavy rain
had brought on an attack of fever, which confined her
to her bed, where she lay helpless and cross, and sometimes delirious.   She would have no one with her but Magdalen.   Every other person made her nervous, she said.   Magdalen's hands were soft; Magdalen's step was light; Magdalen
knew what to do; and so Magdalen stayed by her constantly,
glad of an excuse to keep away from Frank, with whom she had
held but little intercourse since that night in the library, which
she remembered with so much regret.   Hester's illness she
looked upon as a godsend, and stayed all day by the fretful old
woman's bedside, only leaving the room at meal time, or to
make a feint of watching Mrs. Walter Scott, for whom Hester
evinced a strong dislike or dread.

"Snoopin', pryin' thing," she said to Magdalen.   "She'll
be up to all sorts of capers now that I'm laid up and can't head

her off. I've found her there more than once ; I knew what she was after, and took it away, and then like a fool lugged it back again, and it's there now, and you must get it, and put it — put it — oh, for the dear Lord's sake what nonsense be I talkin'. What was I sayin', Magdalen ? "

Hester came to herself with a start, and stared wildly at Magdalen, who was bending over her, wondering what she meant, and what it was which she must bring from the garret and hide. Whatever it was, it troubled Hester Floyd greatly, and when she was delirious, as was often the case, she was sure to talk of it, and beg of Magdalen to get it, and put it beyond the reach of Mrs. Walter Scott.

" How am I to get it when I don't know what it is nor where it is," Magdalen said to her one night when she sat watching by her, and Hester had insisted that she should go to the garret, and " head off that woman. She's there, and by and by she'll find that loose board in the floor under the rafters where I bumped my head so hard. Go, Magdalen, for Heaven's sake, if you care for *Roger.*"

Magdalen's face was very white now, and her eyes like burning coals as she questioned Hester. At the mention of Roger a sudden suspicion had flashed upon her, making her grow faint and cold as she grasped the high post of the bedstead and asked, " How she could get it when she did not know what it was, nor where it was."

The sound of her voice roused the old woman a little, but she soon relapsed into her dreamy, talkative mood, and insisted that Mrs. Walter Scott was in the garret and Magdalen must " head her off."

" I'll go," Magdalen said at last, taking the candle which Hester always used for going about the house. " Hush !" she continued, as Hester began to grow very restless ; " I'm going to the garret. Be quiet till I come back."

" I will, yes," was Hester's reply, her eyes wide open now, and staring wildly at Magdalen, whose dress she tried to clutch with her hand as she whispered, "The loose board, way down under the eaves. You must get on your knees. Bring it to me, and never tell."

The house was very quiet, for the family had long since retired, and the pale spring moonlight came struggling through the windows, and lighting up the halls through which Magdalen went on her strange errand to the garret. The stairs which led to it were away from the main portion of the building, and she felt a thrill of something like fear as she passed into the dark, narrow hall, and paused a moment by the door of the stairway. What should she find, — was Mrs. Walter Scott there, as Hester had averred; and if so, what was she doing, and what excuse could Magdalen make for being there herself?

" I'll wait, and let matters take their course," she thought; and then summoning all her courage, she opened the door, and began the ascent of the steep narrow way, every stair of which creaked with her tread, for Magdalen did not try to be cautious. " If any one is there, they shall know I am coming," she thought; and she held her candle high above her head, so that its light might shine to the farthest crevice of the garret and give warning of her approach.

But there was no one there, and only the accumulated rubbish of the house met her view, as she came fully into the garret and cast her eyes from corner to corner and beam to beam. Through the dingy window at the north the moon was looking in, and lighting up that end of the garret with a weird, ghostly kind of light, which made Magdalen shiver more than utter darkness would have done. She knew she was alone; there was no sign of life around her, except the huge rat, which, frightened at this unlooked-for visitation, sprang from Magdalen knew not where, and running past her disappeared in a hole low down under the eaves, reminding Magdalen of what Hester had said of "the loose plank under the rafters where you have to stoop."

At sight of the rat Magdalen had uttered a cry, which she quickly suppressed, and then stood watching the frightened animal, until it disappeared from sight.

" There can be no harm in seeing if there *is* a loose board there," Magdalen thought ; and setting her candle upon a little table she groped her way after the rat, bumping her head once as old Hester had bumped hers ; and then crouching down upon her knees, she examined the floor in that part of the gar-ret, growing faint and cold and frightened when she found that far back under the roof there *was* a board, shorter than the others, which looked as if it might with a little trouble be lifted from its place.

It fitted perfectly, and, but for what old Hester had said, might never have been discovered to be loose and capable of being moved from its position. Magdalen was not quite sure, even now, that she could raise it, and if she could, did she wish to, and for what reason? Was there anything hidden under it, and if so, *was it —?* "

Magdalen did not dare repeat the last word even ·to herself, and, as she thought it, there came rushing over her a feeling as if she were already guilty of making Roger Irving a beggar.

" No, no, I can't do that. If there is anything under there, — which I do not believe, — it may remain there for all of me," she said ; and her face was very pale as she drew back from be-neath the roof, and took the candle in her hand.

The moon had passed under a cloud, leaving the garret in darkness, and Magdalen heard the rising wind sweeping past the windows as she went down the stairs and out again into the hall, where she breathed more freely, and felt less as if there were a nightmare's spell upon her. Mrs. Walter Scott's door stood ajar just as it had done when Magdalen passed it on her way to the garret, and, impelled by a feeling she could not re-sist, she looked cautiously in. The lady was sleeping soundly, with her hair in the hideous curl papers, and her white hands resting peacefully outside the counterpane. She had not been near the garret. She knew nothing of the loose plank under the roof, and with a feeling that injustice had been done to the sleeper, Magdalen passed on toward Hester's room, her heart beating rapidly and the blood rushing in torrents to her face and neck as she heard Hester's sharp, querulous tones mingled with another voice which seemed trying to quiet her. It was a man's voice,— Roger's voice,— and Roger himself was bending over the restless woman and telling her that Magdalen would soon be back, and that nobody was going to harm him.

"Here she is now," he continued, as Magdalen glided into the room, looking like some ghost, for the blood which had crimsoned her face a moment before had receded from it, leaving it white as marble, and making her dark eyes seem larger and brighter and blacker than their wont. "Why, Magda," Roger exclaimed, coming quickly to her side, "what is the matter? Have you, too, been hearing burglars?"'

"Burglars!" Magdalen repeated, trying to smile as she put her candle upon the table and hastened to Hester, who was sitting up in bed, and who demanded of her, "Did you find it? Was she there?"

"No, no. There was nobody there," Magdalen said, soothingly; and then as Hester became quiet, and seemed falling away to sleep as suddenly as she sometimes awoke, Magdalen turned to Roger, who was looking curiously at her, and as she fancied with a troubled expression on his face. "You spoke of burglars. What did you mean?" she asked.

"Nothing," he replied, laughingly. "Only I have been restless all night, — too strong coffee for dinner, I dare say. Suppose you see to it yourself to-morrow. I remember a cup you made me once, and I never tasted better."

"Yes; but what of the burglars, and why are you up?" Magdalen continued.

She knew there was some reason for Roger's being there at that hour of the night, and she wished to get at it.

"I could not sleep," he replied, "and I thought I heard some one about the house. The post-office was entered last week, and as it would not be a very improbable thing for the robbers to come here, I dressed, and fearing that you might be alarmed at any unusual sound about the house, I came directly here, and learned from Hester that you were *rummaging*, —

you or somebody. I could hardly understand what she did mean, she was so excited."

"I rummaging!" Magdalen stammered. "Hester has queer fancies. She took it into her head that Mrs. Irving was rummaging, as she calls it, and insisted that I should go and see; so I went, to quiet her."

"And got a cobweb in your hair," Roger added, playfully brushing from her hair the cobweb which she had gotten under the roof, and which he held up before her.

"Oh, Mr. Irving!" Magdalen exclaimed, in real distress, for she did not like the expression of the eyes fastened upon her. "I don't know what Hester may have said to you, but she has such queer ideas, and she would make me go where she said Mrs. Irving was, and I went; but I meant no harm, believe me, won't you?"

Her cheeks were scarlet, and her eyes were filling with tears as they looked up to Roger, who laughed merrily, and said:

"Of course I believe you; for what possible harm could there be in your going to the garret after Mrs. Irving, or what could Hester think she was there for?"

He knew then where she had been. Hester had let that out, but had she told him anything further? Magdalen did not know. She was resolved, however, that she would tell him nothing herself, so she merely replied:

"Hester is often out of her head, and when she is she seems to think that Mrs. Irving meditates some harm to you."

"I discovered that from what she said while you were gone," Roger rejoined; and then, looking at the clock, he saw it was nearly one, and asked Magdalen if she would not like him to watch while she slept.

If he knew of the loose plank, or had a thought of the will, he gave no sign of his knowledge; he only seemed anxious about Magdalen, and afraid that she would over-exert herself, and when she refused to sleep, he insisted upon sitting with her and sharing her vigils.

"It must be tedious to watch alone," he said, and then he

brought the large chair he was accustomed to read in, and made Magdalen sit in it, and found a pillow for her head, and bade her keep quiet and try to rest.

It was pleasant to be cared for, especially as she was tired and worn, and Magdalen sat very still, with her head upon the pillow and her face in the shadow, until her eyelids began to droop and her hands to slide down into her lap, and when Roger asked if it was time for the medicine, he received no answer, for Magdalen was asleep.

"Poor child," he said, as he stood looking at her. "She has grown pale and thin with nursing Hester. I must get some one to take her place, and persuade Hester to be reasonable for once. Magda must not be allowed to get sick if I can help it. How very beautiful she is, with the long eyelashes on her cheek and her hair rippling away from her forehead! I wonder are all young girls as beautiful in their sleep as Magda."

Roger was strangely moved as he stood looking at the tired sleeping girl.. Little by little, day by day, week by week, she had been growing into his heart, until now she filled every niche and corner of it, and filled it so completely, that to have torn her from it would have left it bleeding and desolate. She was not his daughter now, nor his ward, nor his sister. She was *Magda*, his princess, his queen, whose bright eyes and clear, ringing voice thrilled him with a new sense of happiness, and made him long to clasp her in his arms and claim her for his own in the only way she could ever satisfy him now. And he did not greatly fear what her answer might be, for he had noted the bright flush which always came to her cheek, and the kindling light in her starry eyes when he appeared suddenly before her. He did not believe he was indifferent to her, and as he sat by her until the gray dawn broke, he resolved that ere long he would end his suspense, and know from her own lips if she could love him enough to be his wife. Gradually, as her slumber grew more profound, the pillow slipped, and her head dropped into a position which looked so uncomfortable, that Roger ventured to lift it up and place it more easily against

the back of the chair. An hour later and Magdalen woke
with a start, exclaiming when she saw the daylight through the
shutters and Hester's medicine untouched upon the table,
"Why didn't you wake me ? Hester has not taken her medicine, and the doctor will blame me."

"Hester is just as well without it," Roger answered. "She
has slept quietly every moment, and sleep will do her more
good than drugs. My word for it she will be better when she
wakes ; but, Magda, I shall get her a nurse to-day, and relieve
you. I cannot let you grow pale and thin. You are looking
like a ghost now. Come with me into the open air, which
you need after this close room."

He wrapped a shawl around her, and taking her hood from
the table in the hall tied it upon her head and then led her out
upon the wide piazza, where the fresh breeze from the river
was blowing, and where he walked up and down, with her hand
on his arm, until the color came back to her cheeks, and her
eyes had in them their old, restless brightness, as she stood by
him and looked off upon the hills just growing red in the light
of the rising sun.

It was too early yet for many flowers, but the April winds
had melted the snow from off the Millbank grounds, and here
and there patches of green grass were beginning to show, and
the golden daffodil was just opening its leaves upon the borders
of the garden walk. Millbank was nothing to what it would be
a few weeks later, but it was handsome even now, and both
Roger and Magdalen commented upon its beauty, while the
former spoke of some improvements he had in contemplation,
and should commence as soon as the ground was settled. A
fountain here, and a terrace there for autumn flowers, and
another winding walk leading to the grove toward the mill he
meant to have, he said, and a pretty little summer-house down
by the brook, like one he had seen in England.

And as he talked of the summer-house by the brook, with its
rustic seats and stands, the sun passed into a bank of clouds,
the wind began to freshen and blow up from the river in raw,

7

chilling gusts, which made Magdalen shiver, and brought to her mind last night's adventure in the garret where the loose plank was. And with thoughts of that plank there crept over her a deeper chill, — a feeling of depression, as if the brightness of Millbank was passing away forever, and that the change was somehow being wrought by herself.

CHAPTER XIX.

THE BEGINNING OF TROUBLE.

HESTER was better. Her long sleep had done her good, and when she awoke it was evident that her fever was broken and the crisis of her disease passed. She was perfectly rational, and evidently retained no recollection of what she had said of the garret and Mrs. Walter Scott. Indeed, she was very civil to that lady, who, on her way to breakfast, came in to see her, looking very bright and fresh in her black wrapper, trimmed with scarlet, and her pretty little breakfast cap set on the back of her head. Good fare, which she did not have to pay for, — pure country air, and freedom from all care, had had a rejuvenating effect on Mrs. Walter Scott, and for a woman of forty-seven or thereabouts, she was remarkably handsome and well preserved. This morning she complained of feeling a little languid. She could not have slept as well as usual, she said, and she dreamed that some one came into her room, or tried to come in, and when she woke she was sure she heard footsteps at the extremity of the hall.

"It was Roger, most likely," Hester rejoined. "Like the good boy he is, he got up about twelve, or thereabouts, and stayed up the rest of the night with me and Magdalen."

"Oh-h," Mrs. Irving replied, and her eyes had in them a puzzled look as she left Hester's room and repaired to the breakfast-table.

" Hester tells me that you spent the night with her, or with Magdalen, — which was it ? " she said to Roger playfully, as she leisurely sipped her cup of coffee.

There was no reason why Magdalen should have colored scarlet as she did, or why Roger should stammer and seem so confused as he replied, " Yes, Hester was very restless, and Magdalen very tired, and so I stayed with them."

" And proved a very efficient watcher, it seems ; for Hester is better and Magdalen as blooming as a rose," was Mrs. Irving's next remark, as she shot a quick, curious glance at Magdalen, whose burning cheeks confirmed her in the suspicion which until that morning had never entered her mind.

Magdalen cared for Roger, and Roger cared for Magdalen, and at last she had the key to Magdalen's refusal of her son.

Mrs. Irving had heard from Frank of his ill success, and while expressing some surprise, had told him not to despair, and had promised to do what she could for the furtherance of his cause. It was no part of her plan to speak to Magdalen then upon the subject, but she was more than usually kind and affectionate in her manner towards the girl, hoping that by this means the mother might succeed where the son had failed. Now, however, an unlooked-for obstacle had arisen, and for once Mrs. Walter Scott was uncertain what to do. She had never dreamed that *Roger* might fancy Magdalen, he was so much older and seemed to care so little for women ; but she was sure now that he did, and the hundred thousand dollars she had looked upon as eventually sure seemed to be fading from her grasp. There were wrinkles in her forehead when she left the breakfast table, and her face wore a kind of abstracted look, as if she were intently studying some new device or plan. It came to her at last, and when next she was alone with Frank, she said, " I have been thinking that it might be well for you to get *Roger's* consent for you to address Magdalen."

" Roger's consent ! " Frank repeated, in some surprise. " I should say Magdalen's consent was of more consequence than Roger's."

"Yes, I know," and the lady smiled meaningly. "You said to me once that you loved Magdalen well enough to take her on any terms, and wait for the affection she withholds from you now."

"Yes, I said so; but what of it?" Frank asked; and his mother replied, "I think I know Magdalen better than you do. She has implicit confidence in Roger's judgment, and an intense desire to please him. Let her once believe he wishes her to marry you, and the thing is done. At least, it is worth the trial, and I would speak to Roger without delay and get his consent. Or stay," she added, as she reflected that Frank would probably make a bungle and let out that Magdalen had refused him once, "I will do it for you. A woman knows so much better what to say than a man."

· Frank had but little faith in his mother's scheme, and he was about to tell her so, when Magdalen herself came in. She had just returned from accompanying Roger as far as the end of the avenue on his way to his office. He told her that a walk in the bracing air would do her good, and had taken her with him to the gate which was the entrance to the Millbank grounds. There they had lingered a little, and Roger had seemed more lover-like than ever before, and Magdalen's eyes had shone on him like stars and kept him at her side long after he knew he ought to be at his office, where some of his men were waiting for him. At last, warned by the striking of the village clock of the lateness of the hour, he said a final good-by, and Magdalen returned to the house, flushed with excitement and radiant with happiness, which showed itself in her eyes and face, and in her unusual graciousness towards Frank. Now that she began herself to know what it was to love, and how terrible it would be to lose the object of her love, she pitied Frank so much, and never since that night in the library had she seemed to him so much like the Magdalen of old as she did, when, with her large straw hat upon her arm, she stood talking with him a few moments, mingling much of her old coquetry of manner with what she said, and leaving him at last perfectly willing that his mother should do anything which would further his cause with Magdalen.

That night, when dinner was over and Magdalen was with Hester, who was recovering rapidly, Mrs. Walter Scott took her balls of worsted and her crocheting, and knocking softly at the door of the library, where she knew Roger was, asked if she might come in. He thought it was Magdalen's knock, and looked a little disappointed when he found who his visitor was. But he bade her come in, and bringing a chair for her near to the light, asked what he could do for her.

"I want to talk with you about Frank and Magdalen," Mrs. Irving said. "You must of course have seen the growing affection between the young people?"

Mrs. Walter Scott pretended to be very busy counting her stitches, but she managed to steal a side glance at her companion, who fairly gasped at what he had heard, and whose fingers fluttered nervously among the papers on the table, on one of which he kept writing, in an absent kind of way and in every variety of hand, the name of Magdalen. He had *not* noticed the growing affection between the young people; that is, he had seen nothing on Magdalen's part to warrant such a conclusion. Once, just after his return from Europe, he had thought his nephew's attentions very marked, and a thought had crossed his mind as to what might possibly be the result. But all this was past, as he believed, and his sister's intelligence came upon him like a thunderbolt, stunning him for an instant, and making him powerless to speak. Those were fierce heart-pangs which Roger was enduring, and they showed themselves upon his face, which was very pale, and the corners of his mouth twitched painfully, but his voice was steady and natural as he said at last, —

"And Magdalen, — does she — have you reason to believe she would return a favorable answer to Frank's suit?"

Mrs. Irving was sure now that what she had suspected was true, and that nothing but a belief in Magdalen's preference for another would avail with him, so she replied unhesitatingly, —.

"Certainly I do. I have suspected for years that she was strongly attached to Frank, and her manner towards him fully warrants me in that belief. She is the soul of honor, and never professes what she does not feel."

"Ye-es," Roger said, with something between a sigh and a long-drawn breath, assenting thus to what his sister said, and trying to reconcile with it Magdalen's demeanor toward himself of late.

If she was attached to Frank, and had been for years, why that sudden kindling of her eyes, and that lighting up of her whole face whenever he was with her, and why that sweet graciousness of manner towards him which she had of late evinced? Was Magdalen a coquette, or was that the way of girls? Roger did not know, — he had never made them a study, never been interested in any girl or woman except Magdalen; and now, when he must lose her, he began to feel that he had loved her always from the moment when he took her as his child and first held her baby hands in his, and laid her soft cheek against his own. She *was* his, — he had a better right to her than Frank, and he wrote her name all over the sheet of paper on the table, and thought of all the castles he had built within the last few weeks, — castles of the time when Magdalen would be really his and he could lavish upon her the love and tender caresses he would be coy of giving any one who was not his wife. Roger was naturally very reserved, — and in his intercourse with Magdalen he had only shown her glimpses of the deep, warm love he felt for her. He held peculiar notions about such things, and he was sorry now that he did,— sorry that he had not improved his opportunities and won her for his own before Frank appealed to him, as he had done through his mother, and thus sealed his lips forever. He was thinking of all this, and was so absorbed in it that he forgot his sister was there watching him narrowly, but veiling her watchfulness with her apparent interest in her worsted work, which became strangely tangled and mixed, and required her whole attention to unravel and set right. But she could not sit still all the

evening and let Roger fill that sheet of foolscap with " Magda·
len ; " she must recall him to the point at issue, and so she said
at last, —

" Frank will do nothing without your sanction, and what he
wants is your permission, as Magdalen's guardian, for him to
address her.   Can he have it ? "

Then Roger looked up a moment, and the pencil which had
been so busy began to trace a long black line through every
name as if he thus would blot out the sweetest dream of his
life.

" Have my permission to address Magdalen ?   Yes — certainly, if he wants it.   I had thought — yes, I had hoped — I
had supposed — "

Here Roger came to a full stop, and then, as the only thing
he could do, he added, —

" I thought I had heard something about a Miss Grey of
New York, and that probably has misled me.   Was there nothing in that report ? "

" Nothing," Mrs. Irving replied.   " Frank knew her in New
Haven and met her abroad, and so it was only natural he should
call upon her in New York.   There is nothing in that rumor ;
absolutely nothing.   Frank's mind was too full of Magdalen for
him to care for a hundred Miss Greys.   Poor foolish boy, it
brings my own youth back to me to see him so infatuated.   I
must go to him now, for I know how anxiously he is waiting
for me.   Thank you for the favorable answer I can give him."

She hurried from the room and out into the hall, never stopping to heed the voice which called after her, —

" Helen, oh, Helen ! "

Roger did not know what he wanted to say to her.   His call
was a kind of protest against her considering the matter settled
as wholly as she seemed to think it was.   He could not give
Magdalen up so easily, — he must make one effort for himself,
— and so he had tried to call his sister back, but she did not
hear him, and went on her way, leaving him alone with his
great sorrow.

Frank was in his own room, lazily reclining in his easy chair, and about finishing the second cigar in which he had indulged since dinner.   He took his third when his mother came in, for he saw that she had something to tell him, and he could listen so much better when he was smoking.   With a faint protest against the atmosphere of the room, which was thick with the fumes of tobacco, Mrs. Walter Scott began her story, telling him that he had Roger's consent to speak to Magdalen as soon as he liked, but not telling him of her suspicions that Roger, too, would in time have spoken for himself, if his nephew had not first taken the field.   It was strange that such a possibility had never occurred to Frank.   He, too, had a fancy that Roger was too old for Magdalen, — that he was really more her father than her lover, and he never dreamed of him as a rival.

"I wish you could arrange it with Magdalen as easily as you have with Roger," he said ; and his mother replied, "She will think better of it another time.   Girls frequently say no at first."

"But not the way Magdalen said it," Frank rejoined.   "She was in earnest.   She meant it, I am sure."

"Try her with Roger's consent.   Tell her *he* wishes it ; not that he is *willing*, but that he *wishes* it.   You will find that argument all-powerful," Mrs. Irving said.

Being a woman herself she knew how to work upon another woman's feelings, and she talked to and encouraged her son until he caught something of her hopefulness, and saw himself the fortunate possessor of all the glorious beauty and sprightliness embodied in Magdalen, who little dreamed of what lay before her, and who next morning, at the breakfast table, wondered at Frank's exhilaration of spirits and Roger's evident depression.   He was very pale, and bore the look of one who had not slept ; but he tried to be cheerful, and smiled a faint, sickly kind of smile at Magdalen's lively badinage with Frank, whom she teased and coquetted with something after her olden fashion, not because she enjoyed it, but because she saw there was a cloud somewhere, and would fain dispel it.   She never joked with Roger as she did with Frank ; but this morning, when she met him in the hall, where he was drawing on his gloves preparatory to going out, she asked him what was the matter, and if he had one of his bad headaches coming on.

" His throat was a little sore," he said ; "he did not sleep much last night, but the walk to the village would do him good."

Magdalen had taken a long scarf from the hall-stand, and holding it toward him, said, " It's cold this morning, and my teeth fairly chattered when I went out on the piazza for my run with old Rover. Please wear this round your throat, Mr. Irving. Let me put it on for you."

There was a soft light in her eyes and a look of tender in-terest in her face, and Roger bent his head before her and let her wind the warm scarf round his neck and throw the fringed ends over his shoulder. Roger was tall, and Magdalen stood on tiptoe, with her arms almost meeting round his neck as she adjusted the scarf behind, and her face came so near to his that he could feel her breath stir his hair just as her presence stirred the inmost depths of his heart, tempting him to take her in his arms and beg of her not to heed Frank's suit, but listen first to him, who had the better right to her. But Roger was a prudent man ; the hall was not the place for love-making, so he restrained himself, and only took one of Magdalen's hands in his and held it while he thanked her for her thoughtfulness.

" You are better than a physician, Magda. I don't know what I should do without you. I hope you will never leave Millbank."

So much he did say, and his eyes had an earnest, pleading look in them, which haunted Magdalen all the morning, and made her very happy as she flitted about the house, or dashed off one brilliant piece after another upon her piano, which seemed almost to talk beneath her spirited touch.

Meanwhile, Roger and Frank were alone in the office. The brisk wind which was blowing in the morning had brought on an April shower of sleet and rain, and there was not much prospect of visitors or clients. Roger sat by his desk, pretend-

7*

ing to read, while Frank at his table was doing just what Roger had done the previous night, viz., writing Magdalen's name on slips of paper, and adding to it once the name of Irving, just to see how it would look ; and Roger, who got up for a book which was over Frank's head, saw it, and smiled sadly as he remembered that he, too, had written " Magdalen Irving," just as Frank was doing.   There was a little mirror over the table, where Frank had placed it for his own use ; for he was vain of his personal appearance, and his hair and collar and necktie needed frequent fixing.   Into this mirror Roger glanced and then looked down upon his nephew, who at that moment seemed a boy compared with him.   Frank's light hair and skin, and whitish, silky mustache, gave him a very youthful appearance and made him look younger than he was, while Roger had grown old within the night.   There were no gray hairs, it is true, among his luxuriant brown locks ; but he was haggard and pale, and there were dark circles beneath his eyes, and he felt tired·and worn and old, — too old to mate with Magdalen's bright beauty.   Frank was better suited to her in point of age, and Frank should have her if she preferred him.   Roger reached this conclusion hastily, and then, by way of strengthening it, pointed playfully to the name on the paper, and asked, " Have you spoken to her yet ? "

Frank was glad Roger had broached the subject, and he began at once to tell what he meant to do and be, if Magdalen would but listen favorably to him.   He would study so hard, and overcome his laziness and his expensive habits, and be a man, such as he knew he had not been, but such as he felt he was capable of being with Magdalen as his leading star.   He had *not* spoken to her yet, he said, but he should do so that night,.and he was glad to have Roger's approval, as that would surely bias Magdalen's decision.   Frank grew very enthusiastic, and drove his penknife repeatedly into the table, and ran his fingers through his hair, and pulled up his collar and looked in the glass ; but never glanced at Roger, to whom every word he

uttered was like a stab, and whose face was wet with perspiration as he listened and felt that his heart was breaking.

"I'd better go away for a day or two, until the matter is
settled, for if I stay I might say that to Magdalen which would
hardly be fair to say, after Frank's confiding in me as he has,"
Roger thought; and, after the mail came in, and he had some
pretext for doing so, he announced his intention of going to
New York in the afternoon train. "I shall not go to the
house," he said, "as I have some writing to do; so please tell
your mother where I have gone, and that I may not return
until day after to-morrow."

With all his efforts to seem natural, there was something
hurried and excited in his manner, which Frank observed and
wondered at, but he attributed it to some perplexity in business
matters, and never suspected that it had anything to do with
him and his prospective affairs.

Roger talked but little that morning, but busied himself at
his own desk, until time for the train, when, with some direc-
tions to Frank as to what to do in case certain persons called,
he left his office and went on his way to New York.

After Roger's departure, Frank grew tired of staying alone.
The day had continued wet and uncomfortable, and few had
dropped in at the office, and these for only a moment. So,
after a little, he started for Millbank, resolving, if a good opportunity occurred, to speak to Magdalen again on the subject
uppermost in his mind. He did not see his mother as he entered the house, but he met a servant in the hall and asked for
Magdalen.

"Miss Lennox was in Mrs. Floyd's room," the servant said,
and Frank went there to find her.

"I sent her up garret to shet a winder and hain't seen her
sense," Hester said in answer to his question. "She's some-
wheres round, most likely. Did you want anything particular?"

"No, nothing very particular," was Frank's reply, as he left
the room and continued his search for Magdalen, first in the

parlors, and then in the little room at the end of the upper hall, which had been fitted up for a fernery.

Not finding her there and remembering what Hester had said about the garret, he started at last in that direction, though he had but little idea that she was there. If she had come down, as he supposed, she had left the door open behind her, and he was about to shut it, when a sound met his ear, which made him stop and listen until it was repeated. It came again ere long, — a sound half way between a moan and a low, gasping sob, and Frank ran swiftly up the stairs, for it was Magdalen's voice, and he knew now that Magdalen was in the garret.

CHAPTER XX.

WHAT MAGDALEN FOUND IN THE GARRET.

AGDALEN had not forgotten "the loose plank," but since the night of her adventure in the garret she had never been near that part of the building, though sorely tempted to do so every day and hour of her life. It seemed to her as if some powerful influence was urging her on toward the garret, while a still more powerful influence to which she gave no name was constantly holding her back. She had puzzled over the loose plank, and dreamed of it, and speculated upon it, and wondered if there was anything under it, and if so, was it —, she never quite said *what*, even to herself, for it seemed to her that she should in some way be wronging Roger if she breathed the name of *will*. Of one thing, however, she felt certain; if there *was* a paper secreted in the garret, old Hester knew of it, and had had a hand in hiding it; and once she thought of quizzing Aleck to see if he too knew about it. She could not have done much with him, for had he known of the will, he would, if questioned with regard to it, have been so deaf that everybody in the house would have heard the conversation. Aleck was not fond of talking, and in order to avoid it, had a way, as Hester said, of affecting to be deafer than he was, and so was usually left in peace. He always heard Roger, and generally Magdalen; but to the rest of the household he was as deaf as a post unless it suited him to hear. It was useless to question him, and so Magdalen kept her own counsel for two weeks after that memorable night when Roger had shared her vigils, and from which time Hester's recovery had been rapid.

She was able now to sit up all day, but had not yet been to the kitchen, and when she asked Magdalen to go and shut the garret window which she had left open in the morning and into which she was sure the rain was pouring, Magdalen expressed a good deal of surprise that she should have ventured into the garret, and asked why she went there.

"I wanted to look over them clothes in the chest; I knew they needed airin'," Hester said, and Magdalen accepted the explanation and started for the garret.

It was raining fast, and as she opened the door which led up the stairs, a gust of wind blew down into her face, and she heard the heavy rain drops on the roof. The window was open as Hester had said, and Magdalen shut it, and then stood a moment looking off upon the river and the hills over which the April shower was sweeping in misty sheets. To the right lay the little village of Belvidere, where Roger's office was. She could see the white building nestled among the elms in one corner of the common, and the sight of it made her heart beat faster than its wont, and brought before her the scene of the morning when Roger had held her hand in his, and looked so kindly into her eyes. She could feel the pressure of his broad, warm hand even now, and she felt her cheeks grow hot beneath the look which seemed to beam upon her here in the gloomy garret where there was only rubbish, and rats, and barrels, and chests, and loose planks under the roof. She started, almost guiltily, when she remembered the latter, and turned her face resolutely from that part of the room, lest she should go that way and see for herself what was hidden there.   Hester had said, "I went to air the clothes in the old chest," and Magdalen turned to the chest and looked at it, carelessly at first, then more closely, and finally went down on her knees to examine some-thing which made her grow cold and faint for a moment.

It was nothing but a large cobweb, but it covered the entire fastening of the chest, stretching from the lid down across the keyhole, and showing plainly that the chest had not been open in weeks.   It could not be opened without disturbing the cob-web, for Magdalen tried it, and saw the fleecy thing torn apart as she lifted the lid.   There was a paper package lying on top of the linen, and from a rent in one corner Magdalen saw a bit of the dress she had worn to Millbank.   It was years since she had seen it, and at the sight of it now she felt a thrill of pain, and turned her head away.   There was too much of mystery and humiliation connected with that little dress for her to care to look at it; and she shut the lid quickly, and said to herself, as she turned away:

"Hester has not opened the chest to-day.   What, then, was she here for?"

Then, swift as lightning, the answer came:

"She was here to look after whatever is hidden under that loose plank, and probably to remove it."

Yes, that was the solution of the mystery.   If there *had* been anything under the floor, it had been transferred to some other hiding-place, and, woman-like, Magdalen began to feel a little sorry that she had lost her chance for knowing what was there.

"There can be no harm in looking now, if it is really gone," she said; and following some impulse she did not try to resist, she went toward that part of the garret, putting a broken chair out of her way, and bending down beneath the slanting rafters.

It was raining hard, and she went back a step or two, and glanced at the window against which the storm was beating. She was not afraid there, in broad daylight; but a strange feel-ing of awe and dread began to creep over her, mingled with a firmer determination to explore that spot under the floor. She did not believe she should find anything, but she *must* look, — she must satisfy herself, let the consequence be what it might. She did not think of Roger, nor the will, nor Frank, but, strange to say, a thought of *Jessie* crossed her mind, — Jessie, the drowned woman, who seemed so near to her that she involuntarily looked over her shoulder to see if a spectre were there. Then she bent low under the beams, — went nearer to the loose plank, — had her hands upon it, and knew that it did not fit as perfectly as on that night when she first discovered it. It had been moved. Somebody had been there recently, and, trembling with excitement, Magdalen grasped the plank, and drew it up from its position, shrinking a little from the dark opening which looked so like a grave. Gradually, as she saw clearer, she could distinguish the lath and plastering, with bits of chips and shavings and sawdust, and signs that the rats lived there. Then, leaning forward, she peered down under the floor, looking to the north, looking to the east, then to the south, and lastly to the west, where, pushed back as far as possible from sight, was a little box, the cover of which was tied firmly down with a bit of white Marseilles braid, such as Magdalen was trimming her dress with a few days before in Hester Floyd's room. She had missed about half a yard, which could not at the time be found, but she had found it now, and she grew dizzy and faint as she reached for the box, and brought it out to the daylight.

Whatever the mystery was, she had it in her hands, and she sat down upon a chair to recover her breath, and decide what she should do.

"Put it back where you found it," was suggested to her; but she could not do that, and seemingly without an effort on her part her fingers nervously untied the hard knot, then slowly unwound the braid, which she examined to see if it was soiled, and if there was not enough for the pocket of her sack, if she decided to have one.

She thought there was, and she laid it on her lap and then opened the lid!

There were two packages inside, and both were wrapped in thick brown paper, which Magdalen removed carefully, and without the least agitation now. Her excitement had either passed or was so great that she did not heed it, and she was conscious of no emotions whatever as she sat there removing the paper wrappings from what seemed to be a *letter*, an old, yellow, soiled letter, directed to "Master Roger L. Irving," in a handwriting she did not know. She did not open the letter, but she read the name and whispered it to herself, and thought by some strange accident of that morning by the river when Roger had spoken of working for her with his hands, and of her helping him in case he should lose Millbank. Why she should recall that incident she could not tell any more than she could guess that she held in her hands that which would eventually lead to just such an alternative as Roger had suggested.

She put the letter down, and took the other package and removed its wrappings and turned it to the light, uttering a cry of terror and surprise at what was written there. She must read it, — she *would* read it and know the worst, and she opened the worn document, which was dated back so many years, and read it through while her fingers seemed to grow big and numb, and she felt her arms prickle to her shoulders. Once she thought of paralysis, as the strange sensation went creeping through her whole system, and she was conscious of feeling that she merited some such punishment for the idle curiosity which had resulted so disastrously.

She read every word that was written on the paper, and understood it, too, — that is, understood what the dead old man had done, but not *why* he had done it. That was something for which she could find no excuse, no reason. Doubtless the letter directed to Roger contained the explanation, if there was one; but that was sacred to her, — that was Roger's alone. She could not meddle with that; she would give it to him just as she had found it.

" Poor wronged Roger; it will kill him," she moaned; "and to think that I should be the instrument of his ruin."

She was rocking to and fro in her distress, with her hands locked together around her knees, and her head bowed in her lap. What could she do? What should she do? she asked herself, and something answered again, " Put it where you found it, and keep your own counsel."

Surely that advice was good, and Magdalen started to follow it, when suddenly there came back to her the words, " If I believed it, I would move heaven and earth to find it."

Roger had spoken thus on that summer morning, which seemed so long ago. Roger was honest; Roger was just; Roger would bid her take that dreadful paper to him, though total ruin was the result.

Twice Magdalen started for the dark opening under the roof and as often stopped suddenly, until at last, overcome with excitement and anguish, she crouched down upon the floor, and moaned piteously, " Oh, Roger, Roger, if you must be ruined, I wish it had fallen to the lot of some other one to ruin you. Was it for this you brought me here? for this you have been so kind to me? Oh, Roger, I cannot live to see you a beggar. Why was it done? What was it for?"

The words she uttered were not intelligible, and only her sobbing moans met Frank's ear and sent him up the steep stairway to where she sat with her face buried in her lap and the fatal paper clutched firmly in her hand.

" Magdalen, what is it? What has happened to you?" Frank asked, and then Magdalen first became aware of his presence.

Uttering a low scream she struggled to her feet, and turned toward him a face the expression of which he never forgot, it was so full of pain and anguish, of terror and mute entreaty. There was no escape now, for he was there with her, — the heir, the supplanter of poor Roger. Heaven would not suffer her to hide it as she might have done if left alone a little longer. It had sent Frank to prevent the wrong, and she must do the

right in spite of herself. Magdalen thought all this during
the moment she stood confronting Frank, — then reaching
toward him the soiled yellow paper, she whispered hoarsely:
"Take it, Frank. It is yours, *all yours;* but oh, be merciful
to Roger."

Mechanically Frank took the paper from her, and the next
moment she was on her knees before him trying to articulate
something about "Roger, poor Roger," but failing in the effort.
The sight of that paper in Frank's hands, and knowing that
with it he held everything which Roger prized so dearly, took
sense and strength away, and she fainted at his feet.

MAGDALEN HAD FOUND THE WILL!

CHAPTER XXI.

FRANK AND THE WILL.

FRANK knew she had found the will, but he did not at
all realize the effect which the finding of it would have
upon his future. He had not read it like Magdalen,
— he did not know that by virtue of what was recorded there,
he, and not Roger, was the heir of Millbank. He only knew
that Magdalen lay unconscious at his feet, her white forehead
touching his boot, and one of her hands clutching at his knee
where it had fallen when she raised it imploringly toward him,
with a pleading word for Roger. To lift her in his arms and bear
her to the window, which he opened so that the wind and rain
might fall upon her face and neck, was the work of an instant;
and then, still supporting her upon his shoulder, he rubbed and
chafed her pale fingers and pushed her hair back from her face,
and bent over her with loving, anxious words, which she did
not hear and would scarcely have heeded if she had. Gradually as the rain beat upon her face she came back to conscious·

ness, and with a cry tried to free herself from Frank's embrace. But he held her fast, while he asked what was the matter, — what had she found or seen to affect her so powerfully?

"Don't you know? Haven't you read it?" she gasped; and Frank replied, "No, Magdalen, I have not read it. My first care was for you, — always for you, darling."

She freed herself from him then, and struggling to her feet stood before him with dilating nostrils and flashing eyes. She knew that the tone of his voice meant *love*, — love for her who had refused it once, — aye, who would refuse it a thousand times more now than she had before. He could not have Millbank and her too. There was no Will on earth which had power to take her from Roger and give her to Frank, and by some subtle intuition Magdalen recognized for a moment all she was to Roger, and felt that possibly he would prefer poverty with her to wealth without her; just as a crust shared with him would be sweeter to her than the daintiest luxury shared with Frank, who had called her his darling and who would rival Roger in everything. Magdalen could have stamped her foot in her rage that Frank should presume to think of love then and there, when he must know what it was she had found for him, — what it was he held in his hand. And here she wronged him; for he did not at all realize his position, and he looked curiously at her, wondering to see her so excited.

"Are you angry, Magdalen?" he asked. "What has happened to affect you so? Tell me. I don't understand it at all."

Then Magdalen *did* stamp her foot, and coming close to him, said, "Don't drive me mad with your stupidity, Frank Irving. You know as well as I that I have found what when a child you once asked me to search for, — you to whom Roger was so kind, — you, who would deal so treacherously with Roger in his own house; and I promised I would do it, — I, who was ten times worse than you. I was a beggar whom Roger took in, and I've wounded the hand that fed me. I have found the will; but, Frank Irving, if I had guessed what it contained I would have plucked out both my eyes before they should have looked for it. You deceived me. You said it gave you a *part*, — only a part. You told me false, and I hate you for it."

She was mad now with her excitement, which increased as she raved on, and she looked so white and terrible, with the fire flashing out in gleams from her dark eyes, that Frank involun tarily shrank back from her at first, and kept out of reach of the hands which made so fierce gestures toward him as if they would do him harm. Then as he began to recover himself, and from her words get some inkling of the case, he drew her gently to him, saying as he did so, " Magdalen, you wrong me greatly. Heaven is my witness that I always meant to give you the same impression of the will which I received from my mother, though really and truly I never had much idea that there was one, and am as much astonished to find there is as you can be. I have not read it yet, and I am not responsible for what there is in it. I knew nothing of it, had nothing to do with it ; please don't blame me for what I could not help."

There was reason in what he said, and Magdalen saw it, and softened toward him as she replied, " Forgive me, Frank, if in my excitement I said things which sounded harshly, and blamed you for what you could not help. But, oh ! Frank, I am *so* sorry for Roger, poor Roger. Say that you won't wrong him. Be merciful ; be kind to him as he has been to you."

Frank's perceptions were not very acute, but he would have been indeed a fool if in what Magdalen said he had failed to detect a deeper interest in Roger than he had thought existed. He did detect it, and a fierce pang of jealousy shot through his heart as he began to see what the obstacle was which stood between himself and Magdalen.

" I do not understand why you should be so distressed about Roger, or beg of *me* to be merciful," he said ; but Magdalen interrupted him with a gesture of impatience.

" Read that paper and you will know what I mean. You

will see that it makes Roger a beggar, and gives you all his fortune. He has nothing, — nothing comparatively."

Frank understood her now. He knew before that the lost
will was found, and he supposed that possibly he shared equally
with Roger, but he never dreamed that to him was given all,
and to Roger nothing; and as Magdalen finished speaking he
opened the paper nervously and read it through, while she sat
watching him, her eyes growing blacker and brighter and more
defiant, as she fancied she saw a half-pleased expression flit
across his face when he read that *he* was the lawful heir of
Millbank. He had been defrauded of his rights for years, had
murmured against his poverty and his dependence, and thought
hard things of the old man in his grave who had left him only
five thousand dollars. But that was over now. Poverty and
dependence were things of the past. The old man in his grave
had willed to Frank, his beloved grandchild, all his property
except a few legacies similar to those in the older will, and the
paltry sum left to "the boy known as Roger Lennox Irving."
That was the way it was worded, not "My son Roger," but
"the boy known as Roger Lennox Irving." To him was be-
queathed the sum of Five Thousand dollars, and the farm
among the New Hampshire hills known as the "Morton"
place. That was all Roger's inheritance, and it is not strange
that Frank sat for a moment speechless. Had he shared
equally with Roger he would not have been surprised; but why
he should have the whole and Roger nothing, he did not understand. The injustice of the thing struck him at first quite
as forcibly as it did Magdalen, and more to himself than her,
he said, "There must be some mistake. My grandfather would
never have done this thing in his right mind. Where did you
find it, Magdalen?"

He did not seem elated, as she feared he might. She had
done him injustice, and with far more toleration than she had
felt for him at first, Magdalen told him where she had found it
and why she chanced to look there, and pointed to the signa-
tures of Hester and Aleck Floyd as witnesses to the will.

"Hester hid it," she said, "because she knew it was unjust, and it was the fear of its being found which troubled her so much."

"That is probable," Frank rejoined; "but still I can see no reason for my grandfather's cutting Roger off with a mere pittance. It is cruel. It is unjust."

"Oh, Frank," Magdalen cried, and the tears which glittered in her eyes softened the fiery expression they had worn a few moments before. "Forgive me; I was harsh towards you at first, but now I know you mean to do right. You *will*, Frank. You certainly *will* do right."

Magdalen had recovered her powers of speech and she talked rapidly, begging Frank to be generous with Roger, to leave him Millbank, to let him stay in the beautiful home he loved so much. "Think of all he has done for you," she said, clasping her hands upon his arm and looking at him with eyes from which the tears were dropping fast. "Were you his son he could hardly have done more; and he has been so kind to me, — me who have requited his kindness so cruelly. Oh, Roger, Roger, I would give my life to spare him this blow!"

She covered her face with her hands, while Frank sat regarding her intently, his affection for her at that moment mastering every other emotion and making him indifferent to the great fortune which had so suddenly come to him. Love for Magdalen was the strongest sentiment of which he was capable, and it was intensified with the suspicion that Roger was preferred to himself. He could interpret her distress and concern for his uncle in no other way. Gratitude alone could never have affected her as she was affected, and Frank's heart throbbed with jealousy and fear and intense desire to secure Magdalen for himself. There had been a momentary feeling of exultation when he thought of his poverty as a thing of the past, but Magdalen's love was worth more to him than a dozen Millbanks, and in his excitement no sacrifice seemed too great which would secure it.

"Oh, Roger, Roger, I would give my life to spare him this

blow!" Magdalen had cried; and with these words still ringing in his ears, Frank said to her at last, "Magdalen, you need not give your life; there is a far easier way by which Roger can be spared the pain of knowing that Millbank is not his. He never need to know of this will; no one need to know of it but our-selves, — you and me, Magdalen. We will keep the secret to-gether, shall we?"

Magdalen had lifted up her head, and was listening to him with an eager, wistful expression in her face, which encouraged him to go on.

"But, Magdalen, my silence must have its price, and that price is *yourself!*"

She started from him then as if he had stung her, but soon resumed her former attitude, and listened while he continued:

"I asked you once, and you refused me, and I meant to try and abide by your decision, but I cannot give you up; and when I found that Roger favored my suit and would be glad if you could give me a favorable answer, I resolved to try again, and came home this very afternoon with that object in view."

Frank stopped abruptly, struck with the look of anguish and pain and surprise which crept into Magdalen's eyes as he spoke of "Roger's favoring his suit."

"Roger consent; oh no, not that. Roger never wished that," Magdalen exclaimed, in a voice full of bitter disappoint-ment. "Did Roger wish it, Frank? *Did* he say so, sure?"

Few men, seeing Magdalen moved as she was then, would have urged their own claims upon her; but Frank was different from most men. He had set his hopes on Magdalen, and he must win her, and the more obstacles he found in his way the more he was resolved to succeed. He would not see the love for Roger which was so apparent in all Magdalen said and did. He would ignore that altogether, and he replied, "Most cer-tainly he wishes it, or he would not have given his consent for me to speak to you again. I talked with him about it the last thing this morning before he started for New York. Did I tell you he had gone there? He has, and expects it to be settled before his return.   I am well aware that this is not the time or place for love-making, but your great desire to spare Roger from a knowledge of the will wrung from me what otherwise I would have said at another time.   Magdalen, I have always loved you, from the morning I put you in your candle-box and knelt before you as my princess.   You were the sweetest baby I ever saw.   You have ripened into the loveliest woman, and I want you for my wife.   I have wanted money badly, but now that I have it, I will gladly give it all for you.   Only say that you will be mine, and I'll burn this paper before your eyes, and swear to you solemnly that not a word regarding it shall ever pass my lips.   Shall I do it?"

Magdalen was not looking at him now.   When he assured her of Roger's consent to woo her for himself, and that he "expected it to be settled before his return," she had turned her face away to hide the bitter pain she knew was written upon it.   She had been terribly mistaken.   She had believed that Roger cared for her, and the knowing that he did not, that he could even give his consent for her to marry *Frank*, was more than she could bear, and she felt for a moment as if every ray of happiness had, within the last hour, been stricken from her life.

"Shall I do it? only speak the word, and every trace of the will shall be destroyed."

That was what Frank said to her a second time, and then Magdalen turned slowly toward him, but made him no reply. She scarcely realized what he was asking, or what he meant to do, as he took a match from his pocket and struck it across the floor.   Gradually a ring of smoke came curling up and floated toward Magdalen, who sat like a stone gazing fixedly at the burning match, which Frank held near to the paper.

"Tell me, Magdalen, will you be my wife, if I burn the will?" he asked again; and then Magdalen answered him, "Oh, Frank, don't tempt me thus.   How can I?   Oh, Roger, Roger!"

She was beginning to waver, and Frank saw it, and too much excited himself to know what he was doing, held the match so near the paper that it began to scorch, and in a moment more would have been in a blaze. Then Magdalen came to herself, and struck the match from Frank's hand, and snatching the paper from him, said, vehemently, "You must not do it. Roger would not suffer it, if he knew. Roger is honorable, Roger is just. *I* found the paper, Frank. *I* will carry it to Roger, and tell him it was I who ruined him. I will beg for his forgiveness, and then go away and die, so I cannot witness his fall."

She had risen to her feet, and was leaving the garret, but Frank held her back. He could not part with her thus; he could not risk the probable consequences of her going to Roger, as she had said she would. But one result could follow such a step, and that result was death to all Frank most desired. Millbank weighed as nothing when compared with Magdalen, and Frank made her listen to him again, and worked upon her pity for Roger until, worried and bewildered, and half-crazed with excitement, she cried out, "I'll think about it, Frank. I will love you, if I can. Give me a week in which to decide; but let me go now, or I shall surely die."

She tore herself from him, and was hurrying down the stairs with the will grasped in her hands, when suddenly she stopped, and, offering it to Frank, said to him, "Put it under the floor where I found it. Let it stay there till the week is up."

There was hope in what she said, and Frank hastened to do her bidding, and then went softly down the stairs, and passed unobserved through the hall out into the rain, which seemed so grateful to him after his recent excitement. He did not care to meet his mother just then, and so he quietly left the house, and walked rapidly down the avenue toward the village, intending to strike into the fields and go back to Millbank at the usual dinner-hour, so as to excite no suspicions.

To say that Frank felt no elation at the thought of Millbank belonging to him, would be wrong; for, as he walked along, he was conscious of a new and pleasant feeling of importance, mingled with a feeling that he was very magnanimous, too, and was doing what few men in his position would have done.

"All mine, if I choose to claim it," he said to himself once, as he paused on a little knoll and looked over the broad acres of the Irving estate, which stretched far back from the river toward the eastern hills. "All mine, if I choose to have it so."

Then he looked away to the huge mill upon the river, the shoe-shop farther on, and thought of the immense revenue they yielded, and then his eye came back to Millbank proper, — the handsome house, embowered in trees, with its velvety lawn and spacious grounds, and its ease and luxury within. "All his," unless he chose to throw it away for a girl, who did not love him, and who, he believed, preferred Roger and poverty and toil, to luxury and Millbank and himself. Had he believed otherwise, had no suspicion of her preference for Roger entered his mind, he might have hesitated a moment ere deciding to give up the princely fortune which had come so suddenly to him. But the fact that she was hard to win only enhanced her value, and he resolutely shut his eyes to the sacrifice he was making for her sake, and thought instead how he would work for her, deny himself for her, and become all that her husband ought to be.

"She *shall* love me better than she loves Roger. She shall never regret her choice if she decides for me," he said, as he went back to the house, which he reached just as dinner was announced.

Mrs. Walter Scott had not seen him when he first came home in the afternoon, but she saw him leave the house and hurry down the avenue, while something in his manner indicated an unusual degree of perturbation and excitement. A few moments later she found Magdalen in her own room, lying upon the sofa, her face as white as marble, and her eyes wearing so scared a look that she was greatly alarmed, and asked what was the matter.

"A headache; it came on suddenly," Magdalen said, while her lip quivered and her eyes filled with tears, which ran down

her cheeks in torrents, as Mrs. Irving bent to kiss her, smoothing her forehead and saying to her, " Poor child, you look as if
you were suffering so much. I wish I could help you. Can
I ? "

" No, nobody can help me, — nobody. Oh, is it a sin to wish
I had never been born ? " was Magdalen's reply, which confirmed Mrs. Walter Scott in her suspicion that Frank had something to do with her distress.

Frank had spoken again and been refused, and they might lose
the hundred thousand after all. Mrs. Walter Scott could not
afford to lose it. She had formed too many plans which were
all depending upon it to see it pass from her without an effort
to keep it, and bringing a little stool to Magdalen's side, she
sat down by her and began to caress, and pity, and soothe her,
and at last said to her, " Excuse me, darling, but I am almost
certain that Frank has had more or less to do with your headache. I know he has been here ; did you see him ? "

Magdalen made no reply, only her tears fell faster, and she
turned her face away from the lady, who continued, in her
softest, kindest manner, " My poor boy, I know all about it ;
can't you love him ? Try, darling, for my sake as well as his.
We could be so happy together. Tell me what you said to
him."

" No, no, not now. Please don't talk to me now. I am so
miserable," was Magdalen's reply, and with that Mrs. Walter
Scott was obliged to be content, until she found herself alone
with her son at the dinner table.

Dismissing the servant the moment dessert was brought in,
she asked him abruptly " what had transpired between him
and Magdalen to affect her so strangely."

Frank's face was very pale, and he betrayed a good deal of
agitation as he asked in turn what Magdalen herself had said.

He had a kind of intuition that if his mother knew of the
will, no power on earth could keep her quiet. He believed
she liked Magdalen, but he knew she liked money better ; and
he was alarmed lest she should discover his secret, and be the

instrument of his losing what seemed more and more desirable as one obstacle after another was thrown in his way.

Mrs. Irving repeated all that had passed between herself and Magdalen, and then Frank breathed more freely, and told on his part what he thought necessary to tell.

"Magdalen had been a good deal excited," he said, "and had asked for a week in which to consider the matter, and he had granted it. And mother," he added, "please let her alone, and not bother her with questions, and don't mention me to her above all things. 'Twill spoil everything."

Frank had finished his pudding by this time, and without waiting for his mother's answer he left the dining room and went at once to his own chamber, where he passed the entire evening, thinking of the strange discovery which had been made, wondering what Magdalen's final decision would be, and occasionally sending a feeling of longing and regret after the fortune he was giving up.

CHAPTER XXII.

MRS. WALTER SCOTT AND THE WILL.

ROGER came from New York the next evening. He could not stay from Millbank any longer. He had made up his mind to face the inevitable. He would make the best of it if Magdalen accepted Frank, and if she did not, he would speak for himself at once. Roger was naturally hopeful, and something told him that his chance was not lost forever, that Frank was not so sure of Magdalen. He could not believe that he had been so deceived or had misconstrued her kind graciousness of manner toward himself. A thousand little acts of hers came back to his mind and confirmed him in the belief that unless she was a most consummate coquette, he was not indifferent to her. On reaching Belvidere, he went straight to Millbank without stopping at the office. He was impatient to see Magdalen, but she was not on the steps to meet him as was her custom when he returned from New York or Boston, and only Mrs. Walter Scott's bland voice greeted him as he came in.

" Magdalen was sick with one of her neuralgic headaches," she said, " and had not left her room that day."

Roger would not ask *her* if it was settled. He would rather put that question to Frank, who soon came in and inquired anxiously for Magdalen. A person less observing than Roger could not have failed to see that the Frank of to-day was not the same as the Frank of yesterday. He did not mean to appear differently, but he could not divest himself wholly of the feeling that by every lawful right he was master where he had been so long a dependent, and there was in his manner an air of assurance and independence, and even of patronage, toward Roger, who attributed it wholly to the wrong source, and when his sister left the room for a moment, he said, " I suppose I am to congratulate you, of course ? "

Frank wanted to say yes, but the lie was hard to utter, and he answered, " I think so. She wishes time to consider. Girls always do, I believe."

Roger knew little of girls, he said, and he tried to smile and appear natural, and asked who had called at the office during his absence, and if his insurance agent had been to see about the mill and the shoe-shop.

Frank answered all his questions, and made some suggestions of his own to the effect that if he were Roger he would insure in another company, and do various other things differently.

" I am something of an old fogy, I reckon, and prefer following in my father's safe track," Roger said, with a laugh, and then the conversation ceased and the two men separated.

Magdalen's headache did not seem to abate, and for several days she kept her room, refusing to see any one but Hester and Mrs. Walter Scott, who vied with each other in their attentions to her. Mrs. Walter Scott did a good deal of tender nursing during those few days, and called Magdalen by every pet name there was in her vocabulary, and kissed her at least a dozen times an hour, and carried messages which she never sent to Frank, who was in a state of great excitement, not only with regard to Magdalen, but also the Will, thoughts of which drove him nearly frantic. Every day of his life he mounted the garret stairs, and groping his way to the loose plank, went down on his knees to see that it was safe. The Will had a wonderful fascination for him ; he could not keep away from it, and one morning he took it from the box, and carrying it to the window, sat down to read it again, and see if it really *did* give everything to him. For the first time then he noticed the expression, "To the boy known as Roger Lennox Irving."

It was a very singular way to speak of one's child, he thought, and he wondered what it could mean, and why his grandfather had, at the very last, made so unjust a will; and he became so absorbed in thought as not to hear the steps on the stairs, or see the woman who came softly to his side and stood looking over his shoulder.

Magdalen had, at last, asked to see Frank. She had made up her mind, and insisted upon being dressed, and meeting him in her little sitting-room, which opened from her chamber.

" Do you feel quite equal to the task ? " Mrs. Walter Scott had said, kissing and caressing the poor girl, whose face was deathly pale, save where the fever spots burned upon her cheeks. " You don't know how beautiful you look," she continued, as she wrapped the shawl around Magdalen, and then, with another kiss, went in quest of Frank.

No one had seen him except Celine, who remembered having met him in the little passage leading to the garret stairs.

"He was there yesterday and the day before," she said, and then passed on, never dreaming of all which was to follow those few apparently unimportant words.

"That is a strange place for Frank to visit every day," Mrs.

Walter Scott thought, and, curious to know why he was there, she, too, started for the garret. She always stepped lightly, and her soft French slippers scarcely made a sound as she went up the stairs. Frank's back was toward her, and she advanced so cautiously that she stood close behind him before he was aware of her presence. She saw the soiled paper he held in his hand, read a few words, and then uttered a cry of exulta-tion, which started Frank to his feet, where he stood confront-ing her, his face as white as marble, and his eyes blazing with excitement. His mother was scarcely less pale than himself, and her eyes were fixed on his with an unflinching gaze.

" Ah ! " she said, and in that single interjection was em-bodied all the cruel exultation and delight and utter disregard for Roger, and defiance of the world, which the cold, hard wo-man felt.

Anon there broke about her mouth a peculiar kind of smile, which showed her glittering teeth, and made Frank draw back from her a step or two, while he held the paper closer in his hand, and farther away from her. She saw the motion, and there was something menacing in her attitude as she went close to him, and whispered,—

"I was right, after all. There *was* another Will, which somebody hid. Where did you find it ? "

" Magdalen found it," Frank involuntarily rejoined, mentally cursing himself for his stupidity when it was too late.

"Magdalen found it ? And is that what ails her ? Let me see it, please."

For a moment Frank was tempted to refuse her request, but something in her face compelled him to unfold the paper and hold it while she read it through.

" Why, Frank, it gives you *everything*," she exclaimed, with joy thrilling in every tone, as she clutched his arm, and looked into his face. " I never supposed it quite as good as this."

" Mother," Frank said, drawing back from her again, " are you a fiend to exult so over Roger's ruin ? Don't you see it gives him a mere nothing, and he the only son ? "

All the manhood of Frank's nature was roused by his mother's manner, and he was tempted for a moment to tear the will in shreds, and thus prevent the storm which he felt was rising over Millbank.

"There may be a doubt about the 'only son,'" Mrs. Walter Scott replied. "A father does not often deal thus with his only surviving son. What do you imagine *that* means?" and she pointed to the words, "the boy known as Roger Lennox Irving."

Frank knew then what it meant; knew that in some way a doubt as to Roger's birth had been lodged in his grandfather's mind, but it found no answering chord in his breast.

"Never will I believe that of Roger's mother. He is more an Irving than I am, everybody says. Shame on you for crediting the story, even for a moment, and my curse on the one who put that thought in the old man's heart, for it *was* put there by somebody."

He was cursing *her* to her face, and he was going on to say still more when she laid her hand over his mouth, and said, —

"Stop, my son. You don't know whom you are cursing, nor any of the circumstances. You are no judge of Jessie Morton's conduct. Far be it from me to condemn her now that she is dead. She was a silly girl, easily influenced, and never loved your grandfather, who was three times her age. We read that the parents' sin shall be visited upon the children, and if she sinned, her child has surely reaped the consequences, or will when this Will is proved. Poor Roger! I, too, am sorry for him, and disposed to be lenient; but he cannot expect us to let things go on as they have done now that everything is reversed. How did Magdalen happen to find it?"

She was talking very gently now, by way of quieting Frank, who told her briefly what he knew of the finding of the Will, and then, little by little as she adroitly questioned him, he let out the particulars of his interview with Magdalen, and Mrs. Walter Scott knew the secret of Magdalen's distress. Her face was turned away from Frank, who did not see the cold, remorse-

less expression which settled upon it, as she thought of Mag
dalen's pitting herself against the Millbank fortune. Magdalen's
value was decreasing fast. The master of Millbank could surely
find a wife more worthy of him than the beggar girl who had
been deserted in the cars, and that Magdalen Lennox should not
marry her son was the decision she reached at a bound, and
Frank must have suspected the nature of her thoughts, as she
sat nervously tapping her foot upon the floor, and looking off
through the window, with great wrinkles in her forehead and
between her eyes.

"Mother," he said, and there was something pleading as well
as reproachful in his voice, "I did not mean that you should
know of this, and now that you do, I must beg of you to keep
your knowledge to yourself. I shall lose Magdalen if you do
not, and I care more for her than a hundred fortunes."

His mother turned fully toward him now and said, sneer-
ingly, "A disinterested lover, truly. Perhaps when you promised
to destroy the Will you forgot the hundred-thousand which, if
Roger remained master here, would come to you with Magdalen,
and you made yourself believe that you were doing a very unselfish and romantic thing in preferring Magdalen and poverty to
Millbank."

"Mother," Frank cried, "I swear to you that a thought of
that hundred thousand never crossed my mind until this moment. My love for Magdalen is strong enough to brave poverty in any form for her sake."

"And you really mean to marry her?"

She put the question so coolly that Frank gazed at her in
astonishment, wondering what she meant.

Of course he meant to marry her if she would take him; he
would prefer her to a thousand Millbanks. "And mother," he
added, "you shall not tell her that *you* know of the Will until
after to-morrow. She is to give me her answer then. Promise,
or I will destroy this cursed paper before your very eyes."

He made a motion as if he would tear it in pieces, when,

with a sudden gesture, his mother caught it from him and held it fast in her own hands.

"The Will is not safe with you," she said. "I will keep it for you. I shall not trouble Magdalen, but I shall go at once to Roger. I cannot see you throw away wealth, and ease, and position for a bit of sentiment with regard to a girl whose parentage is doubtful, to say the least of it, and who can bring you nothing but a pretty face."

She had put the Will in her pocket. There was no way of getting it from her, except by force, and Frank saw her depart without a word, and knew she was going to Roger. Suddenly it occurred to him that Roger might not have left the office yet, and he started up, exclaiming, "I am the one to tell him first, if he must know. I can break it to him easier than mother. I shall not be hard on Roger."

Thus thinking, Frank started swiftly across the fields in the direction of Roger's office, hoping either to meet him, or to find him there, and trying to decide how he should break the news so as to wound his uncle as little as possible, and make him understand that he was not in fault.

CHAPTER XXIII.

ROGER AND THE WILL.

HE office was closed, the shutters down, and Roger gone. Frank had come too late, and he swiftly retraced his steps homeward, hoping still to be in time to tell the news before his mother. But his hopes were vain. Roger had entered the house while Frank was in the garret, and Mrs. Walter Scott heard him in his room as she passed through the hall after her interview with her son. But she was too much agitated and too flurried to speak to him just then.

She must compose herself a little, and utterly forgetful of Magdalen, who was waiting for Frank, and growing impatient at his delay, she went to her own room and read the Will again to make sure that all was right and Frank the lawful heir. She could not realize it, it had come so suddenly upon her; but she knew that it was so, and she bore herself like a queen when she at last arose, and started for Roger's room. It was the Mrs. Walter Scott of former days resurrected and intensified who swept so proudly through the hall, just inclining her head to the servant whom she met, and thinking, as she had once thought before, how she would dismiss the entire household and set up a new government of her own. There had been some uncertainty attending the future when she made this decision before, but now there was none. She held the document which made her safe in her possessions; she was the lady of Millbank, and there was a good deal of assurance in the knock, to which Roger responded "Come in."

He was in his dressing-gown, and looking pale and worn just as he had looked ever since his return from New York. Beside him in a vase upon the table was a bouquet, which he had arranged for Magdalen, intending to send it to her with her dinner. And Mrs. Walter Scott saw it and guessed what it was for, and there flashed into her mind a thought that she would make matters right between Roger and Magdalen; she would help them to each other, and save Frank from the possibility of a *mésalliance*. But Mrs. Walter Scott was a very cautious woman; she always kept something in reserve in case one plan should fail, and now there came a thought that possibly Roger might contest the Will and win, and if he did, it might be well to reconsider Magdalen and her hundred thousand dollars, so she concluded that for the present it would be better not to throw Magdalen overboard. That could be done hereafter, if necessary.

She was very gracious to Roger, and took the seat he offered her, and played with her watch-chain, wondering how she should begin. It was harder than she had anticipated, — telling a

man like Roger that all he had thought his, belonged to an-
other·; and she hesitated, and grew cold and hot and withal a
little afraid of Roger, who was beginning to wonder why she was
there, and what she wanted to say.

"Can I do anything for you, Helen?" he asked, just as he
had once before, when she came on an errand which had caused
him so much pain.

Then she had come to tear Magdalen from him; now she was
there to take his fortune, his birthright away; and it is not strange
that, cruel as she was, she hesitated how to begin.

"Roger," she said, in reply to his question, "I am here on a
most unpleasant errand, but one which, as a mother whose
first duty is to her son, I must perform. You remember the
WILL which at your father's death could not be found."

She was taking it from her pocket, and Roger, who was quick
of comprehension, knew before she laid the worn paper upon
the table, that *the lost Will was found!* With trembling haste
he snatched it up, and she made no effort to restrain him. She
had faith in the man she was ruining. She knew the Will was
safe in his hands; he would neither destroy nor deface it. He
would give it its due consideration, and she sat watching him
while he read it through, and pitying him, it must be confessed,
with all the little womanly feeling she had left. She would have
been a stone not to have pitied one whose lips uttered no sound
as he read, but quivered and trembled, and grew so bloodless
and thin, while his face dripped with the perspiration which
started from every pore and rolled down his chin in drops. She
thought at first they were tears, but when he lifted his eyes to
hers as he finished reading, she saw that they were dry, but oh,
so full of pain and anguish and surprise, and wounded love and
grief, that his father should have disinherited him for such a
cause. He knew what the clause "the boy known as Roger
Lennox Irving" implied, and that hurt him more than all the
rest.

Why had his father believed such a thing of his mother, and
who had told him the shameful story? Leaning across the

table to his sister he pointed to the clause, and moving his finger slowly under each word, said to her in a voice she would never have recognized as his, "Helen, who poisoned my father's mind with that tale?"

Mrs. Walter Scott did not know of the letter in Magdalen's possession, or how much Hester Floyd had overheard years before, when, with lying tongue, she had hinted things she knew could not be true, and made the old man mad with jealousy. She did not think how soon she would be confronted with her lie, and she answered, "I do not know. It is the first intimation I have heard of Squire Irving's reason for changing his Will."

She had forgotten her language to Lawyer Schofield the night after the funeral when the other Will was the subject of debate; but Roger remembered it, and his eyes rested steadily on her face as he said, "You do not know? You never heard it hinted that my mother was false, then?"

"Never," she felt constrained to say, for there was something in those burning eyes which threatened her with harm if by word or look she breathed aught against the purity of poor Jessie Morton.

"Who found this Will, and where?" Roger asked her next, and with a mean desire to pay him for that look, Mrs. Walter Scott replied, "Magdalen found it. She has hunted for it at intervals, ever since she was a child and heard that there was one."

But she repented what she had said when she saw how deep her blow had struck.

"Magda found it; oh, Magda, I would a thousand times rather it had been some one else."

That was what Roger said, as with a bitter groan he laid his head upon the table, while sob after sob shook his frame and frightened his sister, who had never dreamed of pain like this. Tearless sobs they were, for Roger was not crying; he was writhing in anguish, and the sobs were like gasping moans, so terrible was his grief. He remembered what Magdalen had told him once of looking for the Will when she was a child, and remembered how sorry she had seemed. Had she deliberately deceived him, and, after he had told her that it was supposed to give Frank nearly everything, had she resumed her search, hoping to find and restore to her lover his fortune? Then he thought of that night with Hester, and the cobweb in Magdalen's hair. She had been to the garret, according to her own confession, and she had looked for the missing will then and "at inteivals" since, until she had found it and sent it to him by Mrs. Walter Scott, instead of bringing it herself?

And he had loved her so much, and thought her so innocent and artless and true, — his little girl through whom he had been so terribly wounded. If she had come herself with it and given it into his hands and told him all about it, he would not have felt one half so badly as to receive it from another, and that other the cruel, pitiless woman whose real character he recognized as he had never done before. He had nothing to hope from her, nothing to hope from Frank, nothing from Magdalen. They were all leagued against him. They would enjoy Millbank, and he would go from their midst a ruined, heartbroken man, shorn of his love, shorn of his fortune, and shorn of his name, if that dreadful clause, "the boy known as Roger Lennox Irving," really meant anything. He knew it was false; he never for a moment thought otherwise; but it was recorded against him by his own father, and after Magdalen, it was the keenest, bitterest pang of all.

Could that have been stricken out and could he have kept Magdalen, he would have given all the rest without a murmur.

As the will read, it was right that Frank should come into his inheritance, and Roger had no thought or wish to keep him from it. He did not meditate a warfare against his nephew, as his sister feared he might. He had only given way for a few moments to the grief, and pain, and humiliation which had come so suddenly upon him, and he lay, with his face upon the table, until the first burst of the storm was over, and his sobs changed to long-drawn breaths, and finally ceased entirely, as he lifted up his head and looked again at the fatal document before him.

Shocked at the sight of his distress, his sister had at first tried to comfort him. With a woman's quick perception she had seen that Magdalen was the sorest part of all, and had said to him soothingly :

"It was by accident that Magdalen found it. She was greatly disturbed about it."

This did not tally with her first statement, that "Magdalen had sought for it at intervals," and Roger made a gesture for her to stop. So she sat watching him, and trembling a little, as she began dimly to see what the taking of Millbank from Roger would involve.

"Excuse me, Helen," he said, with all his old courtesy of manner, as he wiped the sweat drops from his beard. "Excuse me if, for a moment, I gave way to my feelings in your presence. It was so sudden, and there were so many sources of pain which met me at once, that I could not at first control myself. It was not so much the loss of my fortune. I could bear that —"

"Then you do not intend to contest the will?" Mrs. Walter Scott said.

It was a strange question for her to ask then, and she blushed as she did it ; but she must *know* what the prospect was, while underlying her own selfish motives was a thought that if Roger did *not* mean to dispute the right with Frank, she would brave the displeasure of her son, and then and there pour balm into the wound, by telling Roger of her belief that he was, and always had been, preferred to Frank by Magdalen. But she was prevented from this by the abrupt entrance of Frank himself. He had heard that his mother was with Roger, and had hastened to the room, seeing at a glance that the blow had been given ; that Roger had seen the will ; and for a moment he stood speechless before the white face and the soft blue eyes which met him so wistfully as he came in. There was no reproach in them, only a dumb kind of pleading as if for pity, which touched Frank's heart to the very core, and brought him to Roger's side.

Roger was the first to speak. Putting out his hand to Frank, he tried to smile, and said :

"Forgive me, boy, for having kept you from your own so long. If I had believed for a moment that there was such a will, I would never have rested day or night till I had found it for you. I wish I had. I would far rather I had found it than — than —— "

He could not say "Magdalen," but Frank knew whom he meant, and, in his great pity for the wounded man, he was ready to give up everything to him *but* Magdalen. He must have *her*, but Roger should keep Millbank.

"I believe that I am more sorry than you can be that the will is found," he said, still grasping Roger's hand. "And I want to say to you now that I prefer you should keep the place just as you have done. There need be no change. Only give me enough to support myself and — and —— "

He could not say Magdalen either, for he was not so sure of her, but Roger said it for him.

"Support yourself and Magdalen. I know what you mean, my boy. You are very generous and kind, but right is right. When I thought Millbank mine, I kept it. Now that I know it is not mine, I shall accept *no part of it*, however small."

He spoke sternly, and his face began to harden. He was thinking of the clause, "the boy known as Roger Lennox Irving." He could take no part of the estate of the man who had dictated those cruel words. He was too proud for that; he would rather earn his bread by the sweat of his brow than be beholden to one who could believe such things of his mother. Frank saw the change in his manner, and anxious to propitiate him, began again to urge his wish that Roger would, at least, allow him to divide the inheritance in case the will was proved, but Roger stopped him impatiently.

"It is not you, my boy, whose gift I refuse. If you cannot understand me, I shall not now explain. I've lived on you for years. I can never repay that, for I feel as if all my energies were crippled, so I will let that obligation remain, but must incur no other. As to proving the will," and Roger smiled bitterly when he saw how eagerly his sister listened, and remembered the question she had asked him just as Frank came in, and which he had not yet answered, "As to proving the will, you will have no trouble there. I certainly shall make none. You will find it very easy stepping into your estate."

Mrs. Walter Scott drew a long breath of relief and sank into her chair, in the easy, contented, languid attitude she always assumed when satisfied with herself and her condition. She roused up, however, when Roger went on to say :

"One thing I must investigate, and that is, *who* hid this will, and why. Have you any theory?" and he turned to his sister, who replied, "I have always suspected Hester Floyd. She was a witness, with her husband."

"Why did you always suspect her, and what reason had you for believing there was a later will than the one made in my favor ?" Roger asked, and his sister quailed beneath the searching glance of his eyes.

She could not tell him all she knew, and she colored scarlet and stammered out something about Mrs. Floyd's strange manner at the time of the Squire's funeral, nearly twenty years ago.

"Frank, please go for Hester," Roger said. "We will hear what she has to say."

Frank bowed in acquiescence, and, leaving the room, was soon knocking at Hester Floyd's door.

CHAPTER XXIV.

HESTER AND THE WILL.

ESTER was sitting by her fire knitting a sock for Roger, and Aleck was with her, smoking his pipe in the corner, and occasionally opening his small, sleepy eyes to look at his better half when she addressed some remark to him. They were a very quiet, comfortable, easy-looking couple as they sat there together in the pleasant room which had been theirs for more than forty years, and their thoughts were as far as possible from the storm-cloud bursting over their heads, and of which Frank was the harbinger.

"Mrs. Floyd, Mr. Irving would like to see you in the library," Frank said a little stiffly, and in his manner there was a tinge of importance and self-assurance unusual to him when addressing the *head* of Millbank, Mrs. Hester Floyd.

Hester did not detect this manner, but she saw that he was agitated and nervous, and she dropped a stitch in her knitting as she looked at him and said, "Roger wants me in the library? What for? Has anything happened that you look white as a rag?"

Frank was twenty-seven years old, but there was still enough of the child about him to make him like to be first to communicate news whether good or bad, and to Hester's question he replied, "Yes. *The missing will is found.*"

Hester dropped a whole needle full of stitches, and she was whiter now than Frank as she sprang to Aleck's side and shook him so vigorously that the pipe fell from his mouth, and the stolid, stupid look left his face for once as she said: "Do you hear, Aleck, the will is found! The will that turns Roger out-doors."

Aleck did not seem so much agitated as his wife, and after gazing blankly at her for a moment, he slowly picked up his

pipe and said, with the utmost nonchalance, "You better go
and see to't. You don't want me along."

She did *not* want him; that is, she did not need him; and
with a gesture of contempt she turned from him to Frank, and
said, "I am ready. Come."

There was nothing of the deference due to the heir of Millbank in her tone and manner. Frank would never receive
that from her, and she flounced out into the hall, and kept a
step or two in advance of the young man, to whom she said,
"Who is with Roger? Anybody?"

As she came nearer to the library she began to have a little
dread of what she might encounter, and visions of lawyers and
constables, armed and equipped to arrest her bodily, flitted uneasily before her mind; but when Frank replied, "There is no
one there but mother," her fear vanished, and was succeeded
by a most violent fit of anger at the luckless Mrs. Walter
Scott.

"The jade!" she said. "I always mistrusted how her
snoopin' around would end. If I'd had my way, she should
never have put foot inside this house, the trollop."

"Mrs. Floyd, you are speaking of my mother. You must
stop. I cannot allow it."

It was the master of Millbank who spoke, and Hester turned
upon him fiercely.

"For the Lord's sake, how long since you took such airs?
I shall speak of that woman how and where I choose, and you
can't help yourself."

By this it will be seen that Hester was not in the softest of
moods as she made her way to the library, but her feelings
changed the moment she stood in the room where Roger was.
She had expected to find him hot, excited, defiant, and ready,
like herself, to battle with those who would take his birthright
from him. She was not prepared for the crushed, white-faced
man who looked up at her so helplessly as she came in, and
tried to force a smile as he pointed to a chair at his side, and
said, —

"Sit here by me, Hester.   It is you and I now.   You and I alone."

His chin quivered a little as he held the chair for her to sit down, and then kept his hand on her shoulder as if he felt better. stronger so.   He knew he had her sympathy, that every pulsation of her heart beat for him, that she would cling to him through weal and woe, and he felt a kind of security in having her there beside him.   Hester saw the yellow, soiled paper spread out before him, and recognized it at a glance.   Then she looked across the table toward the proud woman who sat toying with her rings, and exulting at the downfall of poor Roger.   At her Hester glowered savagely, and was met by a derisive smile, which told how utterly indifferent the lady was to her and her opinion.   Then Hester's glance came back, and rested pityingly on her boy, whose finger now was on the will, and who said to her, —

"Hester, there *was* another will, as Helen thought.   It is here before me.   It was found under the garret floor.   Do you know who put it there ? "

He was very calm, as if asking an ordinary question, and his manner went far toward reassuring Hester, who, by this time, had made up her mind to tell the truth, and brave the consequences.

"Yes," she replied.   "I put it there myself, the day your father died."

"I told you so," dropped from Mrs. Walter Scott's lips ; but Hester paid no heed to her.

She was looking at Roger, fascinated by the expression of his eyes and face as he went on to question her.

"Why did you hide it, and where did you find it ? "

"It was lying on the table, where Aleck found him dead, spread out before him, as if he had been reading it over, as I know he had, and he meant to change it, too, for he'd asked young Schofield to come that night and fix it.   Don't you re-member Schofield said so ? "

Roger nodded, and she continued :

"And I know by another way that he meant to change it. 'Twas so writ in his letter to you."

"His letter to *me*, Hester? There was nothing like that in the letter," Roger exclaimed; and Hester continued:

"Not in the one I gave to you, I know. That he must have begun first, and quit, because he blotched it, or something. Any ways, there was another one finished for you, and in it he said he was goin' to fix the will, add a cod-cil or something, because he said it was unjust."

"Why did you withhold that letter from me, Hester, and where is it now?"

Roger spoke a little sternly, and glad of an excuse to turn his attention from herself to some one else, Hester replied,—

"It was in the same box with t'other paper, and I s'pose *she's* got it who snooped till she found the will."

She glanced meaningly at Mrs. Walter Scott, who deigned her no reply, but who began to feel uneasy with regard to the letter of which she had not before heard, and whose contents she did not know.

Neither Roger nor Frank wished to mix Magdalen up with the matter, if possible to avoid it, and no mention was made of her then, and Hester was suffered to believe it was Mrs. Walter Scott who had found the will.

"You read the letter, Hester. Tell me what was in it," Roger said.

And then Hester's face flushed, and her eyes flashed fire, as she replied, —

"There was in it that which had never or' to be writ. He giv the reason why he made this will. He was driv to it by somebody who pisoned his mind with the biggest, most impossible slander agin the sweetest, innocentest woman that ever drawed the breath."

Roger was listening eagerly now, with a fiery gleam in his blue eyes, and his nostrils quivering with indignation.

Mrs. Walter Scott was listening, too, her face very pale,

except where a bright spot of red burned on her cheeks, and her lips slightly apart, showing her white teeth.

Frank was listening also, and gradually coming to an under standing of what had been so mysterious before.

Neither of the three thought of interrupting Hester, who had the field to herself, and who, now that she was fairly launched, went on rapidly :

" I'll make a clean breast of it, bein' the will is found, which I never meant it should be, and then them as is mistress here now can take me to jail as soon as they likes. It don't matter, the few days I've got left to live. I signed that fust Will, me and Aleck, twenty odd year ago, and more, and I knew pretty well what was in it, and that it was right, and gin the property to the proper person ; and then I thought no more about it till a few months before he died, when Aleck and me was called in agin to witness another will, here in this room, standin' about as I set now, with the old gentleman where *that* woman is, Aleck where you be, and Lawyer Schofield where Mr. Franklin stands. I thought it was a queer thing, and mistrusted some-thin' wrong, particularly as I remembered a conversation I overheard a week or so before about you, Roger, and your mother, compared to who, that other woman ain't fit to live in the same place ; and she won't neither, she'll find, when we all get our dues."

Both Roger and Frank knew she referred to Mrs. Walter Scott, who, if angry glances could have annihilated her, would have done so. But Hester was not afraid of her, and went on, not very connectedly, but still intelligibly, to those who were listening so intently :

" She pisoned his mind with snaky, insinuatin' lies, which she didn't exactly speak out, as I heard, but hinted at, and made me so mad that I wanted to throttle her then, and I wish I had bust into the room and told her it was all a lie, as I could prove and swear to ; for, from the day Jessie Morton married Squire Irving until the summer she went to Saratoga, when you, Roger, was quite a little shaver, she never laid eyes on that man, who was her ruin afterward. I know it is so, and so does others, for I've inquired ; and if the scamp was here, he'd tell you so, which I wish he was, and if I knew where to find him, I'd go on my hands and knees to get his word, too, that what this good-for-nothing snake in the grass told was a lie ! "

Human nature could endure no more, and Mrs. Walter Scott sprang to her feet, and turning to her son, asked, —

" If he, a man, would sit quietly, and hear his mother so abused ? "

" You have a right to stop her," she said, as she saw Frank hesitate. " A right to turn her out of the house."

" I'd like to see him do it," Hester rejoined, her old face aglow with passion and fierce anger.

" Hush, Hester, hush," Roger said, in his quiet, gentle way ; " and you, Helen, sit down and listen. If I can bear this, you certainly can."

The perspiration was rolling from his face in great drops a second time, and something like a groan broke from his lips as he covered his eyes with his hands and said, " My mother, oh, my mother, that I should hear her so maligned."

" She wan't maligned," Hester exclaimed, misinterpreting the meaning of the word. " It was a lie, the whole on't. She never left this house except for church or parties, and only three of them, one to Miss Johnson's, one to Squire Schofield's, and one to Mrs. Lennox's, and a few calls, from the time she came here till after you was born ; I know, I was here, I was your nurse, I waited on her, and loved her like my own from the moment she cried so on my neck and said she didn't want to come here. She was too young to come as his wife. She was nothin' but a child, and when she couldn't stan' the racket any longer she run away."

Roger was shaking now as with an ague fit. Here was some-thing which Hester could not deny. Jessie had run away and left him, her baby boy. There was no getting smoothly over that, and he shivered with pain as the old woman went on :

" I don't pretend to excuse her, though there's a good deal

to be said on both sides, and it most broke her heart, as a body who see her as I did that last night at home would know."

" Hester," Roger said, and his voice was full of anguish, "why must you tell all this. It surely has nothing to do with the matter under consideration, and I would rather be spared, if possible, or at least hear it alone."

" I must tell it," Hester rejoined, "to show you why I hid the will, and why he made it, and how big a lie *that woman* told him."

There was the most intense scorn in her voice every time she said " that woman," and Mrs. Walter Scott winced under it, but had no redress then ; her time for that would be by and by, she reflected, and assuming a haughty indifference she was far from feeling she kept still while Hester went on :

" The night she went away she undressed her baby herself ; she wouldn't let me touch him, and all the time she did it she was whispering, and cooing, and crying-like over him, and she kissed his face and arms, and even his little feet, and said once aloud so I in the next room heard her, ' My poor darling, my pet, my precious one, will you ever hate your mother ? ' "

" Hester, I cannot hear another word of that. Don't you see you are killing me ? " Roger said, and this time the tears streamed in torrents down his face, and his voice was choked with sobs.

Hester heeded him now, and there were tears on her wrinkled face as she laid her hand pityingly on his golden brown hair and said, " Poor boy, I won't harrer you any more. I'll stick to the pint, which is that your mother, after you was asleep, and just afore I left her for the night, came up to me in her pretty coaxin' way, and told me what a comfort I was to her, and said if anything ever was to happen that Roger should have no mother, she would trust me to care for him before all the world, and she made me promise that if anything should happen, I would never desert Roger, but love him as if he was my own, and consider his interest before that of any one else. I want you to mind them words, ' consider his interest before any one else,' for that's the upshot of the whole thing. I promised to do it. I *swore* I would do it, and I've kep' my word. Next mornin' she was gone, and in a week or so was drownded dead off Cape Hattrass, where I hope I'll never go, for there's allus a hurricane there when there ain't a breath no wheres else. I sot them words down. I've read 'em every Sunday since as regular as my Bible, and that fetches me to the mornin' the Squire was found dead.

"That woman had been here a few months before, workin' on his pride and pisenen' his mind, till he was drove out of his head, and you not here, either, to prove it was a lie by your face, which, savin' the eyes and hair, is every inch an Irving. He acted crazy-like, and mad them days, as Aleck and me noticed, and he made another will, after that woman was gone to Boston, and a spell after she went home for good. Aleck went up in the mornin' to make a fire here in this very room, and, sittin' in his chair, he found the Squire stark dead, and cold and stiff, and he come for me who was the only other body up as good luck would have it, and I not more'n half dressed. There was the will, lyin' open on the table, as if he had been readin' it, and I read it, and Aleck, too ; 'twas this same will, and my blood biled like a caldron kittle, and Aleck fairly swore, and we said, what does it mean ? There was a letter on the table, too, a finished letter for Roger, and I read it, and found the reason there. The Squire's conscience had been a smitin' him ever since he did the rascally thing, and at last he'd made up his mind to add a cod-cill, and he seemed to have a kind of forerunner that he should never see Roger agin, and so he tried to explain the bedivelment and smooth it over and all that, and signed himself, 'Your affectionate father.' "

"Did he, Hester ? Did he own me at last ?" Roger's voice rang through the room like a bell, its joyful tones thrilling even Mrs. Walter Scott, who was growing greatly interested in Hester's narrative, while Frank stood perfectly spellbound, as if fearful of losing a word of the strange story.

"Yes, I'm pretty sure he did," Hester said, in reply to

9

Roger's question. "Any way, he said he had forgiven your mother, and he would leave *her* letter with his, for you, in case he never see you, and I gin you your mother's, but kept his, because that would have told you about the will, which I meant to hide. We both thought on't to once, Aleck and me, but I spoke first, bein' a woman, and mentioned the promise to consider Roger's interest before any body's else, and Jessie seemed to be there with us, and haunted me, with the great blue eyes of hern, till I made up my mind, and took the pesky thing and the letter, and put 'em away safe up in the garret under the floor, where I'd had a piece sawed out a spell before, so as to put pisen under there for the rats. Then I moved an old settee over the place, and chairs and things, so that it would look as if nobody had been there for ages. He must have begun another letter first and blotched it, for the sheet lay there, and I took it as a special Providence and kept it for Roger, as his father's last words to him. I knew t'other will was not destroyed, for I'd seen it not long before, and I found it in his writing desk, sealed up like a drum, and left it there, and then *she* came with her lofty airs, and queened it over us, as if she thought she was lord of all ; but her feathers drooped a bit when the will was read, and she thought the old Harry was in it, and hinted, and snooped, and rummaged the very first night, for I found her there, with her night gownd on, and more than forty papers stickin' in her hair, though why she thought 'twas there, is more than I know ; but she's hunted the garret ever since by turns, and I moved it twice, and then carried it back, and once she set Magdalen at it, she or *he*, it's little matter which."

Magdalen was a sore point with Roger, and he shuddered, when her name was mentioned, and thought of the letter, and wondered if she had it, and would ever bring it to him.

"I was easy enough when that woman wasn't here," Hester continued, "and I did think for a spell she'd met with a change, she was so soft and so velvety and so nice, that butter couldn't melt in her mouth if it should try. Maybe she's forgot what she sprung from, but I knew the Browns, root and branch; they allus was a peekin', rummagin' set, and her uncle peeked into a money drawer once. She comes honestly by her snoopin' that found the will."

Mrs. Walter Scott had borne a great deal of abuse from Hester, and borne it quietly after her appeal to Frank, but now she could keep still no longer, and she half rose from her chair, and exclaimed:

"Silence, old woman, or I will have you put out of the house, and I hold Frank less than a man if he will hear me so abused. I never found the will. It was Magdalen Lennox who found it, just where you told her it was when you were crazy."

"Magdalen found it, and brought it to *you* instead of burnin' it up!" old Hester exclaimed, raising her hands in astonishment, and feeling her blood grow hot against the poor girl. "Magdalen found it, after all he has done for her! She's a *viper* then; and my curse be —"

She did not finish the sentence, for both Roger and Frank laid a hand upon her mouth, and stopped the harsh words she would have spoken.

"You don't know the circumstances. You shall not speak so of Magdalen," Roger said, while Frank, glad of a chance to prove that he *was* a man even if he had allowed his mother to be abused, said sternly: "Mrs. Floyd, I have stood quietly by and heard my mother insulted, but when you attack Magdalen I can keep still no longer. *She* must not be slandered in my presence. I hope she will be my wife."

Hester gave a violent start, and a sudden gleam of intelligence came into her eyes, as she replied, "Oh, I see now. She wasn't content to have you alone, and I don't blame her for that. It would be a sickening pill to swaller, you and that woman too but she must take advantage of my crazy talk, and find the will which makes her lover a nabob. That's what I call gratitude to me and Roger, for all we've done for her. Much good may her money and lover do her!"

Thus speaking, Hester rose from her chair and went toward

Roger, who had sat as rigid as a stone while she put into words what, as the shadow of a thought, he had tried so hard to fight down.

"I'm done now," she said. "I've told all I know about the will. I hid it, Aleck and me, and I ain't sorry neither, and I'm ready to go to jail any minit the new lords see fit to send me."

She started for the door, but came back again to Roger, and, laying her hand on his hair, said soothingly, and in a very different tone from the one she had assumed when addressing Frank or his mother: "Don't take it so hard, my boy. We'll git along somehow. I ain't so very old. There's a good deal of vim in me yet, and me and Aleck will work like dogs for you. We'll sell the tavern stand, and you shall have the hull it fetches. Your father give us the money to buy it, you know."

Roger could not fail to be touched by this generous unselfishness, and he grasped the hard-wrinkled hand, and tried to smile, as he said: "Thank you, Hester, I knew you would not desert me; but I shall not need your little fortune. I can work for us all."

It was growing dark by this time, and the bell had thrice sent forth its summons to dinner. As Roger finished speaking, it rang again, and, glad of an excuse to get away, old Hester said, "What do they mean by keepin' that bell a dingin' when they might know we'd something on hand of more account than victuals and drink. I'll go and see to't myself."

She hurried out into the hall, and Frank shut the door after her, and then came back to the table, and began to urge upon Roger the acceptance of a portion, at least, of the immense fortune, which a few hours before he had believed to be all his own. But Roger stopped him short.

"Don't, Frank," he said. "I know you mean it now, and, perhaps, would mean it always, but so long as that clause stands against me, I can take nothing from the Irvings."

He pointed to the words "the boy known as Roger Lennox Irving," and Frank rejoined, "It was a cruel thing for him to do."

"Yes; but a far wickeder, crueller thing, to poison his mind with slanders, until he did it," Roger replied, as he turned to his sister, and said, "Helen, I hold you guilty of my ruin, if what Hester has told us be true; but I shall not reproach you; I will let your own conscience do that."

Mrs. Irving tried to say that Hester had spoken falsely, that she had never worked upon the weak old man's jealousy of his young wife; but she could not quite utter so glaring a falsehood, knowing or believing, as she did, that Magdalen had the letter, which might refute her lie. So she assumed an air of lofty dignity, and answered back that it was unnecessary to continue the conversation, which had been far more personal than the questoins involved required, — neither was it needful to prolong the interview. The matter of the will was now between him and Frank, and, with his permission, she would withdraw. Roger simply inclined his head, to indicate his willingness for her to leave, and, with a haughty bow, she swept from the room, signalling to Frank to follow. But Frank did not heed her. He tarried for a few moments, standing close to Roger, and mechanically toying with the pens and pencils upon the table. He did not feel at all comfortable, nor like a man who had suddenly become possessed of hundreds of thousands. He felt rather like a thief, or, at best, an usurper of another's rights, and would have been glad at that moment had the will been lying in its box under the floor, where it had lain so many years. Roger was the first to speak.

"Go, Frank," he said; "leave me alone for to-night. It is better so. I know what you want to say, but it can do no good. Things are as they are, and we cannot change them. I do not blame you. Don't think I do. I always liked you, Frank, always, since we were boys together, and I like you still; but leave me now. I cannot bear any more."

Roger's voice trembled, and Frank could see through the fast gathering darkness how white his face was and how he wiped the sweat-drops from his forehead and lips, and wringing his hand nervously, he, too, went away, and Roger was alone.

CHAPTER XXV.

MAGDALEN AND ROGER.

AGDALEN had waited for Frank until she grew so nervous and restless that she crept back to her couch, and, wrapping her shawl about her, lay down among the pillows, still listening for Frank's footsteps and wondering that he did not come. She had made up her mind at last. After days and nights of throbbing headache and fierce heart-pangs and bitter tears, she had come to a decision. She would die so willingly for Roger, if that would save Millbank for him. She would endure any pain or toil or privation for him, but she could not *sin* for him. She could not swear to love and honor one, when her whole being was bound up in another. She could not marry Frank, but she hoped she might persuade him to let Roger keep Millbank, while he took the mill and the shoe-shop, and the bonds and mortgages. He would surely listen to that proposition, and she had sent for him to hear her decision, and then she meant next day to take the will from its hiding place, and carry it to Roger, with the letter she guarded so carefully. This was her decision, and she waited for Frank until two hours were gone and the spring twilight began to creep into the room, and still no one came near her. She heard the dinner-bell, and knew it was not answered, and then, as the minutes went by, she became conscious of some unusual stir in the house among the servants, and grasping the bell-rope at last, she rang for Celine, and asked where Mrs. Irving was.

"In the library with Mr. Irving and Mr. Frank and Hester. They are talking very loud, and don't pay any attention to the dinner bell," was Celine's reply, and Magdalen felt as if she was going to faint with the terrible apprehension of evil which swept over her.

"That will do. You may go," she said to Celine; and then,

the moment the girl was gone, she rose from the couch, and
knotting the heavy cord around her dressing gown, and adjust
ing her shawl, went stealthily out into the hall, and stealing
softly down the stairs, soon stood near the door of the library

It was closed, but Hester's loud tones reached her as she
talked of the will, and with a shudder she turned away, whisper
ing to herself:

"Too late! He'll never believe me now."

Then a thought of Aleck crossed her mind. She did not
think he was in the library; possibly he was in Hester's room;
at all events she would go there, and wait for Hester's return.
An outside door stood open as she passed through the rear hall
which led to Hester's room, and she felt the chill night air blow
on her, and shivered with the cold. But she did not think of
danger to herself from the exposure. She only thought of
Roger and what was transpiring in the library, and she entered
Hester's room hurriedly, and uttered a cry of joy when she saw
Aleck there. He was not smoking now. He was sitting
bowed over the hearth, evidently wrapped in thought, and he
gave a violent start when Magdalen seized his arm, and asked
him what had happened.

He heard her, though she spoke in a whisper, and turning his
eyes slowly toward her, replied :

"Somebody has found the will, and Roger is a beggar."

"Oh, Aleck, I wish I was dead," Magdalen exclaimed, and
then sank down upon the floor at the old man's feet, sobbing
in a piteous kind of way, and trying to explain how she had
found it first, and how she would give her life if she never had
done so.

In the midst of her story Hester came in, and Magdalen
sprang up and started toward her, but something in the expression of the old woman's face stopped her suddenly, and grasping the back of a chair, she stood speechless, while Hester gave
vent to a tirade of abuse, accusing her of ruining Roger, taunt-
ing her with vile ingratitude, and bidding her take herself and

her lover back to where she came from, if that spot could be found.

Perfectly wild with excitement Magdalen made no effort to explain, but darted past Hester out into the hall, where the first person she encountered was Frank, who chanced to be passing that way. She did not try to avoid him ; she was too faint and dizzy for that, and when asked what was the matter, and where she was going, she answered :

"To my room. Oh, help me, please, or I shall never reach it."

He wound his arm around her, and leaning heavily upon him she went slowly down the hall, followed by Hester Floyd, who was watching her movements. Not a word was spoken of the will until her chamber was reached ; then, as Frank parted from her, he said :

"I think you know that Roger has the will; but I did not give it to him. I would have kept it from him, if possible, and it shall make no difference, if I can help it."

He·held her hand a moment; then suddenly stooped and kissed her forehead before she could prevent the act, and walked rapidly away, leaving her flushed and indignant and half fainting, as she crept back to the couch. No one came near her to light her lamp. No one remembered to bring her food or drink. Everybody appeared to have forgotten and forsaken her, but she preferred to be alone, and lay there in the darkness until Celine came in to ask what she would have.

"Nothing, only light the lamp, please," was her reply.

Then, after a moment, she asked :

"Are the family at dinner ? "

"Yes ; that is, Mrs. Irving and Mr. Frank. Mr. Irving is in the library alone," Celine said.

And then Magdalen sat up and asked the girl to gather up her hair decently, and give it a brush or two, and bring her a clean collar, and her other shawl.

Magdalen was going·to the library to see Roger, who sat just where Frank had left him, with his head bowed upon the fatal paper which had done him so much harm. The blow had fallen so suddenly, and in so aggravating a form, that it had stunned him in part, and he could not realize the full extent of his calamity. One fact, however, stood out distinctly before his mind, "Magdalen was lost forever!" Frank had said openly that she was to be his wife! She had come to a decision. She would be the mistress of Millbank, without a doubt. But he who had once hoped to make her that himself, would be far away, — a poor, unknown man, — earning his bread by the sweat of his brow. Roger did not care for that contingency. He was willing to work; but he felt how much easier toil would be if it was for Magdalen's sake that he grew tired and worn. He was thinking of all this when Magdalen came to his door, knocking so softly that he did not hear at first; then, when the knock was repeated, he made no answer to it, for he would rather be left alone. Ordinarily, Magdalen would have turned back without venturing to enter; but she was desperate now. She *must* see Roger that night, and she resolutely turned the door-knob and went into his presence.

Roger lifted up his head as she came in, and then sprang to his feet, startled by her white face and the change in her appearance since he saw her last. Then she had stood before him in the hall, winding the scarf around his neck, her face glowing with health and happiness and girlish beauty, and her eyes shining upon him like stars. They were very bright now, unnaturally so he thought, and there was a glitter in them which reminded him of the woman in the cars who had left her baby with him.

"Magdalen," he said, as he went forward to meet her. "I did not think you had been so sick as your looks indicate. Let me lead you to the sofa."

He laid his hand on her shoulder, but she shook it off and sank into a chair close beside the one he had vacated.

"Don't touch me yet, Roger, oh Roger," she began, and Roger's heart gave a great leap, for never before had she called him thus to his face. "Excuse me for coming here to-night.

9*

I know it is not maidenly, perhaps, but I must see you, and tell you it was all a horrible mistake. I did not know what I was doing. Hester talked so much about that loose board in the garret and something hidden under it, that once, a week ago or more, it seems a year to me, I went up to shut a window; my curiosity led me to look under the floor, and I found it, Roger, and read it through, and Frank came and surprised me, and then the secret was no longer mine, and I — oh, Mr. Irving, I wanted to keep it from you, till — till — I cannot explain the whole, and I don't know at all how it came into your hands. Can you forgive me, Roger? I could have burned it at once or had it burned, but I dared not. Would you have liked me better if I had destroyed it?"

She stopped speaking now, and held her hands toward Roger, who took them in his own and pressed them with a fervor which brought the blood back to her cheeks and made her very beautiful as she sat there before him.

"No, Magda," he said, "I am glad you did not destroy it. I would rather meet with poverty in its direct form than know that you had done that thing; for it would have come to light some time, and I should have felt that in more ways than one I had lost my little girl."

He was speaking to her now as he had done when she was a child, and one of his hands was smoothing her soft hair; but he was thinking of Frank, and there was nothing of the lover in his caress, though it made Magdalen's blood throb and tingle to her finger tips, for she knew he did not hate her as she had feared he might.

"The will should never have been hidden," he said. "Hester did very wrong. Do you know the particulars?"

"I know nothing except that I found it and you have it," Magdalen replied, and briefly as possible Roger told her the substance of Hester's story, smoothing over as much as possible Mrs. Irving's guilt, because she was to be Magdalen's mother-in-law.

Before he spoke of the letter left by his father, Magdalen

had taken it from her pocket and held it in her hand. He knew it was the missing letter, but did not offer to take it until his recital was ended, when Magdalen held it to him and said, " This is the letter; it was in the box, and I kept it to give to you myself in case you should ever know of the will. I have not read it. You do *not* believe I would read it," she added in some alarm, as she saw a questioning look in his face.

Whatever he might have suspected, he knew better now, and he made her lie down upon the sofa, and arranged the cushions for her head, and then, standing with his back to her, opened the letter, and read that message from the dead. And as he read, he grew hard and bitter toward the man who could be so easily swayed by a lying, deceitful woman. He knew Magdalen was watching him, and probably wondering what was in the letter, and knew, too, that she could not fully believe in his mother's innocence without more proof than his mere assertion. Of all the people living he would rather Magdalen should think well of his mother, and after a moment's hesitancy he turned to her, and said :

" I want you to see this, Magda. I want you to know why I was disinherited, and then you must hear my poor mother's letter, and judge yourself if she was guilty."

He turned the key in the door, so as not to be interrupted, and then came back to Magdalen, who had risen to a sitting posture, and who took the letter from his hand while he adjusted the shade so that the glare of the lamp would not shine directly in her eyes as she read it.

CHAPTER XXVI.

'SQUIRE IRVING'S LETTER.

I T was dated the very night preceding the morning when Squire Irving had been found dead by Aleck Floyd, and it commenced much like the one which Roger had guarded so religiously as his father's last message to him :

"MILLBANK, April —.

"MY DEAR BOY,— For many days I have been haunted with a presentiment that I have not much longer to live. My heart is badly diseased, and I may drop away any minute, and as death begins to stare me in the face, my thoughts turn toward you, the boy whom I have been so proud of and loved so much. You don't remember your mother, Roger, and you don't know how I loved her, she was so beautiful and artless, and seemed so innocent, with her blue eyes and golden hair. Her home was among the New Hampshire hills, a quarter of a mile or so from the little rural town of Schodick, whose delightful scenery and pure mountain air years ago attracted visitors there during the summer months. Her father was poor and old and infirm, and his farm was mortgaged for more than it was worth, and the mortgage was about to be foreclosed, when, by chance, I became an inmate for a few weeks of the farmhouse. I was stopping in Schodick, the hotel was full, and I boarded with Jessie's father. He had taken boarders before,— one a young man, Arthur Grey, a fast, fashionable, fascinating man, who made love to Jessie, a mere child of sixteen. Her letter, which I inclose, will tell you the particulars of her acquaintance with him, so it is not needful that I go over with them. I knew nothing of Arthur Grey at the time I was at the farmhouse, except that I sometimes heard him mentioned as a reckless, dashing young man. I was there during the months of August and September. I had an attack of heart disease, and Jessie nursed me through it, her soft hands and gentle ways and deep blue eyes weaving around me a spell I could not break. She was poor, but a lady every whit, and I loved her better than I had ever loved a human being before, and I wanted her for my wife. As I have said, her father was old and poor, and the farm was mortgaged to a remorseless creditor. They would be homeless when it was sold, and so I *bought* Jessie, and her father kept his home. I know now that it was a great mistake ; know why Jessie fainted when the plan was first proposed to her, but I did not suspect it then. Her father said she was in the habit of fainting, and tried to make light of it. He was anxious for the match, and shut his eyes to his daughter's aversion to it.

"I brought her to Millbank in December, and within the year you were born. I heard nothing of Arthur Grey. I only knew that Jessie was not happy; satins and pearls and diamonds could not drive that sad, hungry look from her eyes, and I took her for a change to Saratoga, and there she met the villain again, and as the result she left Millbank to go with him to Europe. In a few days she was drowned, and her letter written on the 'Sea Gull' was sent to me by that accursed man who, when she tried to escape him, followed her to the ship bound for Charleston. I believe that part, and a doubt of your legitimacy never entered my heart until Walter's wife put it there. I had made my will, and given nearly all to you, when Helen, who was here a few months ago, began one day to talk of Jessie, very kindly, as I remember, and seemed trying to find excuses for what she called her sin, and then said she was so glad that I had always been kind to the poor innocent boy who was not to blame for his mother's error. I came gradually to understand her, though she said but little which could be repeated, but I knew that she doubted your legitimacy, and she gave me reason to doubt it too, by hinting that Arthur Grey had been seen in Belvidere more than once after Jessie's marriage. Her husband, Walter, was her informant ; but she had promised secrecy, as he wished to spare me,

and so she could not be explicit.   But I had heard enough to
drive me mad with jealousy and rage, and I made another will,
and gave you little more than the Morton farm, which, when
Jessie's father died, as he did the day when you were born, I
bought to please your mother.   I was wild with anger when I
made that will, and my love for you has ever since kept tug·
ging at my heart, and has prevented me from destroying the
first will, as I twice made up my mind to do.   To-day I have
read your mother's letter again, and I have forgiven Jessie at
last, though Helen's insinuations still rankle in my mind.   But
I have repented of leaving you so little, and have sent for
young Schofield to change my last will, and make you equal
with Frank.

"Perhaps I may never see you again, for something about
my heart warns me that my days are numbered, and what I do
for you must be done quickly.   Heaven forgive me if I wronged
your mother, and forgive me doubly, trebly, if in wronging her
I have dealt cruelly, unnaturally by you, my darling, my pride,
my boy, whom I love so much in spite of everything; for I do,
Roger, I certainly do, and I feel even now that if you were
here beside me, the sight of your dear face would tempt me to
burn the later will and reacknowledge the first.

"Heaven bless you, Roger.   Heaven give you every possible good which you may crave, and if in the course of your
life there is one thing more than another which you desire, I
pray Heaven to give it to you.   I wish Schofield was here
now.   There is a dreadful feeling in my head, a cold, prickling
sensation in my arms, and I must stop, while I have power to
sign myself,

"Yours lovingly and affectionately,

"WILLIAM H. IRVING."

This was the letter, and the old man must have been battling with death as he wrote it, and with the tracing of Roger's
name the pen must have dropped from his nerveless fingers,
and his spirit taken its flight to the world where poor, wronged

Jessie had gone before him. The fact that she was innocent did not prevent her child from receiving the punishment of her seeming guilt, and at first every word of his father's letter had been like so many stabs, making his pain harder than ever to bear. Magdalen comprehended it in full, and pitied him now more than she had before.

"Oh, I am so sorry for you, Mr. Irving; sorrier than I was about the will," she said, moving a little nearer to him.

He looked quickly at her, and guessing of what he was thinking, she rejoined:

"Don't imagine for a moment that I distrust your mother. I know she was innocent and I hate the woman who breathed the vile slander against her."

"Hush, Magda, that woman is Frank's mother," Roger said, gently, and Magdalen replied:

"I know she is, and your sister-in-law. I did not think of the relationship when I spoke, or suppose you would care."

She either did not or *would* not understand him, and she went on to speak of Jessie and the man who had been her ruin.

"Grey," she repeated, "Arthur Grey! It surely cannot be Alice's father?"

Roger did not know. He had never thought of that. "I never saw him," he said, "and never wish to see him or his. I could not treat him civilly. There is more about him here in mother's letter. She loved him with a woman's strange infatuation, and her love gives a soft coloring to what she has written. I have never shown it to a human being, but I want you to read it, Magda, or rather let me read it to you."

He was not angry with her, Magdalen knew, and she felt as if a great burden had been lifted from her as she listened to the letter written thirty years before.

CHAPTER XXVII.

JESSIE'S LETTER.

T was dated on board the "Sea Gull" and began as follows :

"My husband : — It would be mockery for me to put the word *dear* before your honored name. You would not believe I meant it when I have sinned against you so deeply and wounded your pride so sorely. But oh, if you knew all which led me to what I am, you would pity me even if you condemned, for you were always kind, too kind by far to a wicked girl like me. But I am not so bad as you imagine. I have left you, I know, and left my darling baby, and *he* is here with me, but by no consent of mine. I am not going to Europe. I am going to Charleston, where Lucy is, and shall mail this letter from there. Every word I write will be true, and you must believe it and teach Roger to believe it, too, for I have not sinned as you suppose, and Roger need not blush for his mother except that she deserted him. I am writing this quite as much for him as for you, for I want him to know something of his mother as she was years ago, when she lived among the Schodick hills, in the dear old house which I have dreamed about so often, and which even here on the sea comes up so vividly before me, with the orchard where the mountain shadows fell so early in the afternoon, and the meadows where the buttercups and clover-blossoms grew. Oh, I grow sick, and faint, and dizzy when I think of those happy days and contrast myself as I was then with myself as I am now. I was so happy, though I knew what poverty meant ; but that did not matter. Children, if surrounded by loving friends, do not mind being poor, and I did not mind it either until I grew old enough to see how it troubled my father. My mother, as you know, died before I could remember her, and my aunt Mary, my father's only sister, and cousin Lucy's mother, took her place and cared for me.

"The summer before you came to us, I met *Arthur Grey*. He was among the visitors who boarded at the hotel. He was said to be very rich, very aristocratic, very fastidious. You never saw him, and cannot understand the strange fascination there was about him, or how his manner, when he chose to be gracious, was calculated to win upon a simple girl like me. I met him, and, ere I was aware of it, he taught me how to love him. He became an inmate of our house at last, and thus our growing fondness for each other was hidden from the public, which would have said that I was no match for him. I *know* that he loved me. I never doubted that for a moment. Deception can assume many garbs, but never the guise he wore when he won my girlish love. He asked me to be his wife one autumn night, when the Indian summer haze was on the hills, and the mountain tops were gorgeous with scarlet and gold. I had never dreamed that a human being could be as happy as I was when, with him at my side, I walked back across the fields to our home. The very air around seemed full of the ecstatic joy I felt as I thought of a life spent with *him*. He wished me to keep our betrothal a secret for a time, he said, as he did not care to have his mother and sisters know of it just then. They were at the hotel for a few weeks, and I used to see them at church ; and their cold, haughty manner impressed me disagreeably, just as it did every one who came in contact with them. I should not live with them, Arthur said. I should have a home of my own on the Hudson. He had just bought a residence there, and he described it to me until I knew every tree, and shrub, and winding walk upon the place.

"Then he went away, and the dreary winter came, and his letters, so frequent at first, began to come irregularly, but were always loving and tender, and full of excuses for the long delay. Once I heard of fierce opposition from his mother and sister, and a desire on their part to persuade him into a more brilliant marriage. But I trusted him fully until the spring, when after a longer interval of silence than usual there came a letter from his mother, who wrote at her son's request, as he was ill and unable to write himself. I was still very dear to him, she said, but considering all things he thought it better for us both tha. the engagement should be broken. I had been brought up sd differently, that he did not believe I would ever be happy in the society in which he moved, and it was really doing me a kind-ness to leave me where I was; still, if I insisted, he was in honor bound to adhere to his promise, and should do so.

"I pass over the pain, and bitter disappointment, and dread-ful days, when, in the shadow of the woods where I had walked so often with him, I laid my face in the grass and wished that I could die. I did not write him a word, but I sent him back his letters, and the ring, and every memento of those blissful hours; and the few who knew of my engagement guessed that it was broken, and said it had ended as they expected.

"Then *you* came, just when my heart was so sore, and you were kind to father, and sought me of him for your wife, and he begged me to consider your proposal, and save him his home for his old age. Then I went again into the shadow of those woods, and crept away behind a rock, under a luxuriant pine, and prayed that I might know what was right for me to do. My father found me there one day and took me home, and said I need not marry you. He would rather end his days in the poorhouse than see me so distressed. But the sight of his dear old face growing so white, and thin, as the time for the foreclosure drew near, was more than I could bear, and it mattered little what I did in the future; so I went to you and said 'I will be your wife, and do the best I can; but you must be patient with me. I am only a little girl.'

"I ought to have told you of Arthur, but I did not, and so trouble came of it. We were married in the morning, and went to Boston, and then back for a few days to Schodick, where there was a letter for *me*, from *Arthur*. It was all a terrible deception: he had had a long, long illness, and his mother, — a cruel, artful woman, — took advantage of it, and wrote me that cruel letter. Then, when my package reached her, and she found there was no word of protest in it, she gave it to him, and worked upon him in his weak condition until he believed me false, and the excitement brought on a relapse which lasted longer and was more dangerous than his first illness had been As soon as he was able to hold his pen, he wrote to me again ; but his mother managed to withhold the letter, and so the time went on until, by chance, he discovered the deception, but it was too late. *I was your wife.* I am your wife now, and so I must not tell you of that terrible hour of anguish in my room at home, when cousin Lucy, who was then at our house, found me fainting on the floor with the letter in my hand. I told *her* everything, for we were to each other as sisters ; but with that exception, no living being has ever heard my story. I asked her to send him a paper containing the notice of my marriage, and that was all the answer I returned to his letter.

"Then you took me to Millbank, and I tried to do my duty, even though my heart was broken. After Roger came, I was happier, and I appreciated all your kindness, and the pain was not so hard to bear, till we went to Saratoga that summer, where I met *him* again.

"He loved me still, and we talked it over together, sometimes when you were sleeping after dinner, and nights when you were playing billiards. There is so much of that kind of thing at Saratoga that one's sense of right and wrong is easily blunted there, and I was so young ; still this is no excuse. I ought not to have listened for a moment, especially after he began to talk of *Italy* and a cottage by the sea, where no one would know us. I was his in the sight of Heaven, he said. I was committing sin by living with you. I was more his wife than yours, and he made me believe that if once I left you, a divorce could easily be obtained, and then there would be nothing in the way of our marriage. I caught at that idea and listened to it, and from that moment my fate was sealed. But I never contemplated anything but marriage with him, when at last I consented to leave you. I wanted to take Roger, and went on my knees to him, begging that I might have my baby, but he would not consent. A child would be in the way, he said, and I must choose between him and my boy. His influence over me was so great that I would have walked into the fire with him then, had he willed it so.

"I left Millbank at night, intending to meet Arthur in New York, and go at once to the steamer bound for Liverpool, but on the way thoughts of my baby sleeping in his crib, with that smile on his lips when I kissed him last, came to save me, and at New Haven I left the train and took the boat for New York, and went to another hotel than the one where he was waiting for me. I scarcely knew what I meant to do, except to avoid him, until, as I sat waiting for a room, I heard some people talking of the 'Sea Gull,' which was to leave the next day for Charleston. Then, I said, 'Heaven has opened for me that way of escape. I dare not go back to Millbank. My husband would not receive me now. Lucy is in Charleston. She knows my story. I will go to her,' and so yesterday, when the 'Sea Gull' dropped down the harbor, I was in it, and *he* was there too; but I did not know it till we had been hours upon the sea, and it was too late for me to go back. He had wondered that I did not come according to appointment, and was walking down Broadway when he saw me leave the hotel, and called a carriage at once and followed me to the boat, guessing that it was my intention to avoid him. I have told him of my resolve, and when Charleston is reached, we shall part forever.

"This is the truth, my husband, and I want you to believe it. I do not ask you to take me back. You are too proud for that, and I know it can never be, but I want you to think as kindly of me as you can, and when you feel that you have forgiven me, show this letter to Roger, if he is old enough to understand it. Tell him to forgive me, and give him this lock of his mother's hair. Heaven bless and keep my little boy, and grant that he may be a comfort to you and grow up a good and noble man. Perhaps I may see him sometime. If not, my blessing be with him always."

"This is all of mother's letter, but there is a postscript from *him*. Shall I read that, too?" Roger asked, and Magdalen said yes; and then, as he held the letter near to her, she saw the bold, masculine handwriting of Arthur Grey, who had written :

"SQUIRE IRVING — DEAR SIR — It becomes my painful duty to inform you that not long after the inclosed letter from your wife was finished, a fire broke out and spread so fast that all hope of escape except by the life-boats was cut off. Your wife felt from the first a presentiment that she should be drowned, and brought the letter to me, asking that if I escaped, and she did not, I would forward it at once to Millbank. I took the letter and I tried to save her, when the sea ingulfed us both, but a tremendous wave carried her beyond my reach, and I saw her golden hair rise once above the water and then go down forever. I, with a few others, was saved as by a miracle, — picked up by a vessel bound for New York, which place I reached yesterday. I have read Jessie's letter. She told me to do so, and to add my testimony to the truth of what she had written. Even if it were not true, it would be wrong to refuse the request of one so lovely and dear to me as Jessie was, and I accordingly do as she bade me, and say to you that she has written you the truth.

"I have the honor, sir, to be
"Your obedient servant,
"ARTHUR GREY."

Not a word of excuse for himself, or regret for the part he had had in effecting poor Jessie's death. He could scarcely have written less than he did, and the cold, indifferent wording of his message struck Magdalen just as it did Roger. She had wept over poor Jessie's story, and pitied the young, desolate creature who had been so cruelly wronged. And she had pitied Arthur Grey at first, and her heart had gone out after him with a strange, inexplicable feeling of sympathy. But when it came to Saratoga and Italy, and all the seductive arts he must have used to tempt Jessie from her husband and child, and when she heard the message he had sent to the outraged husband, her blood boiled with indignation, and she felt that if she were to see him then, she must curse him to his face. While Roger had been reading of him, her mind had, for some cause, gone back to that Saturday afternoon, in the graveyard, when she met the handsome stranger whose courteous manners had so fascinated her, and who had been so interested in everything pertaining to the Irving family. Suddenly it came to her that *this* was *Arthur Grey*, and, with a start, she exclaimed : "I have seen that man, — I know I have. I saw him at your father's grave years and years ago."

Roger looked inquiringly at her as she explained the circumstances of her interview with the stranger, telling of his questions with regard to Mrs. Irving and his apparent interest in her, and when she had finished her story, he said, "Is it your impression that he was ever in Belvidere before ?"

"I know he never was," Magdalen replied. "He told me so himself, and I should have known it without his telling, he seemed so much a stranger to everything and everybody."

Roger knew that every word his sister had breathed against his mother was a lie, but Magdalen's involuntary testimony helped to comfort and reassure him as nothing else had done. The clause which read "the boy known as Roger Lennox Irving" did not especially trouble him now, though he could not then forgive the father who had wronged him so, and when he thought of him there came back to his face the same sad, sorry look it had worn when Magdalen first came in, and which while talking to her had gradually passed away. She detected it at once, and connecting it with the will said to him again, "Oh, Mr. Irving, it would have been better if I had never come here. I have only brought sorrow and ruin to you."

"No, Magda," Roger replied, "it would not have been better if you had never come here. You have made me very happy, so happy that—" he could not get any further for something in his throat which prevented his utterance.

She *had* brought him sorrow, and yet he would not for the world have failed of knowing how sweet it was to love her even if she could not be his. If he could have kept her and taken her with him to his home among the hills, he felt that he would have parted willingly with his fortune and beautiful Millbank. But that could not be. She belonged to Frank; everything was Frank's, and for an instant the whole extent of his calamity swept over him so painfully that he succumbed to it, and laying his face upon the table sobbed just as piteously as he had done in the first moment of surprise and pain when he heard that both fortune and name were gone. Magdalen could not understand all the causes of his distress. She did not dream that every sob and every tear wrung from the strong man was given more to her than to the fortune lost, and she tried to comfort him as best she could, thinking once to tell him how willingly she would toil and slave to make his new home attractive, deeming no self-denial too great if by its means he could be made happier and more comfortable. But she did not dare do this until she knew whether she was wanted in that home among the Schodick hills where he said he was going. Oh, how she wished he would give some hint that he expected her to go with him; but he did not, and he kept his face hidden so long that she came at last to his side, and laid her hand on his shoulder and bent over him with words of sympathy. Then, as he did not look up, she knelt beside him, and her hand found its way to his, and she called him Roger again, and begged him not to feel so badly.

"You will drive me mad with remorse," she said, "for I know I have done it all. Don't, Roger, it breaks my heart to see you so distressed. What can I do to prove how sorry I am? Tell me and I will do it, even to the taking of my life."

It did not seem possible that this girl pleading thus with him could be another's betrothed, and for a moment Roger lost all self-control, and forgetting Frank and his rights snatched her to his arms and pressing her to his bosom rained kiss after kiss upon her forehead and lips, saying to her, "My darling, my darling, you have been a blessing and a comfort to me all your life, but there's nothing you can do for me now. Once I hoped — oh, Magda, my little girl, that time is far in the past ; I hope for nothing now. I am not angry with you. I could not be so if I would. I bless you for all you have been to me. I hope you will be happy here at Millbank when I am gone ; and now go, my darling. You are shivering with cold and the room is very damp. God bless you, Magda."

He led her out into the hall, then closed the door upon her, and went back again to his solitude and his sorrow, while Magdalen, bewildered and frightened and wearied out, found her way as best she could to her own room, where a few moments later Celine found her fainting upon the floor.

CHAPTER XXVIII

THE WORLD AND THE WILL.

THE world, or that portion of it represented by Belvidere, did not receive it kindly, and when the new heir appeared in the street on the day succeeding the events narrated in the last chapter, he was conscious of a certain air of constraint and stiffness about those whom he met, and an evident attempt to avoid him. It was known all over town by that time, for Roger had made no secret of the matter, and an hour after Magdalen left him, he had sent for all the servants, and told them briefly of his changed condition. He entered into no particulars ; he merely said :

"My father saw fit to make a later will than the one found at the time of his death. In it he gave Millbank and all its appurtenances to Frank, as the child of his eldest son, my brother Walter. This later will, of whose existence I did not know, has recently been found, and by virtue of it everything goes to Frank, who is the rightful owner of Millbank, or will be when the will is proved. You have served me faithfully, some of you for years, and I shall never forget your unvarying kind ness and fidelity. The amount of wages due each of you I shall venture to pay from money kept for that purpose. My nephew will allow me to do that, and then, so far as I am concerned, you are at liberty to seek new situations. Our relations as employer and servant are at an end. I do not wish you to talk about it, or to express your sympathy for me. I could not bear it now, so please do not trouble me."

This last he said because of the murmur of discontent and surprise and dissatisfaction which ran through the room when those assembled first learned that they must part with their master, whom they had loved and respected so long.

" We will not leave you, Mr. Irving. We will go where you go. We will work for you for less wages than for anybody else," was what the house servants said to him, and what many of his factory and shop hands said when next day he met them in front of the huge mill where they were congregated.

He had told his servants not to talk of his affairs, but they did not heed him ; while Hester Floyd, whom no one could control, discussed the matter freely, so that by noon the little town was rife with rumors of every kind, and knots of people gathered at the corners of the street, while in front of the cotton mill a vast concourse had assembled even before the bell rang for twelve, and instead of going home to the dinner they would hardly have found prepared that day, they stood talking of the strange news, which had come to them in so many different forms. That there had been some undue influence brought to bear upon Squire Irving, they knew ; and that the mother of the new heir was the guilty party who had slandered the Squire's unfortunate young wife, they also knew ; and many and loud were their imprecations against the woman whose proud haughty bearing had never impressed them favorably, and whom they now disliked with all the unrestrained bitterness common to their class.

All had heard of Jessie Irving, and a few remembered her as
she was when she first came among them, in her bright, girlish
beauty, with those great, sad blue eyes, which always smiled
kindly upon her husband's employes when she met with them.
As people will do, they had repeated her story many times, and
the mothers had blamed her sorely for deserting her child, while
a few envious ones, when speaking of "the grand doings at
Millbank," had hinted that the original stock was "no better
than it should be," and that the Irving name was stained like
many others.

But this was all forgotten now.   Jessie Irving was declared
a saint, and an angel, and a martyr, while nothing was too
severe to say against the woman who had maligned her, and
influenced the jealous old Squire to do a thing which would de-
prive the working classes in Belvidere of the kindest, most considerate, and liberal of masters.   The factory hands could *not*
work after they heard of it, and one by one they stole out upon
the green in front of the large manufactory, where they were
joined by other hands from the shoe shop, until the square was
full of excited men and boys, and girls, the murmur of their
voices swelling louder and louder as, encouraged by each other,
they grew more and more indignant toward the "new lords," as
they called Frank and his mother, and more enthusiastic in
their praises of Roger.

One of their number proposed sending for him to come himself and tell them if what they had heard was true, and to hear
their protest against it; and three of the more prominent men
were deputed to wait upon him.

There was no mistaking the genuine concern, and sympathy,
and sorrow written on their faces, when Roger went out to
meet them, and the sight of them nearly unmanned him again.
He had been very calm all the morning; had breakfasted with
his sister and Frank, as usual; had said to the latter that it
would be well enough to send for Lawyer Schofield, who was
not now a resident of Belvidere, but was practising in Springfield; and had tried to quiet old Hester, who was giving loose

rein to her tongue, and holding herself loftily above the "per-
tenders," as she called them. He had also remembered Mag
dalen, and sent her a bouquet of flowers by Celine, who represented her as feverish and nervous, and too tired to leave her
bed. Roger did not gather from Celine's report that she was
very ill, only tired and worn ; so he felt no particular anxiety
for her, and devoted himself to standing between and keeping
within bounds the other members of his household, and in so
doing felt a tolerable degree of quiet, until the men came up
from the mill, when the sight of their faces, so full of pity, and
the warm grasp of their friendly hands, brought a sudden rush
of tears to his eyes, and his chin quivered a little when he first
spoke to them.

"We've heard about it, Mr. Irving," the speaker said, "and
we don't like it, any of us, and we hope it is not true, and we
are sent by the others who are down on the green, and who
want you to come and tell us if it is true, and what we are to
do."

Mrs. Walter Scott, sitting by her chamber window, saw the
three men walk down the avenue, with Roger in their midst,
and saw, too, in the distance the crowd congregated in front of
the mill, and felt for a moment a thrill of fear as she began to
realize, more and more, what taking Millbank from Roger
meant. She would have felt still more uneasy could she have
seen the faces of the crowd, and their eager rush for Roger
when he appeared.

The women and the young girls were the first to pounce
upon him, and were the most voluble in their words of sorrow,
and surprise, and indignation, while the men and boys were not
far behind.

Bewildered and too much overcome at first to speak, Roger
stood like some father in the midst of his children, from whom
he is soon to be separated. He had been absent from them
for years, but his kindness and generosity had reached them
across the sea. They had lighter tasks, and higher wages,
and more holidays, and forbearance, and patience than any class

of workmen for miles and miles around, and they knew it all came from Roger's generosity, and the exceeding great kindness of his heart, and they were grateful for it.

A few, of course, had taken advantage of his goodness, and loitered, and idled, and complained of their hard lot, and talked as if to work at all were a great favor to their employer. But the majority had appreciated him to the full, and given him back measure for measure, working for his interest, and serving him so faithfully, that few manufactories were as prosperous or yielded so large an income as those in Belvidere. And now these workmen stood around their late master, with their sad faces upturned, listening for what he had to say.

"It is all true," he said. "There was another will made by my father a few months before he died."

Here a few groans for Squire Irving were heard from a knot of boys by the fence, but these were soon hushed, and Roger went on :

"This will Hester Floyd saw fit to hide, because she thought it unjust, and so for years —— "

He did not get any further, for his voice was lost in the deafening cheers which went up from the groaning boys for *Hester Floyd*, whom they designated as a *trump* and a *brick*, hurrahing with all their might, " Good for her. Three cheers and a tiger for Hester Floyd."

The cheers and the tiger were given, and then the boys settled again into quiet, while Roger tried to frame some reasonable excuse for what his father had done. But they would not listen to that, and those nearest him said, " It's no use, Mr. Irving. We've heard the reason and we know whom to thank for this calamity, and there's not one of us but hates her for it. We can never respect Mrs. Walter Irving."

The multitude caught the sound of that name, and the boys by the fence set up a series of most unearthly groans, which were in no wise diminished when they saw coming toward them *Frank*, the heir, and their new master, if they chose to serve him. Frank's face was very pale, and there was something

like fear and dread upon it when he met the angry glances of
the crowd, and heard the groans and hisses with which they
greeted him. Making his way to Roger's side, he whispered,
" Speak to them for me. They will listen to you when they
would only insult me. Tell them I am not in fault."

So it was Roger who spoke for Frank, explaining matters
away, and trying to make things as smooth as possible.

" My nephew is not to blame," he said. " He had nothing
to do with the will. He knew nothing of it, and was as much
surprised as you are when he found there was one."

" Yes, and would have burned it, too ; tell them that," Frank
said, anxious to conciliate a people whose enmity he dreaded.

Roger repeated the words, which were received with incredu-
lity.

" Stuff!" " Bosh !" " Can't make me swaller that !"
" Don't believe it !" and such like expressions ran through the
crowd, till, roused to a pitch of wild excitement, Frank sprang
upon a box and harangued the multitude eloquently in his own
defence.

" It *is* true," he said. " I did try to burn the will, and
would have done so if it had not been struck from my hand.
I held a lighted match to it, and Roger will tell you that a part
of it is yellow now with the smoke and flame."

" Yellow with time more like," a woman said, while a son of
Erin called out, " Good for you, Misther Franklin, to defind
yourself, but plase tell us who struck the match from yer
hand."

" An' sure who would be afther doin' the mane thing but his
mither, bad luck to her," interrupted another of Ireland's sons,
and Frank rejoined, " It was not my mother. Roger will tell
you that it was some one whom you love and respect, and who
was just as desirous that the will should be destroyed as I was,
but who did not think it right and dared not do it. I am sorrier about it than you are, and I've tried to make Roger keep
Millbank, and he refuses. I can no more help being the heir
than I could help being born, and I do not want to be blamed.

I want your good will more than anything else. I have not Roger's experience, nor Roger's sense; but I'll do the very best I can, and you must stand by me and help me to be what Roger was."

Frank was growing very eloquent, and his pale, boyish face lighted up and his eyes kindled as he went on telling what he meant to be if they would only help him instead of hindering and disliking him, until the tide began to set in his favor and the boys by the fence whispered to each other:

"Let's go in for white-hair, jest for fun if nothing more, — he talks reasonable, and maybe he'll give us half holidays when the circus is in town. Mr. Irving never done that."

"Yes, but he let us go to see the *hanimals*, and gin Bob 'Untley a ticket," said a red-faced English youth.

But the circus clique carried the day, and there rose from that part of the green a loud huzza for " Mr. Franklin Irving," while the faces of the older ones cleared up a little, and a few spoke pleasantly to Frank, who felt that he was not quite so obnoxious to the people as he had been. But they kept aloof from him, and followed their late master even to the gates of Millbank, assuring him of their readiness to go with him and work for him at lower rates than they were working now. And Roger, as he walked slowly up the avenue, felt that it was worth some suffering and trial to know that he stood so high in the estimation of those who had been employed by him so long.

All over town the same spirit prevailed, pervading the higher circles, and causing Mrs. Johnson to telegraph to Springfield for Lawyer Schofield, who she hoped might do something, though she did not know what. He came on the next train, and went at once to Millbank and was closeted with Roger for an hour and looked the ground over and talked with Hester Floyd and screamed to Aleck through an ear trumpet and said a few words to Frank and bowed coldly to Mrs. Walter Scott, and then went back to the group of ladies assembled in Mrs. Johnson's parlor, and told them there was no hope. The will was perfectly good. Frank was the rightful heir, and

Roger too proud to receive anything from him more than he had received. And then his auditors all talked together, and abused Mrs. Walter Scott and pitied Roger and spoke slight ingly of Frank, and wondered if there was any truth in the rumor that Magdalen was to marry him. They had heard so, and the rumor incensed them against her, and when Lawyei Schofield said he thought it very possible, they pounced upon the luckless girl and in a very polite way tore her into shreds, without, however, saying a word which was not strictly lady. like and capable of a good as well as of a bad construction.

CHAPTER XXIX.

POOR MAGDA.

OBODY paid any attention to her on the morning fol-lowing her visit to the library, except Celine, and Frank and Roger. The latter had sent her a bou-quet which he arranged himself, while Frank, remembering that this was the day when she was to give him her answer, had asked if she would see him, and Celine, through whom the message was sent, had brought him word that "Miss Lennox was too sick to see any one." Then Frank had begged his mother to go to her and ascertain if she were seriously ill, and that lady had said she would, but afterward found it convenient to be so busy with other matters, that nursing a sick, girl who was nothing to her now except a person whom she must if possible remove from her son's way, was out of the question. She did not care to see Magdalen just then, and she left her to the care of Celine, who carried her toast and tea about nine o'clock and urged her to eat it. But Magdalen was not hun-gry, and bade the girl leave her alone, as she wanted rest more than anything. At eleven Celine went to her again and found her sleeping heavily, with a flush on her cheeks, and her head occasionally moving uneasily on the pillow. Celine was not accustomed to sickness, and if her young mistress was sleeping she believed she was doing well, and stole softly from the room. At one she went again, finding Magdalen still asleep, but her whole face was crimson, and she was talking to herself and rolling her head from side to side, as if suffering great pain. Then Celine went for Mrs. Walter Scott, who, alarmed by the girl's representations, went at once to Magdalen. She was awake now, but she did not recognize any one, and kept moaning and talking about her head, which she said was between two planks in the garret, where she could not get it out. Mrs. Walter Scott saw she was very sick, and though she did not pet or caress or kiss the feverish, restless girl, she did her best to soothe and quiet her, and sent Celine for the family physician, who came and went before either Roger or Frank knew that danger threatened Magdalen.

" Typhoid fever, aggravated by excitement and some sudden exposure to cold," was the doctor's verdict. "Typhoid in its most violent form, judging from present symptoms ;" and then Mrs. Walter Scott, who affected a mortal terror of that kind of fever, declared her unwillingness to risk her life by staying in the sick room, and sent for Hester Floyd.

The old woman's animosity against Magdalen had cooled a little, and when she heard how sick she was she started for her at once.

" She nussed me through a fever, and I'd be a heathen to neglect her now, let her be ever so big a piece of trumpery," she said to herself as she went along the passage to Magdalen's room.

But when she reached it, and saw the moaning, tossing girl, and heard her sad complaints of her head wedged in between the boards, and her pleadings for some one to get it out, her old love for the child came surging back, and she bent over her lovingly, saying to her softly, "Poor Maggie, old Hester will get your head out, she will, she will — there — there — isn't it a bit easier now?" and she rubbed and bathed the burning head, and gave the cooling drink, and administered the little globules in which she had no faith, giving eight instead of six and sometimes even ten. And still there was no change for the better in Magdalen, who talked of the will, which she was trying to burn, and then of Roger, but not a word of Frank, who was beside her now, his face pale with fear and anxiety as he saw the great change in Magdalen, and how fast her fever increased.

Roger was the last to hear of it, for he had been busy in the library ever since Lawyer Schofield's departure, and did not know what was passing in the house until Hester went to him, and said:

"She thinks her head is jammed in between them boards in the garret floor, and nobody but you can pry it out. I guess you had better see her. Mr. Frank is there, of course, as he or' to be after what I seen in the hall yesterday."

"What did you see?" Roger asked, and Hester replied:

"I found her in my room when I went from here and I spoke my mind freely, I s'pose, about her snoopin' after the will when you had done so much for her, and she gave a scart kind of screech, and ran out into the hall, where Mr. Frank met her, and put his arm round her and led her to her own door, and kissed her as he had a right to if she's to be his wife."

Roger made no reply to this, but tried to exonerate Magdalen from all blame with regard to the will, telling what he knew about her finding it, and begging Hester to lay aside her prejudice, and care for Magdalen as she would have done six weeks ago.

And Hester promised, and called herself a foolish old woman for having distrusted the girl, and then went back to the sickroom, leaving Roger to follow her at his leisure. Something in Magdalen's manner the previous night had led him to hope that possibly she was not irrevocably bound to Frank; there might be some mistake, and the future was not half so dreary when he thought of her sharing it with him. But Hester's story swept all that away. Magdalen was lost to him, lost

10*

forever and ever, and for a moment he staggered under the knowledge just as if it were the first intimation he had received of it. Then recovering himself he went to Magdalen's bedside, and when at sight of him she stretched her arms towards him and begged him to release her head, he bent over her as a brother might and took her aching head upon his broad chest and held it between his hands, and soothed and quieted her until she 'fell away to sleep. Very carefully he laid her back upon the pillow, and then meeting in Frank's eye what seemed to be reproach for the liberty he had taken, he said to him in an aside, "You need not be jealous of your old uncle, boy. Let me help you nurse Magda as if she was my sister. She is going to be very sick."

Frank had never distrusted Roger and he believed him now, and all through the long, dreary weeks when Magdalen lay at the very gates of death, and it sometimes seemed to those who watched her as if she had entered the unknown world, he never lost faith in the man who stood by her so constantly, partly because he could not leave her, and partly because she would not let him go. She got her *head* at last from between the boards, but it was Roger who released it for her, and with a rain of tears, she cried, "It's out; I shall be better now;" then, lying back among her pillows, she fell into the quietest, most refreshing sleep she had known for weeks. The fever was broken, the doctor said, though it might be days before her reason was restored, and weeks before she could be moved, except with the greatest care. When the danger was over and he knew she would live, Roger absented himself from the sick-room, where he was no longer needed. She did not call for him now; she did not talk at all, but lay perfectly passive and quiet, receiving her medicines from one as readily as from another, and apparently taking no notice of anything transpiring around her. But she was decidedly better, and knowing this Roger busied himself with the settlement of his affairs, as he wished to leave Millbank as soon as possible.

CHAPTER XXX.

LEAVING MILLBANK.

T was in vain that Frank protested against the pride which refused to receive anything from the Irving estate. Roger was firm as a rock.

"I may be foolish," he said to Lawyer Schofield, who was often at Millbank, and who once tried to persuade him into some settlement with Frank. "I may be foolish, but I cannot take a penny more than the terms of the will give to me. I have lived for years on what did not belong to me. Let that suffice, and do not try to tempt me into doing what I should hate myself for. I have been accustomed to habits of luxury, which I shall find it difficult to overcome; just as I shall at first find it hard to settle down into a steady business, and seek for patronage with which to earn my bread. But I am comparatively young yet. I can study and catch up in my profession. I passed a good examination years ago. I have tried by reading not to fall far behind the present age. I shall do very well, I'm sure." Then he spoke of Schodick, where he had decided to go. "Some men would choose the West as a larger field in which to grow, and at first I looked that way myself; but Schodick has great attractions for me. It was my mother's home. I shall live in the very house where she was born. You know my father gave me the farm, and though it is rocky and hilly and sterile, — much of it, — I would rather go there than out upon the prairies. I shall be very near the town, which is growing rapidly, and there is a chance of my getting in with a firm whose senior member has recently died. If I do, it will be the making of me, and you may yet hear of Roger Irving from Schodick as a great man."

Roger had worked himself up to quite a pitch of enthusiasm, and seemed much like his olden self as he talked of his plans to Lawyer Schofield, who had never admired or respected him so much as he did when he saw him putting the best face upon matters and bearing his reverses so patiently. Everybody knew now that he was going to Schodick, in New Hampshire, and. that Hester and Aleck were going with him. Both seemed to have renewed their youth to a most marvellous degree, and Hester's form was never more erect, or her step more elastic, than during those early summer days, when, between the times of her ministering to Magdalen, of whom she still had the care, she went over the- house, selecting here and there articles which she declared were *hers*, and with which Mrs. Walter Scott did not meddle.

Full of her dread of the fever, that lady had scrupulously kept aloof from Magdalen, and when she began to fear lest the few for whose opinion she cared should censure her for neglect she affected symptoms of the disease and stayed in her own room, where she received the visits of the doctor, in white line wrap--pers elaborately trimmed, and a scarlet shawl thrown across her shoulders. Frank visited her several times a day, and once, when his heart was heaviest with the fear lest Magdalen would die, he went to her for sympathy, and laying his head on the pillow beside her, wept like a child. There was no pity in her voice, for she felt none for him, and her manner was cold and indifferent as she said she apprehended no danger, — and added that she hoped Frank would not commit himself too far or allow his feelings to run away with his judgment. He must remember that Magdalen had never promised to marry him, and that if one woman could read another she did not believe she ever would.

"She loves Roger," she said, "and he loves her, and I have made up my mind to explain to him a few things, and thus prevent you from throwing yourself away on a girl whose parentage is so doubtful."

Then Frank dried his tears, and so far forgot himself as to swear roundly that so sure as she went to Roger with such a tale, or in any way interfered between him and Magdalen, just so sure would he *deed* every penny of the Irving property to

Roger, and if he refused to take it, he would deed it to Magdalen, and if she refused it too, he would make donations to
every charitable institution in the land, until the whole was
given away, and he was poorer than before the will was found.
Mrs. Walter Scott was afraid of Frank in his present defiant
mood, and promised whatever he required, but suggested that
it might be well for him not to assume too much the character
of Magdalen's lover, until her own lips had given him the right
to do so. Frank knew this was good advice, and, to a certain
extent, he followed it; and when the crisis was past, he, too,
absented himself from the sick-room, and spent his time with
Roger in trying to understand the immense business which was
now his to manage, and which he no more comprehended than
a child.

"It is not well to trust too much to agents and overseers.
Better attend to it yourself," Roger said.

And then he spoke of one agent in particular whom he distrusted and had intended to discharge, and advised Frank to
see to it at once, and have but little to do with him. And
Frank promised to do so, remembering the while, with regret,
that between this man and himself there existed the most
friendly relations and perfect sympathy with regard to *horses*,
— Frank's great weakness — which only want of money kept in
abeyance.

Like his mother, Frank was disposed to let Hester Floyd
take whatever she chose in the way of bedding and table-linen,
and offered no objections when she laid claim to the spoons and
silver tea-set which had been bought for Jessie, and were marked
with her initials. Spoons and forks of a more modern style, with
only "Irving" marked upon them, were next appropriated by
the greedy old woman, who kept two men busy one entire
day packing boxes for Schodick, N. H. She was going at
once to the old farm-house, which the present tenant had,
for a consideration, been induced to vacate, and her preparations went rapidly forward, until, at last, the day but one
came, when, with her boxes and Aleck and Matty, her grand-

niece, who went as maid of all work, she was to start for the
Schodick hills, while Roger went West for a few weeks, thus
leaving the old lady time to get things "straightened out and
tidied up" before he came. This had been Frank's idea, conveyed to Roger in the form of a suggestion that a little travel
would do him good, and his home in Schodick seem a great
deal pleasanter if he found it settled than if he went to it when
all was disorder and confusion. All the better, kindlier qualities of Frank's nature were at work during those last days, and
even Hester brought herself to address him civilly, and thank
him cordially when, to her numerous bundles and boxes, he
added a huge basket of the choicest wines in the cellar.

"To be sure, he was only offering to Roger what was already
his own," she said; "but then it showed that what little milk of
human kindness he had wasn't sourer than swill, as his mother's
was."

Roger had seen to the packing of but one article, and this he
had done by himself and then carried it to the back stoop where
the other baggage was waiting. Hester saw the long, narrow
box and wondered what it was. Frank saw it too, *guessed*
what it was, went to the garret to reconnoitre, and then knew
that it was the cradle candle-box, in which Magdalen had been
rocked. It had stood for years in a corner of the garret, surrounded with piles of rubbish and covered with dirt and cob-
webs; but Roger had hunted it out and it was going with him
to his new home, sole memento of the young girl he had loved
so dearly, and who, all through the long bright summer days
when he was so busy, lay quiet and still, knowing nothing, or at
most comprehending nothing, of what was passing around her.

It was a strange state she was in, but the doctor said she
was mending, that the danger was past, and a week or two of
perfect quiet would restore her to a more natural condition.
Had he said otherwise, Roger would not have gone, but now it
was better for him to leave her while she was unconscious of
the pain it cost him to do so; and on the night before his departure for the West he went to look at her for the last time

Only Celine was with her and she thoughtfully withdrew, leaving him alone with Magdalen, whose pale lips he kissed so passionately and on whose face he dropped tears of bitter anguish. Years after, when her eyes were shining upon him full of love and tenderness and trust, he told her of that parting scene ; but she knew nothing of it then, and only moved a little uneasily and muttered something he could not understand. She had no farewell word for him, and so he kissed her lips and forehead once more and drew the covering smoothly about her, and buttoned the cuff of her night-dress, which he saw was unfastened, and moved the lamp a little more into the shadow, because he thought it hurt her eyes, and then went out and left her there alone.

They were astir early at Millbank the next morning, and a most tempting breakfast, prepared by Hester herself, awaited Roger in the dining-room. But he could not eat, and, after a few ineffectual attempts to swallow the rich, golden-colored coffee, he rose from the table and left the dining-room.

Knowing that he would, of course, come to say good-by to her, and dreading an interview with him when no one was present, Mrs. Walter Scott had made a "great effort" to dress herself, and come down to breakfast. But she *panted* hard, and seemed too weak to talk, and kept her hand a good deal on her left side, where she said she experienced great pain since her illness, and sometimes feared her lungs were affected. With all her languor and weakness, she could not quite conceal her elation at the near prospect of being entirely alone in her glory, and it showed itself in her face and in her eyes, which, nevertheless, tried to look so sorry and pitiful when, at last, Roger turned to her to say good-by.

She had nothing to fear from him now. He had given up quietly. Success was hers, with riches and luxury. It could matter little what Roger thought of her. His opinion could not change her position at Millbank. Still, in her heart she respected him more than any man living, and would rather he thought well of her than ill. So, with that look in her eyes which they always wore when she wanted to be particularly interesting, she held his hand between her own and said, —

"I can't let you go without hearing you say that you forgive me for any wrong you imagine me to have done, and that you will not cherish hard feelings toward me. Tell me this, can't you, *dear brother?*"

He dropped her hand then, as if a viper had stung him, and a gleam of fire leaped to his eyes as he replied :

"Don't call me *brother*, now, Helen. That time is past. You have wronged me fearfully, and but for you I should never have met this hour of darkness. If God can forgive me for all my sins against Him, I surely ought to try and forgive you, too. But human flesh is weak, and I cannot say that I feel very kindly towards you, for I do not."

He had never said so much to her before, and the proud woman winced a little, but tried to appear natural, and, for appearance sake, went with him to the door, and stood watching the carriage until it left the avenue and turned into the highway.

In perfect silence Roger passed through the grounds, so beautiful now in their summer glory, but as the carriage left the park behind, he leaned from the window for a last look at his old home. The sun was just rising and the dew-drops were glittering on the grass and flowers, while the thousands of roses with which the place was adorned filled the air with perfume. It seemed a second Paradise to the heart-broken man, whose thoughts went back to the dream he once had of just such a day as this when he was leaving Millbank. In the dream, however, there was this difference : Magdalen was with him ; her hand lay in his, her eyes shone upon him, and turned the midnight into noonday. Now he was alone, so far as she was concerned. Magda was not there ; she would never be with him again, unless she came the wife of Frank, who sat opposite, with an expression of genuine sympathy on his boyish face. Frank was sorry that morning, so sorry that he could not talk ;

but when, as they lost sight of Millbank, Roger groaned aloud, and leaned his head against the side of the carriage, he went over to him, and sitting down beside him took his hand in his own and pressed it nervously.

There was a crowd of people at the station; the whole village, Frank thought, when he saw the moving multitude which pressed around Roger to say good-by and assure him of their willingness to serve him. There were mills in Schodick, they had heard, and shoe shops, too ; and a few were already talking of following their late master thither.

"It would be worth something to see him round even if they did not work for him," they said.

And Roger heard all and saw all, and said good-by to all, and took in his arms the little baby boy named for him ten months before, and said playfully to the mother, "He shall have the first *cow* I raise on my farm."

And then the train came round the river bend and the crowd fell back, and Frank went with Roger into the car and waited there until the train began to move, when with a bound he sprang upon the platform, and those nearest to him saw that he was very white and that there were traces of tears in his eyes. No one spoke to him, though all made way for him to pass to his carriage, which drove rapidly back to Millbank, which was now his beyond a doubt.

Hester Floyd went later in the day, and to the last stood out against Mrs. Walter Scott, whom she did not deign to notice by so much as a farewell nod. Over Magdalen she bent lovingly, trying to make her comprehend that she was going away, but Magdalen only stared at her a moment with her wide open eyes, and then closed them wearily, and knew nothing of Hester's tears or the great wet kiss which was laid upon her forehead.

'She's to be the lady of Millbank, I s'pose, but I don't begrutch her her happiness with that old sarpent for a mother-in-law and that white-livered critter for a husband," Hester thought as she stole softly from the room and went down to where the drayman was loading her numerous boxes and bundles. Frank offered her the use of the carriage to carry herself and Aleck to the station; but she declined the offer, and took a fierce kind of pride in seeing the village hack drive up to the side door. "She as't no odds of nobody," she said, and tying on her six years' old straw bonnet, and pinning her brown shawl with a darning-needle, she saw deposited in the hack her old-fashioned work-basket and her satchel and bird cage and umbrella, and her bandbox tied up in a calico bag, and her palm-leaf fan, and Aleck, and Matty, who carried two beautiful Malta kittens in a basket as her own special property. Then, with a quick, sudden movement, and an indifference she was far from feeling, she shook the hands of all her fellow-servants over whom she had reigned so long, and hoping they would never find a *"wus"* mistress than she had been, sprang into the hack with an alacrity which belied her seventy summers, and was driven to the depot.

From her window Mrs. Walter Scott watched the fast receding vehicle, and felt herself breathe freer with every revolution of the wheels. When Roger went, a great weight had been lifted from her spirits, but so long as old Hester Floyd remained she could not feel altogether free; and now that the good dame was really out of the house she sat perfectly still until she heard the whistle of the engine, and saw the white smoke of the train which carried the enemy away. Then she rose up from her sitting posture, and her long graceful neck took a prouder arch, and her step was more firm, her manner more queenly, as she went directly to the kitchen, and summoning the servants to her presence told them they were at liberty to leave her employ within a month, as she should by that time have provided herself with other help. Very civilly they listened to her, and when she was through informed her that she need not wait a month before importing her new coterie of servants, as each one of them was already supplied with a situation, and was intending to leave her that night, with the exception of Celine, who had promised Mrs. Floyd to stay till Miss Lennox's mind was restored.

With a haughty, " Very well, do as you like," Mrs. Walter Scott swept out of the kitchen and made the circuit of the handsome rooms which were now her own. Frank, too, had watched the hack as it drove away, and listened for the signal by which he should know that Hester Floyd was gone, for not till then could *he* feel perfectly secure in his possessions. . But as the loud, shrill blast came up over the hills and then died away amid the windings of the river, there stole over him a pleasurable sense of proprietorship, and he thought involuntarily of the familiar lines, " I am monarch of all I survey, my right there is none to dispute." Frank liked to feel comfortable in his mind, and as he reviewed the steps by which he had reached his present position, he found many arguments in his own favor which tended to silence any misgivings he might otherwise have experienced. He was not to blame for his grandfather's will, nor to blame for hiding it. Everybody knew that. Roger said he was not, and Roger's opinion was worth everything to him. He had been willing to burn the will, and when he could not do that, he offered repeatedly to divide with Roger, and was willing to divide now and always would be. Surely he could do no more than he had done. He was a pretty good fellow after all, and he began to whistle "Annie Laurie" and think of the agent whom Roger had warned him against, and wished it had been anybody but *Holt*, who was such a good judge of horses, and had such a fine high-blood for sale, which he offered cheap, because he needed a little ready money. As the war steed scents the battle from afar, and pricks up his ears at the smell of blood, so Frank felt his love of horse flesh growing strong within him. There could be no harm in riding over to *see* Holt's horse. He would have to go there any way if he dismissed the man, as Roger had advised, and he would go at once and have a bad job off his mind. Accordingly, when lunch time came Mrs. Walter Scott lunched alone, and when the dinner hour came she dined alone, and when the stable doors were closed that night they shut into his new home Firefly, "the swiftest horse in the county," which Frank had bought for eleven hundred dollars.

Holt, the agent, was not dismissed!

CHAPTER XXXI.

THE HOME IN SCHODICK.

T was a quiet, old-fashioned farm-house, with gables and projections and large rooms and pleasant fire-places and low ceilings and small windows, looking some of them toward the village, with its houses of white nestled among the trees, and some of them upon the hills, whose shadows enfolded the farm-house in an early twilight at night, and in the morning reflected back the warm sunshine which lay so brightly upon their wooded sides. There was a kitchen with a door to the north, and a door to the south, and a door to the east, leading out into the woodshed, and there were stairs leading to an upper room, and a fire-place "big enough to roast an ox," Hester said, when, with her basket and bandbox and umbrella and camlet cloak and bird cage and kittens and Aleck, she was dropped at her new home and began to reconnoitre, deciding, first, that the late tenants of the place were "shiffless critters, or they would never have lived there so long with only a wooden latch and a wooden button on the outside door," and second, that they were "dirty as the rot, or they would never have left them stains on the buttry shelf, that looked so much like cheese-mould."

Hester was not altogether pleased with the house. It came a little hard to change from luxurious Millbank to this old brown farm-house, with its oaken floors and stone hearth and tiny panes of glass, and for a time the old lady was as home-sick as she could be. But this only lasted until she got well to work in the cleaning process, which occupied her mind

so wholly that she forgot herself, and only thought how to
make the house a fitting place for her boy to come to after his
travels West. Roger had given her money with which to
furnish the house, and she had added more of her own, while
Frank, when parting with her, had slipped into her hands one
hundred dollars, saying to her, "Roger is too proud to take
anything from me, and I want you to use this for the house."

And so it was owing partly to Frank's thoughtfulness and
Hester's generosity that the farm-house, when renovated with
paper and paint, and furnished with the pretty, tasteful furniture
which Hester bought, looked as well and inviting as it did.
The most pains had been taken with Roger's room, the one
his mother occupied when a girl. Hester had ascertained
which it was from an inhabitant of Schodick, who had been
Jessie's friend, and slept with her many a time in the room
under the roof, which looked off upon the pond and up the
side of the steep hills. The prettiest carpet was put down
there, and curtains were hung before the windows, and the bed
made up high and clean with ruffled sheets and pillow-cases,
mementos of Millbank, and Jessie's picture was hung on the
wall, the blue eyes seeming to look sadly round upon a spot
they had known in happier days than those when the portrait
was taken. There were flowers, too, in great profusion, — not
costly, hot-house flowers, like those which decked the rooms at
Millbank, but sweet, home-flowers, like those which grow
around the doors and in the gardens of so many happy New
England homes, — the fragrant pink and old-fashioned rose.
and honeysuckle and heliotrope, with verbenas and the sweet
mignonette.

And here Roger came one pleasant July afternoon, when a
heavy-thunder-storm had laid the dust, and cooled the air, and
set every little bird to singing its blithest notes, and, alas!
soured the rich, thick cream, which Hester had put away for
the few luscious wild strawberries which, late as it was for
them, Mattie had found in the meadow, by the fence, and
picked for Mr. Roger. With the exception of this little draw-

back, Hester was perfectly happy, and her face was radiant when she met her boy at the door, and welcomed him to his new home, taking him first to his own room, because it looked the prettiest, and would give him the best impression.

Roger had been in Schodick once or twice when a boy, but everything now was new and strange, while, struggle as he might against it, the contrast between the old home and the new affected him painfully at first, and it was weeks before he could settle down quietly, and give his time and attention to the firm of which he at once became a member. For days and days he found his chief solace in wandering over the hills where his mother once had been, and exploring the shadowy woods, and hunting out the rock under the overhanging pine, where she had crept away from sight, and prayed that she might die, when the great sorrow was in her heart, just as it was now in his. He found the spot at last, just under the shadow of one great rock and on the ledge of another, where the ground was carpeted thickly with the red pine of last year's growth, and the green, tasselated boughs above his head seemed to whisper softly, and try to comfort him.

Here poor Jessie had knelt, and felt that her heart was breaking. And here Roger sat, and felt that *his* heart was broken.

He had tried not to think much of Magdalen, and during the novelty and excitement of travelling he had not felt the bitter pain tugging at his heart as it was tugging now, causing him to cry out, in his anguish:

"Oh, Magda, my darling! how can I live without you?"

He had his father's letter with him, and he read it again there in the dim light, and was struck, as he had never before been, with that clause which said:

"And if, in the course of your life, there is one thing more than another which you desire, I pray Heaven to grant it to you!"

He had read these lines many times, but they never impressed him so forcibly as now. It was his father's last invocation to Heaven in his behalf. The one thing more than another which he desired was Magdalen, and why had God withheld her from him? Why had He not heard and answered the father's prayer? Why had He dealt so harshly by the son, taking from him everything which had hitherto made life desirable?

These were hard questions for a creature to ask its Creator. And Roger felt hard and rebellious as he asked them, with his face among the cones and withered pines, and from the pitiless skies above him there came no answer back, for it is not thus that God will have His children question Him.

Roger could not be submissive then, and for hours he sat there alone, battling with his sorrow, and never trying to pray until at the very last, when with a cry such as a wayward child gives when the will is finally broken, he covered his face with his hands and prayed earnestly to be forgiven for all the wicked, rebellious feelings he had cherished, and for strength to bear whatever the future had in store for him. After that he never gave way again as he had done before, though he went often to that rock under the pine, and made it a kind of Bethel where, unseen by mortal eye, he could tell his troubles to God, and go away with the burden somewhat lightened.

They heard at the farmhouse that Magdalen was improving slowly, and then there came a rumor in a roundabout way, that the day for the bridal was fixed, and that Mrs. Walter Scott was in New York selecting the bridal trousseau. Roger's face was very white for a few days after that, and nothing had power to clear the shadow from his brow, until one morning there came a letter to Hester Floyd from Magdalen herself, with the delicate perfumery she always used lingering about it, and her pretty monogram upon the seal. How Roger pressed the inanimate thing in one hand and caressed it with the other, and how fast he carried it to Hester, who was in the midst of working over her morning's churning, but who put the tray aside at once and washed her hands, and adjusted her spectacles, while Roger stood by inwardly chafing at the delay and ionging to know what Magdalen had written. It was very short indeed, and formal and stiff, and did not sound at all like Magdalen. She was quite well now, and she wanted to thank Mrs. Floyd for all the care she had taken of her before leaving Millbank.

"Mrs. Irving tells me you were very kind to me," she wrote, "and though I have no recollection that you or any one but Celine came near me, I am grateful all the same, and shall always remember your kindness to me both then and when I was a child, and such a care to you; I am deeply grateful to all who have done so much for me, and I wish them to know it, and remember me kindly as I do them. I am going away soon, and I want to take with me all I brought to Millbank. I have the locket, but the little dress I cannot find. Mrs. Irving thinks you took it in the chest. Did you, and if so, will you please send it to me at once by express, and oblige,

"Yours truly,

"MAGDALEN."

That was the letter. Not one word in it to Roger, except as the sentence beginning with "I am deeply grateful to *all* who have done so much for me," was supposed to refer to him. She wished him to remember her kindly as she did him, and she was going away from Millbank, but *where*, or how, or with whom, Roger could not tell. Hester *knew* she was going to be married, though why "she should want to lug that dud of a slip round with her finery was more than she could divine," she said, as she brought down the little spotted crimson dress, and wrapping it in thick brown paper gave it to Roger to direct.

"Maybe you'll write her a line or two for me; my hand is too shaky and cramped," she said to Roger, who shook his head and replied, "You must answer your own letters, Hester;" but he directed the little parcel to "Miss Magdalen Lennox, Belvidere," and sent it on its way to Millbank.

CHAPTER XXXII.

MAGDALEN'S DECISION.

T was a warm morning in early August when Magdalen came fully to herself and looked around her with a feeling of wonder and uncertainty as to where she was and what had happened to her. The last thing she could remember distinctly was of being cold and chilly, and that the night wind blew upon her as she groped her way back to her room. Now the doors and windows were opened, and the warm summer rain was falling on the lawn outside and sifting down among the green leaves of the honeysuckle which was trained across the window. There were flowers in her room, —summer flowers, — such as grew in the garden beds, and it must be that it was summer now, and many weeks had passed since that dreadful night whose incidents she finally recalled, knowing at last what had happened in part. *She* had found the will, and Mrs. Walter Scott had carried it to Roger, who was not as angry as she had feared he might be. Nay, he was not angry at all, and his manner towards her when she went to him in the library had belied what Frank had said, and her cheeks flushed and her pulse throbbed with delight as she felt again the kisses Roger had rained upon her lips and forehead and hair, and heard his voice calling her — "Magda, my darling, my darling." He had done all this on that night which must have been so long ago, and that meant *love*, and Frank was mistaken or wished to deceive her, and she should tell him so and free herself wholly from him and then wait for Roger to follow up his words and acts, as he was bound in honor to do. Of all this Magdalen thought, and then she wondered what had been done about the will, and if Roger would really go away from Millbank ; and if so, would he take her with him or leave her for awhile and come for her again. That he *had* gone she never for a moment suspected. She had been delirious, she knew, but not so much so that some subtle influence would not have told her when Roger came to say good-by. He was there still. He had arranged those beautiful bouquets which looked so fresh and bright, and had set those violets just where she could see them. He had remembered all her tastes, and would come soon to see her and be so glad when he found how much better she was. At last there was a step in the hall ; somebody was coming, but it was not Roger, nor Frank, nor yet Celine. *She* had finally been sent away, though she had stood her ground bravely for a time in spite of Mrs. Walter Scott's lofty ways and cool hints that Miss Lennox would do quite as well with a stranger, inasmuch as she did not know one person from another. She called her *Miss Lennox* now altogether. *Magdalen* would have been too familiar and savored too much of relationship, real or prospective, and this the lady was determined to prevent. But she said nothing as yet. The time for talking had not come, and might never come if Magdalen only had sense enough to answer Frank in the negative. He was still anxious, still waiting for that torpor to pass away and leave Magdalen herself again. In his estimation she was already his, for surely she could not refuse him now when everybody looked upon the marriage as a settled thing, and he insisted that everything should be done for her comfort, and every care given to her which would be given to Mrs. Franklin Irving. And in this his mother dared not cross him. His will was stronger on that point than her own, and hence the perfect order in the sick-room, and the evidences of kind, thoughtful attention which Magdalen had been so quick to detect. In one thing, however, Mrs. Walter Scott had had her way. She had dismissed Celine outright, and put in her place a maid of her own choosing, and it was her step which Magdalen heard, coming towards her room. She was not a bad-faced girl, and she smiled pleasantly as she spoke to Magdalen and said, " You are better this morning, Miss Lennox."

" Yes, a great deal better. Have I been sick long, and

where are they all? Who are you, and where is Celine?"
Magdalen asked, and the girl replied, "She left here some two
weeks ago and I came in her place; I am Sarah King; can I
do anything for you?"

"Nothing but answer my questions. How long have I been
sick, and where are Hester Floyd and Mr. Irving?"

She meant Roger, but the girl was thinking of Frank, and
replied, "Mr. Irving went to Springfield yesterday, but will be
home to-night, I guess, and so glad to find you better; he has
been so concerned about you, and is in here two or three times
a day."

"Is he?" and Magdalen's face flushed at this proof of
Roger's interest in her.

"Don't you remember anything about it?" the girl asked,
and Magdalen replied, "Nothing; it is all like a long, disturbed
sleep. Where is Hester, did you say?"

"You mean Mrs. Floyd, I suppose; she has been gone some
time, — to Schodick, or some such place. She went with *old*
Mr. Irving, Mr. Franklin's uncle, I believe. He is West somewhere now, I heard madam say. I have never seen him, nor
Mrs. Floyd."

She meant Roger by *old Mr. Irving*, and ordinarily Magdalen would have laughed merrily at the mistake, but now she
was too much surprised and pained to give it more than a
thought.

"Roger, Mr. Roger Irving gone, and Hester, too?" she cried.
"When did they go, and why did they leave me here so sick?
has everybody gone? Tell me, please, all you know about it."

Sarah knew very little, but that little she told, and then
Magdalen knew that of all the once happy household at Millbank she was left alone. Hester was gone, the old servants
gone, and Roger was gone, too. That was the hardest part of
all, and the tears sprang to her eyes as a feeling of homesickness came stealing over her.

"I'd better call Mrs. Irving," Sarah said, puzzled to know
why Magdalen should cry, and she left the room to do so.

Fifteen minutes later and Mrs. Walter Scott came in, habited in white, with puffs and tucks and rich embroidery wherever there was a place for it, and on her head a jaunty little morn-ing cap of the softest Valenciennes, with a bit of lavender rib-bon to relieve it. She was not all smiles and tenderness now, and there was about her a studied politeness wholly different from her old caressing manner toward Magdalen.

"Sarah tells me you are better this morning, and you do look greatly improved," she said, standing back a little from the bed and feigning not to see the hand which Magdalen held toward her.

Magdalen felt the change in a moment and understood the cause. Mrs. Irving was now the undisputed mistress of Mill-bank, and she the poor dependant, left there on the lady's hands, a burden and a drag whom nobody wanted. That was the way Magdalen put it, and her tears fell like rain as she re-plied, "Yes, I am better, but I, — I — don't understand it at all, or why I should be left here alone; why didn't they take me with them?"

"I suppose because you were too sick to be moved, though I knew but little about their movements. Mrs. Floyd was so very rude and ill-bred that I kept out of her way as much as possible, and as Roger avoided me, I saw but little of them. It is not worth while to distress yourself unnecessarily," the cruel woman went on as she saw how Magdalen cried. "We have taken every possible care of you and shall continue to do so until you are well, when, if you, wish to join your friends in Schodick, we will provide the means for you to do so."

Nothing could be cooler than her tone and manner and words, and but for her face, which there was no mistaking, Mag-dalen would have doubted her identity with the oily-tongued woman who used to caress and pet her so much, and to whom at one time she had paid a kind of child-worship. But it *was* the same woman, and she stood a moment longer, looking coldly at Magdalen, and picking a dried leaf or two from the vase of flowers on the stand; then consulting her watch she said, "You must excuse me now, as I have an engagement at ten. Sarah will see that you have everything you want. You will find her an excellent nurse. I chose her myself from a dozen applicants for the place. I'll see you again by and by. I wish you good-morning."

For a few moments Magdalen lay like one stunned; then, as she began to reason upon the matter and to understand it more clearly, her pride came to her aid; and when at last Sarah went back to her, she found her with flushed cheeks and a resolute, determined look in her eyes, which flashed and sparkled with much of their former fire.

Frank did not return till the next night. There was a horse-race in Springfield and he had Firefly there and put him on the course and won a bet and made for himself quite a reputation as a horse-jockey; and he paid Holt's bills at the Massasoit House, and sent bottles of champagne to sundry other "good fellows" who had praised his skill in driving and praised his horse and flattered him generally. Then he promised to look at another horse which somebody recommended as unsurpassed in the saddle, and took several shares in a new speculation which was sure to go if "the rich Mr. Irving patronized it," and which if it went was sure to pay double. Judge Burleigh, of Boston, who was stopping at the Massasoit, had sought him out and introduced his daughter Bell, a handsome, haughty girl, who had made fun of his light mustache and boyish face before she knew who he was, and then been very gracious to him after. Bell Burleigh was poor and fashionable and extravagant, and on the lookout for a husband. Frank Irving was rich, and master of the finest residence in the county, and worth cultivating, and so she expended upon him every art known to a thorough woman of the world, and walked with him through the halls and sat with him in the parlor in the evening, and went out in the morning to see him drive Firefly round the course, and had her father ask him to their table at dinner time, and flattered and courted him until he began to wonder why other people beside Bell Burleigh had not discovered what

an entertaining and agreeable man he was! But through it all
he never for a moment wavered in his allegiance to Magdalen.
Bell's influence could not make him do that; but it inflated his
pride and made him less able to bear the humiliation to which
Magdalen was about to subject him.

After her first interview with Magdalen, Mrs. Walter Scott
did not see her again until her son returned, though she sent
twice to know how she was feeling and if she would have anything. To these inquiries Magdalen had answered that she
was doing very well and did not want anything more than she
already had, and this was all that had passed between the two
ladies when Frank came home from Springfield. He heard
from Sarah of the change in Magdalen; but heard, too, that
she could not see him that night, as she had been sitting up
some little time and was very tired. The next day it was the
same, and the next. She was too weak to talk, and would
rather Mr. Irving should wait before she saw him. And so
Frank waited and chafed and fretted and lost his temper with
his mother, who maintained through all the utmost reserve with
regard to Magdalen, feeling intuitively that matters were adjust-
ing themselves to her satisfaction. She guessed what the delay
portended, and on the strength of it went once or twice to the
sick room, and was a little more gracious than at first. But
Magdalen was very reserved toward her now, barely answering
her questions, and seeming relieved when she went away.

Frank saw her at last. She was sitting up in her easy chair,
and her face was very pale at first, but flushed and grew crimson as Frank bent over her and kissed her forehead and called
her his darling, and told her how glad he was to find her better,
and how miserable he had been during the last few days because he could not see her.

"It was naughty in you to banish me so long. Don't you
think so, darling?" he said playfully, as he stooped again to
kiss her.

He was taking everything for granted, and Magdalen gasped

for breath as she put up both hands to thrust him aside, for she felt as if she were smothering with him so near to her.

"Sit down, Frank," she said, "sit there by the window," and she pointed to a seat so far from her that more kisses were out of the question.

Something in her tone startled him, and he sat where she bade him sit and then listened breathlessly while she went over the whole ground carefully, and at last, as gently as possible, for she would not unnecessarily wound him, told him she could not be his wife.

"I decided that before I knew Roger had the will," she said, "and I sent for you to tell you so on that dreadful day when so much happened here. I like you, Frank, and I know you have been very kind to me, but I cannot be your wife; I do not love you well enough for that."

It was in vain that Frank begged her to consider, to take time to think. She surely did not know what she was doing when she refused *him;* and he thought of Bell Burleigh and all the flattery he had received in Springfield, and wished Magdalen could know how highly some people esteemed him.

Magdalen understood him in part, and smiled a little derisively as she replied: "I know well what I am doing, Frank; I am refusing one who, the world would say, was far above me, — a poor girl, with neither home, nor friends, nor name."

"What, then, do you propose to do?" Frank asked, "if, as you say, you are without home or friends."

"I don't know. Oh, I don't know. Some way will be provided," Magdalen answered sadly, her heart going out in a longing cry after Roger.

As if divining the thought, and feeling jealous and angry on account of it, Frank continued:

"You surely would not go to Schodick now. Even your love for Roger would not allow you to do so unmaidenly a thing as that."

He spoke bitterly, for he felt bitterly, and when he saw how white Magdalen grew, and how she gasped for breath, he went on pitilessly,—"I think I know what stands between us. You fancy you love Roger best."

"Hush ! Frank, hush !" Magdalen cried, and the color came rushing back into her face. "If I *do* love Roger best, *it* is not to be mentioned between us, and you must respect the feeling. He does not care for me, or he would not have left me here so sick, without a word of farewell to be given when I could understand it. *Did* he leave any message, Frank ? "

Had Magdalen been stronger, she would never have admitted what she was admitting to Frank, who, still more piqued and irritated, answered her, "None that I ever heard of."

"Or come to see me either ? Didn't he do so much as that ? "

Frank could have told her of the many nights and days when Roger never left her side, except as it was absolutely necessary ; but he would not even tell her that ; he merely said : " I dare say he looked in upon you before he left, but I do not know. He was very busy those last few days, and had a great deal to do."

Magdalen's lip quivered, but she made a great effort not to show how much she was pained by Roger's seeming indifference and neglect. Still, it did show upon her face, for she was weak, and tired, and worn, and the great tears came dropping from her eyes, as she thought how mistaken she had been, and how desolate and alone she was in the great world. And Frank pitied her at last, and tried to comfort her, but would not say a word which would give her hope, with regard to Roger. He should not consider her answer as final, he said, when she begged him to leave her. She would feel differently by and by, when she saw matters as they really were. She had no other home but Millbank, as she, of course, would not follow Roger to Schodick. He placed great emphasis on the word *follow*, and Magdalen felt her blood tingle to her finger tips as he went on to say, that, let her decision be what it might, her rightful place was there at Millbank, which he wished her to consider her home, just as she always had done. She surely ought to be as willing to look to him for support as to Roger, who was in no condition now to enlarge his household, even if he wished to do it.

He left her then, and went at once to his mother. He had staked his all on Magdalen, and he must not lose her, — for aside from the great trial it would be to him, there was the bitter mortification he would be compelled to endure, for he had suffered the people of Belvidere to believe in his engage- ment, and Magdalen must be won, or at least kept at Mill- bank, and in order to do this there must be a perfect under- standing between himself and his mother. And after a half hour's interview there *was* a perfect understanding, and Mrs. Walter Scott knew that if by word or sign she helped Mag- dalen to a knowledge of Roger's love for her, and so sep- arated her from Frank, just so sure would he carry out his former threat, of deeding Millbank away. That point was settled, and another too, which was, that Magdalen should be treated with all the kindness and attention due to an inmate of the house, and one who might, perhaps, be its mistress.

"But whether she is or not, mother, you've got to come down from your stilts, and treat her as you did before the con- founded will was found, or, by the Harry, I'll do something you'll be sorry for."

Frank's recent intercourse with horse-jockeys, and men of the race-course, had not improved his language ; but he was in earnest, and his mother promised whatever he required, and kept her promise all the more readily, because she knew that do what he would, and plead as he might, Magdalen would nev- er be his wife.

11*

CHAPTER XXXIII.

THE BEGINNING OF THE END.

WANTED, — A young woman of pleasing address, and cultivated manners, as companion for a young lady who suffers greatly from ill health and nervous depression. It is desirable that the applicant should be both a good reader and good musician.

"Address, for four weeks,

"Mrs. Penelope Seymour,

'St. Denis, New York.'

This advertisement was in the *Herald*, which Frank laid upon the table in the room where both his mother and Magdalen were sitting. It was four weeks since Magdalen's first awakening to perfect consciousness after her long illness, and in that time she had improved rapidly. She went to the table now, and had ridden two or three times with Mrs. Walter Scott, between whom and herself there was a kind of tacit understanding that, so long as they remained together, each was to be as civil and polite to the other as possible, knowing the while that each would be glad to be relieved of the other's society. Frank had made several efforts to ride with Magdalen. He wanted to exhibit her in town with his new bays, which he had bought for an enormous sum. But Magdalen always made some excuse ; and without seeming to do it, Mrs. Walter Scott helped her to avoid him, so that he had had no opportunity for seeing her alone, since the interview in her chamber, when she told him her answer was final, and he had refused to consider it as such. He had been invited to join a party of young men from Hartford and Springfield, who were going on a fishing excursion to the Thousand Islands and from thence into Canada, if there should prove to be good hunting there, and when he brought the *Herald* into the sitting-room, he came also to say good-by to his mother and Magdalen.

"Perhaps I shall be gone six weeks," he said, in reply to his mother's questions as to his return, and he looked at Magdalen to see how she would take it.

She was relieved rather than sorry, and he saw it, and felt a good deal chagrined, as he shook her hand at parting, and received her kind wishes for a pleasant trip. After he was gone, she took up the *Herald*, and ran her eye over its columns, till she reached the list of "Wanted." She had studied that list before, for she had it in her mind to find some situation, as teacher or governess, which would take her from Millbank and make her independent of every one. She saw the advertisement for a young woman, who was "a good reader, and good musician." She knew she was both, and knew, too, that she was of "pleasing address" and "cultivated manners." She did not object to being a companion for an invalid. It would be easier than a teacher's life, and she would write to "Mrs. Penelope Seymour" and see what that lady had to say. Accordingly, the very next mail which went to New York from Belvidere carried a letter of inquiry from Magdalen to Mrs. Seymour, whose reply came at once; a short note, written in a plain, square hand, and directly to the point. There had been many applications for the situation, but something in Miss Lennox's manner of expressing herself had turned the scale in her favor, and Mrs. Seymour would be glad to see her at the St. Denis, as soon as possible. Terms, five hundred dollars a year, with a great deal of leisure.

Five hundred dollars a year seemed a vast amount of money to Magdalen, who had never earned a penny since the berries picked for that photograph sent to Roger, and she began at once to think how she would lay it up, until she had enough to make it worth giving to Roger, who should not know from whence it came, so adroitly would she manage. She had in her own mind accepted the situation, but, before she wrote again to Mrs. Seymour, it would be proper to lay the case before Mrs.

Walter Scott, and, for form's sake, ask her advice. That lady was delighted, for now a riddance from Magdalen was sure without her intervention, but she kept her delight to herself and seemed, for several minutes, to be considering. Then she said something about its not being what her son expected or wished, and asked if Magdalen was fully resolved not to marry Frank.

Magdalen knew this to be a mere ruse, done for politeness' sake, and she bit her lip to keep from answering hastily.

Her decision was final, she said. She should probably never marry any one certainly not Frank ; and she could not remain at Millbank longer than was absolutely necessary. Mrs. Irving must know how very unpleasant it was, and what an awkward position it placed her in.

Mrs. Irving did know, and fully appreciated Magdalen's nice sense of propriety, and she was very gracious to the young girl, and said she was welcome to stay at Millbank as long as she liked, but, if she preferred to be less dependent, she respected the feeling, and thought, perhaps, Mrs. Seymour's offer was as good as she would have, and it might be well to accept it.

And so it was accepted, and Magdalen made haste to get away, before Frank's return. She hunted for the little dress, impelled by a feeling that somewhere in the wide world, into which she was going, she might find her mother, and she would have every possible link by which the identity could be proven. Mrs. Walter Scott had told her that Hester Floyd took the chest of linen in which the dress was laid and so she wrote to Hester the letter we have seen. Once she thought to send some word direct to Roger, but her pride came up to prevent that. He had never written to *her*, or sent to inquire for her that she knew of, for Frank had not told her of a letter written on the prairies, in which Roger had inquired anxiously for her and asked to be remembered. Roger did not care for her messages, she thought, and she wrote as formally as possible, and then, with a strange inconsistency, expected that Roger would answer the letter. But only the package came, directed in his handwriting, and Magdalen could have cried when she saw there was nothing more. She cut the direction out, and put it away in a little box, with all the letters Roger had written her from Europe, and then went steadily on with her preparations for leaving Millbank.

It was known, now, in town, that Magdalen was going away, and it created quite a sensation among her circle of friends. She was *not* to marry Frank. She was not as mercenary as many had believed her to be, and the tide turned in her favor, and Mrs. Johnson called with her daughter Nellie, now Mrs. Marsh, of Boston, and all the *élite* of the town came up to see her, and without expressing it in words, managed to let her know how much she had risen in their estimation by the step she was taking. They could not quite understand it all, but they spoke encouragingly to her, and invited her to their houses, whenever she chose to come, and went to the depot to see her off, on the bright autumnal day when she finally left Millbank for a home with Mrs. Penelope Seymour.

CHAPTER XXXIV.

MRS. PENELOPE SEYMOUR.

MAGDALEN felt herself growing very nervous and uneasy as the long train came slowly into New York, and car after car was detached and drawn away by horses. She was in the last of all, and was feeling very forlorn and homesick and half inclined to cry, just as a voice by the door asked : "Is Miss Lennox, from Belvidere, here?"

There was reassurance in the tone of the voice, and reassurance in the expression of the frank, open face of the young man, who, as Magdalen rose from her seat, came quickly to her side, and doffing his hat, said : "Miss Lennox, I presume? I am Guy Seymour, Aunt Pen's nephew, or as she would tell

you, her husband's nephew, and she has kept me in a constant
state of worry the entire day on your account. I was at the
depot at least an hour before there was any possible hope of
the train, and as you are an hour behind, that makes two hours
I have waited, so you see I have done my duty. Allow me to
take your satchel and umbrella. You haven't a bandbox, have
you?"

The comical look in the saucy brown eyes, which turned
upon Magdalen, betrayed the fact that he was quizzing her a
little. But Magdalen did not mind it. She felt a kind of
security with him, and liked him at once in spite of the bandbox thrust.

"This way, please; perhaps you'd better take my arm," he
said, as he made his way through the crowd to a carriage, which
was waiting for him.

When once fairly seated, Magdalen had leisure to study her
vis-à-vis more closely. He was apparently twenty-five or
twenty-six years of age, a young man who had seen a great deal
of fashion and society, and who still retained about him a certain air of frankness and candor and simplicity, which opened
a way for him at once to every stranger's heart. There was
something in the wave of his hair and the cast of his head which
reminded Magdalen of Roger, and made her feel as if she had
found a friend. He was inclined to be quite sociable, and after
exhausting the weather, he said to her, "You are from Belvidere, I believe? Do you know a Mr. Irving there, the one
who has so recently come into a fortune?"

Magdalen looked quickly up, and her face was scarlet as she
replied, "I know him, yes. Is he an acquaintance of yours?"

"I was two years behind him in college, but sophs and seniors are as widely apart as the poles. I wonder if he is greatly
improved. I used to think him a kind of a prig."

"I may as well start with a right understanding at once,"
Magdalen thought, and she answered a little haughtily. "Mr.
Frank Irving is a friend of mine. I have known him ever since
I can remember. Millbank is the only home I have ever had."

Magdalen thought her companion came near whistling in his surprise, and she felt sure that he was regarding her more curiously than he had done before, while for some reason he seemed more attentive and polite, and by the time the St. Denis was reached, she felt as if she had known him months instead of a brief half hour.

" You must not mind if you find Aunt Pen a little stiff at first. She has a great deal of starch in her composition," he said as he ran up the stairs and down the hall in the direction of No. —.

And stiff, indeed, Magdalen did find Aunt Pen, as the nephew called her. A little, short, straight, square-backed woman of sixty or thereabouts, with iron-gray hair, arranged in puffs around her forehead, — a proud, haughty, wrinkled face, and round bright eyes, which seemed to look straight through Magdalen as Guy ushered her into the room.

" Miss Lennox, Auntie Pen," he said, and taking Magdalen by the arm he led her up to his aunt, who felt constrained to offer her jewelled hand, but who did it in such a way that Magdalen felt the conventional gulf there was between them in the lady's mind, and winced under it.

" I hope you'll order dinner at once," Guy continued. " The train was an hour behind, and Miss Lennox is fearfully tired. I'll ring myself," and he touched the bell rope while Mrs. Seymour was saying something about being glad to see Miss Lennox, and hoping she was not very tired.

Oh how strange and lonely Magdalen felt, when at last she was alone in her room for a few moments, while she arranged her hair and made herself more presentable for dinner ! The windows looked out into a dreary court, and tears sprang to Magdalen's eyes as she felt the contrast between these dingy brick walls and that damp, mouldy pavement, and the fresh green grass and wealth of flowers and shrubbery and forest trees which for years had been hers to gaze upon. Suppose she was to live at the St. Denis for years, and to occupy that room into which the sun never penetrated. And for aught she knew,

such was to be her fate. She had made no inquiries as to
where she was to live, whether in city or country, hotel or
private house. Her orders were to come to the St. Denis, and
there she was, and her heart was aching with homesickness, and
a longing to be away,—not at Millbank, but with Roger, wherever
he was. With him was home and happiness and rest, such as
Magdalen felt she should never find again. But it would not
do now to indulge in feelings like these. There was dinner
waiting for her, as Guy's cheery voice announced outside her
door. "Never mind stopping to dress to-night. It won't pay,
and Aunt Pen don't expect it. She is dressed enough for both,"
he said ; then he went away, and Magdalen heard him whistling
a part of a favorite opera, and felt glad and grateful that at the
very outset of her career she had met Guy Seymour to smooth
away the rough places for her as he was doing in more ways
than she knew of, or ever would know. To him she owed it
that she was not left to find her way alone from the depot to the
hotel.

"There is no need of your going for her. People of her class
can always find their way," his aunt had said to him in the
morning, when he asked what time she expected her *Yankee
school-ma'am* to arrive, saying he wished to know so as to have
nothing in the way of his going up to meet her.

To his aunt's suggestion that "people of her class could
usually find their way," he gave one of his pet whistles, and said,

"How do you know she is one of the 'people of her class?'
And supposing she is, she is a woman, and young and possibly
good looking, and New York is an awful place for a young, good-
looking woman to land in, an entire stranger. So, *ma chère*
auntie, I shall meet her just as I should want some chap of a
Guy Seymour to meet my sister if I had one. And, auntie, I
beg of you to unbend a little, and try to make her feel at home.
I've no doubt she'll be as homesick as I was the first time I
ever visited you when I was a boy, and cried so hard to go
home that I vomited up that quart of green gooseberries I had
eaten surreptitiously out in the garden. Do you remember it?'

And so kind-hearted Guy had his way, and when he told Magdalen that his aunt had kept him in a constant worry on her account, he had reference to a widely different state of affairs from what his words implied and what he meant they should imply. He had been fighting for her all day and insisting that if she was a lady she should be treated as a lady, and when he met her at the depot, he felt that he had been wholly right in the course he had pursued.

She *was* a lady, and pretty, too, as nearly as he could judge through the drab veil which covered her face. The veil was off when she came out to dinner, and Guy, who met her at the door and conducted her to the table, started a little to see how beautiful and graceful she was, and how like a queen she bore herself toward his aunt, who took her in now, from her black, shining hair to the sweep and cut of her fashionable travelling dress.

"That is last spring's style. It must have been made in New York," was Mrs. Seymour's mental comment, and she felt a growing respect for one whose dress bore so unmistakably the New York stamp upon it.

She was dressed in satin, — soft, French gray satin, — whose heavy folds stood out from her slender figure and covered up the absence of hoops, which she never wore. There was a point lace coiffure on her head and point lace at her throat and wrists, and diamonds on her fat white hands, and she looked to the full a lady of the high position and blood which she professed, and she was very kind to Magdalen, albeit there was a certain stiffness in her manner which would have precluded the slightest approach to anything like familiarity had Magdalen attempted it.

Evidently there was something about Magdalen which riveted her attention, for she omitted no opportunity for looking at her when Magdalen did not know it, and at certain turns of the head and flashes of the large, restless eyes which sometimes met hers so suddenly, she found herself perplexed and bewildered, and wondering when or where she had seen eyes like these whose glance she did not like to meet, but which never-theless kept flashing upon her, and then turning quickly away. Guy, too, caught now and then a familiar likeness to something seen before; but it was not in the eyes or the turn of the head, — it was more in the expression of the mouth and the smile which made Magdalen so beautiful, while there was some-thing in the tone of her voice like another voice which in all the world made the sweetest music for him. He knew of whom Magdalen reminded him, though the faces of the two were no more alike than a brilliant rose and a fair, white water-lily. Still the sight of Magdalen and the silvery ring of her voice brought the absent one very near to him, and made him still kinder and more attentive to the young girl whose champion he had undertaken to be.

"Is it still your intention to leave New York to-morrow, or will you give Miss Lennox a day in the city for sight-seeing? I dare say she would like it better than plunging at once into that solitude of rocks and hills and running rills," Guy said to his aunt, who replied: "I had intended to leave to-morrow. I am beginning to long for the solitude, as you call it, and unless Miss Lennox is very anxious to see the city —"

"Of course she is. Every young girl wants to see the Park and Broadway and the picture galleries, especially if she has never been in New York before. But I beg your pardon, Miss Lennox; for aught I know you were born here."

Magdalen had been a close listener to the conversation be-tween the aunt and nephew, and gathered from it that her destination was the country, and she was not to live in the noisy city, which would seem so dreary to her from contrast with the gayeties of last winter, when she was there under very different auspices. She had no desire to see Broadway, or the Park, or the pictures. She had seen them all, with Roger as her escort, and they would look so differently now. So to Mr. Seymour's suggestion that she was possibly born in New York, she replied:

"I was here last winter, and saw, I think, all there is worth seeing. I would rather go at once to 'the rocks and hills and running rills.' I feel most at home with nature."

She flashed a bright smile on Guy, who felt his blood tingle a little, while his aunt thought, "I knew her clothes were made in New York;" then to Magdalen she said, "I have many acquaintances in the city. Possibly you may have met some of them, if you were *in society.*"

She laid great stress upon the last two words, and Magdalen colored, while Guy, who saw his aunt's drift, said laughingly, "Don't pray drive Miss Lennox into telling whether she was a belle or a student, copying some picture, or perfecting herself in music. You'll be asking next if she knew the Dagons and Draggons, whom not to know is to be nobody indeed."

He spoke sarcastically now, and Magdalen's face was scarlet, though she could not help laughing at his allusion to the "Dagons and Draggons" whom she had met, and so was not lacking in that accomplishment. She knew it was very natural that Mrs. Seymour should wish to know something of her antecedents, and she said, "I was *not* here to copy pictures. I came with friends, and saw, I suppose, what is called society; at least I met the *Dagons* and *Draggons*, if that is any proof. I was chaperoned by Mrs. Walter Irving, of whom you may have heard."

"Mrs. Walter Scott Irving, of Lexington avenue," Mrs. Seymour exclaimed; "I have heard of her. Are you a relative of hers?"

"No, madam, not a relative. I was adopted by her husband's half brother, Mr. Roger Irving, when I was a very little child. He was as kind to me as if I had been his sister. I have always lived at Millbank, and always intended to live there until circumstances occurred which made it desirable for me to seek a home elsewhere and earn my own livelihood. There was found a later will than the one proven at the time of Squire Irving's death, and by virtue of that will Mr. Roger's nephew, Frank, came into possession of the estate, and Roger went away, while I preferred not to be dependent."

She had told all of her history which it was necessary to tell, and after a little more conversation she bade her new acquaintance good-night and retired to her room.

"Well, Guy, what do you think of her?" Mrs. Seymour said, coming to her nephew's side.

"I think she's splendid," he replied; "but who the deuce is it she looks like? She has evidently been as delicately brought up as Alice herself. It's the finding of that will which has turned her adrift upon the world, no doubt, and I pity her, for she is every inch a lady; and, Aunt Pen, don't for gracious, sake put on airs with her, as if you were the great Mogul, and she some Liliputian. Remember from what a height she has fallen! Think of her knowing the Dagons and Draggons!"

He was teasing her now, but however much of a scapegrace she might think him to be, Auntie Pen was pretty sure to consider and follow his advice, and the next morning she was very polite to Magdalen, and offered of her own accord to stay another day in New York if she liked, saying Guy should drive them to the Park, or wherever she wished to go. But Magdalen longed to be out of the city, and an hour or two after breakfast the carriage came round to take them to the train.

Mrs. Seymour had not been very communicative with regard to Beechwood, the place to which they were going. She had said merely that it was on the Hudson. That it was her niece who was the invalid; that they had been some years abroad; that the house was very pleasant; that for certain reasons they saw but little company; and then had asked abruptly if Miss Lennox was nervous. Guy, who was not to accompany them, had asked the same question in connection with something he was saying of Beechwood, but Magdalen did not heed the question then, or attach to it any importance. She was very anxious to be off, and was glad when, at last, the car began to move, and she knew she was leaving New York.

It was a warm, still day in early October, and Magdalen enjoyed the ride along the beautiful river, and was sorry when at last it came to an end, and she was left standing on the same platform where, years before, another young girl had stood looking about her, half sadly, half regretfully, and wishing herself away. It was a different carriage now which was waiting for the travellers, — a new, stylish carriage, drawn by two beautiful horses, which would have driven Frank Irving wild, and John, the coachman, in high-crowned hat and white gloves, was very deferential to Mrs. Seymour, and touched his hat to Magdalen, and saw them both into the carriage, and then, closing the door, mounted to his seat, and started up the mountain road, over which *Alice Grey* had ridden many a time, for it was to her that Magdalen was going. She knew it at last, for as they rode up the mountain side she said to Mrs. Seymour :

" I do not think you have told me the name of your niece. I have heard you call her Alice, and that is all I know of her."

" Surely, you must excuse me;" Mrs. Seymour replied ; " I thought I had told you that her name was Alice Grey. You may have heard of her from Mr. Irving. We met him abroad, and again in New York."

" Yes, I have heard of her," Magdalen replied, her face flushing, and her heart beating rapidly as she thought of the strange Providence which was leading her to one of whom she had heard so much, and of whom when a little girl she had been so jealous.

" Hers is a most lovely character, and you are sure to like her," Mrs. Seymour continued. " She has been sorely tried. We are all sorely tried. You told me, I think, that you were not nervous ? "

This was the second time she had put the question to Magdalen, who was not now quite so certain of her nerves as she had been when the question was asked her before ; but Mrs. Seymour did not wait for an answer, for just then they came in sight of the house, which she pointed out to Magdalen, who thought of Millbank as she rode through the handsome grounds and caught glimpses of the river in the distance. The carriage stopped at last at a side door, and conducting Magdalen into a little reception-room Mrs. Seymour asked the servant who met them, "where Miss Grey was?"

Magdalen could not hear the answer, it was so low; but she saw a cloud on Mrs. Seymour's brow and divined that something was wrong.

"Show Miss Lennox to her room, the one next to my niece's," the lady said, and Magdalen followed the girl to a large upper room the windows of which looked out upon the river and the country beyond.

It was very pleasant there, and Magdalen threw off her hat and shawl and was just seating herself by the window for a better view of the charming prospect, when there came a gentle knock at her door, and a sweet musical voice said softly, "Please, may I come in?"

CHAPTER XXXV.

ALICE AND MAGDALEN.

MAGDALEN gave one anxious glance at herself in the mirror as she sprang up, and then hastened to unbolt the door and admit Alice Grey. She knew it was Alice, though she had never imagined her one half so beautiful as she seemed now in her white dress, with her chestnut hair falling in soft curls about her face and neck, and her great dreamy blue eyes, which had something so pitiful and pleading in their expression. She was very slight and not as tall as Magdalen, who felt herself a great deal larger and older than the little, pale-faced girl, whose white cheeks had in them just the faintest coloring of pink as she held out her hand and said, "You are Miss Lennox, I know. Auntie wanted me to wait till she could introduce me, or till you came down to dinner, but I was anxious to see somebody young and new, and fresh. I go out so little that I get tired of the faces seen every day."

" Perhaps you will get tired of mine," Magdalen suggested, laughingly.

" Perhaps I may, but it will be a long time first," Alice replied, leading Magdalen to the window where she could see her more distinctly.

There was an expression of surprise or wonder, or both, in her face now, as she said, " Where have I met you before, Miss Lennox ? "

" I do not think we have ever met before ; at least not to my knowledge," Magdalen replied, while Alice continued :

" I must have seen you or somebody like you. I can't be mistaken in those eyes. Why, they are like — "

Alice stopped suddenly, and the color all faded from her cheeks and lips, while Magdalen looked curiously at her.

" You've never been abroad ? " Alice asked, after a moment, during which she had studied Magdalen closely.

" Never," was the reply, and Alice continued :

" And I have been away seven years, and so it cannot be ; but you do not seem a stranger, and I am so glad. I opposed your coming at first, — that is, I was opposed to having any one come just to entertain me, and when auntie wrote from New York that she had engaged a Miss Lennox, I saw you directly, some tall, lank, ugly woman, who wore glasses and would bore me terribly.

" Do I come up to your ideal," Magdalen asked, her heart warming more and more toward the young girl, who replied :

" You are seeking for a compliment, for of course you know just how beautiful and brilliant and sparkling you are ; only that sudden turn of your head and flash of your eyes does bother me so. And you are young, too. As young as I am, I guess. I am twenty-one."

" And I am nineteen," Magdalen rejoined, while Alice exclaimed :

" Only nineteen ! That *is* young to be doing for one's self ; young to come here, to care for me, in *this* house."

She seemed to be talking in an absent kind of way, and her

eyes, which were looking far off across the river, had in them a sad, sorry expression, as if to care for *her*, in *that* house, was a lot not to be envied. Turning suddenly to Magdalen, she asked: "*Are you nervous, Miss Lennox?*"

That was the fourth time this question had been put to Magdalen, who laughed a little hysterically as she replied:

"I never supposed I was, but fear I shall be if questioned again upon the subject. Your aunt asked me twice if I was nervous, and Mr. Guy Seymour once."

As she said the last name, Alice colored a little, but she merely answered:

"You saw cousin Guy in New York; auntie's husband was his uncle, but I call him cousin just the same. Did he say when he was coming to Beechwood?"

"At Christmas, I believe," Magdalen replied, wondering that Alice paid no heed to what she had said of her nervousness.

She was standing with her hands clasped, and the same expression in her eyes which Magdalen had observed before. She was evidently thinking of something foreign to Guy Seymour, or nervousness, and she stood thus until Magdalen heard in the hall outside the opening of a door, and caught the faintest possible sound like a human cry. She might not have noticed it at all but for the effect it had on Alice, who started suddenly from her dreamy attitude, and said:

"I must go now, Miss Lennox. I shall see you at dinner, which will be served in an hour. I am so glad you have come to me. I feel stronger with you already, — feel as if you would do me good, — do us all good, perhaps. *Au revoir*, till dinner time."

She flitted from the room, and Magdalen heard again the quick closing of a door down the hall. Then all was still, and the house was as silent as if she were its only occupant. It had not occurred to her that there was any mystery at Beechwood, any grief or shame which the family tried to cover up, but the moment Alice was gone she felt a weight settling down upon her, a feeling of loneliness and desolation, which she

called homesickness, and burying her face among the pillows of
the tempting-looking bed, she wept bitterly for a few moments.
Then, remembering dinner, she dried her eyes and commenced
unpacking her trunks, which had been sent up while Alice was
with her.

"I shall not be expected to dress much. This will do very
nicely," she thought, as she shook out the folds of a heavy black
silk, made the winter before by Mrs. Irving's dressmaker.

It was trimmed with the softest, daintiest lace, for everything
pertaining to her wardrobe had been perfect, and she looked fit
to grace any assemblage when at last Alice came to take
her down to the parlor, where Arthur Grey was waiting for
them.

CHAPTER XXXVI.

MR. GREY AND MAGDALEN.

MR. GREY had heard from his sister that Magdalen came
from Millbank, where she had lived in the Irving family
until the finding of the will, and for a few moments he
had felt as if he could not have her there at Beechwood, recalling by her presence what he would so gladly have forgotten.
Why was it that the Irvings, or some one connected with them,
were always crossing his path. Surely he had been sufficiently
punished for poor Jessie's death. His most implacable enemy
could have asked no greater sorrow for him than he had experienced for years, save at times when in foreign scenes he forgot in part the horror and the burden which since his return to
America had pressed heavier than before.

"The girl is a lady and very handsome too, though of a far
different style from Alice. I hope you will try to like her,

Arthur," his sister had said to him, as she saw a shadow on his face and felt that in some way he was displeased.

"Of course I can have nothing against the girl," Mr. Grey replied, "though there are reasons why any thing connected with the Irvings should be distasteful to me, and I would rather Miss Lennox had come from some other family."

He left his sister then, and went to his own room, where on the wall was still hanging that little pencil sketch of the grave-yard in Belvidere, and the barefoot girl standing in the grass with the basket of flowers on her arm. That Miss Lennox was the original of that picture, Mr. Grey did not doubt. She had told him that her name was Magdalen, and that she had always lived at Millbank, so there could be no mistake. He had scarcely thought of that incident for years, but it came back to him now and struck him as very strange that this same barefoot girl should have come there as companion to his daughter.

"Should she ever enter this room, and there's no knowing where Alice may take her, she will see this picture and recog-nize it at once, and wonder where I found it and possibly rec-ognize me as the stranger who talked with her in the graveyard. It is better out of sight," he said, as he took the drawing from the wall and laid it away in the drawer where the lock of golden hair was, and the faded bouquet which the "wretch of a Jim Bartlett" once had the credit of stealing. And all this time the man trod softly, as if fearful of being heard and called for, and he looked often toward the door which opened into the adjoin-ing room. But everything was still ; the *Burden* was sleeping at last, lulled into quiet by the sweet music of " Allie's " voice and the touch of " Allie's " hands.

Having put the picture away, Mr. Grey made himself ready for dinner, and then going down to the parlor, he stood before the grate, waiting for his daughter and Miss Lennox. The door was open into the hall, and he saw them as they came, with their arms interlaced, and Magdalen's head bent towards Alice, who was smiling up at her.

"Strong friendship at once," he thought, feeling for a moment vexed that his high-bred daughter, should so soon have fallen in love with her hired companion.

But this emotion of pride passed away forever with Mr. Grey's first full inspection of Magdalen Lennox, whose brilliant beauty startled and surprised him, and whose bright, restless eyes confounded and bewildered him, carrying him back to the Schodick hills, and the orchard where the apple blossoms were growing. But not there could he find the solution of the strange feeling which swept over him and kept him silent, even after Alice had introduced her friend.

"Miss Lennox, father," Alice said, a second time, and then he came to himself, and said, " Excuse me, Miss Lennox, something about you, as you came in, sent me off into the fields of memory, in quest of some one who must have been like you. You are very welcome to Beechwood, and I am glad to see you here."

With a courtly grace he offered her his arm, and led her to the dining room, followed by Alice and his sister, both of whom were delighted to see him take so kindly to a stranger.

To Mrs. Seymour it showed an acknowledgment on his part of her good taste and judgment in selecting so fitting a person for Alice's companion, and a willingness to follow her advice, and make the best of it, even if Miss Lennox was connected with the Irvings. *She* knew something of Jessie's story. She saw her once in Schodick, and she had done what she could to separate her brother from her, but she did not know of the tragic ending, and she gave no thought to the poor, drowned woman, who, all through the formal dinner, was so constantly in Magdalen's mind. She had at once identified Mr. Grey with the stranger in Belvidere, though he seemed older than she had thought him then. Still, there was no mistaking him, and when his sister casually addressed him as "Arthur," it came over her, with a great shock, that this man was none other than the "Arthur Grey" who had been poor Jessie's ruin, and whom Roger hated so cordially. There could be no mistake; she was positive that she was right in her conclusions, and felt for a moment as if she were smothering. What strange fatality was it which had brought her into the very household of the man she had hated, for Roger's sake, and longed to see that she might tell him so. She *had* seen him, at last! he was there, at her side, speaking to her so kindly, and making her feel so much at home, that she could *not* hate him, and before dinner was over she had ceased to wonder at Jessie's infatuation, or to blame her for listening to him. He was very polite to her, but seemed to be studying her face as intently as Alice had done at first, and once, when she poised her head upon one side, while her eyes flashed suddenly upon him, and then were quickly withdrawn, the blood came rushing to his face and crept up under his hair, for he knew now of whom that motion reminded him. He had thought it so charming once, and the eyes which shone upon him as Magdalen's did had been so beautiful, and soft, and liquid, and given no sign of the fierce wildness with which they had many a time glared on him since.

"It is only a resemblance, but I would rather it did not exist," he thought, as he met that look again, and shivered as if he was cold.

Dinner being over they returned to the parlor, where, at Alice's request, Magdalen seated herself at the piano. Her home-sickness was passing away, and she no longer felt that a nightmare was oppressing her, but rather that she should find at Beechwood peace and quiet and a home, and she sang with her whole soul, and did not hear the sound outside, which caught Alice's attention so quickly, and took her from the room. She knew, however, when Alice went out, and a moment after was conscious of some confusion by the door, and heard Alice's voice, first in expostulation and entreaty, then calling hurriedly for her father to come. Then Mr. Grey went out, and Mrs. Seymour was left alone with Magdalen, who finished her song and left the piano, wondering what it was which had taken both Mr. Grey and Alice so suddenly from the room, and kept them away for half an hour or more. Indeed, Mr

Grey did not return at all, and when, at last, Alice came back, she was very white, and said something to her aunt, which sounded like, "It was the music, which affected her, I think."

Was there a mystery at Beechwood, Magdalen thought; a something hidden from view, and was it this which made Alice look so sad even while she tried to smile, and appear gay and cheerful, by way of entertaining her new friend?

They had the parlor to themselves ere long, for Mrs. Seymour went out, and then Alice took her seat on the couch, where Magdalen was sitting, and nestled close to her, as a child nestles to its mother when it is tired and wants to be soothed.

Passing her arm around the slender waist, Magdalen drew the curly head down on her bosom, and gently smoothed the chestnut hair, and passed her hand caressingly across the fore-head, where the blue veins showed so plainly.

Magdalen was not given to sudden friendships, and she could not account for the love and tenderness she felt growing so fast within her for this young girl, who lay encircled in her arms, and who she knew at last was crying, for she felt the hot tears dropping on her hand. She could not offer sympathy in words, for she did not know what to say, but she stooped and kissed the flushed cheek wet with tears. Alice understood her, and the silent crying became a low, piteous sobbing, which told how keenly her heart was wrung.

"Pray excuse me, for giving way so foolishly," Alice said at last, as she lifted up her head. "I was ill so long in Europe, and the voyage home was rough and stormy, and I kept my berth the entire two weeks we were out at sea, so that by the time New York was reached I could not stand alone. I am better now; home scenes and mountain air have done me good, but — but — oh, Miss Lennox, I cannot tell you now of the shadow which has cast a gloom over my whole life. Why, I have seen the time when my beautiful home had scarcely a charm for me, and in my wickedness I accused God of dealing too harshly with me. But He has been so good to me, who do not deserve kindness from Him. When I knew you were

coming I went away among the hills and prayed that I might
like you, — that your presence would do me good, — and I am
certain the prayer was answered.   I do like you.   I feel a firm
conviction that in some way you are destined to do us all an
untold good.   You do not seem like a stranger, but rather like
a familiar friend, or I should not be talking to you as I am.
Have you sisters, Miss Lennox?"

The moment which Magdalen dreaded had come, when she
was to be questioned by Alice with regard to her family, and
she resolved to be perfectly frank, and keep nothing back which
it was proper for her to tell.

"I have no sisters that I am aware of," she said.   "I was
adopted, when a little baby, by Mr. Roger Irving, who lived at
Millbank, and was himself a boy then.   The circumstances of
my adoption were very peculiar, and such as precluded the
possibility of my knowing anything of my family friends, if I had
any.   I have never known a sister's love or a brother's, or a
father's or mother's, though I have been as kindly and tenderly
cared for as if I had been the petted child of fond parents, and
only an adverse turn in the wheel of fortune sent me from the
home I loved so much."

She paused here, and Alice rejoined, "Mr. Irving?   Millbank?   Why, both are familiar names to me, and have been
since I was a little girl at school in New Haven and knew Mr.
Franklin Irving.   And *you*, — why, yes, —" and Alice's manner grew more and more excited, "you are the very Magdalen Frank used to tell me about and of whom I was sometimes
jealous.   You know Frank," she continued, misconstruing the
expression of Magdalen's face.

"Yes, I know Frank," Magdalen replied, "and I, too, have
heard a great deal of *you*, and was jealous of you at one time,
I believe."

"You had no cause," Alice replied, thinking of the "Piccola
Sentinella," rather than of New Haven; "I liked Mr. Irving
very much as a boy, and when we met him abroad I was very
glad to see him and rather encouraged his visits than otherwise,

but father disliked him thoroughly, or seemed to, and treated him so cavalierly that I wondered he could come to us at all. But he did, and then father took me away, and I saw Mr. Irving no more till he called upon me in New York. I was sick then and did not go out, but I heard of a Miss Lennox who was with the Irvings and said to be very beautiful, and that was you."

"I was with the Irvings," Magdalen replied, and Alice continued : "I fancied, then, that Mr. Irving would eventually marry you and speculated a good deal upon the matter. It seems so funny that *you* are *here !* I do not understand it at all, or why you should leave Millbank. Mr. Frank Irving is the heir now, is he not ? "

Magdalen hesitated a moment, and then thinking it better to do so, told briefly of her life at Millbank until that luckless day when she discovered the will.

"After that Roger went to Schodick," she said, "and I — I might have stayed there, but I did not like Mrs. Irving's manner towards me when she became the mistress, and I could not be dependent upon Frank, and so I came away."

Alice knew that Magdalen was withholding something from her, and with a woman's wit guessed that it concerned Frank ; but she would not question her, and turned the conversation into another channel, and talked of the books she had read and the authors she liked best.

It was comparatively early when Magdalen went up to her room, a door of which communicated with Alice's. This the latter desired should stand open.

"I like to feel that some one is near me when I wake in the night, as I often do," Alice said, and then she added, "I shall be obliged to leave you for a time, but do you go straight to bed. I know you must be tired. I shall come in so softly that you will not hear me. Good night."

She kissed Magdalen and then went from the room and down the hall toward the door, which Magdalen had heard open and shut so many times. Magdalen *was* very tired, and was soon

sleeping so soundly that she did not hear Alice when she came
back, but she dreamed there were angels with her clad in white,
and with a start she woke to find the moonlight streaming into
her chamber, and making it so light that she could see distinctly the young girl in the adjoining room was kneeling
by the bed, her hands clasped together and her upturned
face bathed in the silvery light, which made it like the face of
an angel. She was praying softly, and in the deep stillness of
the night every whisper was audible to Magdalen, who heard
her asking Heaven for strength to bear the *burden* patiently,
and never to get tired and weary and wish it somewhere else.
Then the nature of the prayer changed, and Magdalen knew
that Alice was thanking Heaven for sending her to Beechwood.
"And if anywhere in the world there are still living the friends
she has never known, oh, Father, let her find them, especially
her mother, — it is so terrible to have no mother."

That was what Alice said, and Magdalen's tears fell like rain
to hear this young girl pleading for her as she had never
pleaded for herself. She had prayed, it is true. She always
prayed both morning and at night, but they were mere formal
prayers, and not at all like Alice's. Hers were earnest, hers
were heartfelt, and Magdalen knew that she was speaking to a
real, living presence ; that the Saviour to whom she talked was
there with her in the moonlit room as really as if she saw him
bodily. Alice's was a living faith, which brought Heaven down
to her side, and Magdalen felt that there *were* indeed angels
abiding round about her, and that Alice was one of them.

CHAPTER XXXVII.

LIFE AT BEECHWOOD.

HE next morning was bright and beautiful, as mornings in early October often are, when the summer seems to linger amid flower and shrub, as if loth to quit the glories its own sunshine and showers had created.

The mist still lay in soft clouds upon the river and on the mountain sides, when Magdalen arose, and, leaning from her window, drank in the bracing morning air, and acknowledged to herself that Beechwood was almost as beautiful as Millbank. She had slept quietly, and felt her old life and vigor coming back to her again as she hastened to dress herself.

She had heard no sound as yet, except the tread of a servant in the yard, and the baying of the Newfoundland dog up the mountain path.

Alice was not in her own room. She must have dressed and gone out before Magdalen awoke, and the latter was hesitating whether to go down to the parlor, or to remain where she was, when Alice appeared, her blue eyes shining brightly, and a faint flush upon her cheek.

"I slept *so* well because you were here near me," she said as she linked her arm in Magdalen's, and started for the dining-room.

As they passed through the hall, Magdalen noticed at the farther extremity a green baize door, which seemed to divide that part of the hall from the other, and which she knew by the location was the door which she had heard shut so many times. Where did it lead to? What was there behind it? What embodiment of sorrow and pain was hidden away in that portion of the building? That there was *somebody* there, Magdalen was sure; for, just as she reached the head of the stairs she saw a servant girl coming up a side staircase, bearing in her arms a silver tray, on which was arranged a tempting breakfast for an invalid.

"I shall know all in good time," she thought, and she pretended not to see the girl, and kept on talking to Alice until the dining-room was reached, where Mr. Grey and his sister were waiting for them. Both seemed in unusually good spirits, and Mr. Grey kissed his daughter fondly as she nestled close to him and smiled up into his face with all the love of a trusting, affectionate daughter. The sight for a moment smote Magdalen with a keen sense of desolation and loneliness. Never had she known, — never could know the happiness of a father's watchful love and care, and never had she felt its loss as keenly as she felt it now, when she saw the caressing tenderness which Mr. Grey bestowed upon his daughter and the eagerness with which it was returned. They were both very kind to her, and treated her more like a guest than one who had come to them as a hired companion.

It was a delightful day for driving; and after breakfast was over, Alice asked for the carriage and took Magdalen to all her favorite resorts, down by the river and up among the hills, where she said she often went and sat for hours alone. They were firmer friends than ever before that drive was over, and Alice had dropped "Miss Lennox" for the more familiar "Magdalen," and had asked that she should be simply "Alice," and not that formal "Miss Grey."

That afternoon Magdalen wrote a short letter to Hester Floyd, telling her where she was, explaining how she chanced to be there, and going into ecstasies over the loveliness and beauty of Alice Grey, but never hinting at Mr. Grey's identity with the man who had tempted Jessie to sin. It was as well to keep that to herself, she thought, inasmuch as the telling it would only awaken bitter memories in Roger's heart. Once she determined not to speak of Roger at all, but that would be too marked a neglect, and so she asked to be remembered to him, and said she should never forget his kindness to her, or cease to regret the meddlesome curiosity which had resulted so

disastrously for him. She made no mention of either Mrs
Walter Scott or Frank. She merely said she left Millbank at such
a time, and expressed herself as glad to get away, it seemed
so changed from the happy home it used to be in other days.

"Mrs. Hester Floyd. Care of Roger Irving, Esq., Schodick, N. H.," was the direction of the letter which Magdalen
gave to Mr. Grey, who was going to the post-office and offered
to take it for her. Very narrowly she watched him as he
glanced at the superscription, and she half pitied him when she
saw his lips quiver and turn pale for a moment as he read the
name of a place which he remembered so well. Once in his
life *he* had sent letters to that very town, and the Schodick
post-mark was not an unfamiliar one to him. Now she to
whom he had written was dead, and he held a letter directed
to the care of her son. How he longed to ask something concerning him, and finally he did so, saying in a half indifferent
tone, " Schodick ? — I once spent a summer there, and I have
heard of Mr. Irving. Does he live in the village ?"

" No, sir, he lives at his mother's old home. They call it
the Morton farm. Did you know his mother, Jessie Morton ?"

Magdalen put the question purposely, but regretted it when
she saw the look of intense pain which flitted across Mr. Grey's
face.

" I knew her, yes. She was the most beautiful woman I
ever saw," he replied, and then he turned away and walked
slowly from the room with his head bent down, as if his thoughts
were busy with the past.

The days succeeding that first one at Beechwood went rapidly by, and each one found Magdalen happier and more contented with her situation as companion of Alice, who strove in
so many ways to make her feel that she was in all respects her
equal, instead of a person hired to minister to her. Indeed,
the hired part seemed only nominal, for nothing was ever required of Magdalen which would not have been required of her
had she been a daughter of the house and Alice her invalid

sister. They rode together, and walked together, and read together, and slept together at last, for Alice would have it so, and every morning of her life Magdalen was awakened by the soft touch of Alice's hand upon her cheek, and the kiss upon her brow.

To Magdalen this was a new and blissful experience. At Millbank she had always been alone, so far as girls of her own age were concerned, and Alice Grey seemed to her the embodiment of all that was pure and beautiful, and she loved her with a devotion that sometimes startled herself with its intenseness. The mystery, if there was one, was very quiet now, and though Alice went often down the hall and through the green baize door, she never looked as sad and tired when she came back as she had done on that first day at Beechwood. Mr. Grey, too, frequently passed the entire evening with the young girls in the parlor, where Magdalen, who was a very fine reader, read to them aloud from Alice's favorite authors. But after the first night she was never asked to *sing*. Alice often requested her to play, and they had learned a few duets which they practised together, but songs were never mentioned, and Magdalen would have fancied that there was something disagreeable in her voice were it not that when alone with Alice among the hills and down by the river, whither they often went, her companion always insisted upon her singing, and would sit listening to her as if spell-bound by the clear, liquid tones.

At last there came a letter from Hester Floyd, who, in her characteristic way, expressed herself as pleased that Magdalen "had grit enough to cut loose from the whole coboodle at Millbank, and go to do for herself. I was some taken aback," she wrote, " for I s'posed by the tell that you was to marry that pimpin, white-faced Frank, and I must say you showed your good sense by quittin' him, and doin' for yourself. Me and Roger would have been glad for you to come here ; that is, I *b'leeve* Roger would, though he never sed nothin' particklar. He's some altered, and don't talk so much, nor 'pear so chipper as he used to do, and I mistrust he misses *you* more'n he does his money. He's a good deal looked up to, both in the town and in the church, where they've made him a vestry-man in place of a man who died, and 'twould seem as if he'd met with a change, though he allus was a good man, with no bad habits ; but he's different like now, and don't read news-papers Sunday, nor let me get up an extra dinner, and he has family prayers, which is all well enuff, only bakin' mornins it does hender some."

Then followed a description of the house and Schodick gen-erally, and then a break of two days or more, after which the old lady resumed her pen, and added : "Roger's got a letter from Frank, askin' if he knew where you was. He said you left while he was away unbeknownst to him, and had never writ a word, by which I take it you and he ain't on the fust ratest terms. Roger talked the most that day that he has in a month, and actually whistled, but then he'd just gained a suit, and so mabby it was that, though I b'leeve it wouldn't do no harm if you were to drop him a line in a friendly way. It's leap-year, you know."

This was Hester's letter, over which Magdalen pondered long, wondering if the old lady could have suspected her love for Roger, and how far she was right in thinking he missed her more than his money. Magdalen read that sentence many times, and her heart thrilled with delight at the thought of be-ing missed by Roger ; but from Hester's suggestion that she should write him a friendly line, she turned resolutely away. The time was gone by when she could write to Roger without his having first written to her. After that interview in the library, when his kisses had burned into her heart, and his pas-sionate words, "Magda, my darling," had burned into her memory, she would be less than a woman to make the first ad-vances. Concessions, if there were any, must come from him now. He knew how sorry she was about the will ; he had exonerated her from all blame in that matter, and now, if he had any stronger feelings for her than that of a friend, he must make it manifest. This was Magdalen's reasoning over the

Roger portion of Hester's letter, and then she thought of Frank, and felt a nervous dread lest he might follow her, though that seemed hardly possible, even if he knew where she was. Still he would undoubtedly write as soon as he could get her address from Roger, and she was not at all disappointed when, a week or two after the receipt of Hester's letter, Mr. Grey brought her one from Belvidere, directed in Frank's well known hand-writing. After obtaining her address he had written at once, chiding her for having left so suddenly without a word for him, and begging of her to return, or at least allow him to come for her, and take her back to her rightful place at Millbank.

"I can't imagine what freak of fortune led you to the Greys," he wrote. "It is the last place where I could wish you to be. Not that I do not respect and esteem Miss Grey as the sweetest, loveliest of women, but I distrust both her father and her aunt. For some reason they have never seemed to like me, and may say things derogatory of me; but if they do, I trust it will make no difference with you, for remember *you* have known me all your lifetime."

Magdalen wrote next day to Frank, who, as he read her letter, began for the first time to feel absolutely that she was lost to him forever. He was sure of that, and for a moment he wept like a child, thinking how gladly he would give up all his money if that would bring him Magdalen's love. But it was not in his nature to be unhappy long, and he soon dried his eyes and consoled himself with a drive after his fast bays, and in the evening when his mother mentioned to him the names of two or three young ladies from New York who were coming to Millbank for the holidays, and asked if there was any one in particular whom he wished to invite, he mentioned Miss Burleigh, whom he had met in Springfield. And so Bell was invited, and hastened to reply that she should be delighted to come, but feared she could not, as "pa never liked to be separated from his family at that time, and sister Grace would be home from school, and could not, of course, be left behind.'

She was so sorry, for she had heard such glowing accounts of Millbank, and its graceful mistress, that she ardently desired to see and know both, but as it was she must decline.

As might be supposed, the invitation to Miss Bell Burleigh was repeated, including this time the Judge and Grace, both of whom accepted, Grace for the entire holidays, and the Judge for a day or two, as he did not wish to crowd. And so Christmas bade fair to be kept at Millbank with more hilarity than ever it had been before. Every room was to be occupied, Bell and Grace Burleigh taking Magdalen's, for which Frank ordered a new and expensive carpet and chamber set, just as he had ordered new furniture for many of the other rooms. He was living on a grand scale, and had his income been what his principal was he could scarcely have been more munificent or lavish of his money. He was at the head of every charitable object in Belvidere and Springfield, and gave so largely that his name was frequently in the papers which he sent to Magdalen, with his pencil mark about the flattering notices ; and Magdalen smiled quietly as she read them and then showed them to Alice, who once laughingly remarked, "Suppose you refer him to Matthew vi. 2. It might be of some benefit to him." And that was all the good Frank's ostentatious charity did him in that direction.

Meantime the tide of life moved on, and Christmas came, and the invited guests arrived at Millbank, where there were such revellings and dissipations as the people of Belvidere had never seen, and where Bell Burleigh's bold, black eyes flashed and sparkled and took in everything, and saw so many places where a change would be desirable should Millbank ever have another mistress than Mrs. Walter Scott.

Guy Seymour, too, had his holidays at Beechwood, which seemed a different place with his great, kind heart, his quick appreciation of another's wants, his unfailing wit and humor, his merry whistle and exhilarating laugh, his good-natured teasing of Auntie Pen, and his entire devotion to Alice, who was rather reserved toward him, but who talked a great deal of him to Magdalen when they were alone, and *cried* when at last he went away.

CHAPTER XXXVIII.

THE MYSTERY AT BEECHWOOD.

 DAY or two after Guy's return to New York there came to Beechwood a tall, muscular-looking woman, whom Alice called Mrs. Jenks, and for whom Magdalen could see no possible use. She did not consort with the family, nor with the servants, and Magdalen often met her in the upper hall, and saw her disappearing through the green baize door. It was about this time, too, that Mr. Grey left home for Cincinnati, and the household settled down into a state of quiet and loneliness, which, contrasting as it did with the merry holidays when Guy Seymour was there, seemed to both girls very hard to bear.

Alice was unusually restless, and when at last Guy wrote telling of a famous singer who had just appeared in New York, and asking them all to come down for a few days and hear for themselves, she caught eagerly at it, and overruling every objection, won her aunt's consent to going. Magdalen was to accompany them, and she was anticipating the trip and what it might bring about, for Hester Floyd had written that *Roger* was in New York. But when the morning fixed upon for their journey came she was suffering with a prevailing influenza which made the trip impossible for her. She, however, insisted upon Alice's going without her, and so for a few days she was left alone in the house so far as congenial companionship was concerned. Mrs. Jenks she never saw, though she knew she was there; for as she grew better and able to be about the parlors and library she heard the servants speak of the amount of *wine* she ordered with her dinner, while one of them added in a whisper, "Suppose she should get drunk and there should be a row, wouldn't we be in a pretty mess. Nobody could contro. her."

Magdalen was not timid, but after this she kept her dooi locked at night, while during the day she frequently caught herself listening intently as if expecting something to happen. But nothing did happen until one night when she went as usual to the parlor, where she sat down to the piano and tried a new piece of music which Guy had sent to Alice. Finding it rather difficult, she cast it aside and dashed off something more familiar to her. On the music stand were piles and piles of songs, some her own, some Alice's, and she looked them over, and selecting one which had always been her favorite, she began to sing, feeling much as an imprisoned bird must feel when it finds itself free again, for since her first night at Beechwood she had never been asked to sing with the piano. Now, however, she was alone, and she sang on and on, her voice, which had been out of practice so long, gathering strength and sweetness until the whole house was full of the clear, liquid tones, and the servants, still dawdling over their supper, commented upon the music and held their breath to listen. One of them had brought a lamp into the room before going to her tea, and this with the fire in the grate was all the light there was; but it answered every purpose for Magdalen, who enjoyed the dim twilight and the flickering shadows on the wall, and kept on with her singing, while through the upper hall there came stealing softly the figure of a woman with her white night-dress trailing on the carpet, and her bare feet giving back no echo to her stealthy footsteps. She had come through the green baize door, and she paused there a moment and turned her ear in the direction whence she had come. But all was quiet. There was no one watching her, and with a cunning gleam in her restless, black eyes, she shut the door softly, then opened it again, and went back down the long hall until she reached a door which was partly ajar. This she also shut, and turning the key took it in her hand and started again for the music which had set her poor brain to throbbing, and quickened the blood in her veins until every nerve was quivering with excitement.

"I am coming, oh, I'm coming. Don't you hear me as I come?" sang Magdalen, while down the stairs and through the hall came the unseen visitor until she reached the parlor door, where she stood for a moment in the attitude of listening, while her eyes were fixed upon Magdalen with a curious, inquiring look.

Then they rolled restlessly about the room, and took in every thing from the picture on the wall to the fire in the grate, and then went back again to the young girl, still singing her song of summer. The music evidently had a soothing effect upon the poor, crazed creature, and her eyes were soft and pleasant and moist with tears as she drew near to Magdalen, who at last felt the hot breath upon her neck, and knew there was some one behind her. There was a violent start, then a sudden crash among the keys, as Magdalen felt not only the breath, but the touch of the long, white fingers, which clasped her shoulder so firmly. She could see the fingers as they held to her dress, but only the outline of a human form was visible, and so she did not scream until she turned her head and saw the white-robed woman, with the long hair falling down her back, the peculiar look of insanity in every feature. Then a shriek, loud and unearthly, rang through the house, followed by another and still another, as she felt the woman's arm twining itself around her neck, and heard the woman's voice saying to her, "What are you, angel or devil, that you can move me so?"

Roused by the terrific shrieks, the servants came rushing to the parlor, where they found Magdalen fainted entirely away, with the maniac bending over her and peering into her face. When Magdalen came to herself, she was in her own room, and the girl, Honora, who waited on her in the absence of Pauline, was sitting by and caring for her. She did not seem inclined to talk, and to Magdalen's inquiries, "Oh, what was it, and shall I see it again?" she merely replied, "You'll not be troubled any more. It was the fault of Mrs. Jenks. She drank half a bottle of wine since noon and is drunk as a beast."

That was all the explanation Magdalen could get, and as she recovered rapidly from the effects of her fainting fit, she signified her wish to be left alone ; but she did not venture to the parlor again that night, and she saw that both the doors leading from her room and Alice's into the hall were locked, and bolted, too. Then she tried to reason herself into a tolerable degree of calmness and quiet, as she thought over the events of the evening and wondered who the maniac was.

"Alice's mother, most likely," she said, and a great throb of pity swept over her for the young girl whose life had been so darkened and who had possibly never known a mother's love any more than she herself had done.

And then her thoughts went out after her own mother, with a longing desire such as she had seldom felt. Where was she that wintry night ? Was she far from or was she near to the daughter who had never seen her face to remember it ? Was she living still, or was the snow piled upon her grave, and would not Magdalen rather have her thus than like the babbling maniac who had startled her so in the parlor? She believed she would. In one sense Alice was more to be pitied than herself, and she sat thinking of the young girl and the shadow on her life until the fire burned out upon the hearth, and she crept shivering to bed. But not to sleep. She could not do that for the peculiar cry, half human, half unearthly, which from time to time kept coming to her ears, and in which she recognized tones like the voice heard an instant in the parlor before consciousness forsook her. There was evidently a great commotion throughout the house, the servants running to and fro ; but no one came near her until the early dawn was stealing into the room, and giving definite shapes and forms to the objects about her. Then there was a tap at her door, and Honora's voice said :

"Miss Lennox, will you come with me and see what you can do to quiet her ? She's kept screeching for you all night, and Mrs. Jenks, who is in her senses now, says maybe you can influence her. Strangers sometimes do. I'll wait outside till you

are ready. You needn't be afraid, — she never hurt any
body."

Magdalen trembled in every joint, and her teeth fairly chat
tered as she hastened to dress herself.

"It's because I'm cold; there certainly is nothing to fear,"
she thought, as she bound her hair under a net and knotted
her dressing-gown around her waist.

She had never been through the baize door, and as Honora
held it for her to pass she felt for a moment as if trespassing
upon forbidden ground. But the door swung to behind her.
She was shut into a narrow hall, with two doors on the right
hand side, and one of them ajar. The mystery she was going
to confront was beyond that door, she knew, for a moaning cry
of "Let me go to her, I tell you," met her ear, and made her
draw a little closer to Honora, who said to her, reassuringly,
"There is nothing to fear; she is perfectly harmless."

"Yes; but tell me, please, who it is," Magdalen said, clutch
ing the arm of the girl, who replied:

"Oh, I supposed you knew. It is *Mrs. Grey.*"

Magdalen's conjectures were correct, and she went fearlessly
up to the door, which Honora opened wide and then shut behind
her, leaving her standing just across the threshold in the room
which held the Mystery at Beechwood.

CHAPTER XXXIX.

MAGDALEN AND THE MYSTERY.

 MYSTERY no longer, but a living, breathing, panting
woman, with wild, rolling eyes, masses of jet-black
hair streaked with gray streaming down her back, and
long white arms and hands, which beat the air helplessly as she
tried to escape from the firm grasp of her attendant, Mrs.
Jenks. It was Magdalen's first close contact with a maniac,

and she drew back a step or two, appalled by the wild out-cry with which the woman greeted her, and the desperate spring she made toward the spot where she was standing. For an instant she was tempted to flee from the room, but Mrs. Jenks had her patient under control by virtue of superior strength. There was no escaping from the vice-like grasp of her strong arms, and so Magdalen stood still and gazed spell-bound upon the terrible spectacle.

"Come nearer and see what effect your speaking to her will have. She has asked for you all night; she will not hurt you," Mrs. Jenks said, and Magdalen went up to the poor, restless, tossing creature, and sitting down upon the bed took in her own the hot hand which was extended toward her.

"Can I do anything for you, Mrs. Grey?" she said, softly caressing the wasted hand which held hers so tightly.

Quick as lightning a gleam of anger shot from the black eyes as the woman replied :

"Don't insult *me* by calling me *Mrs. Grey.* That name has been a curse to me from the moment I bore it. Call me *Laura,* or nothing!"

"Well, then, Laura, can I do anything to make you better?" Magdalen said, and the woman replied, "Yes, stay with me al-ways, and sing as you did last night when I thought the angels called me ; and put your hand on my head ; — feel how hot it is. There is a lost baby's soul in there, burning up for my sin."

She carried Magdalen's hand to her forehead, which was hot with fever and excitement, and Magdalen could feel the blood throbbing through the swollen veins.

"Poor Laura," she said, "poor, sick woman! I am so sorry for you. I would have come before if I had known you wanted me."

"Yes but don't waste time in words. I've had a plenty of those all my life. Sing! sing! sing!— that is what I want," in-terrupted the crazy woman, and sitting on the bed, with the hot hand grasping hers, Magdalen tried to think what she could sing that would soothe her excited patient.

There was a trembling in her joints and a choking sensation in her throat which seemed to preclude the possibility of her singing, but she made a great effort to control herself, and at last began the beautiful hymn, "Peace, troubled soul," her voice growing in steadiness and sweetness and volume as she saw the effect it had upon poor Laura, whose eyes grew soft and gentle, and finally filled with tears, which rolled in great drops down her sunken cheeks.

Mrs. Jenks had relaxed her vigilance now, and Laura lay perfectly still, listening with rapt attention to the song, and keeping her eyes fixed upon Magdalen's face, as if there were some spell to hold them there.

"Who are you?" she asked, when the song had ceased. "Where did you come from and what is your name?"

I came to live with Alice. You know Alice," Magdalen said, — "she is your daughter."

"Yes, one of them; but not *that* one, over there in the cradle. Please give it a little jog. I can't have my baby waking up and crying, for that disturbs Arthur, and he might send it away to goat's milk and a wet nurse. Give it a jog, please."

She pointed to the head of her bed, and for the first time Magdalen observed a pretty little rosewood crib, with dainty pillow-cases, ruffled and fluted, and snowy Marseilles quilt, spotlessly white and clean. But there was no infant's head upon the pillow, no little hands outside the spread, or sound of infant's breathing.

The crib was empty, and Magdalen glanced inquiringly at Mrs. Jenks, who said:

"You may as well rock it first as last. She will give you no peace till you do. It's a fancy of hers that there's a baby there, and she sometimes rocks it day and night. She is always quiet when she is on that tack, but sometimes the baby gets out of the cradle into her head, and then there is no pacifying her. Her tantrum is over now, and, if you are willing, I'll leave her with you a few moments. I shan't be out of hearing. My room is across the hall."

She was evidently anxious to get away; and Magdalen, who would not confess to any fear, was left alone with the crazy woman. She had drawn the crib nearer to her, and with her foot upon the rocker kept it in motion, while Laura commenced a low, cooing sort of lullaby of "Hush, my darling! mother's near you!"

The novelty of her situation, and the wakefulness of the previous night, began to have a strange effect on Magdalen, and, as she rocked the cradle to the sound of that low, mournful music, it seemed to her as if it were her own self she was rocking, herself far back in that past of which she knew so little. There was a dizzy feeling in her head, a humming in her ears, and for a few moments she felt almost as crazy as the woman at her side. But as she became more accustomed to the room and the situation, she grew calmer and less nervous, and could think what it was better to reply to the strange questions her companion sometimes put to her.

"If a person killed something and didn't know it, and didn't mean to, and didn't know as they had killed it, would God call them a murderer, as He did Cain?"

This was one question, and Magdalen replied at random, that in such a case it was no murder, and God would not so consider it.

"Then why has He branded me here in my head, where it keeps thump, thump! just like the beating of a drum, and where it is so hot and snarled?" Laura asked. Then, before Magdalen could reply, she continued: "I did not mean to kill it, and I don't think I did. I put it somewhere, or gave it to somebody; but the more I try to think, the more it thumps, and thumps, and I can't make it out; only I didn't; didn't truly mean to kill it. Oh, baby! No, no! I didn't! I didn't!"

She was sobbing in a pitiful kind of way, and Magdalen moved her position so that she could take the poor, tired, "twisted" head upon her bosom, while she soothed and comforted the moaning woman, softly smoothing her tangled hair

and asking her, at last, if she would not like it brushed and put
up out of her way.

" It will look nicer so," she said ; and, as Laura made no objection, she brought the brush and comb from a little basket on
the bureau, and then set herself to the task of combing out the
matted hair, which had been sorely neglected since Alice went
away.

" Allie will be glad to know I am so nice. She likes me
neat and tidy, but a woman with a child to tend cannot always
keep herself as she would," Laura said, when the hair-dressing
was ended and Magdalen had buttoned her night-dress, and
thrown around her a crimson shawl which hung across the bed.

The woman herself was rocking the cradle now, and signal-
ing Magdalen to be quiet, for baby was waking up. To her
there was a living, breathing child in that empty cradle, and
as her warning " sh-sh " rang through the room, Magdalen shuddered involuntarily, and felt a kind of terror of that crib, as if
it held a goblin child. Suddenly Mrs. Grey turned to her and
said :

" You did not tell me your name, or else I have forgotten."

" My name is Magdalen Lennox," was the reply, and instantly
the black eyes flashed a keen look of curiosity upon the young
girl, who winced a little, but never turned her own eyes away
from those confronting her so fixedly.

" Magdalen," the woman said, " Magdalen. That brings it
back to me in part. I remember now. That was the name I
gave her when she was christened, because I thought it would
please Arthur, who was over the sea. He wanted to call Alice
that, but I was hot, and angry, and worried in those days, and
my temper ran very high, and I would not suffer it, for out of
Magdalen went seven devils, you know, and out of his Magdalen went fourteen, I'm sure. She was a beautiful woman, I
heard, and he loved her better than he did me, — loved her first
when he was young. I found it out when it was too late. His
mother told me so one day when she couldn't think of anything
else to torment me with. The Duchess of Beechwood ! She's

out under the snow now, and her monument is as tall as the
Tower of Babel. She was a dreadful woman, — she and Clarissa both; that was her daughter, and they just worried and
tormented and hunted me down, until I went away. "

Magdalen was gaining some insight into the family history
of the Greys, though how much of what she heard was true she
could not tell. One thing, however, struck her forcibly. She
knew that poor Jessie Morton's second name was Magdalen,
and from some source she had heard that Mr. Grey used frequently to call her by that name, which he preferred to Jessie,
and when Mrs. Grey alluded to the beautiful woman whom her
husband had loved better than his wife, she felt at once that it
was Jessie to whom reference was made, — Jessie who had unwittingly made trouble in this family, — Jessie for whom the
father would have called Alice, his first born, and for whom it
would seem a later child was subsequently named. She wanted
so much to ask questions herself, but a natural delicacy prevented her. She had no right to take advantage of a lunatic's
ravings and pry into family matters, so she sat very quiet for a
few moments watching her patient, who said at last:

"Yes, that brings it back in part. St. Luke's Church, and
mother, and Mr. and Mrs. Storms were sponsors, and we called
one Madeline, and the other Magdalen after the woman that
Arthur liked the best. Did you ever see her?"

"I've seen her picture. I lived in her house," Magdalen
replied:

"Tell me of her. Was she prettier than I am?—though
how should you know that, when you've only seen the gray-
haired, wrinkled, yellow hag they keep shut up so close at
Beechwood? But I was handsome once, years ago, when
mother made those shirts for Arthur and I did them up, and he
came before they were done and sat by the table and watched
me and said my hands were too small and pretty to handle that
heavy iron, — they would look better with rings and diamonds,
and he guessed he must get me some. I wore a pink gingham
dress that day, and hated ironing and sewing after that, and

13

wished I was a lady like those at the hotel where Arthur
boarded, and I took a dollar and bought a ring and put it on
my finger, and the next time he came he laughed and held my
hand while he looked at it, and told me he would get a better
one if I would go with him to the jeweller's. Mother would
not let me, and she had high words with him and ordered him
away and called him a hard name, — a villain, who only wanted
to ruin me. I was sick ever so long after that with something
in my head, though not like what's got into it since. Arthur
sent me flowers and fruit and little notes, and came to the door
to inquire, but still mother would not believe him true. When
I was most well he wrote a letter asking me to meet him, and
I ran away from mother and was married, and had the rings at
last, — a diamond and emerald and the plain gold one, — and a
white satin gown, and we travelled far and wide, and I looked
like a queen when he brought me here to the Duchess and
Lady Clarissa, and then to Penelope, who lived in New York,
and wasn't quite so bad, though she snubbed me some. I was
not as happy as I thought I should be, for Arthur stayed so
much in New York, and his mother was so cold and grand and
stiff, that I lay awake nights to hate her, and when Alice was
born the Duchess sent her out to nurse, because I was low-bred
and vulgar, and Arthur got sick of me and stayed in New York
more than ever, and left me to fight my way alone with the
dragons, and I got so at last that *I did fight good.*"

Her eyes were flashing fiercely, and Magdalen, who had listened breathlessly to the strange story, could readily imagine
just how that black-eyed, high-spirited creature *did fight*, as she
termed it, when once she was fairly roused to action. There
were rage and passion delineated in every feature now, and her
face was a bright purple as she hurled her invectives against
Arthur's mother and sister Clarissa, who, it would seem, had
persecuted her so sorely, and who were now "lying under the
snow."

"Tney gave me no peace day or night. They took Allie
away. They turned Arthur against me; they said I was low

and ignorant and poor, and finally they hinted that I was crazy,
— made so by *temper*, — and *that* I would not stand, so I went
away; and Arthur went East and I West to mother, and the
baby was born, which Arthur knew nothing about, and mother
died, and the other baby died, and I was alone, and went awhile
to Mrs. Storms; and then I drifted back here. I don't know
how, nor when, nor where, nor what happened after I left
Mrs. Storms only I lost baby, but I didn't kill it, Heaven
knows I didn't. I lost it, but Providence sent it back, so I
can see it, though nobody else does, and it's there in the cradle,
and I've rocked it ever since, and worn the carpet through.
Don't you see the white spots? Those are baby's foot-
prints."

She leaned over the side of the bed and pointed to the
breadth of carpet which was worn white and threadbare with
the constant motion of the crib. It was not the first carpet she
had worn out, nor the second, for "she had to rock to keep
the baby quiet, even if it did annoy Arthur so," she said; and
Magdalen's heart ached for the poor, demented creature, while
in spite of all his faults she pitied the man who was designated
as Arthur, and who must suffer fearfully with such a wife.
Laura's story, so long as it pertained to her girlhood and early
married life, had been quite connected and reasonable, and
Magdalen gained a tolerably clear understanding of the matter.
Arthur Grey had accidentally found this woman, who when
young must have been as beautiful as she was poor and lowly
born. The obstacles thrown in his way had only increased his
passion, which finally outweighed every other consideration,
and led to a clandestine marriage, wholly distasteful to the
proud mother and sisters, who had so violently opposed poor
Jessie Morton. That they had made Laura's life very unhappy; that the fickle husband, grown weary of his unsophis-
ticated wife, had cruelly neglected her, until at last in desperation she had gone away, Magdalen gathered from the story told
so rapidly; but after that she failed to comprehend what she
heard. The baby which Laura said had died, and the one

which she did not kill and which she had christened Magdalen, with Mrs. Storrs as sponsor, were enigmas which she could not solve. It struck her as a strange coincidence that she her self and the lost baby of the Greys should have borne the same name, and for the same woman; and she wondered what it was about that child which had affected the mother so strangely and put such wild fancies into her head. Her hand had dropped from the cradle now, the rocking had ceased, and the tired, worn-out woman, who had tossed and shrieked and strug-gled the livelong night, was falling asleep. Once, as her heavy lids began to droop, she started up, and reaching for Magda-len's hand, said to her, "Don't leave me! I am better with you here. Stay and sing more songs to me about the troubled soul. It makes me feel as if I was in Heaven."

She held Magdalen's hand in her own, and Magdalen sang to her again, while the tears rained from Laura's eyes, and rolled down her faded cheeks.

"Let me cry; it does me good," she said, when Magdalen tried to soothe her. "It cools me, and my head seems to grow clearer about the baby. It will come to me by and by, what I did with her. Oh, my child, my darling, God has surely kept her safe somewhere."

She was talking very low and slowly, and Magdalen watched her until the lips ceased to move, and the long eyelashes still wet with tears rested upon the flushed cheeks. She was asleep at last, and Magdalen, looking at her, knew that she must have been beautiful in her early girlhood when Arthur Grey had won her for his bride. Traces of beauty she had yet, in the regular-ity of her features, her well-shaped head, her abundant hair, with just a little ripple in it, her white forehead, and even teeth which showed no signs of decay. She was not old either, and Magdalen thought how young she must have been when she became a wife.

"Poor woman! her life has been a failure," she said, as she drew the covering around the shoulders and over the hands, on one of which the wedding ring and a superb diamond were still shining.

Mrs. Jenks seemed in no hurry to resume her post, and weary from her wakefulness of the previous night, Magdalen settled herself in the large easy chair by the bed, and was soon so fast asleep, that until twice repeated she did not hear Honora, who came to tell her that breakfast was waiting for her.

CHAPTER XL.

A GLIMMER OF LIGHT.

ALL that day Magdalen stayed with Mrs. Grey, who clung to her as a child clings to its mother, and who was more quiet and manageable than she had been in many weeks. Magdalen could soothe and control her as no one else had done since she left the private asylum where her husband had kept her so long, and this she did by the touch of her hand, the sound of her voice, and the glance of her eye, which fascinated and subdued her patient at once.

That night Mrs. Seymour and Alice came home, accompanied by Guy. They had not been expected quite so soon, and Magdalen knew nothing of their arrival until Alice, who had heard from Honora what had transpired during her absence, entered the room. Mrs. Grey was sitting up in her large armchair, her dressing gown and shawl carefully arranged, her hair nicely combed, and a look of content upon her face which Alice had rarely seen. She was rocking still, with one foot on the crib and her eyes fixed on Magdalen, who was repeating to her the Culprit Fay, which she knew by heart, and to which the childish woman listened with all the absorbing interest of a little girl of ten. At sight of Alice there came a sudden gleam of joy over her face, succeeded by a look of fear as she wound both arms tightly around Magdalen's neck, exclaiming:

"Oh, Allie, I'm glad you've come, but you must not take *her* away. She does me good. I'm better with her. Say that she may stay."

There was a momentary look of pain in Alice's eyes at seeing a stranger thus preferred to herself; but that quickly passed, and stooping over her mother, she kissed her tenderly, and said:

"Magdalen shall stay with you as long as she will. I am glad you like her so well. We all love Magdalen."

"Yes, and it's coming back to me. That was baby's name, — the one I gave her to please your father, and by and by I'll think just where it is."

Alice shot a quick, inquiring glance at Magdalen, as if to ask how much of their family history her mother had revealed, but Magdalen merely said:

"She seems to think there is a baby in the cradle, — a baby whom she says she lost or mislaid. It died, I suppose."

"Poor mother, she has suffered so much for that dead child," was Alice's only reply, as she stood caressing her mother's hair.

Then she tried to tell her something of her visit to New York and the rare music she had heard; but Mrs. Grey did not care for that, and said a little impatiently, "Don't bother me now; I'm listening to the story. Go on, Magdalen. He was just going to relight his lamp, and I want it over with, for I know how he felt. My lamp has gone out, and all the falling stars in heaven can't light it."

"I see you are preferred to me," Alice said to Magdalen; "but if you do her good, and I can see that you have already, I bless you for it. Poor, dear mother, who has never known a rational moment since I can remember."

She kissed her mother again, and then left the room, while Magdalen went on with her fairy tale, parts of which she repeated twice, and even thrice, before her auditor was satisfied.

After that Magdalen spent most of her time with the poor lunatic, who, if she attempted to leave her, would say so plead-

ingly, "Stay with me, Magda; don't go. It's beginning to
come back."

She called her *Magda* altogether, and though that name was
sacred to Roger's memory, Magdalen felt as if there was a blessing in the way the poor invalid spoke it, and her heart throbbed
with a strange kind of feeling every time she heard the
"Ma-ag-da," as Mrs. Grey pronounced it, dwelling upon the
first syllable, and shortening up the last.

Mr. Grey was still absent, glad, it would seem, of an excuse
to stay away from the tiresome burden at home. He had gone
to Cincinnati, to look after some property which belonged to
his wife, and as there was some difficulty in proving his claim to
a portion of it, which had more than quadrupled in value and
was now in great demand, it was desirable that all doubts
should be forever settled; so he wrote to Alice, that he should
stay until matters were satisfactorily adjusted. He had heard
of Magdalen's kind offices in the sick room, and he sent a note
to her, adjuring her to stay with Mrs. Grey so long as her influence over her was what Alice had reported it to be.

"Money can never pay you," he said, "if you succeed in doing her good, or even in keeping her quiet for any length of
time; but to show you that I appreciate your services, I will
from this time forward make your salary one thousand dollars
per annum as Mrs. Grey's attendant. It is strange the influence
which some people have over her, and strange that you, a girl,
can control her, as Alice says you do. Perhaps she recognizes
in you something that exists in herself, and so, on the principle
that like subdues like, she is subdued by you. The very first
time I saw you, there was something in your eyes and the toss
of your head which reminded me of her as she was when I first
knew her, but of course the resemblance goes no further. I
would weep tears of blood sooner than have your young life and
bright beauty darkened as Laura's has been."

When Magdalen received this note she was in a state of wild excitement, and hardly realized what Mr. Grey had written, until she
reached the part where he spoke of her resemblance to his wife.

"Something in your eyes and the toss of your head."

She read that sentence twice, and her eyes grew larger and darker than their wont as she too saw *herself* in the motions, and gestures, and even looks of the maniac, whose talk that very day, whether true or false, had sent through her veins a thrill of conjecture so sudden and wonderful, that for an instant she had felt as if she were fainting. Alice had talked but little of her mother's insanity. It was a great grief to them all, she had said, and she had wished to keep it from Magdalen as long as possible, fearing lest the fact of there being a lunatic in the house might trouble her, as it had done others who came to Beechwood. Of the fancy about the baby she had never offered any explanation, and Magdalen had ceased to think much of it, except as the vagary of a lunatic, until the day when she received the note from Mr. Grey. That afternoon Laura had talked a great deal, fancying herself to be in the cars, and sometimes baby was with her and sometimes it was not.

"That is the very last I remember," she said, apparently talking to herself. "I took the train at Cincinnati, and baby was with me ; I left the train, and baby was not with me. I've never seen her since, but I think I gave her to a boy. It was ever so long before I got home, and everything was gone, baggage, baby and all. I can't think any more."

Her voice ceased at this point, and Magdalen knew she was asleep ; but for herself she felt that she too was going mad with the suspicion which kept growing in intensity, as she recalled other things she had heard from Mrs. Grey, and to which she had paid no attention at the time. Once she arose and going to the glass studied her own face intently. Then she stole to the bedside of the sleeping woman and examined her features one by one, while all the time the faintness was increasing at her heart, and the blood seemed congealing in her veins. There was no trace of color in her face that night when she met the family at dinner, and Alice half shrunk from the eyes which fastened so greedily upon her and scarcely left her face a moment.

"What is it, Magdalen ?" she asked after dinner, when they

were standing alone before the parlor fire, and she felt the burning eyes still on her. "What is it, Magdalen? Is anything the matter?"

Then Magdalen's arms twined themselves around the young girl's neck in an embrace which had something almost fierce in its fervor.

"Oh, Alice, my darling; if it could be, if it could be!"

That was the answer Magdalen made, and her voice was choked with tears, which fell in torrents upon Alice's upturned face.

"Excuse me, do I!" she added, releasing the young girl, and recovering her composure. "I am nervous to-night. I can't go back to your mother. I shall be as mad as she is in a little while. Will you take my place in her room just for this evening?"

Alice assented readily, and after a few moments she left the parlor, and Magdalen was alone. But she could not keep quiet with that great doubt hanging over her and that wild hope tugging at her heart. Rapidly she walked up and down the long parlors, while the perspiration started about her forehead and lips, which were so ashy pale that they attracted the attention of Mrs. Seymour, when she at last came in, bringing her crocheting with her.

"Are you sick, Miss Lennox?" she asked in some alarm; and then Magdalen's resolution was taken, and turning to the lady, whose shoulder she grasped, she said, "Please come with me to my room, where we can be alone and free from interruption. There is something I wish you to tell me." And without waiting for an answer she led the astonished woman into the hall and up the stairs in the direction of her own room.

*13

CHAPTER XLI.

MRS. SEYMOUR AND MAGDALEN.

AVING locked the door, Magdalen brought a chair to Mrs. Seymour, and said:

"You are out of breath; sit there, but let me stand. I should suffocate if I were sitting down. I feel as if a hundred pairs of lungs were rising in my throat."

She was paler now than when Mrs. Seymour first met her in the parlor, and her eyes flashed and sparkled and glowed as only one pair of eyes had ever done before in Mrs. Seymour's presence, and for an instant a doubt of the young girl's sanity crossed that lady's mind, and she glanced uneasily at the door, as if contemplating an escape. But Magdalen was standing before her, and Magdalen's eyes held her fast. She dared not go now if she could, and she asked nervously what Miss Lennox wanted of her.

"I want you to tell me what it is about the child of whom Mrs. Grey talks so much. *Was* there a child born after Alice, say nineteen or twenty years ago, and did it die, or was it lost; and if so, when, and how; and was Mrs. Grey here when it was born, or was she somewhere else, in Cincinnati or vicinity? Tell me that. Tell me all about it."

Mrs. Seymour was very proud and haughty, and very reticent with regard to their family matters, especially the matters pertaining to her brother's marriage and his wife's insanity. She never talked of them to any one except Guy, from whom she had no secrets; and her most intimate friends, the Dagons and Draggons of New York society, knew nothing except what rumor told them of the demented woman who made Beechwood a prison rather than a paradise. How, then, was she startled, and shocked, and astonished, when this young girl, — this hired companion for her niece, — demanded of her a full recital of

what she had never told her most familiar friends.   Not *asked*
for it, but demanded it as a right, and enforced the demand with
burning eyes and the half-menacing attitude of one determined
to have her way.   Ordinarily Mrs. Seymour would have put
this girl down, as she termed it, and given her a lesson in good
breeding and manners, but there was something about her now
which precluded all that, and after a moment she said :

"Your conduct is very strange, Miss Lennox.   Very strange
indeed, and what I did not expect from you.   I suppose I may
be permitted to ask your right to a story which few have ever
heard ? "

"Certainly," Magdalen replied ; "question my right as much
as you like, only tell me what I want to know.   *Was* there a
child, and did it die ?"

"There *was* a child, and it *did* die," Mrs. Seymour said, and
Magdalen, nothing daunted, continued : "How do you know
it died?   Did you see it dead ?   She says she left it in the cars ;
she told me so to-day.   Oh, Mrs. Seymour, tell me, please
what you know about that child before I, too, go mad ! "

Magdalen was kneeling now before Mrs. Seymour, on whose
lap her hands were clasped, and her beautiful face was all aglow
with her excitement as she continued :

"I know a girl who was left in the cars somewhere in Ohio
almost nineteen years ago ; — left with a young boy, and the
mother, who took the train at Cincinnati, never came back, and
he could not find her.   He thinks she was crazy.   She had
very black hair and eyes, he said, and was dressed in mourning.
Perhaps it was Mrs. Grey.   Did she come from Cincinnati
about that time ?   It was April, 18—, when the baby I mean
was left in the cars."

Mrs. Seymour was surprised out of her usual reserve, and
when Magdalen paused for her reply, she said :

"My brother's wife came from Cincinnati in May, not
April ; but we thought she had been a long time on the road.
As to its being 18—, I'm not so sure ; but it was nineteen

years ago in May, I know, for husband died the next July, and mother the winter after."

" And what of the child? And how did it happen that Mrs. Grey was left to travel alone? Where had she been, and where was Mr. Grey?" Magdalen asked, and Mrs. Seymour replied, "My brother was in Europe, — sent there by unhappy domestic troubles at home. Laura had been in Cincinnati, and came back to Beechwood after the death of her mother and the child, of whose birth we had never heard."

" Never heard of its birth!" Magdalen exclaimed. "Then, perhaps, you do not know certainly of its death. She says she left it in the cars with a boy, and Roger was a boy; the child I told you of was left with him."

"Who was that child, and where is she?" Mrs. Seymour asked, and Magdalen replied, "*I* am that child, and didn't you say I reminded you of some one. Didn't Guy and Alice and your brother say the same; and I, too, can see the resemblance to that crazy woman in *myself*."

Her eyes were full of tears, and as she looked up at Mrs. Seymour her head poised itself upon one side just as Laura's had done a thousand times in the days gone by. Mrs. Seymour was interested now; that familiar look in Magdalen's face had always puzzled her, and as she saw her flushed, and excited, and eager, she was struck with the strong resemblance she bore to Laura as she was when she first came to Beechwood, and more to herself than to Magdalen she said:

" It is very strange, but still it cannot be, — though that child business was always more or less a mystery to me. Miss Lennox," and she turned to Magdalen, " would you mind telling me the particulars of your having been left in the car?"

Very rapidly Magdalen repeated the story of her desertion as she had heard it from Roger, while Mrs. Seymour listened intently and seemed a good deal moved by the description given of the mother.

" Was there nothing about you by which you might be identified? That is, did they keep no article of dress?" she asked, and Magdalen sprang up, exclaiming, "Yes, — the dress I wore ; a crimson delaine, dotted with black. I have it with me now."

"A crimson delaine, dotted with black," Mrs. Seymour repeated, while her hands began to tremble nervously and her voice to grow a little unsteady. "There was *such* a dress in Laura's satchel ; baby's dress, she told us, and Alice has it in her drawer."

"Get it, get it, and we will compare the two," Magdalen cried, and seizing Mrs. Seymour's hand she dragged rather than led her to the door of Alice's room ; then, going hastily to her trunk, she took from it the dress which she had worn to Mill-bank. "Here it is," she cried, turning to Mrs. Seymour, who came in with another dress, at sight of which Magdalen uttered a wild exultant cry, while every particle of color faded from Mrs. Seymour's face, and her eyes wore a frightened kind of look. *The dresses were alike!* The same material, the same size, the same style, except that Mrs. Seymour's was low in the neck, while Magdalen's was high, and what was still more confirmatory that they had belonged to the same person, the buttons were alike, and Magdalen pointed out to the astonished woman the same peculiarity about the button holes and a portion of the work upon the dresses. The person who made them must have been left-handed, as was indicated by the hems where left-handed stitches would show so plainly.

"I am astonished, I am confounded, I am bewildered, I feel like one in a dream," Mrs. Seymour repeated to herself.

Then she dropped panting into a chair, and wiping the perspiration from her face, continued :

"The coincidence is most remarkable ; the dresses *are* alike ; and still it is no proof. Was there nothing else ? "

"Yes. Do you recognize this? Did you ever see it before ? " Magdalen said, holding up the little locket which had been fastened about her neck when she came to Millbank.

Mrs. Seymour took it in her hands and examined it closely, then passed it back with the remark, "I never saw it before, to my knowledge."

"But the initials, 'L. G.' — did you notice those?" Magdalen continued, and then Mrs. Seymour took the locket again,
and glancing at the lettering whispered rather than said aloud :

"'L. G.' That stands for Laura Grey. It may be. I wish
Arthur was here, for I don't know what to think or do."

"You can at least tell me about the child," Magdalen persisted, and Mrs. Seymour, who by this time was considerably
shaken out of her usual reticence and reserve, replied, "Yes,
I can do that, trusting to your honor as a lady never to divulge
what I may tell you of our family affairs. My brother always
had a *penchant* for pretty faces, and while he was young had
several *affairs du cœur* which came to nothing. When he was
forty, or thereabouts, he went to Cincinnati, where he stayed a
long time, and at last startled us with the announcement of his
marriage with Laura Clayton, a young girl of seventeen, whose
beauty, he said, surpassed anything he had ever seen. She
was not of high blood, as we held blood, he wrote, but she was
wholly respectable, and pure, and sweet, and tolerably well
educated, and he wanted us to lay aside our prejudices and
receive her as his wife should be received. I was in favor of
doing so, though perhaps this feeling was owing in part to my
husband's sensible reasoning and partly to the fact that I did
did not live here then and would not be obliged to come in
daily contact with her. My home was in New York, and so I
only heard from time to time of the doings at Beechwood. It
transpired afterward that Laura's mother was a widow, who
lived much by herself, without relatives and only a few acquaintances. She had come from New Orleans the year before,
and bought a house and quite a large lot of land in the
suburbs of Cincinnati. There was Spanish blood in her veins,
and it shows itself in Laura. The mother did some plain
sewing for Arthur, who in that way saw the daughter and finally
married her against her mother's wishes. I think Mrs. Clayton
was a sensible woman, or perhaps she feared that Arthur only
sought her daughter's ruin ; for she tried to keep them apart,
and so made the matter worse and drove them into a clandes-

tine marriage. Mother and sister Clarissa were here then. Clarissa was never married, and from her I learned the most I know about the trouble. She deeply regretted afterward the course they pursued toward Laura, whom they did not understand, and whose life they made so wretched with their coldness and pride. She was naturally high-spirited, but she bore patiently for a long time whatever they laid upon her and tried, I believe, to please them in all things. Clarissa herself told me that the girl never really turned upon them, except as her eyes would sometimes blaze with anger, until Alice was born, and mother wanted her put out to a wet nurse, who lived so far away that for Laura to see her baby every day was impossible. Then she rebelled openly, and there was a terrible scene, but mother carried her point, as she usually did when she had Arthur where she could talk to him. Laura fought like a tigress when the last moment came, and mother took the baby from her by force, and then locked her in her room for fear she would go down to the river and drown herself, as she threatened to do. Arthur was in New York, or I think he would have interfered when he saw how it affected Laura. I was sorry for the poor girl when I heard of it from Clarissa. I had lost a dear little baby and could sympathize with Laura. I think it makes a woman harder and less considerate not to have a husband or children of her own, and Clarissa had neither."

Mrs. Seymour forgot that her mother had both husband and children, and that therefore the thing which would excuse Clarissa could not be applied to her. But Magdalen did not forget it, and her fists were involuntarily clinched as if to smite the hard old woman who had torn Laura's baby from her.

"Does Alice know this?" she asked, and Mrs. Seymour replied, "She does not, of course. There could be no reason for harrowing up her feelings with a recital of the past, and I hardly know why I am telling *you* the story so fully as I am."

"Never mind, go on ;" Magdalen exclaimed eagerly, and Mrs. Seymour continued :

"After the baby went away a kind of melancholy mood came

over Laura and she would sit for hours and even days without speaking to any one ; then she would have fits of crying, and again was irritable and quarrelsome, so that it was a trial to live with her. After two or three months she ceased to speak of her child, and when Arthur offered to take her to see it flew into so fierce a passion that he took the next train to New York and left her with mother.

" It was a habit of his to go away from anything disagreeable, and most of his time was spent from home. He was always very fickle. To possess a thing was equivalent to his tiring of it, and even before Alice's birth he was weary of his young wife ; and so matters went on from bad to worse till Alice was nearly a year old, and Arthur began to talk of going abroad, while Laura proposed a separation, or that she should be allowed to go to Cincinnati while her husband was away. They would all be happier, she said ; and his mother and Clarissa favored the plan. Arthur consented, and went with her himself to Cincinnati, and settled a yearly allowance upon her, and at her mother's request bought three or four vacant lots which adjoined hers and were for sale, and which she wanted to hold so as to prevent shanties from being built upon them."

"And didn't Mrs. Grey see her baby before she went ? " Magdalen asked, and Mrs. Seymour replied :

"Yes, once. It was brought to the house, but she took little notice of it, and said it belonged to the *Greys*, not to *her*. We think now she was crazy then, though they did not suspect it at the time. She expressed no regret whatever when Arthur left her, but on the contrary seemed relieved to have him go. He sailed for Europe the next week, and was gone a year and a half, or more. Laura wrote to him quite regularly at first, but never held any communication with Beechwood. After a while there was a break in her letters, and when at last she wrote she told him something of which he had no suspicion at the time of his leaving home. He ought to have come back to her then, but he did not, though he sent her money and advised her to return to Beechwood. This she would not do. She preferred to stay with her mother, she said ; and he heard no more from her for three or four months, when she wrote a few hurried lines, telling him her baby *Madeline* died when she was four weeks old, and adding that she presumed he would not care, as it would save him the trouble of taking the child from her as he had taken Alice. That roused him a little to a sense of his duty, and he wrote kindly to her and told her he was sorry, and advised her again to return to Beechwood, where he said he would join her. To this she did not reply for a long time, and when at last she wrote she said that her mother was dead, and that after visiting a friend she was going back to Beechwood. The next he heard from her she was here at Beechwood, where she had arrived wholly unexpected by mother and Clarissa, who did not know that she was coming, and who judged that she must have been weeks on the road. Her baggage was lost, and she had nothing with her but a little satchel, in which was a child's dress and a few other articles. She was dressed in black, and told them her mother was dead, but said nothing of the child of whose birth they had never heard, she having insisted that Arthur should not tell them of it. She was very quiet for a few days, never speaking unless spoken to, and then she did not always answer. Occasionally they heard her muttering to herself, ' One is dead, and one is safe. They will never find it, — never,' but what she meant, they could not guess.

"Alice was spending a few days with her foster-mother up the river, and did not return till Laura had been home a week. In all that time she had never mentioned her child, and when at last she came, and Clarissa said to her, ' Your baby is here, Laura. Would you like to see her ? ' she sprang to her feet and her eyes glared like a maniac's.

" ' Baby was hid,' she said. ' Baby was gone where they could not find it.'

"Then her mood changed, and she raved for the baby till Alice was brought to her ; but that only made her worse, and she became perfectly furious, telling them this was not the baby whom she had lost, and whom she insisted upon their finding.

"Clarissa wrote at once to Arthur, who hastened home, finding his mother and sister at their wit's end, and his wife raving mad, and calling continually for the baby she had lost, or hid. That was her constant theme — 'lost, or hid, or left somewhere.' Arthur did his best to soothe her, telling her the baby was dead, and asking if she did not remember writing to him about it. But it did no good. Her reply was always the same : 'One is dead, and one is not.'

"For hours she would sit repeating these words in a kind of moaning, half sobbing way, 'one is dead, and one is not ;' and never from that time has she known a rational moment. Hunting out Alice's cradle, she took it to her room, and rocked it day and night, saying her lost baby was in it, and raving fearfully if the family made a noise in the room.

"This annoyed Arthur terribly. He likes quiet, and ease, and luxury, and, as he could not have these in his own house, he sought them elsewhere, and has travelled almost over the world. Twice Laura has been in a private asylum. She was there all the time we were abroad ; but after our return Alice begged so hard for her to be allowed to come to Beechwood, that Arthur brought her back, and will never move her again.

"Mother died the winter after Laura's return, and Clarissa the year following. As my husband was dead, and I alone in the world, I came here to care for my brother and Alice. Poor girl ! Her life has been a sad one, though she knows nothing, or comparatively nothing, of the early domestic trouble between her parents, and how her mother was received at Beechwood."

Mrs. Seymour paused here, and Magdalen, who had listened eagerly, asked, "If that child which died when it was four week sold had lived, how old would it have been when Mr. Grey came home ? "

Mrs. Seymour could hardly tell, for the reason that in her

letter to her husband Laura did not give the date of its birth, but as nearly as they could judge it must have been nine or ten months old, possibly more.

"Yes," Magdalen said; "and the dress in the satchel, — did it never occur to you that it could not have been made for a four weeks' old baby. It was meant for a larger child. And did you never think there might be a meaning in the words, 'One is dead, and one is not,' Mrs. Seymour?" and Magdalen grew more earnest and vehement. "There must have been two children instead of one, — twins, one of whom died and the other she left in the cars. I know it, I believe it. I shall prove it yet. She has always talked to me of two, and one she said was Madeline and one was Magdalen, and Mr. Irving told me that the woman in the cars called me something which sounded like Magdalen. Don't you see it? Can't you understand how it all might be?"

Mrs. Seymour was confounded and bewildered, and answered faintly, "Oh, I don't know; I wish Arthur was here."

"I am going to him," Magdalen exclaimed, starting to her feet, — "going at once, and have him help me solve this mystery. Alice must not know till I come back, and not then, if I fail. I shall start for Cincinnati to-morrow. A woman can oftentimes find out things which a man cannot. Do you think your nephew will go with me?"

She talked so fast, and with so much assurance, that Mrs. Seymour was insensibly won to think as she did and assent to whatever she suggested; and the result was that in less than half an hour's time Guy, who had been invited up to Magdalen's room, had heard the whole of the strange story. *He* believed it, and indorsed Magdalen at once, and hurrahed for his new cousin, and winding his arm around her waist waltzed with her across the room, upsetting his Aunt Pen's work-basket, and when she remonstrated he caught her in his other arm and took her with him in his mad dance. Exhausted, panting, and half indignant at her scape-grace nephew, Auntie Pen released herself from his grasp, and after a time Magdalen succeeded in stopping him, but he kept fast hold of her hands, while she explained what she wantsd of him, and asked if he would go with her.

" Go with you? Yes, the world over, *ma belle* cousin," he said, and greatly to the horror of prim Mrs. Penelope, he sealed his promise to serve her with a kiss upon her brow.

Mrs. Seymour was shocked, and half doubted the propriety of sending Magdalen off alone with Guy; but Magdalen knew the kiss was given to Alice as her possible sister rather than to herself, and so did not resent it.

They were to start the next day, but it was not thought best to let Alice know of the journey until morning. Then they told her that a matter of importance, which had recently come to Magdalen's knowledge, made it necessary for her to go to Cincinnati, and that Guy was going with her. Alice knew they were keeping something from her, but would not question them, and without a suspicion of the truth she bade Magdalen and Guy good-by, and saw them start on their journey to Cin cinnati.

CHAPTER XLII.

IN CINCINNATI.

M R. GREY was breakfasting in that leisurely, luxurious kind of way which he enjoyed so thoroughly. His morning papers were on the table beside him. He had glanced them through, and read every word in them about poor Laura's property, which was now secured to her and her heirs forever. He had succeeded in making his claim clear, and Laura and her heirs were richer by some thirty thousand dollars than they were when last the crazy woman was in the city. To a man with nearly half a million thirty thousand dollars were not so very much; but Mr. Grey was glad to get it, and had decided that it should be invested for Alice, just as his breakfast appeared, and in dispatching that, he forgot the city lots and houses, and the days when he had gone so often to one of them, now a long time torn down to make room for a large and handsome block. He had finished his first cup of coffee, and was waiting for his second, when a hand was laid familiarly upon his shoulder, and Guy Seymour's handsome face confronted him.

"Why, Guy, how you frightened me!" he said. "Where did you come from? Is anything the matter at home? Is it Alice?"

She was nearest his heart, and he asked for her first, while his cheek paled for a moment; but Guy quickly reassured him.

There was nothing the matter with Alice; nothing the matter with any one, he said. He had come on business, and as soon as Mr. Grey was through with his breakfast he would like to see him alone. Then Mr. Grey proceeded with his coffee and mutton chop, and omelette and hot cakes, and Guy grew terribly impatient and nervous with waiting. Mr. Grey's appetite was satisfied at last, and he invited Guy to his room and asked what he could do for him. Guy had the story at his tongue's end. He had repeated it to himself several times so as to be sure and make himself understood, and after half an hour or so he *was* understood, and Mr. Grey knew why he was there, and who was with him. To say that he was startled would convey but a faint idea of the effect Guy's story had upon him. Laura's ravings about "the one that was dead and the one that was not," had come back to him with a new meaning and helped to prove the *twin* theory correct, and he was struck dumb with amazement, and tried in vain to speak as some question he wished to ask presented itself to his mind. He could not speak, his tongue was so thick and lay so heavy in his mouth, while the blood rushed in such torrents to his head and face that he plucked at his cravat as if to tear it off, so he could breath more freely, and made a motion toward the window for air.

"Apoplexy, it has almost given me that," he whispered as the fresh air blew gratefully upon him, and he drank the water

Guy brought to him. Then leaning his head against the back of his chair, he said : " I am greatly shocked by this story you have told me. It seems reasonable and may be true, though I do not deserve it. I've been a villain, a rascal. I abused and neglected Laura ; I ought to have come home when she first wrote about the baby, and should have done so but for that devilish trait of mine, to follow a pretty face. I had an Italian woman in tow and it blunted every other feeling, and when. I heard the child was dead I did not care so very much, though I wrote to her kindly enough ; and now, to have this great good come so suddenly upon me is too much, — too much," —

Guy believed in Magdalen, and his belief had so colored his story that Mr. Grey believed in her, too, at first. Then a doubt began to creep into his mind, as was very natural, and he asked, " Where is she, and how does she propose to prove it ? "

" She is in No. —. She wishes to see you first. Will you go to her now ? " Guy said ; and Mr. Grey arose, and leaning on Guy started for the room where Magdalen was waiting for him.

When the first great shock came upon her Magdalen had thought only of Alice, the darling sister it might be, and of the poor worn-out wreck which, though a wreck, might be her mother still, and her heart had gone out after them both and enfolded them with all a daughter's and sister's love, but in this sudden gush of affection Mr. Grey had had little part. So great had her excitement been, and so rapidly had she acted upon her convictions, that she had scarcely thought of him in any other capacity than that of her employer. But as she sat waiting for him, there suddenly swept over her the consciousness that if what she hoped was true, then he was her own father, and for a moment she rebelled against it as against some impending evil.

" Roger is his sworn enemy," she whispered faintly, as her mind went back to the time when Roger had cursed him as his mother's ruin. " Roger will never forgive my being *his* daughter," she thought, and for an instant she wished she had never told her suspicions to a human being, but had kept them locked

in her own bosom. Then she thought of Alice, and that comforted her, and made her calm and composed when she heard
the knock at her door and saw Guy coming in with Mr. Grey.

He was very pale, and came toward her, with an eager,
questioning look in his eyes, which scanned her curiously.
She had risen, and was standing with her hands locked together, her head unconsciously poised upon one side, and her
body bent slightly forward. It was Laura's attitude exactly,
Laura had stood just this way that night she met him outside
her mother's house and he persuaded her to the clandestine
marriage. Save that there was about Magdalen more refine-
ment, more culture, and a softer style of beauty than had ever
belonged to Laura Clayton, he could have sworn it was the
Laura of his mature manhood's love, or passion, who stood
upon the rug by the fire, her dark eyes meeting his with a wistful, earnest gaze. In an instant the forgot his doubts; —
his faith was strong as Guy's, and he reached his arms toward
her, and his lips quivered as he said:

"You are so much like Laura that you *must* be my child."

She knew he expected her to go to him, but Jessie and Laura,
and the uncertainty as to herself and his right to claim her, rose
up a mighty barrier between them, and she made no movement
towards him ; she only said:

"It is not sure that I am your child. We must prove it beyond a doubt," and in her voice there was a tone which Mr.
Grey understood.

She knew Laura's story. Penelope had told her, and she resented the injury done to one who might be her mother. It
was a part of his punishment, and he accepted it, and put down
the tenderness and love which kept growing in his heart for the
beautiful girl before him.

"No, it is not proved," he said, "though I trust that it may
be. Tell me, please, your own story as you have heard it from
Mr. Irving, and also what you wish me to do."

He had heard the whole from Guy, but the story gained new
force and reality as told by Magdalen, whose eyes and face and

gestures grew each moment more and more like Laura Clayton as she was years ago. Guy had forgotten the locket, but Magdalen did not, and she showed it to Mr. Grey, who examined it closely, then staggered a step or two toward her, and steadied himself against the mantel, as he said :

"It *was* Laura's.   I remember it perfectly and where I bought it.   I gave it to her myself.   My likeness was in it then.   You see it has been taken out," and he pointed to the inside of the ornament from which a picture had evidently been removed. "Magdalen, I do not need stronger proof.   Will you let me call you daughter?"

The tears were streaming down his face, and Magdalen felt herself beginning to relent, but there must be no mistake, — no shadow on which to build a doubt hereafter.   She could not take her place in the hearts of that family as a rightful daughter of the house and then suddenly be displaced by some other claimant.   She must know to a certainty that she was Magdalen Grey, and she replied :

"I am not satisfied; we must investigate farther than we have. Your wife talked of a Mrs. Storms who was sponsor for her baby.   Did you ever know it was baptized?   Did she write you to that effect?"

" Never.   She only said that baby Madeline was dead," Mr. Grey replied, and after a moment's hesitation Magdalen continued, " Tell me, please, if you ever wished to give Alice another name than the one she bears, and did your wife oppose it?"

Mr. Grey's face was scarlet, but he answered promptly, —

" I *did* propose calling Alice after a dear friend of mine whose second name was Magdalen."

"Then Mrs. Grey was right so far," Magdalen rejoined, "and may have been correct in her other statements to me, also. She told me one was Madeline, and that to please you she called the other "Magdalen," after the friend for whom you wished Alice named, and that a Mr. and Mrs. Storms were sponsors.   Do you know any such people?"

Mr. Grey did not, and Magdalen continued :

"We must find them. Is it of any use to inquire in the vicinity where Mrs. Grey once lived?"

"None whatever. Every house has been pulled down, and every family is gone," was the unpromising answer, but Magdalen was not disheartened.

"The christening must have been in church. Can you tell which one it was likely to be?"

Mr. Grey thought it was St. Luke's, as Mrs. Clayton was an attendant there. They might ——

He did not finish the sentence, for Magdalen started quickly, exclaiming:

"There must be a Parish Register, and there we shall find it recorded, and possibly trace Mrs. Storms. Let us go at once to the Rectory, if there is one."

Her bonnet and shawl were on in a trice, a carriage was called, and the three were soon on their way to the house of the Rev. Henry Fowler, Rector of St. Luke's. He was a young man, who had only been there for a year or two, but Magdalen's beauty and excitement enlisted his sympathy at once, and he went with them to the church and took from a dusty shelf an old worn-looking volume, wherein he said was recorded the births, deaths, and baptisms of twenty and twenty-five years ago. It was Magdalen who took the book in her own hands, and sitting down upon the chancel steps with her bonnet falling back from her flushed face and her white lips compressed together, turned the pages eagerly, while the three men stood looking at her. Suddenly she gave a cry, and the three came near her.

"Look," she said, "it's here. There was a child baptized," and she pointed to the record of the baptism of "Magdalen Laura," daughter of Arthur and Laura Grey. Sponsors, "Mr. and Mrs. James Storms, Cynthiana, Kentucky."

Then suddenly a cloud passed over her face as she said sadly, ' But there is only *one*. Where is *Madeline*?"

"Turn to the deaths," Guy said, and with trembling fingers Magdalen did as he bade her, but found no trace of Madeline. Only Mrs. Clayton's death was recorded there, and the tears

14

gathered in Magdalen's eyes and dropped upon the register as she felt that her hopes were being swept away. It was Guy who comforted and reassured her by suggesting that Madeline might have died before the christening, and Magdalen caught eagerly at it, and springing up exclaimed, "Yes, and they neglected to record her death ; that's it, I know ; we will find this Mrs. Storms ; we will go at once to Cynthiana. Is it far? Can we reach it to-day ?"

It was not very far, the clergyman said. It was on the railroad between Cincinnati and Lexington, but he did not believe she could go that day, as the train was already gone.

It seemed an age to wait until the morrow, but there was no help for it ; and Magdalen passed the day as best she could, and when the morning came and they started for Cynthiana, she was almost sick with excitement, which increased more and more the nearer she drew to Mrs. Storms, who was to confirm her hopes or destroy them forever.

CHAPTER XLIII.

IN CYNTHIANA.

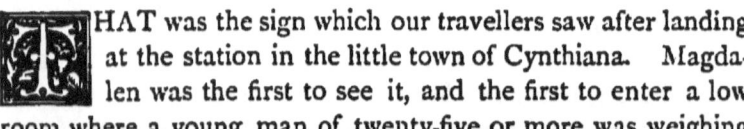

GEORGE P. STORMS & CO.,
DEALERS IN
DRY GOODS, GROCERIES & PROVISIONS.

HAT was the sign which our travellers saw after landing at the station in the little town of Cynthiana. Magdalen was the first to see it, and the first to enter a low room where a young man of twenty-five or more was weighing a codfish for a negress with a blue turban bound around her head.

Magdalen was taking the lead in all things, and Mr. Grey and Guy let her, and smiled at her enthusiasm and the effect she produced upon the young man. He was not prepared for this apparition of beauty in so striking contrast to old Hannah and her codfish, and he blushed and stammered in his reply to her question as to whether "Mrs. James Storms was a relative of his, and lived near them."

"She is my mother, and lives just down the street. Did you wish to see her?" he said, and Magdalen replied:

"Yes; that is, if she is the Mrs. Storms I am after. Is she a church woman, and has she ever been in Cincinnati?"

"She is a church woman, and has been in Cincinnati," the young man said, and then he followed Magdalen to the door and pointed a second time to his mother's house, and stood watching her as she sped like a deer along the muddy street, leaving Mr. Grey and Guy very far behind her.

A very respectable-looking woman answered Magdalen's knock, and inviting her to enter, stood waiting for Mr. Grey and Guy, who had just reached the gate

It was Magdalen who did most of the talking, — Magdalen who, without taking the chair offered her, broke out impetu-ously, "Are you Mrs. James Storms, and did you years ago, — say nineteen or twenty — know a Mrs. Clayton, in Cincinnati, and her daughter, Mrs. Grey, — Laura they called her?"

The woman, who seemed to be naturally a lady, cast a wondering glance at Magdalen, and replied:

"I am Mrs. Storms, and I knew Laura Clayton, or rather Mrs. Grey. Are you her daughter? You look like her as I remember her."

Magdalen did not answer this question, but went on vehemently:

"Were you much with Mrs. Grey, and can you tell me anything about her starting for her home in New York, and if she had a baby then, and how old it was, and what dress did it wear? Try to remember, please, and tell me if you can."

Mrs. Storms was wholly bewildered with all these interrogatories of a past she had not recalled in years, and looked inquiringly at Mr. Grey, who was standing by Magdalen, and who said with a smile :

"Not quite so fast. You confuse the woman with your rapid questions. Ask her one at a time ; or perhaps it will be better for me to explain a little first."

Then as briefly as possible he repeated what he thought necessary for Mrs. Storms to know of the business which had brought them there, and asked if she could help them any.

For a moment Mrs. Storms was too much surprised to speak, and stood staring, first at Magdalen and then at Mr. Grey, in a dazed, helpless kind of way.

" Lost her baby, — the little child I stood for ! Didn't have it when she got home, nor her baggage either ! it takes my breath away ! Of course she was crazy. I can see it now, though I did not suspect it then. I only thought her queer at times."

"Yes, but tell us ; begin at the beginning," Magdalen exclaimed, too impatient to wait any longer. And thus entreated, Mrs. Storms began :

" I knew Mrs. Clayton in New Orleans, before she moved to Cincinnati, or I was married and came here. I had seen Laura when a little girl, but did not know much of her until she came home after her marriage. Then I saw her every time I was at her mother's, which was quite often, considering the distance between here and Cincinnati, and the tedious way we had then of getting there by stage. My husband, who is dead now, and myself were sponsors for her baby, whom she called Magdalen."

"Was there *one* or *two* children ? Tell me that first, please," Magdalen said, and when Mrs. Storms replied, "She had *two*, but one died before it was christened," she gave a sudden scream, and staggered a step towards Mr. Grey, who, almost as white and weak as herself, laid his hand with a convulsive grasp upon her shoulder and said, "Two children ! twins ! and I never knew it !"

"Never knew it!" Mrs. Storms repeated. "I wrote it to you myself the day after they were born. I happened to be there, and Laura asked me to write and tell you, and I did, and di·rected my letter to Rome."

"I never received it, which is not strange, as I journeyed so much from place to place and had my mail sent after me," Mr. Grey rejoined, and Mrs. Storms continued, "I remember now that after my letter was sent Laura grew worse, — crazy like, we thought, and seemed sorry I had written, and said the Greys did not like children and would take her babies from her, and when the little sickly one died she did not seem to feel so very badly and said it was safe from the Greys. She was always queer on that subject, though she never said a word against her husband. She had plenty of money, and, I supposed, was going back to Beechwood as soon as you returned. I was not with her when Mrs. Clayton died; it was sudden, — very, and I only went to the funeral. Laura told me, then, she was going home, but said she wished first to visit me. I consented, of course, though I wondered that she did not go at once. She came to me after the funeral, and stayed some time with her child, and appeared very sad and depressed, and cried a great deal at times, and then, again, was wild, and gay, and queer."

"But the child, — the little girl — How did she look?" Magdalen asked.

And Mrs. Storms replied:

"She was very healthy and fat; a pretty creature, with dark eyes, like her mother's, and dark hair too. A beautiful baby I called her, who might easily grow to be just like you, miss."

She was complimenting Magdalen, whose face flushed a little as she asked:

"Do you remember what the child wore when she went away? Would you know the dress if you saw it?"

Mrs. Storms hardly thought she would. Mrs. Grey was in mourning, but about the baby she did not know.

"Was the dress like this?" Magdalen asked, taking from

her satchel the dress she had worn to Millbank, and the one found in Laura's bag.

Mrs. Storms looked at them a moment, and then a sudden gleam of intelligence broke over her face as she exclaimed :

"I do remember them perfectly now. I made them myself for Mrs. Grey."

"And you are left-handed ? " interrupted Magdalen.

"Yes, I am left-handed. You knew that by the hems ? You would make a capital lawyer," Mrs. Storms said, laughingly. Then, excusing herself a moment, she left the room, but soon returned, bringing a patch-work quilt, made from bits of delaine.

Conspicuous among these were blocks of the same material as the two spotted dresses. To these blocks Mrs. Storms called Magdalen's attention.

"I had a baby then, a boy, Charlie, he is dead now, and these are pieces of the dress Mrs. Grey gave to him. She bought enough for him and her baby, too, and I made them both and then found there was still material for another, provided the sleeves were short and the neck low. So I made that at the very last, and as Laura's trunk was full she put it in her satchel."

Mr. Grey's hand deepened its grasp on one whom he now knew to be his child beyond a doubt, and who said to Mrs. Storms :

"Did she go from here alone to Cincinnati, and about what time ? "

"It was in April, and must have been nineteen years ago. I know by Charlie's age. I had hurt my ankle and Mr. Storms was going with her, but at the last something happened, I don't remember what, and he did not go. She said a great many harsh things about her mother-in-law and sister, and about their taking her baby from her, and the night before she went was more excited than I ever saw her, but I did not think her crazy. There was no railroad then, and she went by stage, and from Cincinnati sent me a note that she was safely there and about to start for the East. I wondered a little she never wrote to me, but fancied she was with her grand friends and in her handsome house and had forgotten poor folks like us, and I would not write first. Then I had a great deal of trouble pretty soon.

"Charlie died, and Mr. Storms' lungs gave out, and I went to Florida with him and buried him there, and after six years came back to Cynthiana. So you see there was a good deal of one thing and another to put Laura out of my mind."

Many more questions were asked and explanations and suggestions made until it was preposterous for Magdalen to require more testimony. She *was* Mr. Grey's daughter, — she believed it now, and her heart throbbed with ecstasy when she remembered Alice, whom she already loved so much. There was also a feeling of unutterable tenderness and pity for the poor crazy woman who had suddenly come up in the capacity of her mother. She could, aye, she did love her, all wrecked and shattered and imbecile as she was; but she could not so soon respond to the affection which showed itself in every lineament of Mr. Grey's face and thrilled in the tone of his voice as he wound his arm around her neck, and drawing her closely to him said, with deep emotion :

"Magdalen, my daughter, my darling child! Heaven has been better to me than I deserved."

He stooped and kissed her lips, but she did not give him back any answering caress, except as she suffered him to hold her in his embrace. He felt the coldness of her manner, and it affected him deeply, but there was no opportunity then for any words upon the subject. The train was coming which would take them to Cincinnati, and so after a little further conversation with Mrs. Storms, whom Mr. Grey resolved to remember in some substantial form, they bade her good-by and were soon on their way to the city.

CHAPTER XLIV.

FATHER AND DAUGHTER.

HERE was no longer a shadow of doubt that Mr. Grey and Magdalen bore to each other the relation of father and child. He had been satisfied with far less testimony than Magdalen required, and even she was satisfied at last, though she suggested the propriety of ascertaining from Roger if his remembrances of the woman who had left her with him tallied with Mrs. Storms' description of Mrs. Grey as she was when she left Cynthiana. To this Mr. Grey assented, and proposed that as personal interviews were always more satisfactory than letters, Guy should go to Schodick, leaving himself and Magdalen to rest a day or so in Cincinnati, and then return to Beechwood, where Guy would join them with his report. Magdalen had half hoped he might go himself, though she knew how he must shrink from a meeting with Roger Irving, and mingled with her happiness in having found both parents and sister was a keen sense of pain as she thought how the gulf between herself and Roger was widened by the discovery of her lineage.

"Roger will hate me now, perhaps," she said to herself, when alone in her room at the hotel she sat down to rest and tried to realize her position.

Guy was going early the next morning before she was up, and if she would send any message to Roger it must be written that night. Once she thought to write him a long letter, begging him for her sake and Alice's, whom he was sure to love, to forgive her father all the wrong he had done, and to come to them at Beechwood, where he would receive a cordial welcome. But after a moment's reflection she felt that she was hardly warranted in writing thus. His cordial welcome from all parties was not so certain. Mr. Grey had not intimated a wish to see him or hinted at anything like gratitude for all Roger had done for her. It would be pleasanter both for Roger and her father never to meet. She could not invite him to Beechwood and so with a gush of tears she took her pen and wrote to him hastily :

" Mr. Irving : Can you forgive me when you hear who I am, and will you try to think of me as you did in the days which now seem so very far in the past. I have been your ruin, Roger. I have brought to you almost every trouble you ever knew, and now to all the rest I must add this, that I am the child of your worst enemy, Arthur Grey. Don't hate me for it, will you ? Alice, who is much better than I, would say it was God's way of letting you return good for evil. I wish you would think so, too, and I wish I could tell you all I feel, and how grateful I am to you for what you have done for me. If I could I would repay it, but I am only a girl, and the debt is too great ever to be cancelled by me. May Heaven reward you as you deserve.

" Your grateful   Magdalen.

" P. S. — Mr. Seymour will tell you the particulars of my strange story. You will like him. There is not a drop of Grey blood in his veins."

This was Magdalen's letter, which she handed to Guy in her father's presence when she went to say good-night to the two gentlemen in the parlor.

" Will you write to Mr. Irving, too ? " she asked Mr. Grey, who shook his head, while a look of embarrassment and pain flitted across his face.

" Not now, — some time perhaps I may. I am truly grateful to him, and Guy must tell him so. Guy will know just what to say. I leave it in his hands."

Mr. Grey was not quite like himself that night, and when next morning Magdalen met him at breakfast, he still seemed abstracted and absent-minded, and but little inclined to talk. When breakfast was over, however, he went with her to her room, and sitting down beside her grasped her hands in his, and said :

" Magdalen, my child, I never expected to see this day, — never thought there was so much happiness in store for me, — a happiness I have not deserved, and which still is not unmixed with pain and humiliation. Magdalen, my daughter," he continued, "there is something between us which should not be between a father and his child. I feel it in your manners, and see it in your face, and hear it in your voice. What is it, Magdalen ? "

He was talking very kindly, and sadly too, and the tears glittered in Magdalen's eyes, but she did not reply. She could not tell him all the hard things she had written against him in her heart, before she knew him to be her father, but he guessed them in part, and continued :

" Penelope told you something of your mother's story. I wonder if she told you all ? "

" Yes, all that I ever care to hear," Magdalen replied. " I know of her clandestine marriage, her wretched life at Beech-wood, of their taking Alice from her, and of — of your cruel neglect of her."

She said the last hesitatingly, for there was something in the blue eyes fastened upon her which prevented her saying as hard things as she felt.

"Yes, it's all true, and more," Mr. Grey replied. "Penelope could not tell you as bad as it was, for she never knew all. I did neglect your mother when she needed me the most. I liked my ease. I could not endure scenes. I was afraid of mother. I acted a coward's part, and Laura suffered for it. She was beautiful once, — oh, so beautiful when I first met her in her sweet young girlhood ! She was much like you, and I loved her as well as I was capable of loving then. I had been thwarted and crossed, and had done things for which I have always been sorry, but never as sorry as since I have known you were my child, for there is something in your face which seems continually to reproach me for the past, and until I have made you my

confession, I feel that there cannot be perfect confidence be
tween us. I think I had seen you before you came to Beech
wood."

"Yes, in Belvidere, at Mrs. Irving's grave, though I did not
know who you were. I had not heard of you *then*."

She knew about Jessie, — Mr. Grey was sure of that, and with
something between a sigh and a groan, he said :

"You have heard of that sad affair too, I see ; but perhaps
you don't know all, and how I was deceived."

"Yes, I know all. I have seen Mrs. Irving's letter — the
one she wrote on board the 'Sea Gull,' and to which you
added a postscript. Mr. Grey, why did you write so coldly ?
Why did you express no sorrow for what you had done ? Why
did you leave a doubt of Jessie to sting and torment poor
Roger, the truest, the best man that ever lived ? "

Magdalen was confronting her father with poor Jessie's
wrongs, and he felt that, if possible, she resented them more
than those done to her mother.

"I was a fiend, a demon in those days," he said. "I hated
the old man who had won the prize I coveted so much. I did
not care how deeply I wounded him. I wanted him to feel as
badly as I felt when I first knew I had lost her. I was angry
with fate, which had thwarted me a second time and taken her
from me just as I thought possession secure. I did not despair of coaxing her to go with me at last, — that is, I hoped I
might, for I knew her pliant nature ; but death came between
us, and even in that terrible hour, when the water around me
was full of drowning, shrieking wretches, I cursed aloud when
I saw her golden hair float on the waves far beyond my reach,
and then go down for ever."

He shuddered as if with cold, was silent a moment, and then
went on :

"I loved Jessie Morton as I have never loved a woman
since, not even your mother. I went to Belvidere just because
she had once lived there. I met you in the graveyard, and
was struck with your eyes, which reminded me of Laura. I

never dreamed you were my child, but I was interested in you, and made you a part of the little pencil sketch I drew of the yard. That picture has often excited Alice's curiosity, for it was hung in my room at home. When you came and I heard you were from Millbank I hid the sketch away, lest you should see it and recognize the place and wonder how I came by it. You see I am telling you everything, and I may as well con· fess that when Penelope told me you were from Millbank I wished you had never come to us. We usually hate what we have injured, and anything connected with the Irvings has been very distasteful to me, and I could not endure to hear the name."

"But you would like Roger; he is the best, the noblest of men!" Magdalen exclaimed, so vehemently that her father must have been dull indeed if he had failed to see how strong a hold Roger Irving had on Magdalen's affections.

He did see it, but could not sympathize with her then, or at once lay aside all his olden prejudice against the Irvings, and it would be long before Magdalen would feel that in her love for Roger she had her father's cordial sympathy.

"I have no doubt you speak truly," he said, "and some time, perhaps, I may see him and tell him myself that his mother was pure, and good, and innocent as an angel; but now I wish to talk of something else, to tell you of my former life, so you may know just the kind of father you have found."

Magdalen would rather not have listened to the story which followed, and which had in it so much of wrong, but there was no alternative. Mr. Grey was resolved upon a full confession, and he made it, and when the recital was finished, he said :

"I have kept nothing from you. I would rather you should know me as I am. I have told you what I could never tell to Alice. She could not bear it; but you are different. Alice leans on me, while something assures me that I can lean on you. I am growing old. I have a heavy burden to bear. I want you to help me ; want you to trust me ; to love me, if you can. I have sinned greatly against your mother ; have helped to make her what she is. But I have tried to be kind to her these many years; and I ask you, her child and mine, to forgive all that is past and try to love me, if only ever so little. Will you, Magdalen?"

He held his hands toward her, and Magdalen took them in hers, and by the kisses and tears dropped upon them, Arthur Grey knew that there was a better understanding between himself and Magdalen than had existed an hour ago; that she knew the worst there was to know of him, and would, in time, see and appreciate the better side of his character, and with this he was content, and seemed much like himself, the courtly, polished gentleman, whose attentions were almost lover-like, and who showed in every look and action how thoroughly he believed in and how fast his love and interest was increasing for the beautiful girl who had been so conclusively proved to be his daughter.

CHAPTER XLV.

AT BEECHWOOD.

IT was not possible for Mrs. Seymour to keep perfectly quiet with regard to the cause of Magdalen's sudden journey to Cincinnati, especially as Alice herself talked and wondered so much about it. Little by little it came out, until Alice had heard the entire story, which made her for a time almost as crazy as Laura herself. A few lines from Guy written hurriedly in the cars, on his way to Schodick, told her at last that what she hoped was true, and then in the solitude of her room she knelt, and amid tears of joy and choking sobs paid her vows of praise and thanksgiving, and asked that she might be made worthy of the priceless gift so suddenly bestowed upon her. The next day a telegram from her father apprised her that he would be home that night "with Magdalen,

your sister ;" and Alice kissed the words "your sister," and repeating them softly to herself went dancing about the house,
now explaining to the astonished servants, and again trying to
convey some definite idea to the darkened mind of her mother.
But Laura's only answer was, "Baby is in the cradle. I see
her if you do not."

She was, however, pleased that Magdalen was coming home,
and asked to be made "tidy and nice, so that Magda would be
glad."

Once, as Alice was buttoning the clean wrapper and arranging the crimson shawl, which gave a soft tint to the sallow,
faded face, the poor creature's lip quivered a little as she said,
"Am I really nice, and will Arthur kiss me, think you ? I
wish he would. It might make me better. Your talk of Cincinnati has brought queer things back to me, and sometimes I
can almost get hold of how it was, then it goes again. I wish
Arthur *would* kiss me."

"I hope he will. I think he will," Alice said, her own kisses
falling in showers upon the wasted face of the invalid, who
seemed more rational than she had for many weeks.

As the day wore on and the hour approached for the travellers to arrive, Alice grew very restless and impatient, and would
not for an instant leave the window where she watched anxiously for the carriage.

"They are coming ; they are here," she cried at last, and
running into the hall she was the first to welcome Magdalen,
whose face was drenched with tears, and whose heart throbbed
with an entirely new sensation of happiness as she felt Alice's
kisses upon her lips and the tight clasp of her arms about her
neck.

Aunt Penelope came next, and though her greeting was more
in accordance with perfect propriety, there was much genuine
affection and kindness in it, and Magdalen knew that she believed in her and accepted her as a niece. Mr. Grey was no-
where to be seen. He had stood an instant and looked on
when Alice and Magdalen first met, then he vanished from sight,

and Alice found him half an hour later in her mother's room, whither he had gone at once. Perhaps the recovery of his daughter had brought back something of his olden love for Laura, or there were really better impulses at work within, for his first thought was for his wife, and when, as he came in, she asked if "She did not look nice," he stooped and kissed her as he had not done in years; and the poor creature, who had known so much suffering, clung to him, and laying her aching head upon his bosom, sobbed and wept like a child, saying to herself, "he did, he did — kiss me, — he did — "

"Laura," Mr. Grey said, softly, when she had grown a little calm, "try to understand me, won't you? The lost baby is found. It is Magdalen, too, whom a kind man took care of. We have seen Mrs. Storms in Cynthiana; you remember her?"

Laura remembered Mrs. Storms, and for a few moments the fixed expression of her eyes and the drawn look about her forehead and mouth showed that reason was making a tremendous effort to grasp and retain what she heard. But it had been dethroned too long to penetrate the darkness now, and when she spoke, it was to assert that "baby was in the cradle over there; Magdalen was too big to be her baby." Hopeless and disheartened, Mr. Grey desisted in his attempts to make her understand, but stayed by her till Alice came to say that dinner waited.

It was thought best that Magdalen should not see Laura until the next morning, when it was hoped that she might convey some definite idea to her mind. They were to meet alone, and after breakfast Magdalen repaired to the sick-room, and entering unannounced, was received by her mother with outstretched arms and a cry of joy.

"You've been gone long, Magda, — so long," she said, "and my head has ached so for you."

"But I've come now to stay always. I have found the baby, too. Let me tell you about it," Magdalen replied, controlling her own emotions with a mighty effort, and keeping as calm and composed as it was possible for her to do. "I'll make it like a story," she said; and Laura listened very quietly while Magdalen, beginning at the funeral of Mrs. Clayton, went over the whole ground correctly, until she reached the *cars* and the *boy* who took the baby.

Then she purposely deviated from the truth, and said it was a *woman* to whom the child was given.

"No, no, not a woman," Laura exclaimed, vehemently. "It was a boy, and I sat with him, and my head was all in a snarl. I fell when I got out of the stage in Cincinnati, and struck it a heavy blow on the pavement, and it set to buzzing so loud."

Here was something of which Magdalen had never heard; the blow on the head would account for the culmination of the queer fancies which must have been gathering in Laura's brain for months and years, and which broke out suddenly into decided insanity. If that were true she could understand better than she did before why she had been abandoned; but she did not stop then to reason about it. She was too anxious to keep her mother to the point, and when she paused a moment she said to her, "You fell and hurt your head on the pavement, and then got into the train."

"Yes, the next day, or the next, I don't know which, my head ached so, and I didn't know anybody to tell, and I had baby to care for, and I thought the Grand Duchess would get her as she did Alice, and shut me up, and the boy looked good and true, and I gave her to him, and got out and thought I'd run away, and there was another train standing there, and I took it and went I don't know where, nor what else, only I was back in Cincinnati again, and after a great while got here to the Grand Duchess, with the baby safe as safe could be. My head was sore a long time, but I did not tell them about the blow for fear they'd say I was crazy, but they said it just the same."

She was getting excited, and anxious to make the most of the present opportunity, Magdalen took up the story herself, and told what the boy did with the child, and how he called her Magdalen, after the same lady for whom Mrs. Grey had named her, and how the child grew to a woman, and came out at last to Beechwood, sent there by Heaven to find her sister, and minister to her poor mother, who did not know her at first, but who would surely know her now.

"Don't you, *mother ;* don't you know I am your daughter Magdalen ? "

For an instant Laura seemed to comprehend her. There was a perplexed look on her face, then her lip began to quiver and her tears to come, and throwing her arms around Magdalen's neck, she said, "Mother, mother, you call me that as Alice does. You say you are the baby, and Arthur said so too. I wish I could remember, but I can't. Oh, I don't know what you mean, but you make me so happy ! "

And that was Magdalen's success, with which she tried to be satisfied, hoping there might come a time when the cloud would lift enough for her to hear her mother call her daughter, and feel that she knew what she was saying.

The next day Guy came from Schodick. Magdalen was the first to meet him, and her eyes asked the question her lips would never have uttered.

"No, *Miss Grey,*" Guy said, laughingly, adopting the name which sounded so oddly to her. "He did not send any written reply to your note. There is some *confounded bother* on his mind, I could not divine what ; something which sealed his lips, though his face and eyes and manner had 'Magdalen, Magdalen,' written all over and through them. Don't look so sorry, cousin," he continued, winding his arm around her waist, " and don't try to look so innocent, either. I guessed the whole thing when you handed me the note, and I know it for certain now. You love Roger Irving, he loves you. There is nothing truer than that, but there is something between you, — what, I don't know, — but I'll find it out. I'll clear it up. He is a splendid fellow, and almost idolized, I judge, by the people of Schodick. Not much like his nephew Frank, ——"

Here Guy stopped suddenly, for Mr. Grey was coming in with Alice, who asked the result of his visit to Mr. Irving.

"I have learned but little that we did not know before," Guy said. "Mr. Irving's description of the woman who left the child tallies exactly with what I should suppose Mrs. Grey might have been at that time. A woman of twenty or thereabouts, medium size, dressed in mourning, carrying a satchel, with black hair and eyes, — the woman I mean, not the satchel, — restless, peculiar eyes they were, and he said he had frequently noticed the same peculiarity about Magdalen's, which means, I take it, that they flash and glow and raise the mischief with a fellow."

He gave a comical look at Magdalen, and did not observe the frown on Mr. Grey's face, but Magdalen did, and felt a throb of pain as she saw a new obstacle laid across the path to Roger. There were many things she wanted to ask Guy about that home in Schodick which she could not ask with her father and Alice present, and she felt as if she must cry outright with pain and disappointment. Guy, however, was not one to lose much of what was passing around him, and after telling Mr. Grey the particulars of his interview with Roger, he sauntered towards the library, knowing that Magdalen would follow him. And she did, and blushed scarlet at the whistle he gave as he said, "I knew you would come. Now what shall I tell you? What do you want to know most?"

He had her secret. There was no use in trying to conceal it, and Magdalen did not try, but said, "Don't laugh at me, Guy. Think what Roger has been to me all these years, and tell me how he looks, and about the house, and does he work very hard? Oh, Guy, he was made poor by *me*, you know, and I have *all* my wages saved up ready to send him, but now I can't earn any more, and what I've got is so little."

Her tears were rolling down her cheeks, but she brushed them away and looked half indignantly at Guy, who laughed merrily as he said: "The absurdity of your sending money to Roger. He does not need it; take my word for that. The

house is old, old as the hills, I reckon, judging from its archi-
tecture, but very comfortable and neat as a lady's slipper. I
saw no marks of poverty. The neighbors did not send in anything while I was there, and we had a grand dinner. I dined
with him, you see, on solid silver, too, with wine and Malaga
grapes; though come to think of it, the grapes were a present
from Frank, who sent a box from New York. That Frank is
living fast and doing the magnificent on a great scale, I reckon,
but I'd rather be Roger than he."

"Didn't Roger say anything to my note?" Magdalen asked,
more interested in that than in Frank and Malaga grapes.

"No, he didn't, except, 'Tell Magdalen I will answer this by
and by,'" Guy said; "but he seemed glad for you in one sense,
and then again he didn't. I should say, if I am any judge of
mankind, that he was afraid that the gulf between the rich
Miss Grey and the poor Mr. Irving was wider than he could
span, but I may be mistaken; at all events it is sure to come
right in time. As I said before, he is a splendid chap, and you
have my consent."

Guy was very hopeful, very comforting, and Magdalen felt
better after this talk with him, and looked anxiously for the
letter which Roger was to send, and which came at last. A
kind, brotherly letter, in which he said how glad he was for her
that she had found her friends, and disclaimed all idea of her
having ever brought trouble to him.

"You have been the source of the greatest happiness I have
ever enjoyed," he wrote; "and I would give a dozen fortunes
rather than not have known you, and enjoyed you for the few
years I called you mine, my sister, my child, my *Magda*. Once
I could have cursed the man who lured my mother to her ruin,
and cursed his children, too; but I did not then dream that
such a curse would cover the beautiful child of my adoption.
Heaven bless you, Magda, in *all* your new relations! Heaven
make you happy in them as you deserve to be! Once I hoped
I might see you at Schodick, and I have thought how I would
take you around the old farm, and to the places hallowed

by my mother's footsteps, and pictured to myself just what you would say, and just how you would look. But that dream is over now. I cannot ask you to come. You would not care to, nor your father care to have you. Remember me to him, if you like. . Since I know he is your father, I feel no bitterness toward him. Good-by! And God bless you, and bring you, at last, to the Heaven where I hope to find my little girl again!"

This was Roger's letter, over which Magdalen wept tears of pain, mingled with tears of joy, — joy, that he loved her still, — for only in that way could she construe some portions of his letter; and pain that he should write as if all intercourse between them was necessarily at an end; that he was probably never to see her; she never to go to Schodick, when she had within the last few days thought so much about it, and planned how she could, perhaps, get her father and Alice to go with her, and thus show Roger to them. That plan had failed, that castle fallen, and Magdalen wept its fall, wondering what had come over Roger, and what he meant by some portions of his letter. She did not know how, for a moment, Roger had writhed under the knowledge that she was the daughter of Arthur Grey; or how the fact had seemed at once to build an iron wall between him and the girl he loved better than his life. Then, just as he was recovering from the first great shock, and hope was beginning to make itself heard again, Guy had unwittingly put his oar into the troubled waters, and made them ten times worse. In his enthusiasm about Magdalen, whom he extolled as all that was lovely and desirable, he gave Roger the impression that between himself and Magdalen there already existed an intimacy which would ripen into relations of a closer nature than mere friends. And Roger listened to him with a face which told no tales, and a heart which throbbed with jealousy and pain; and then, feeling that he must know something definite, said to him, just as he was leaving:

"Excuse me, Mr. Seymour, if I seem impertinent. From what you have said, I gather that you hope, one day, to be more to Mr. Grey than his sister's nephew."

And Guy, thinking only of Alice at that moment, had replied :

"You are something of a Yankee, I *guess*. But you are right in your conjectures. I do hope to be more to Mr. Grey than his sister's nephew; but there's no telling. Girls are riddles, you know."

And then good-natured, kind-hearted Guy had gone his way, leaving in Roger's mind an impression which drifted his life farther and farther away from Magdalen, whose heart went out after him now with a stronger desire than it had ever known before.

CHAPTER XLVI.

THE CLOUDS BREAK OVER BEECHWOOD.

ACKNOWLEDGED by every one as the daughter of the Greys, caressed and idolized by Alice, petted by Aunt Penelope, and treated by Mr. Grey with the utmost tenderness and deference, Magdalen would have been perfectly happy but for one unfulfilled desire which was the skeleton at her side. Between herself and Alice there was perfect confidence, while she was learning daily more and more to respect her father, who omitted nothing which could tend to win her love. To her mother she was the same gentle nurse who never grew weary, but who sat hour after hour by the bedside, repeating over and over again the story of the lost child, until Laura knew it by heart and would correct her at once if she deviated ever so little. There was a change gradually stealing over the invalid, a change both in body and mind. She was far more quiet, and did not rock the cradle as much as formerly, and once, when Magdalen had finished her story for the second time that day, she said to her, "I think I have heard it enough to know that baby is not in the crib, and never has been. . Take it away, — where I can't rock it again and make Arthur so nervous."

They carried it out, — Alice and Magdalen together, — and put it away, each ·feeling, as they left it, as if turning from a little grave. Laura never spoke of it but once, and that was to her husband. Pointing to the place where it had stood so long, she said with a smile, "Do you see it is gone? It will never keep you awake again. Kiss me, Arthur, for I, too, shall be gone before long."

He kissed her, more than once, and put his arms about her, and felt how small and thin she had grown; then looking into her face he saw the change which only Magdalen had noticed. The burden was lifting, the cloud was breaking, and Laura was passing away. There was no particular disease, only a gradual breaking up of the springs of life, and as the days grew longer and warmer she drooped more and more, until at last she never left her bed all day, and rarely spoke except to Magdalen, who was with her constantly. Sometimes it seemed as if there was a gleam of reason struggling through the darkness which had shrouded her mind so long, but it never went much furthei than such expressions as, " I think I do remember the boy with the kind voice and soft blue eyes, to whom I gave Magdalen, but I can't quite make out how that Magdalen and this are one."

" I would not try now; I'd go to sleep and rest," Magdalen would say, and obedient to the voice she always heeded, Laura would grow quiet and fall again into the deep slumber so common to her now.

In this way she lingered on for a few weeks, and then died quietly one morning in early June, when her husband was in New York and only Magdalen and Alice were with her. They knew that she was failing, but they had not thought the end so near, and were greatly shocked when, at a faint call from her, they hastened to her side and saw the pinched look about her nose, the deep pallor about her lips, and the sweat-drops upon her brow.

"Let me go for aunty," Alice said, but her mother answered, "No, Alice, there won't be time. I'm going somewhere, going away from here, and I want you and Magda to stay. It's getting night, and the way is dark, and life is very weary. Give me your hands, both of you, my children."

She acknowledged Magdalen, and with a cry the young girl fell on her knees beside the bed, exclaiming, " Mother, oh mother, you do know I am your child. Call me that once more."

But Laura's mind was going out after one who was not there, and she only whispered, "Where is Arthur? Allie, where is your father?"

"In New York," was the reply, and a shadow flitted over the otherwise placid face, as Laura rejoined, "Always in New York, the old, old story. I wish he was here; tell him, will you, that I am gone, and before I went I left word I was sorry I had troubled him so much. I'd like to kiss him again. *Magda*, let me kiss you for him ; give it to him for me, and if I don't look very bad, ask him to kiss me back, but not unless I'm decent looking. He's fastidious, and fancies pretty faces."

She wound her arms about Magdalen's neck and her cold lips gave the kiss for Arthur. It was their last; they never moved again, and when Magdalen unclasped the clinging arms from her neck and laid the poor head which had ached so long back upon the pillow, she saw that her mother was dead. They telegraphed at once for Mr. Grey, who reached home just at nightfall. They had dressed Laura in white and laid her on the couch with flowers in her hands and flowers on her pillow, and as if in answer to her wishes, the old worn look had passed entirely from her face, which looked smooth and fair and younger than the face of forty is wont to look. Many traces of her soft, girlish beauty clung to her still, and Mr. Grey, when first he went into the room and drew aside the muslin which covered her face, started, and uttered an exclamation of surprise at the unexpected beauty of his wife. He *did* like pretty faces, and he was glad that the Laura, who lay there dead, was like the girl he had loved so passionately for a few brief months. The sight of her as she was now with the placid look on her white face and the long eyelashes shading her cheek, brought back something of his former love for Laura Clayton, and kneeling beside her he wept tears of sorrow and regret for the life which had been so full of sorrow.

"Laura, poor Laura," he said, and his hand fondled the cold cheek which would never again glow beneath his touch, " I wish you could know I am here beside you, and how sorry I am for the past. Dear Laura, I wish you had forgiven me before you died."

"She did, father, and I am here to tell you what she said."

It was Magdalen's voice which spoke and Magdalen who knelt by the weeping man, calling him father for the first time in her life! Passing the open door she had heard his words of grief, and her first impulse was to comfort him. It was very meet that there in the presence of the dead mother she should call him father, and the name fell involuntarily from her lips, sending a thrill of joy through his heart, and causing him to look up as she knelt beside him and press her closely to his heart.

"Bless you, Magdalen, my darling, my daughter ; bless you for calling me by that name. I have longed so for it, have wanted so to hear it. I shall be a better man. I am a better man. I believe in Alice's God, and here by Laura's side, in His presence and yours, I acknowledge my past transgressions. I renounce my infidel notions, in which I really never did believe. I wish to be forgiven. I pray that Jessie and Laura, both of whom I wronged, may have met together in the Heaven to which I am unfit to go."

He was talking more to himself than to Magdalen, who, when he had finished, told him of Laura's last moments, omitting everything which could give him pain and telling him only of the kindly message left for him. "She wanted to kiss you," Magdalen said, "and as you were not here, she gave it to me for you. This was *mother's kiss* for my *father ;*" and Magdalen's lips were pressed against the lips of Mr. Grey, who broke down entirely and sobbed like a little child.

Could Laura have looked into that room, she surely would have been satisfied with the tears and kisses given her by her husband, who sat there until midnight, and whom the early morning found at her side. Had she been always as young and fair and as dearly loved as when he first called her his wife, he could not have seemed more sad or expressed more sorrow than he did. Everything which could be done for a dead person was done for her, and her funeral was arranged with as much care as if she had been a blessing rather than a trouble to the house over whose threshold they bore her, on a beautiful summer's day, out to the little family cemetery on the hillside, where they buried her beside the proud old woman, who made no demur when the plebeian form was laid beside her.

CHAPTER XLVII.

BELL BURLEIGH.

THERE was to be a wedding in St. James's Church, Boston, and the persons most interested were Isabella Helena Burleigh and B. Franklin Irving, whose bridal cards were sent to Beechwood one morning a few weeks after Laura's death. It was to be a most brilliant affair, and was creating considerable excitement both in Belvidere and in Boston, where by virtue of her boasted blood, which she traced back to Elizabeth's time, and by dint of an indomitable will, Miss Burleigh was really quite a belle. It was her *blood* which had won upon Mrs. Walter Scott, who said she thought more of family pedigree than money, and Miss Burleigh's pedigree was without taint of any kind. So Mrs. Walter Scott was pleased, or feigned to be so, and went to Boston, and took rooms at the Revere, at fifteen dollars per day, and had her meals served in her private parlor; and Frank brought down his own horses and carriage, and took another suite of rooms, and paid at the rate of twenty dollars per day for all his ex-.travagances in the way of cigars and wine, and friends invited to dinner. His evenings he spent with his bride-elect in her home on Beacon Street, where everything betokened that the proprietors were not rich in worldly goods, if they were in blood.

The Burleighs were very poor, else the spirited Bell, who had more brains than heart, had never accepted Frank Irving. She knew just what he was, and, alone with her young sister Grace, mimicked him, and called him " green," and when she was with him in company, shivered, and grew hot and cold, and angry at some of his remarks, which betokened so little sense.

He was gentlemanly to a certain extent, and knew all the ins and outs of good society; but he was not like the men with whom Bell Burleigh had associated all her life; not like the men she respected for what was in their heads rather than in their purse. But as these men had thus far been unattaina-ble, and the coffers at home were each year growing lower and lower as her father grew older and older, Bell swallowed all senti-ment, and the ideas she had once had of a husband to whom she could look up, and accepted Frank Irving and Millbank.

But not without her price. She made Frank *pay* for her *blood* and charms, and pay munificently, too. First, one hundred thousand dollars were to be settled on herself, to do with as she pleased. Next, sister Grace and her father were both to live with her at Millbank, and Frank was to clothe and sup-port Grace as if she were his own sister. Then, her brother Charlie's bills at college must be paid, and after he was gradu-ated he must come to Millbank as his home until he went into business.

These were Bell's *terms*, and Frank winced a little and hesi-tated, and when she had told him to take time to consider, he took it and did consider, and decided that it would not pay, and went for a few weeks to New York, where at the Fifth Avenue Hotel he came again upon the Burleighs. Bell knew just how to manage him, and ere he had been there three days he was as much in love with her as ever, and madly jealous of every one who paid her marked attentions. The *price* she asked seemed as nothing compared with herself, and one evening after she had been unusually fascinating and brilliant, and had snubbed him dreadfully, he wrote a note accepting her terms, and begging her to name an early day and put him out of torture. In her dressing-gown, with her own hair falling about her shoulders and her braids and curls of false hair lying on the bureau, Bell read the note, and felt for a moment that she despised and hated the man who wrote it, just because he had acceded to her unreasonable demands.

"I wish he had decided otherwise. I would almost rather die than marry him," she thought, while her eyes put on a darker look and her face a paler hue.

Then she thought of the home on Beacon Street, of the pinching poverty, the efforts to keep up appearances, of her father growing so old, and of herself, not so young as she was once, — twenty-eight, the Bible said, though she passed for twenty-five; then she thought of Charlie, her young brother, and glanced at Grace, her only sister, who lay sleeping so quietly before her. All the love Bell Burleigh had was centred in her father, her brother, and in Grace, the fair young girl, with soft blue eyes and golden hair, who was as unlike her sister as possible, and who was awakened by Bell's tears on her face, and Bell's kisses on her brow.

"What is it, Bell?" she asked, sitting up in bed, and rubbing her eyes in a sleepy kind of way.

Bell did not say, "I have sold myself for you." But — "Rejoice, Grace, that we are never again to know what poverty means; never to pinch and contrive and save and do things we are ashamed of in order to keep up. I am going to marry Mr. Irving, and you are all to live with me at Millbank.

Grace was wide awake now, and looking earnestly in her
sister's face for a moment, said :

" *You* marry that Mr. Irving, *you*, Bell ? There is not a thing
in common between you, unless you love him. Do you ?"

" Hush, Grace ; don't speak of *love* to me," and Bell's voice
had in it a hard, bitter tone. " I parted company with that
sentiment years ago, before you could understand. You have
heard — of — Dr. Patterson, missionary to India ? I would
once have gone with him to the ends of the earth, but mother
said I was too young, too giddy, and the *Board* thought so, too.
I was not quite seventeen, and I defied those old fogy ministers
to their faces, and when they asked me so coldly if I supposed
myself good enough to be a missionary, I answered that I was
going for the love I bore to *Fred*, and not to be a missionary,
or because I thought myself good as they termed goodness.
And so it was broken off, and Fred went without me, and as
they said he must have a wife, he took a tall, red-haired woman
many years his senior, but who, to her other qualifications,
added the fact that she was a *professor*, and believed herself
called to a missionary life. She is dead now, and her grave is
on the banks of the Ganges. But Fred's life and mine have
drifted widely apart ; I am no wife for him now. I have grown
too hard, and reckless, and selfish, and too fond of the world,
to share his home in India. And so all I have to remind me
of the past as connected with him is *one* letter, the last he ever
wrote me, and a lock of his hair, — black hair, not *tow color*,"
and Bell smiled derisively, while Grace knew that she was
thinking of Frank, whose hair, though not exactly tow color,
was far from being black.

Bell paused a moment, and then went on :

" You know how poor we are, and how we struggle to keep
up, and how much father owes. Our home is mortgaged for
more than it is worth, and so is every article of any value in it.
I should like brains if I could get them set off with money, but
as I cannot, I have concluded to take the money. I have
counted the cost. I know what I am about. I shall be Mrs.

Franklin Irving, and pay our debts, and keep you all with me, — and — be — happy."

She said the last very slowly, and there was a look of pain in the eyes of this girl who had once thought to be a missionary's wife, and who had in her many elements of a noble woman. She did not tell Grace the price she had put upon herself That was something she would rather her young sister should not know, and when Grace, whose ideas of marriage were more what Bell's had been in the days of the Fred Patterson romance, tried to expostulate, she stopped her short with, — "It's of no use; my mind is made up. I have told you what I have because I knew you would wonder at my choice, and I wanted you to know some of the causes which led me to make it. I want your love, your respect, your confidence, Grace, I want —"

Bell's lip quivered a little, and she bowed her dark head over her sister's golden one, and cried a little; then sat erect, and the old proud, independent look came back to her face, and Bell Burleigh was herself again, — the calm, resolute, cool-headed woman of the world, who had sold herself for money and a home.

They met in the wide entrance hall to the dining-room next morning, Frank and Bell, and while he stood for a moment, waiting for his paper, she said a word to him, and they walked together into breakfast an engaged pair, with quite as much love and sentiment between them as exists in many and many an engagement which the world pronounces so eligible and brilliant.

Bell had some shopping to do that morning, and Frank did not see her again till just before dinner, when he met and escorted her to his mother's private parlor, where she was to receive the priceless boon of Mrs. Walter Scott's blessing. That lady had heard the news of her son's engagement with a good deal of equanimity, considering there was no money to be expected. Like many people of humble birth, Mrs. Walter Scott set a high value on family and blood, and, as Bell's were both of the first water, she accepted her as her future daughter-in-law, wishing to herself that she was not quite so independent, and resolute, and strong-minded, as the absence of these qualities would render her so much more susceptible to subjugation, for Mrs. Walter Scott meant to subjugate her.

As Mrs. Franklin Irving, she would, of course, be the nominal mistress of Millbank; but it would be only nominal. Mrs. Walter Scott would be the real head; the one to whom everybody would defer, even her daughter-in-law. But she said nothing of this to Frank. She merely told him she was willing, that Miss Burleigh was a girl of rare talent and attainments, that she had a great deal of mind, and intellect, and literary taste, and would shine in any society.

Frank did not care a picayune for Bell's talents, or attainments, or literary taste. Indeed he would rather of the two that she had less of these virtues, and did not overshadow him so completely as he knew she did. Still he was in love with her, or thought he was, and extolled her to his mother, but did not speak of the hundred thousand dollars as a marriage settlement, or of the arrangement about the Judge and Charlie and Grace. He would let these things adjust themselves; and he had faith in Bell's ability to manage her own matters quietly, and without his aid.

She was looking very beautiful when he led her to his mother, arrayed in her heavy purple silk with the white ermine on the waist and sleeves, and Mrs. Walter Scott thought what a regal-looking woman she was. There was a deep flush on her cheek and a sparkle in her black eyes, and her white teeth glittered between the full, pouting lips which just touched Mrs. Walter Scott's hand, as she stood to receive the blessing.

When they went into dinner that night after the blissful interview, there was about Frank a certain consciousness of ownership in the beautiful girl who walked beside him and on whose finger a superb diamond was shining, the seal of her engagement, and those who noticed them particularly, and to whom Miss Burleigh was known, guessed at the new relations existing between the two.

This was in the winter, and before Magdalen's parentage was discovered. Since then the course of true love had run pretty smoothly for once, and Frank had only felt a single pang, and that when he heard who Magdalen Lennox was. Then for a moment all his former love for her came back, and Bell Burleigh, who chanced to be at Millbank for a day or so, wondered what had happened to him that he was so absent-minded and indifferent to her blandishments. She was very gracious to him now, feeling that there was something due him for all his generosity to her, and as she could not give him love in its truest sense, she would give him civility at least and kindliness of manner and a show of affection. So when she saw the shadow on his face, and with a woman's intuition felt that something more than mere business matters had brought it there, she spoke to him in her softest manner and sang him her sweetest songs and wore his favorite dress, and twice laid her hand on his, and asked what was the matter that he looked so gloomy ; had he heard, bad news ? He told her no, and kissed her forehead, and felt his blood tingle a little at this unusual demonstration from his *fiancée*, and so fickle and easily soothed was he, that beneath the influence of Bell's smile the shadow began to lift, and in the letter of congratulation which he wrote to Magdalen there was nothing but genuine sympathy and rejoicing that she had found her home at last and a sister like Alice Grey.

He did not tell of his engagement ; he was a little ashamed to have Magdalen know that he was so soon " off with the old love and on with the new ;" and so she did not suspect it until every arrangement was complete and the day for the bridal fixed. Great was the expenditure for silks and satins and laces and jewelry, and not only New York and Boston, but Paris, too, was drawn upon to furnish articles of clothing rare and expensive enough for a bride of Bell Burleigh's fastidious taste and extravagant notions. Frank, who grew more and more proud of his conquest, and consequently more and more in

love with his bride-elect, insisted upon furnishing the bridal
trousseau, and bade her spare neither money nor pains, but
get whatever she wanted at whatever cost.   And Bell accepted
his money, and spent it so lavishly that all Boston was alive
with gossip and wonder.   There were to be six bridesmaids,
and three of them were to accompany the happy pair for a
week or so at Frank's expense; and Frank never flinched a
hair, even when presented with the Paris bill, in which were
charges of one hundred dollars and more for just one article of
underclothing.   All Bell's linen came ready made from Paris,
and such tucks and ruffles and puffs and flutings and laces had
never been seen before in Boston in so great profusion.   And
Bell bore herself like a queen, who had all her life been accustomed to Parisian luxury.   There was no doubt of her gracing
Millbank or any other home, and Frank each time he saw her
felt more than repaid for the piles and piles of money which
he paid out for her.

At Millbank there was also dressmaking proceeding on a
grand scale, and though Mrs. Walter Scott's wardrobe differed
somewhat from Bell's, inasmuch as it was soberer and older, —
the silks were just as heavy and rich, and the laces just as
expensive.   New furniture, new table-linen, and new silver
came almost daily to Millbank, together with new pictures, for
one of which the sum of two thousand dollars was paid.   When
old Hester Floyd heard of that she could keep quiet no longer,
but vowed " she would go to Belvidere and visit Mrs. Peter
Slocum, who was a distant connection, and would be glad to
have her a spell, especially as she meant to pay her way."

When Hester resolved to do a thing she generally did it,
and as she was resolved to go to Belvidere she at once set
herself to prepare for the journey.

CHAPTER XLVIII.

THE WEDDING, AND HESTER FLOYD'S ACCOUNT OF IT.

ROGER had written to Frank, congratulating him upon his approaching marriage, but declining to be present at the wedding. He wished to know as little as possible of the affairs at Millbank, and tried to dissuade Hester from her visit to Mrs. Slocum. But Hester *would* go, and three days before the great event came off she was installed in Mrs. Slocum's best chamber, and had presented that worthy woman with six bottles of canned fruit, ten yards of calico, and an old coat of Aleck's, which, she said, would cut over nicely for Johnny, Mrs. Slocum's youngest boy. After these presents, Hester felt that she was not " spunging," as she called it, and settled herself quietly to visit, and to reconnoitre, and watch the proceedings at Millbank. And there was enough to occupy her time and keep her in a state of great excitement.

The house had been painted brown, and Hester inveighed against that, and scolded about the shrubbery, which had been removed, and cried a little over the trees which, at Bell's instigation, had been cut down to open a finer view of the river from the rooms appropriated to the bride. Into these rooms Hester at last penetrated, as well as into all parts of the house. Mrs. Walter Scott had gone to Boston, and Frank had gone with her. Hester saw them as they drove by Mrs. Slocum's in their elegant new carriage, with their white-gloved colored driver on the box, and she had represented her blood as " bilin' like a caldron kettle, to see them as had no business a-ridin' through the country and spending Roger's money."

She knew where they were going, and that the coast was clear at Millbank, and with Mrs. Slocum, who was on good terms with the housekeeper, she went there that afternoon and saw " such sights as her eyes never expected to see while she lived."

"I mean to write to Magdalen and let her know just what carryin's on there is here," she said to Mrs. Slocum; and she commenced a letter that night, telling Magdalen where she was, and what she was there for, and not omitting to speak of the "things" she had brought, and which would pay for what little she ate for a week or two.

"Such alterations!" she wrote. "The house as brown as my hands, and a picter in it that cost two thousan' dollars, the awfullest daub, I reckon, that ever was got up. Why, I had rather a hundred times have that picter in my room of Putnam goin' in after the wolf; that means somethin', and this one don't. But the rooms for the bride, they are just like a show-house, I'm sure, with their painted walls and *frisky* work, I b'lieve, they call it, and the *lam-kins* at the winders, fifty dollars a winder, as I'm a livin' woman, and a naked boy in one of 'em holdin' a pot of flowers on his head; and then her *boodér* or anything under heavens you are a mind to call that little room at the end of the upper south hall, and which opens out of her sleepin' room. There's a glass as long as she is set in a recess like, and in the door opposite is a lookin'-glass, and in the door on t'other side, — three lookin'-glasses in all, so that you can see yourself before and behind and beside, and silk ottermans, and divans and marble shelves and drawers, and a chair for her to sit in and be dressed, and she's got a French waitin'-maid, right from Paris, they say, and some of her underclothes cost a hundred dollars apiece, think of that, when three yards of factory would make plenty good enough and last enough sight longer. I'm glad I don't have to iron 'em; they've got a flutin'-iron they paid thirty dollars for, and Miss Franklin's bed, that is to be, is hung with silk curtains. I should s'pose she'd want a breath of air; the dear knows I should; and one of the rooms they've turned into a picter gallery, and the likenesses of the *Burleighs* is there now, 'cause Mrs. Franklin must have 'em to look at. There's her granny, a decent-lookin' woman enough, with powdered hair, and her husband took when he was younger, and her mother

in her weddin' close, exactly the fashion, I remember, and her
father and herself when she was younger by a good many years
than she is now, for them as has seen her says she's thirty if
she's a day, and Frank ain't quite twenty-eight."

There was a break just here in Hester's epistle. She had decided to remain with Mrs. Slocum until after the party which
was to be given for the bride at Millbank as soon as she returned from her wedding trip, and so she concluded not to
finish her letter until she had seen and could report the doings.
The wedding day was faultlessly fair; not a cloud broke the deep
blue of the summer sky, and the air had none of the sultry heat
of July, but was soft and balmy, and pure from the effects of the
thunder-shower of the previous day. If the bride be blessed
on whom the sun shines, Bell Burleigh was surely blessed and
ought to have been happy. There was no cloud on her brow,
no brooding shadow of regret in her dark eyes, and if she sent
a thought across the seas after the Fred whose life of toil she
would once have shared so gladly, it did not show itself
upon her face, which belied Hester's hint of thirty years, and
was all aglow with excitement. She made a beautiful bride,
and the length of her train was for days and days the theme of
gossip among the crowd who saw it as she walked from the
carriage to the church upon the carpets spread down for the
occasion. She wore no ornaments, but flowers. Her diamonds, and pearls, and rubies, and amethysts were reserved for
other occasions, and she looked very simple and elegant and
self-possessed, and made her responses in a firmer, clearer
voice than Frank. He was nervous, and thought of Magdalen,
and was glad she and Alice had made their mother's recent death
an excuse for not being present, and wondered if her voice
would have been as loud and steady as Bell's when she said,
"I, Isabel, take thee, Franklin," and so forth. On the whole,
the occasion was a trying one for him; his gloves were too
tight, and his boots were tighter and made him want to scream
every time he stepped, they hurt his feet so badly. He took
them off when he returned from the church, and thus relieved,

felt easier, and could see how beautiful his new wife was, and how well she bore her honors, and felt proud and happy, and did not think again of Magdalen, but rather what a lucky fellow he was to have all the money he wanted and such a bride as Bell.

They were going West for a week or two, then back to Millbank for a few days, and then to Saratoga or the sea-side, just where the fancy led them. Mrs. Walter Scott returned to Millbank and sent out a few cards to the *élite* of the town, the Johnsons, and Markhams, and Woodburys, and the clergyman and her family physician. As for the *nobodys*, they were not expected to call, and they consoled themselves with invidious remarks and watching the proceedings.

On Sunday the Irving pew was graced by Mrs. Walter Scott, who wore a new bonnet and a silk which rustled with every step. She was very devout that day, and made a large thank-offering for her new daughter-in-law, a crisp ten-dollar bill, given so that all who cared could see and know it was a ten. She did not see Hester Floyd until service was out, — then she started a little as the old lady stepped into the aisle before her, but offered her hand cordially, and felt that she was very good, and very pious, and very democratic to walk out of church in close conversation with Hester, whom she invited to come and see the changes they had made in the house, and stop to tea, if she liked, with the housekeeper.

Mrs. Walter Scott had nothing to fear from Hester now, and could afford to be very gracious, but the old lady was neither deceived nor elated with her attention. She had been to the house, she said, rather crisply, and seen all she wanted to, and she did think they might have let some of the rooms alone and not fixed 'em up like a play-house, and she'd cover up that naked boy in Mrs. Franklin's room before she got there, for if she was a modest woman, as was to be hoped, she'd feel ashamed. And then, having reached the new carriage, with its white-gloved driver, the two women said good-day to each other, and Mrs. Walter Scott's dove-colored silk was put carefully into the car-

riage by the footman, and the door was closed and the two shining horses were off like the wind, leaving Hester to watch the
cloud of dust and the flash of the wheels which marked the
progress of the fast-moving vehicle.

The particulars of this interview were faithfully recorded for
Magdalen's benefit, the old lady breaking the Sabbath for the
sake of "writing while the thing was fresh in her mind" and
she could do it justice.

Ten days more went by, and then it was reported in the
street that the workmen in the shoe-shop and factory were to
have a holiday on Thursday in honor of their master's return to
Millbank with his bride.   It was whispered, too, that in his letter to his foreman Frank had hinted that some kind of a demonstration on his arrival would be very appropriate and accept-
able, and if his agents would see to it he would defray any expense they might incur for him. Some of the workmen laughed,
and some sneered, and some said openly they had no demonstration to make, but all accepted the holiday willingly enough,
and a few of the young men, with all the boys, decided to get up
a bonfire and fireworks, on a large scale, inasmuch as the bill
was to be paid by "the Gov."

Accordingly a hundred dollars' worth of fireworks were ordered
from Springfield, and Frank, who came about eight o'clock,
was greeted with a rocket which went hissing into the air and
fell in sparks of fire just over his shoe-shop, the shingles of
which were dry with age and the summer heat.   There was a
crowd after all to honor him, and an impromptu band, which
played "Hail to the Chief," and "Come, Haste to the Wedding," and finished up with a grand flourish of "Dixie," to
which many bare feet kept time upon the lawn in front of Millbank.   A collation, which Hester in her journal-letter called a
"collection," had been prepared for them on the grounds, and
the small boys ate themselves almost sick on ice-cream and
raisins, and then halloed with might and main for the bride, who
appeared, leaning on her husband's arm, smiling and bowing,
and offering her hand to be shaken, while all the while she was

wondering if "the miserable little wretches hadn't warts or some worse disease which she would catch of them."

The collation over, the bridal party returned to the house, and the crowd went back to their fireworks, to which the tired and slightly disgusted Bell hardly gave a look. She had the headache, and went early to her room, and closing her blinds to shut out the glare of the blue and red lights which annoyed her terribly, she fell asleep, and was dreaming of the missionary Fred when the cry of "Fire, Fire," aroused her, and Frank looked in with a white, frightened face, telling her the large shoe-shop was on fire, and bidding her not to be alarmed. Some sparks from the first rocket sent up had fallen on the dry roof of the shoe-shop, and set it on fire, the flames creeping under the shingles, and making great headway before they were discovered. It was a long time since there had been a fire in Belvidere, and the excited people hardly knew how to act. Roger had always been tolerably well prepared for such an emergency, but matters at Millbank were managed differently now from what they were when he was master there. The rotary pump was out of order, the engine would not work well at all, and after half an hour or more of orders and counter-orders, of running to and fro, and accomplishing but little, it was certain that nothing could save the huge building, whose roof was one mass of flame, and from whose windows a light was shining brighter than any bonfire ever yet kindled in honor of a bride. When Frank had hinted at demonstrations, for which he would pay, he never dreamed of a bonfire like this, where jets of flame rose far into the sky and shone across the river upon the hills beyond, and made the village as light as day. Bell never went to fires, she said to Mrs. Walter Scott, who, in her dressing-gown, with her shawl over her head, looked in upon her daughter-in-law on her way to join the multitude in the streets. She was too thoroughly city bred to go to fires, and she saw every member of the household depart, — her bridesmaids, sister Grace and all ; and then, as from her bed she could see the whole, she lay down among her pillows and rather enjoyed watching the flames, as they attacked first one part of the building and then another, making the sight every moment more beautiful and grand. It never occurred to her how much of her husband's fortune might be consuming before her very eyes, and when toward morning he came up to her, pale, smoke-stained, and burned, she merely asked what time it was, and how he could bear to stay so long where he could do no good.

Frank's first thought, when he saw the fire, was of Holt and the insurance. During his wedding tour, he had heard that the company in which his shop was insured had failed, and he had telegraphed at once to Holt "to see to it, and insure in another company." Since his return he had not thought of the matter until now, when something told him that his orders had been neglected, and that if the building burned his loss would be heavy. Taking off his coat, he had worked like a hero, and done much to inspirit his men, who, encouraged by his intrepidity, had followed wherever he led and done whatever he bade them do. But it was all in vain, and Frank went back to Millbank a poorer man by many thousands than the setting of the sun had found him, while a hundred people or more were thrown out of employment, and suddenly found themselves with nothing to do.

In this emergency their thoughts turned to Roger. They had heard that a large shoe manufactory was in process of erection at Schodick, and that Roger was to have the superintendence of it, and never before had there been so heavy a mail sent from Belvidere as there was the day following the fire. More than forty men wrote to Roger, telling him of the disaster, asking for situations under him, and offering to work for less than they had been receiving. To many of these favorable answers were returned, and the consequence was that the tide of emigration from Belvidere to Schodick set in at once, and a number of Frank's houses were left tenantless on his hands. The party, however, came off the following week, and servants were im-

ported from New York, with cake and flowers and fruit, and a
band came out from Springfield, and lights were hung in every
tree upon the lawn and boys hired to watch them, for Frank
had learned a lesson from the still smouldering ruins of his shop,
and was exceedingly nervous and uncomfortable on the subject
of fires and lights, and read a lesson on caution to his mother
and the servants and all the family, *save* his wife.   There was
something in her black eyes which prevented his taking liber-
ties with her, and her lamp was suffered to remain in close
proximity to the lace curtains of her room, and he did not say a
word.

Roger wrote to his nephew immediately after the fire, expressing his sorrow, and consoling him by saying he could
afford to lose the shop and still be the richest man in the
county.   Frank thought of the piles and piles of money he had
spent, and wondered what Roger would say, could he know of
all his extravagances.   But Roger did not know, and his letter
comforted Frank, who, after reading it, felt better than he had
before since the fire, and who was quite like himself on the night
when, with his bride, he stood to receive the congratulations of
his dear four hundred friends who came from Boston and Wor-
cester and Springfield and Hartford and New York, but not
many from Belvidere.   A few only of the citizens were considered good enough to enter the charmed presence and take the
white hand on which a thousand-dollar ring was shining.   Bell
wore her diamonds that night, her husband's bridal present, for
which ten thousand dollars were paid, and she shone and flashed
and sparkled, and turned her proud head proudly, and never
spoke to Frank when she could help it, but talked instead with
her old friends from Boston, — scholars and professors, whose
discourse she found far more congenial than Frank's common-
places were.

It was a grand affair, and old Hester, who was at the house,
and from the kitchen and side passages saw much that was
going on, added to her journal a full account of it, after having
described the fire, which she said was "just a judgment from

the Lord." Hester had rather enjoyed the fire, and felt as if justice was being meted out to *Mrs. Walter Scott,* who cried and wrung her hands, and reproached the people for standing idle and seeing her son's property burned before their eyes. Hester ached to give her a piece of her mind, but contented herself with saying in her presence, "that folks didn't seem very anxious. She guessed if it had been Roger's shop they'd have stepped more lively, and not sat on the fence, a whole batch on 'em, doin' nothin'."

" I *was* a little mad at 'em," she wrote to Magdalen, "and felt pretty bad when the ruff tumbled in, but I didn't screech as *that woman* (meaning Mrs. Walter Scott) did. She nigh about fainted away, and they carried her into Miss Perkins's house and flung water in her face till them curls of hern were just nothin' but strings. T'other one, Miss Franklin, wasn't there, and I heard that she lay abed the whole time and watched it from the winder. That's a nice wife for you. Oh, I tell you, he'll get his pay for takin' the property from Roger, and givin' such a party as he did, and only invitin' fust cut in town, and not all of *them.* There was Miss Jenks, and Miss Smith and Miss Spencer s'posed of course they'd have an invite, and Miss Jenks got her a new gown and had it made in Hartford, and then wan't bid ; and if you'll believe, that sneakin,' low-lived, ill-begotten horse-jockey of a *Holt* was there, and his wife, with a yeller gownd and blue flower stuck in the middle of her forehead. How he came to be bid nobody knows, only they say he and Frank is thick as molasses, and agree on the hoss question. Madam's sister was there, a pretty enough lookin' girl with yellow curls and blue eyes, and it's talked that she's to live there, and the whole coboodle of 'em. A nice time they'll have with Mrs. Walter Scott, who holds her head so high that her neck must sometimes ache. You or'to see 'em ride on horseback to Millbank ; Miss Franklin in black velvet, her sister in blue, and even old madam has gone at it, and I seen her a canterin' by on a chestnut mare that cost the dear knows what. Think on't, a woman of her age, with a round hat and feather, ridin' a hoss. It's just ridiculous, I call it. I'm goin' home to-morrow, for Roger and Aleck is gettin' kind of uneasy. Roger is a growin' man. He's got some agency in the mill to Schodick and the shop, and he's makin' lots of money, and folks look up to him and consult him till he's the fust man in town. I wish you two would come together some day, and I can't help thinkin' you will. Nothin' would suit me better, though I was hard on you once about the will. I was about crazy them days, but that's all got along with, and so good-by.

"HESTER FLOYD."

"There goes the quality from Millbank out to have a picnic, and the young madam is ridin' with another man. Nice doin's so soon, though I don't blame her for bein' sick of Frank. He's growing real fat and pussy-like, and twists up them few white hairs about his mouth till they look like a shoemaker's waxed end.   "Yours again to command,

"H. FLOYD."

CHAPTER XLIX.

HOW THEY LIVED AT MILLBANK.

RS. WALTER SCOTT knew nothing of the hundred thousand dollars settled upon Bell, or of the arrangement for the entire family to live henceforth at Millbank. She was well pleased, however, to have Judge Burleigh and Grace and Charlie there for a few days, with other guests from Boston and New York. They were a part of the wedding festivities, and she enjoyed the *éclat* of having so many young people of style and distinction in the house, and enjoyed showing them off at church and in the street. She enjoyed the grand dinners, too, which occupied three hours and for which the ladies dressed so elaborately, the bride wearing something new each day, and astonishing the servants with the length of her train and the size of her hoops, and she enjoyed for a time the dance and the song, and hilarity in the evening, but she be-gan at last to grow weary of it all, and to sigh for a little quiet; and greatly to Frank's surprise and Bell's delight, she gave up the trip to Saratoga, and saw the bridal party depart without her one morning a few days after the party.

The United States was their destination, and the town was soon teeming with gossip of the bride who sported so exquisite jewelry and wore so magnificent dresses and snubbed her husband so mercilessly. Frank's turn-out, too, was com-mented on and admired, and he had the satisfaction of know-ing that his carriage and his horses were the finest in town; but for any genuine domestic happiness he enjoyed, he might as well have been without a wife as with one.

One day Bell expressed a desire for a glass of water from the spring on the grounds of the Clarendon, and as she knew she was exquisitely dressed, and sure to create a sensation all along the street, she started with Grace and her husband for the spring. The Clarendon was not full, though it had the reputation of entertaining the very *crème de la crème*, those who preferred cool shades, and pure air and fresh furniture and quiet, to the glare and crowd and heat and fashion farther down town. There were but few on the broad piazza that afternoon, but at these Bell looked curiously, especially at the two young ladies who were standing with their backs to her, and whom she at once decided to be somebody. Both wore deep mourning, and one was fair with chestnut hair, while the braids of the other were dark and glossy and abundant. A white-haired man and middle-aged woman were sitting near them, and a tall, fine-looking young man was standing by the shorter of the young ladies, and evidently describing something which greatly interested all, for peals of laughter were occasion-ally heard as the story proceeded, and the girl with the chestnut hair turned her head a little more toward Bell, and also toward Frank. There was a violent start on his part, and then he sug-gested that they return to their hotel. But Bell insisted upon going up the hill and occupying some vacant chairs upon the piazza. She was tired, and it looked so cool and pleasant there, she said in that tone of voice which Frank always obeyed, and with a beating heart he gave her his arm and led her up the steep bank and put her in her chair and brought another for Grace, and fidgeted about and managed to keep his back toward the group which he knew was watching him. The hum of their voices had ceased as he drew near with his magnificent bride, who in her diamonds and costly array presented so striking a contrast to the two plainly-dressed young ladies, whom Bell thought so beautiful, wondering greatly who they were. Frank *knew* who they were, and stood an awkward moment and tried not to see them; then with a great gulp, in which he forced down far more emotion than his wife ever gave him credit for possessing, he turned toward them, accidentally as it seemed, and uttering a well-feigned exclamation of surprise went forward to meet Alice Grey and Magdalen.

"Speak of angels and you hear the rustle of their wings," Guy said, when the first words of greeting were over. "I was talking of you, or rather of Mrs. Irving, whom I saw at the hop last night, and whose beauty and dress I was describing to these rustic country girls."

"Oh, yes, certainly. I should like to present my wife to you," Frank said, his spirits rising as they always did when his wife was complimented.

He was proud of her, and if she allowed it, would have been fond of her, too; and he felt a thrill of satisfaction and pleasure that she was looking so well and bore herself so regally as he led her to his friends and introduced her as "My wife, Mrs. Irving."

Bell had heard of the Greys and knew that Alice and Magdalen were fully her equals, and her manner was very soft and gracious towards them as she expressed her pleasure in meeting them. Frank brought her chair for her and placed it between Alice and Magdalen, and held her parasol, and leaned over her, and admired her so much as almost to forget the cir-

cumstances under which he had last seen Magdalen. Bell was
very ladylike, very gentle, and very bright and witty withal,
and the Greys were perfectly charmed with her, and wondered
how she could have married Frank, who in point of intellect
was so greatly her inferior.

For two or three weeks the Greys remained at Saratoga, and
during that time they saw a great deal of the Irvings, while between Bell and the Misses Grey there sprang up a strong liking,
which was very strange, considering how unlike they were in
almost everything. Once Frank spoke to Magdalen of Roger,
who, he said, was getting on famously, both as to money and
reputation.

"Why don't you two marry?" he asked abruptly. "You
ought to. There's nothing in the way that I can see."

Ere Magdalen could reply, they were joined by Alice, but
Frank had detected that in her manner which convinced him
that her love for Roger was unchanged.

"Then why the plague don't they marry?" he said to himself. "It's Roger's fault, I know. He's afraid she is not willing. I mean to write and tell him she is. I owe them both
something, and that's the way I'll pay it;" and that afternoon
Frank did commence a letter to Roger, but he never finished
it, for dinner came on, and after it a drive, and then a letter
from his mother urging his immediate return, as the hands at the
mill were conducting badly, many of them leaving to go to
Schodick, and others taking advantage of his absence, and a
drunken overseer.

Accordingly, the bridal pair went back to Millbank, and
Grace was with them, and Charlie too; while Mr. Burleigh,
who had been disposing of his affairs in Boston, came in a few
days, and Mrs. Walter Scott heard Mrs. Franklin tell the servant to see that everything was in order in "Judge Burleigh's
room; you know which it is, the one at the end of the hall, adjoining Charlie's."

This looked as if there was an understanding between Mrs.
Franklin and Katy with regard to rooms, while the quantity of

baggage which came from the depot in the express wagon looked very much as if the Burleighs had come for good, with no intention of leaving. This was a condition of things of which Mrs. Walter Scott did not approve ; but there was something in the gleam of Mrs. Bell's black eyes which warned her to be careful what she said. She was a little afraid of Bell and so kept quiet until she heard from her own maid that " the old gentleman" was putting his books on the shelves, which, un-known to her, had been conveyed into his room, and was arranging a lot of *stones*, and *snails*, and *birds*. Then she could keep still no longer, but attacked her son with the question :

" Are *all* the Burleighs to live here in future ? I did not suppose you married the entire family."

Frank had looked forward to a time when some such ques-tion would be propounded to him, and was glad it had come. Once he had been afraid of his mother, and he was still a good deal in awe of her and her opinions, but upstairs was a lady whom he feared more, though she had never spoken to him ex-cept in the mildest, softest manner, and he wisely resolved to let his mother know the worst which had befallen her, and told her, as gently as possible, and with the tone of one who was communicating a piece of good news, that the Burleighs were a rather singular family, very strongly attached to each other ; yes, *very* strongly attached, that they never had been sepa-rated, and that Bell had accepted him only on condition that they should not be separated, but live together at Millbank as they had done at Boston.

There was intense scorn in Mrs. Walter Scott's eyes, and in her voice, as she said, " And so you have taken upon your-self the maintenance of four instead of one ! "

" Why, no, — not exactly, — that is, — Judge Burleigh and Charlie, and — yes, and Charlie — "   ·

Frank was getting matters somewhat confused, and did not quite know how to make it clear to his mother's mind that Charlie would only trouble them till he was set up in business, and that Judge Burleigh's society and the pleasure of having so polished and agreeable a gentleman in the house was a suffi-cient compensation for any expense he might be to them; but she understood him at last, and knew that the Judge and Charlie were there for good, and the rooms they occupied had been fitted up expressly for them without a reference to her or her wishes in the matter. Had she known of the hundred thousand made over to Bell she would have gone mad. As it was, she flew into a towering passion, accusing Frank of being in lead-ing-strings and henpecked, and threatening to leave and go back to New York, as she presumed he wished she would. Frank did not wish any such thing. His mother was more necessary to him now than before his marriage, for he was gen-erally sure of her sympathy, which was more than he could say of his wife. So he soothed and quieted her as best he could, and when she referred to his recent loss by fire, and asked how he could burden himself with so large a family, he told her a lie, and said he should be able to recover a part of the in-surance, and that even if he did not, his income was sufficient to warrant his present style of living, and she need have no fears for him; or if she had, he would *settle* something upon her at once, so that in case *he* failed entirely she would not be penniless. This was a happy thought, and Mrs. Walter Scott consented to be mollified and let the Burleighs remain in quiet in consideration of twenty-five thousand dollars in bonds and mortgages and railroad stock which Frank agreed to give her, and which he did convey that very day. She had at first asked for fifty thousand, but had agreed to be satisfied with twenty-five, and Frank went to his dinner a poorer man by over two hundred thousand dollars than he had been when Millbank came into his possession. His wife's settlement and his mother's, and his recent heavy expenditures, had drawn largely upon his means for procuring ready money whenever he wanted it, and as he sat at his table, loaded with silver and groaning with luxuries, he felt almost as poor as he had done in days gone by, when he had not enough to pay his tailor and furnish himself with cigars.   And still he was rich in lands, and the mill, and houses, and he tried to shake off his feelings of de spondency and to believe himself very happy with that beauti ful wife beside him, who let him pare her peach for her, and took grapes from his own cluster, and playfully pushed the wine bottle aside when he was about to help himself for a second time.

Mrs. Walter Scott was cold as an icicle, and not all the Judge's suavity of manner had power to thaw her.   She had promised not to say anything disagreeable to the Burleighs, but her face was very expressive of her dislike, and she could hardly answer either the Judge or Charlie with common civility. She did not object to Grace; and she was even guilty of wishing Frank's choice had fallen upon the younger rather than the elder sister, against whom she could, as yet, bring no accusation, but whom she distrusted and secretly feared.   Bell thoroughly understood her mother-in-law, and knew tolerably well how to manage her.   As Frank's wife, *she* was mistress of Millbank, and though she made no show of her authority, her power was felt in everything; and after she had reigned a month or more, not a servant, with the exception of Mrs. Walter Scott's own maid, went to their former mistress for orders, but received them from the new lady, who was very popular with them, and who, to a certain extent, was popular in town.   She could not endure most of the people by whom she was surrounded; but she had made up her mind that it was better to be admired than hated, and she adopted the *rôle* of Patroness, or Lady Bountiful, and played her part well, as Frank knew by his purse, so often drawn from when Bell and Grace had some poor family on their hands.

Grace did not go back to school.   Millbank was intolerable to the bride without the presence of her light-hearted, merry little sister; and so Grace stayed and studied at home, under a governess, to whom Frank paid five hundred dollars a year ; and paid it the more willingly when he found that the pretty Miss North admired *him* above all men, and was not averse to receiving compliments from him, even in the presence of his wife. Bell did not care how many governesses he compli-mented, provided he did not say his soft nothings to her. Had he affected a great fondness for her, and bored her with atten-tions and caresses, she would have hated him, but he had sense enough to see that love-making was not her style, and so he contented himself with being the possessor of the beautiful and expensive article, which he knew better than to handle or touch. She was always very polite and gracious towards him, but after a few weeks he ceased to pet or caress her, and almost always called her Mrs. Irving, and studied her wishes in everything, except in the matter of horses and *Holt ;* there he was his own master, and did as he liked, and bought as many horses as he chose, and went to the races, and bet largely, and made Holt his chief man of business, and gave him money to expend on double teams and single teams, and trusted him im-plicitly ; and when people asked where Holt got his means to live as he was living now, Frank had no suspicions whatever, but said, " Joe Holt was a first-rate chap, the best judge and manager of horses he ever saw, and ought to succeed in life."

And so the autumn waned, and the Christmas holidays were kept at Millbank on a grand scale, and young people were there from Boston, — friends of Grace and friends of Bell, — and the festivities were kept up sometimes till two or three o'clock in the morning, and some of the young men became very noisy and unmanageable, and among them Charlie, while Frank was undeniably *drunk*, and was carried to his room and given into the care of his wife ! Then Bell rose in her might, and locked up the wine and sent the fast young men home, and gave Charlie a lecture he never forgot, and made him join the Good Templars forthwith, and what was better, made him keep the pledge. What she did to Frank nobody knew, — locked him up, the servants said. At all events, he kept his room for two days, and only came out of it after the New Yorkers were gone to their respective homes. Then he looked very meek and crestfallen, like a naughty boy who has been punished, and his mother pitied him and tried to sympathize, and made him so very angry that he was guilty of swearing at her, and bidding her let him and Bell and their affairs alone.   And Mrs. Walter Scott did let them alone for a while, and stayed a great deal in her own room, and had her meals served there, and took to writing a book, for which she always thought she had a talent. It was about mismated people, and the good heroine looked very much like Mrs. Walter Scott, and the bad one like Mrs. Franklin Irving, while the villain was a compound of Judge Burleigh, and Charlie, and Holt, the horse jockey.

CHAPTER L.

ROGER.

FRANK had invited Roger to spend Christmas at Mill-bank, but Roger had declined, and had passed the holidays in his usual way at Schodick, where there had come to him a letter from Arthur Grey, who, in referring to the past, exonerated Jessie from all blame, and asked Roger's forgiveness for the great wrong done to him.   Then he thanked him for his kindness to Magdalen, and closed by saying :

"Magdalen has been very anxious for you to come to Beechwood, and I should now extend an invitation for you to do so, were it not that we have decided to leave at once for Europe.   We sail in the 'Persia' next week, immediately after my daughter's marriage, which will be a very quiet affair. Hoping to see and know you at some future time, I am

"Yours truly,   ARTHUR GREY."

This letter had been delayed for some reason, and it did not reach Roger until a week after it was written, and then there came in the same mail a newspaper from New York, directed by Magdalen herself. Around a short paragraph was the faint tracing of her pencil, and Roger read that among the passengers the "Persia" would take out were Mr. Arthur Grey and daughter, Mrs. Penelope Seymour, and Mr. Guy Seymour and lady. Magdalen had underscored the "Mr. Guy Seymour and lady," and upon the margin had written :

"Good-by, Roger, good-by."

When Roger read Mr. Grey's letter he had felt sure that the daughter to whose marriage reference was made was Magdalen herself, and the newspaper paragraph and pencil-marks confirmed him in this belief.

"Good-by, Roger, good-by."

His white lips whispered the words, which seemed to run into each other and grow dim and blurred as the great tears gathered in his eyes and obscured his vision.

"Good-by, Roger, good-by."

Yes, it was good-by forever now, and he felt it in its full force, and bowed his head upon his hands and asked for strength to bear this new pain, which yet was not new, for he had long felt that Magdalen was not for him. But the pain, though old, was keener, harder to bear, and hurt as it had never hurt before, for now the barrier between them, as he believed, was a husband, and that for a time seemed worse than death.

Again the rock under the evergreen on the hillside witnessed the tears and the prayers and the anguish of the man whose face began to look old and worn, and who, the people said, was working too hard and had taken too much upon his hands. He was the superintendent now of the cotton mill, which had been enlarged, and of the shoe-shop erected since his residence in Schodick. His profession, too, was not neglected, and the little office on the green still bore his name, and all the farmers for miles around asked for "Squire Irving," as they called him, when they came into town on business pertaining to the law. His word was trusted before that of any other. What Squire Irving said was true, and no one thought of doubting it. To

him the widows came on behalf of their fatherless children, and
he listened patiently and advised them always for the best, and
took charge of their slender means and made the most of them.
The interests of orphan children, too, were committed to his
care, so that he fortunately had little time to indulge in sentiment or sorrow, except at night, when the day's labor was over,
and he was free to dwell upon the hopes of the past, the bitter
disappointment of the present, and the dreariness of the future.

After that paragraph in the newspaper he had heard no
more of the Greys, and had only mentioned them once. Then
he told Hester of Magdalen's marriage with the young man who
had come to see them, and whom Hester remembered perfectly.

Hester did not believe a word of it, she said ; but Roger replied that Magdalen herself had sent him the paper, while Mr.
Grey had written, so there could be no mistake. Then Hester
accepted it as a fact, and looking in her boy's face and seeing
there the pain he tried so hard to suppress, she felt her own
heart throbbing with a keener regret and sense of loss than she
would have felt if Roger had not cared so much.

"That settles the business for him," she said. "He'll never
marry now, and I may as well send off to the heathen that
cribby quilt I've been piecin' at odd spells, thinkin' the time
might come when Roger's wife would find it handy."

And as she thus soliloquized old Hester washed her tea-
dishes by the kitchen sink and two great tears rolled down her
nose and dropped into the dish water. After that she never
mentioned Magdalen, and as the quilt was not quite finished,
she laid it away in the candle-box cradle which stood in the
attic chamber, and over which she sometimes bent for five minutes or more, while her thoughts were back in the past ; and
she saw again the little girl who had sat so often in that cradle,
and whose dear little feet were wandering now amid the won
ders of the Old World.

And so the winter, and the spring, and the summer went by,
and in the autumn Frank came for a few days to Schedick,

looking almost as old as Roger, and a great deal stouter and redder in the face than when we saw him last; while a certain inflamed look in the eye told that Bell's arguments on the sub-ject of temperance had not prevailed with him as effectually as they had with her brother Charlie. Frank's love of wine had increased and grown into a fondness for brandy, but during his stay in Schodick he abstained from both, and seemed much like himself. Very freely he discussed his affairs with Roger, who pitied him from his heart, for he saw that his life was not a pleasant one.

With regard to his domestic troubles, Roger forbore to make any remarks, but he advised to the best of his ability about the business matters, which were not in a very good condition. The shoe-shop had not been rebuilt; there was always trouble with the factory hands; they were either quitting entirely, or striking for higher wages; and the revenues were not what Frank thought they ought to be. Ready money was hard to get; and he was oftentimes troubled for means to pay the house-hold expenses, which were frightfully large. As well as he could, Roger comforted the disheartened man, and promised to go to Millbank soon and see what he could do toward smooth-ing and lubricating the business machinery, and Frank while listening to him began to feel very hopeful of the future, and grew light-hearted and cheerful again, and ready to talk of something besides himself. And so it came about, as he sat with Roger one evening, he said to him:

"By the way, Roger, do you ever hear from the Greys? Do you know where they are?"

Roger did not; he had never heard from them, or of them, he said, since the letter from Mr. Grey, announcing Magdalen's approaching marriage with Guy Seymour.

"Announcing *what?*" Frank asked. And Roger replied:

"Magdalen's marriage with Guy Seymour. You knew that, of course."

"Thunder!" Frank exclaimed, "have you been so deceived all this time, and is that the cause of those white hairs in your whiskers, and that crow-foot around your eyes? Roger, you are a bigger fool than I am, and Bell has many a time proved to me conclusively that I am a big one. It is *Alice*, not Magdalen, who is Mrs. Guy Seymour. They were married very quietly at home; no wedding, no cards, on account of the mother's recent death. I know it is so, for I saw the happy pair with my own eyes just before they sailed. So what more proof will you have?"

Roger needed none, and Frank could almost see the wrinkles fading out of his face, and the light coming back to his eyes, as he tried to stammer out something about its being strange that he was so deceived. Looking at his uncle, now, and remembering all the past, there came again across Frank the resolution to make a clean breast of what should have been told long ago, and after a moment's hesitancy he began:

"Roger, old chap, there are things I could tell you if I wasn't afraid you'd hate me all your life. I b'lieve I'll take the risk any way, and out with the whole of it."

"I promise not to hate you. What is it?" Roger asked, and Frank continued, "Magdalen always loved *you*, and you were blind not to have seen it. You thought too little of yourself, and so fell into the snare laid for you. Mother knew she loved you, and then got you to assent to my addressing her, and I used you as an argument why she should listen to me, and it almost killed her, as you would have known had you seen her face."

"What do you mean? I don't think you make it quite clear," Roger asked, in a trembling voice; and then as well as he could Frank made it clear, and told of the ways and means he had resorted to in order to win Magdalen, who, through all, showed how her whole heart was given to Roger.

"If you had seen her in the garret, rocking back and forth, and moaning your name, and seen how she started from me when I said if she would marry me I would burn the will and never speak of it, you would have no doubt of her love for you."

"Frank, you have wronged me! oh, you have wronged me terribly!" Roger said, and his voice was hoarse with emotion. "Millbank was nothing to this; but go on, tell the whole; keep nothing from me."

And Frank went on, and told the whole which the reader already knows of his efforts to deceive both Roger and Magdalen, whom he had succeeded in separating.

"And were you never engaged?" Roger asked.

And Frank answered him:

"No, never. She would not listen to me for a moment. She admitted her love for you, and I — oh, Roger, I am a villain, but I am getting my pay. I made her think that you only cared for her as your ward or sister, when by a word I could have brought you together, — and she was proud and thought you slighted her, inasmuch as she never knew how much you were with her when she was sick. You were gone when she came to a consciousness of what was passing around her, and I did not tell her of the message you sent from the West. I wanted her so badly myself, but I failed. She left Millbank in my absence, and fate, — I guess I believe in fate more than in Providence, — led her to the Greys, and you know the rest, and why she has been cold toward you, if she has. She thought you wanted her to marry me, and I do believe she has found that the hardest to forgive, and I don't blame her, neither would Bell. The idea of anybody's marrying *me!*"

Frank spoke bitterly, and struck his fist upon his knee as he mentioned his wife.

But Roger did not heed that; he was thinking of Magdalen and what might have been had Frank spoken earlier. Perhaps 't was not too late now, and his first impulse was to fly across the ocean which divided them and find her; but neither he nor Frank knew where she was, though the latter thought he could ascertain Mr. Grey's address in New York, and would do so the first time he was in the city. He was going to New York soon, he said, and would do all he could to repair the wrong and bring Roger and Magdalen together.

"You deserve her if ever a man did," he continued, "and I hope, — yes, I know it will one day come right."

Frank brought his visit to a close next day, and left the old-fashioned farm-house among the Schodick hills, which seemed a paradise compared with Millbank, where he found his wife cool and quiet and self-possessed as ever, and his mother angry, defiant, and terribly outraged with some fresh slight put upon her by her daughter-in-law. With all his little strength he threw himself into the breach, and showed so much discretion in steering clear of both Scylla and Charybdis, that Bell felt a glow of something like respect for him, and thought that one or two more visits to his uncle might make a man of him. Poor Frank, with all his wealth and elegance, and his handsome wife, was far more to be pitied than Roger, to whom had been suddenly opened a new world of happiness, and whose face ceased to wear the old tired look it had worn so long, and who the people said was growing young every day. He felt within himself new life and vigor, and thanked Heaven for the hope sent at last to lighten the thick darkness in which he had groped so long. Very anxiously he waited for Frank's letter, which was to give him Mr. Grey's address, and when at last it came he wrote at once to Magdalen, and told her of his love and hopes, and asked if she would let him come for her when she returned to America, and take her with him to his home among the hills.

"It is not Millbank," he wrote, "but, save that Millbank is sacred to me for the reason that your dear presence has hallowed every spot, I love this home as well as I did that, or think I do. But you may not, and if you come to me I shall build another house, more in accordance with my bright bird, whose cage must be a handsomer one than this old New England farm-house."

This letter was sent to the care of Mr. Grey, and then, long before he could reasonably hope for an answer, Roger began to expect one, and the daily mail was waited for with an eagerness and excitement painful to endure, especially as constant

disappointment was the only result of that watching and waiting and terrible suspense.

Magdalen did not write, and days and weeks and months
went by, and Roger grew old again, and there were more white
hairs in his brown beard, and he ceased to talk about the new
house he was going to build, and seemed indifferent to everything but the troubles at Millbank, which were upon the increase, and which finally resulted in Mrs. Franklin Irving taking her father and brother and sister, and going off to Europe
on a pleasure tour.   Frank was glad to have them go, and
feeling free once more, plunged into all his former habits of
dissipation, and kept Holt with him constantly as his chief man
of business, and rarely examined his accounts, and knew less
how he stood than did his neighbors, who were watching his
headlong course and predicting that it would soon end in ruin.

CHAPTER LI.

MAGDALEN IS COMING HOME.

THE Greys had been gone little more than three years
and a half, and the soft winds of June were kissing
the ripples of the sea on the morning when they
finally embarked for America.   They had travelled all over
Europe, from sunny France to colder, bleaker Russia, but had
stopped the longest at the Isle of Ischia, where at the "Piccola
Sentinella" another little life came into their midst, and Guy
Seymour nearly went wild with joy over his beautiful little boy,
whose soft, blue eyes and golden brown hair were so much like
Alice's.   Magdalen was permitted to name the wonderful baby,
and without a moment's hesitancy she said, "I would like him
to be called after the best man I ever knew — 'Roger Irving.'"

"Oh, Magdalena mia, you don't forget him, do you ?   Love
16*

once love forever, is your maxim," Guy said, playfully ; but he
approved the name, and so did Alice, who knew more of Magdalen's heart-history now than she once had done, and who
with Guy had revolved many plans for bringing Roger and
Magdalen together.

Mr. Grey did not assent quite so readily to the name, though
he did not oppose it. He merely said, " Roger sounds rather
old for a baby ; but do as you like, — do as you like."

So they called the baby Roger Irving, and Magdalen was
godmother, and her tears fell like a baptismal shower upon the
little face as she thought of her own babyhood, and the man
whom she had loved so long, and who was continually in her
thoughts. She knew he was not married ; she had heard that
from the Burleighs who came one day to the " Piccola Sentinella," bringing news direct from home.

" Not married yet, and is not likely to be," Mrs. Franklin
Irving had said, as she sat talking with Magdalen, whose voice
was rather unsteady when she asked for Roger.

Quick to read expressions of thought and feeling, Bell noted
the flush on the young girl's face, and the tremor in her voice,
and felt that she had the key to Roger's bachelorhood. She
had met him twice, — once in Boston and once at Millbank, —
and had liked him very much, and shown her liking in many
ways, and even laid a little snare, hoping to entangle him for
Grace. This Frank saw, and told her "to hang up her fiddle,
for Roger's heart was disposed of long ago to one who loved
him in return, but who was laboring under some mistake."

Bell had forgotten this, but it came back to her again with
Magdalen at her side, and she told her "rumor said there was
a cause for Roger's celibacy ; that he loved a young girl who
had once lived with him, and that he was only waiting for
chance to bring her in his way again." Then she told how popular he was, and how greatly beloved by the people in Schodick
and vicinity, and how fast he was growing rich.

Oh, how Magdalen longed to go home after that, and how she
wondered that Roger did not write if he really loved her, and

how little she guessed that he *had* written long ago, and that her father had kept the letter from her. To this act Mr. Grey had been prompted by a feeling he did not himself quite understand. Against Roger as a man he had nothing, but he did not think it right that his daughter should marry the son of the woman whose early death had been indirectly caused by himself. Had he known how strong was Magdalen's love for Roger he would never have withheld the letter, for, if possible, Magdalen was dearer to him now than Alice, and he studied her happiness in everything. But she never spoke of Roger, and he hoped that time and absence would weaken any girlish affection she might have cherished for him. So when the letter came, and he saw it was from Schodick, he put it away unopened, and Magdalen knew nothing of it until long after Roger had ceased to expect an answer, and hope was nearly or quite extinct in his heart.

Perhaps she would not have known of it then if death had not invaded their family circle and laid his grasp upon her father, who died in Germany, in a little village on the Rhine. His death was sudden to all but himself. He had long known that he suffered from heart disease, which might kill him at any moment, and as far as his worldly affairs were concerned, he was ready. Every debt in America had been paid, every business matter arranged, and his immense fortune divided equally between his two daughters, with the exception that to Magdalen he gave thirty thousand dollars more than he gave to Alice, this being just the amount of poor Laura's property. He was sick only a day or two and able to talk but little, but he spoke to Magdalen of Roger Irving, and told her of the letter withheld and where to find it, and said to her faintly and at long intervals, "Forgive me, if I did wrong. I thought it would be better for the families not to come together. I hoped you might forget him if you believed yourself forgotten, but I see I was mistaken. I am sorry now for the course I pursued. I would like to see the boy, or man he is now. I saw him once when a little child. Jessie wanted to take him with her, but I

refused.   I hated him, because he was hers and not mine.   I
hated all the Irvings.   I took Alice from New Haven because
I feared she might fancy Frank.   I do not hate them now, and
when I'm dead, go back to Roger and tell him so, and tell —
tell Jessie — if you see her ; — yes, — tell her and Laura, too,
— that I tried — I tried — to pray, and I did pray — and I
hope — "

He did not say what he hoped, for his tongue grew stiff
and paralyzed, and only his eyes spoke the farewell which
was forever.   Alice and Guy were both away at a little
town farther up the river, where Guy had some friends ;
but they hurried back to the vine-wreathed cottage they had
taken for the summer, and where their father now lay dead.
He was an old man, of nearly seventy, and had lived out his
appointed time ; but his children wept bitterly over him, and
kissed his white lips and snowy hair, and then made him ready
for the coffin, and buried him on the banks of the blue Rhine,
where the river, in its ceaseless flow, and the rustling vines of
Germany sing a requiem for the dead.

"Let us go back to America," Magdalen said, when Guy
and Alice asked what her wishes were.

Even before her father was buried from her sight, she had found
Roger's letter, of more than two and a half years ago, and had
read it through, and her heart had leaped across the sea with
the answer she would give.   She knew Roger had not forgotten.   He might have lost faith in her, from her silence ;
but he loved her still, and amid all her sorrow for her father,
there was a spring of joy in her heart as she thought of the
future opening so blissfully before her.   She told Guy and
Alice everything, and while they both felt how deeply she had
been wronged, they uttered no word of censure against the
father, who had wronged her so.   He was dead and gone forever, and they made his grave beautiful with flowers and
shrubs, and placed by it a costly stone, and dropped their tears
upon it ; and then turned their backs on Germany and travelled
night and day until the sea was reached, — the glorious sea, at

sight of which Magdalen wept tears of joy, blessing the dashing waves which were to bear her home to Beechwood and to Roger Irving.

CHAPTER LII.

MILLBANK IS SOLD AT AUCTION.

MILLBANK was to be sold, with all its furniture and the hundred acres of land belonging to it. Five years had sufficed for Frank to run through his princely fortune, and he was a ruined man. Extravagant living, losses by fire and neglect to take advantage of the markets, fast horses, heavy bets, the dishonesty of Holt, his head man and chief adviser, and lastly, his signing of a note of twenty thousand dollars, — every penny of which he had to pay, — had done the business for him; and when the Greys landed in New York the papers were full of the "great failure" at Belvidere, and the day was fixed when Millbank was to be sold.

Guy pointed out the paragraph to Magdalen, and then watched her as she read it. She was very white, and there was a strange gleam in her dark eyes; but she did not seem sorry. On the contrary, her face fairly shone as she looked up and said, " I shall buy Millbank and give it back to Roger."

Guy knew she would do that, and he encouraged her in the plan, and went himself to Belvidere, where he was a stranger, and made all needful inquiries, and reported to Magdalen. Mrs. Frank had already left Millbank with her hundred thousand, not a dollar of which could Frank's creditors touch, or Frank either, for that matter.

Bell held her own with an iron grasp, and so well had she managed that none of the principal had been spent, and when the final crash came and her husband told her he was ruined, it found her prepared and ready to abdicate at any moment

The old home in Boston was sold, but she was able to buy a better one, and she did so, and with her father and sister took possession at once. To do Bell justice, she carried nothing from Millbank but her clothing and jewelry. The rest belonged to Frank's creditors, and she considered that it would be stealing to take it. This she said several times for the benefit of Mrs. Walter Scott, who, less scrupulous than her daughter-in law, was quietly filling her trunks and boxes with articles of value, silver and china, and linen and bedding, and curtains, and whatever she could safely stow away. Mrs. Walter Scott was about to buy a house, too, a cosy little cottage with handsome grounds, just out of New York, on the New Haven road. She, too, had managed well, as she supposed. She had speculated in stocks and *oil* until she thought herself worth forty thousand dollars. There was some of it lying in the bank, where she could draw it at any time, and some of it still in *oil*, which she was assured she could sell at an advance upon the original price. So, what with the forty thousand and what with the household goods she would take from Millbank, she felt quite comfortable in her mind, and bore the shock of her son's failure with great equanimity and patience. She was glad, she said, of something to break up the terrible life they were leading at Millbank. For more than a year, and indeed ever since Bell's return from abroad, scarcely a word had been exchanged between herself and Mrs. Franklin Irving, and each lady had an establishment of her own, with a separate table, a separate retinue of servants, and a separate carriage. There was no other way of keeping the peace, and in desperation Frank himself had suggested this arrangement, though he knew that the entire support of both families would necessarily fall on him. But Frank was reckless, and did not greatly care. He was going to destruction any way, he said to Roger, who expostulated with him and warned him of the sure result of such extravagance. "He was going to ruin, and he might as well go on a grand scale, and better, too, if that would keep peace between *the women.*"

And so he went to ruin, and wrote to Roger one morning,

"The smash has come, and I'm poorer than I was when I depended on you for my bread. Everything is to be sold, and I
can't say I am sorry. It's been a torment to me. I've never
had the confidence of my men; they always acted as if I was
an intruder, and I felt so myself. I wish I could give the thing
back to you as clear as when I took it. I'd rather saw wood
than lead the dog's life I have led for the last five years. Bell
is going to Boston. *She* is rich, and maybe will let me live with
her if I pay my board! That sounds queer, don't it? but I tell
you, old chap, you are better off without a wife. I don't believe
in women any way. Mother is going to New York and I am
going to thunder."

Roger's heart gave one great throb of sorrow for his nephew
when he read this letter, and then beat wildly with the wish that
he could buy Millbank back. But he was not able, and he
could have wept bitterly at the thoughts of its going to strangers.
"Thy will be done," was a lesson Roger had learned thoroughly,
and he said it softly to himself, and was glad his father did not
know that the old place which had been in the family more
than fifty years, was about to pass from it forever.

He went to Millbank and examined Frank's affairs to see if
anything could be saved for the young man, who seemed so
crushed, so hopeless, and so stony. But matters were even
worse than he had feared. There was nothing to do but to sell
the entire property. Roger *could* buy the mill, and the men
were anxious for him to do so, and crowded around him with
their entreaties, which Frank warmly seconded.

"Buy it, Roger, and let me work in it as a common hand. I'd
rather do it a thousand times than live on my wife, even if her
money did come from me."

Frank said this bitterly, and Roger's heart ached for him as
he replied that perhaps he would buy the Mill; he'd think of it
and decide. It was not to be sold till after Millbank, and his
decision would depend on who bought that. This comforted
Frank a little, and he felt a great deal better when he at last

said good-by to Roger, who went back to Schodick the day but one before Guy Seymour's arrival in Belvidere.

Guy did not go to see Frank. He found out all he cared to know from other sources, and reported to Magdalen, who could scarcely eat or sleep, so great was her excitement and so eager was she for the day of the sale.

"Have you answered Roger's letter?" Alice asked, and she replied: "No, nor shall I till Millbank is mine. Then I shall take my answer to him with a deed of the place."

She had it all arranged, — her going to Schodick unannounced to see Roger, her laying the deed before him, and her keen enjoyment of his surprise and astonishment, both at the deed and the sight of herself.

"It is five years since I saw him. I wonder if he will know me, and if he will think me old at twenty-four?" she said as she arose and glanced at herself in the mirror.

Three years of travel had not *impaired* but greatly *improved* her looks and style, and those who thought her handsome when she went away exclaimed now at her matchless loveliness, and Magdalen knew herself that she was beautiful, and was glad for Roger's sake. Every thought and feeling now had a direct reference to him, and when at last the day of the sale arrived, she was sick with excitement, and read Guy's message in bed.

He had promised to telegraph as soon as Millbank was hers, and all through the morning she waited and watched and her head throbbed with pain and she grew more and more impatient, until at last came the telegram.

"Millbank is yours. Mr. Roger Irving neither here nor coming. Guy."

Then Magdalen arose and dressed herself, and seemed like one insane as she flew about the room and packed a small hat-box preparatory for to-morrow's journey. She was going to Millbank to execute the deed, and then on to Schodick with Guy. Alice helped her all she could, and tried to keep her quiet, and make her eat and rest lest her strength should fail entirely.

But Magdalen was not tired, she said, nor sick now. She felt

better than she had done in years, and her eyes were bright as
stars and her cheeks like damask roses when she bade Alice
good-by and started for Belvidere.

Guy met her at the station, and conducted her to the new
hotel, which had been built since she left the place. The windows of her room commanded a view of Millbank, and she
looked with tearful eyes at her old home and Roger's, and
thought, "It will be ours again." She had no doubt of that, no
doubt of Roger, and her heart thrilled with ecstasy as she anticipated the joyous future. There had not been much excitement at the sale, Guy told her ; but few seemed to care for so
large a house, and the bids had ceased altogether when once it
was rumored that *he* was merely bidding for *her*, — for Magdalen.

"I believe they suspected your intention," Guy said, "and
you got Millbank some thousands cheaper than I thought you
would. It is a grand old place, and has not been injured by its
recent proprietors."

Magdalen did not wish to go into the house while Mrs. Walter
Scott was there, but she rode through the grounds in the afternoon, and the next day started with Guy for Schodick, which
they reached about three o'clock.

"Mr. Irving was in town," the landlord said, "and slightly
indisposed, he believed ; at least he was not at his office that
morning, and the clerk said he was at his house, sick."

"I am going to him at once," Magdalen said to Guy. "You
have been there. You can direct me, and within half an hour
after their arrival in Schodick she was on her way to Roger's
house with the deed of Millbank in her pocket.

CHAPTER LIII.

MAGDALEN AT ROGER'S HOME.

T had been some consolation to Roger to know that an Irving was living at Millbank, even if it was no longer his, but to have it pass into the hands of strangers was terrible to him, and on the day of the sale he lived over again the sorrow he had felt when first his fortune was taken from him.

He had requested Frank to inform him at once with regard to the purchaser, and had waited almost as impatiently as Magdalen herself, until Frank's telegram flashed along the wires, " Sold to Guy Seymour, for Magdalen."

Then for a moment Roger's heart gave a great throb of joy, and a hope or expectation of something, he knew not what, flitted through his mind.   He had seen in a paper that Guy Seymour had returned from Europe with his family, and from the same paper learned that Mr. Grey was dead.   There was no bitter- ness then in Roger's heart towards the man whose enemy he had been.   Arthur Grey was dead, and gone to One who would deal justly with him ; and Roger was sorry he had ever felt so hard towards him, for he had been the father of Magdalen, and she was as dear to him now as she had been in the years gone by, when she made the very brightness of his life.   He could not forget her, though her name was never on his lips, save as he bore it night and morning to the Throne of Grace, or whis- pered it to himself in the loneliness of his room, or up among the pines, where she always seemed near to him.   He had given up all hope of ever calling her his own.   His unanswered letter had driven him to that, and still the days were brighter and life seemed far more desirable after he knew that she had returned, that the same sky smiled on them both by day, and the same stars kept watch over them at night.

" Guy Seymour bought it for Magdalen," he said, as he held

the telegram in his trembling hand. "Yes, I see; her father has left her rich, and she has bought Millbank, and means perhaps to live there; but not alone, surely not alone in that great house;" and then Roger went off into a train of speculation as to Magdalen's probable intentions. Was Guy to be there with Alice, or was there a prospective husband across the sea? Roger grew hot and faint when he thought of that, and felt a headache coming on, and said to his partner that he would go home and rest a while. He told Hester of the telegram, and with a woman's ready wit she *guessed* what Magdalen's intentions might be, but gave no sign to Roger. She saw how pale he was looking, and was prepared to hear of his headache, and made him some tea, and told him to keep still and not bother about Frank's affairs.

"You've just tired yourself to death over 'em," she said, "and it's no wonder you are sick."

He was better the next day, and went as usual to his office, but the next morning his headache had returned with redoubled violence. And while Magdalen was making her way to the old-fashioned farm-house covered with vines and surrounded with flowers and shrubs, he was sleeping quietly upon the couch in his room, unmindful of the great happiness in store for him, — the great surprise, coming nearer and nearer as Magdalen hastened her footsteps, her heart beating almost to bursting when at a sudden turn in the road she came upon the house which they told her was Mr. Irving's.

"The first one round the corner. You'll know it by the heaps of flowers, and the pretty yard," a boy had said, and Magdalen had almost run, so eager was she to be there.

"Oh, how beautiful! I should know Roger lived here," she said, as she stopped to admire the velvety turf in which patches of bright flowers were blooming, the fanciful beds, the borders and walks, and the signs of taste and care everywhere visible.

She did not think of the old house, with its low windows and doors, and signs of antiquity. She saw only the marks of cultivation around it, and thought it was Roger's home. The

windows of an upper room were open, and a rustic basket of
ivy and geraniums and verbenas was standing in one of them,
while a book with the paper folder in it was in the other, and
across both white curtains were hanging, the summer wind
moving them in and out with a slow, gentle motion.

"I know that this is Roger's room," Magdalen said, and a
vague desire seized her that he might receive Millbank from
her there.

. . . .

Old Hester Floyd had finished her work and was about to
"tidy herself up a little," when a rustling movement at the
door attracted her attention, and she turned to find Magdalen
standing there, her dark eyes bright as diamonds, her cheeks
flushed and burning with excitement, her lips apart and her
hands clasped together, as she bent slightly forward across the
kitchen threshold. With a scream, Hester bounded toward
her, and dragging her into the room, exclaimed, "Magdalen,
Magdalen, I knew it, I knew it. I said something was going
to happen when the rooster crowed so this morning, — somebody going to come; but I did not dream of you, Magdalen,
oh! Magdalen." She kept repeating the name, and with her
hard, rough hands held and rubbed the soft white fingers she
had clasped; then, as the joy kept growing, she sobbed aloud
and broke down entirely.

"Oh! Magdalen," she said, "I am so glad for *him*. He has
wanted you and missed you all the time, though he never
mentioned your name."

Something in the face or manner of the younger woman
must have communicated itself to the mind of the elder, for
Magdalen had given no reason for her sudden appearance at
Schodick, or sign of what she meant to do. But Hester took
her coming as a good omen for Roger, and kept repeating,
"I'm so glad, so glad for Roger."

"How do you know he wants me, if, as you say, he never
mentions my name?" Magdalen asked, and Hester replied,
"How do we know the sun shines when we can't *hear* it?

We can see and feel, can't we? And so I know you ain't long out of Roger's mind, and ain't been since we moved here, and he brung the candle-box cradle with him just because you once slept in it."

"Did Roger do that? Did he bring my cradle from Mill bank? Why didn't you tell me before?" Magdalen asked, her eyes shining with tears of joy at this proof of Roger's love.

"I thought I did write it to you," Hester replied; "I meant to, but might of forgot but he brought it by express; and it's upstairs now, and in it —"

Hester stopped abruptly, thinking it might be premature to speak of the cribby quilt, which did not now stand so good a chance of reaching the heathen as it had done one hour before.

"Where is Roger?" Magdalen asked, and Hester told her of the headache he had complained of ever since the day of the sale, adding, "He's in his room, which is fixed up as nice as anybody's; his books and pictures and a little recess for his bed, just like any gentleman."

"Does he know who bought Millbank?" Magdalen asked next, and Hester replied:

"Yes, Frank telegraphed that Mr. Seymour bought it for *you*, and Roger was as white as a ghost, and has been sick ever since. Magdalen, what did you buy Millbank for? Be you goin' to git married?"

Hester asked this question a little anxiously, and Magdalen's eyes fairly danced as she replied, "I think so, Hester, but I'm not quite certain. I did not buy Millbank for myself, though, I bought it for Roger, and—"

Hester's hand deepened its grasp on Magdalen's, and Hester's face was almost as white as her cap border, as she bent forward to listen, saying eagerly, "and what, Magdalen? You bought it for Roger and what?"

"And have given it to him. I was the means of his losing it. It is right that I should give it back, and I am here to do so. The deed is in my pocket, made out to him, to Roger, — see," and she held the precious document toward Hester, who was on her knees now, kissing even the dress of the young girl thus making restitution.

She could hardly believe it true, and she took the paper in her hands and pressed it to her lips, then opened it reverently, and glancing at its contents, whispered, "It is, it is. It reads like the deed of the tavern stand. It must be true. Oh, Magdalen, Roger can't live there alone. Who is to live with him?"

"You and I, Hester, if he will let us. Do you think he will?" Magdalen said, with a merry gleam in her bright eyes.

"Do I think he will? Ask him, and see what he says."

Old Hester had risen to her feet, but she still held Magdalen's hand, and leading her into the next room, pointed to the stair door, and said, "He is up there; come on if you want to see him."

At the head of the stairs Hester paused a moment to reconnoitre, — then whispered softly, "He's asleep on the lounge. Shall we go back?"

"No, leave me here with him," Magdalen replied, and nodding assent, Hester stole softly down the stairs, while Magdalen stepped carefully across the threshold of the room, and closing the door behind her stood looking upon Roger.

CHAPTER LIV.

ROGER AND MAGDALEN.

HE was sleeping quietly, and his forehead was fully exposed to view, with the brown curls clustering around it, and an occasional frown or shadow flitting across it as if the pain were felt even in his sleep. How Magdalen's fingers tingled to thread those curls, and smooth that broad, white brow; but she dared not for fear of waking him, and she held her breath and stood looking at him as he slept, feeling a keen throb of sorrow as she saw how he had changed and knew what had changed him. He was much thinner than when she saw him last, and there were lines about his mouth and a few threads of silver in his brown beard, while his eyes, as he slept, seemed hollow and sunken.

There was a stool just at her feet, and she pushed it to his side, and seating herself upon it prepared to watch and wait until his heavy slumber ended. And while she waited she looked around and noted all the marks of a refined taste which Roger had gathered about him, — the books, the pictures, the flowers and shells, and lastly, a little crayon sketch of herself, drawn evidently from memory, and representing her as she sat by the river bank years ago, when first Roger Irving felt that his interest in his beautiful ward was more than a mere liking. It was hanging close to Jessie's picture, and Magdalen sat gazing at it until she forgot where she was, and was back again beneath the old tree by the river bank, with Roger at her side. Suddenly she gave a long, deep sigh, and then Roger awoke, and met the glance of her bright eyes, and saw her face so near to him, and knew that his long night of sorrow was over, else she had never been there, kneeling by him as she was, with her hands holding his and her tears dropping so fast as she tried to speak to him.

"Magda, Magda, my darling," was all he could say as he drew her into his arms and held her there a moment in a close embrace.

Then releasing her he lay down upon his pillow, pale as death and utterly prostrated with the neuralgic pain which the sudden excitement and surprise had brought back again.

"You take my breath away; when did you come, and why?" he asked; and then releasing her hands from his, Magdalen took the deed from her pocket and changing her position held it before his eyes, saying: "*I* came to bring this, Roger; to make restitution; to give you back Millbank, which, but for me,   ·
you would not have lost. See, it is made out to you!. Mill-

bank is yours again. I bought it with my own money, — bought it for you, — I give it to you, — it is yours."

She spoke rapidly and kept reiterating that Millbank was *his*, because of the look on his face which she did not quite understand. He was too much bewildered and confounded to know what to say, and for a moment was silent, while his eyes ran rapidly over the paper, which, beyond a doubt, made him master of Millbank again.

"Why did you do this, Magda ?" he said at last, and his chin quivered a little as he said it.

Then Magdalen burst out impulsively, " Oh, Roger, don't look as if you were not glad. I've thought so much about it, and wanted to do something by way of amends. I saved all my salary, every dollar, before I knew I was Magdalen Grey, and was going to send it to you, but Guy laughed me out of it, and said you did not need it : then, when father died and I knew I was rich, my first thought was of you, and when I heard Millbank was to be sold, I said, 'I'll buy it for Roger if it takes every cent I am worth ;' and I *have* bought it, and given it to you, and you must take it and go back there and live. I shall never be happy till you do."

She stopped here, but she was kneeling still, and her tearful, flushed face was very near to Roger, who could interpret her words and manner in only one way, and that a way which made the world seem like heaven to him.

"Magda," he said, winding his arm around her and drawing her hot cheek close to his own, "let me ask one question. I can't live at Millbank alone. If I take it of you, who will live there with me ? "

Hester had asked a similar question, but Magdalen did not reply to Roger just as she had to the old lady. There was a little dash of coquetry in her manner, which would not perhaps have appeared had she been less sure of her position.

" I suppose *Hester* will live with you, of course," she said. " She does nicely for you here. She is not so very old."

There was a teasing look in Magdalen's eyes, which told Roger he had nothing to fear, and raising himself up he drew her down beside him and said: " I ask you to be candid with me, Magda. We have wasted too much time not to be in earnest now. Your coming to me as you have could only be construed in one way, were you like most girls ; but you are not. You are impulsive. You think no evil, see no evil, but do just what your generous heart prompts you to do. Now, tell me, dar-ling, was it sympathy and a desire to make restitution, as you de-signate it, or was it love which sent you here when I had ceased to hope you would ever come. Tell me, Magda, do you, can you love your old friend and guardian, who has been foolish enough to hold you in his heart all these many years, even when he believed himself indifferent to you ? "

Roger was talking in sober earnest, and his arm deepened its clasp around Magda's waist, and his lips touched the shining hair of the bowed head which drew back a moment from him, then drooped lower and lower until it rested in his bosom, as Magdalen burst into a flood of tears and sobs. For a moment she did not try to speak ; then, with a desperate effort to be calm, she lifted up her head and burst out with, " I never got your letter, never knew it was written until a few weeks ago. Father kept it. Forgive him, Roger; remember he was my father, and he is dead," she cried vehemently, as she saw the dark frown gathering on Roger's face. Yes, he was her father, and he was dead, and that kept Roger from cursing the man who had wronged him in his childhood, through his mother, and touched him still closer in his later manhood, by keeping him so long from Magdalen.

" Father told me at the last," Magdalen said. " He was sor-ry he kept it, and he bade me tell you so. He did not dislike *you*. It was the name, the association ; and he hoped I might forget you, but I didn't. I have remembered you all through the long years since that dreadful day when I found the will, and it hurt me so to think you wanted me to marry Frank. That was the hardest of all."

" But you know better now. I told you in my letter of Frank's confession," Roger said, and Magdalen replied, "Yes, I know better now. Everything is clear, else I had never come here to bring you Millbank, and — and, myself, if you will take me. Will you, Roger? It is leap year, you know. I have a right to ask."

She spoke playfully, and her eyes looked straight into his own, while for answer he took her in his arms, and kissed her forehead and lips and hair, and she felt that he was praying silently over her, thanking Heaven for this precious gift which had come to him at last. Then he spoke to her and said, " I take you, Magda, willingly, gladly; oh how gladly Heaven only knows, and as I cannot well take you without the incumbrance of Millbank, I accept that, too; and darling, though this may not be the time to say it, there has already been so much of business and money and lands mixed up with our love, that I may, I am sure, tell you I am able of myself to buy the mill in Belvidere and the site of the old shoe-shop. Frank wanted me to do it, and I put him off with saying I would wait until I knew who was to live at Millbank. I know now," and again he rained his kisses upon the face of her who was to be his wife and the undisputed mistress, as he was the master, of Millbank.

A long time they talked together of the past, which now seemed to fade away so fast in the blissful joy of the present; and Magdalen told him of little Roger Irving, whose godmother she was, and of her mother and Alice, and the home at Beechwood, where Guy Seymour's family would continue to live.

"It's the same house my father built for Jessie, — for your mother," Magdalen said, softly, and glanced up at the picture on the wall, whose blue eyes seemed to look down in blessing upon this pair to whom the world was opening so brightly.

Then they talked of Frank and Bell and Mrs. Walter Scott, and by that time the summer sun was low in the western horizon, and Hester's tea-table was spread with every delicacy the place could afford; while Hester herself was fine and grand in her second-best black silk, which nothing less than Magdalen's arrival could have induced her to wear on a week-day.

Guy, too, had made his appearance after waiting in vain foi Magdalen's return. Hester remembered him, and welcomed him warmly, and told him "the young folks was up chamber, billin' and cooin' like two turtle doves," whereupon Guy began to whistle "Highland Mary," which Magdalen heard, and start-ing up, exclaimed:

"There's Guy come for me! I must go now back to the hotel."

But she did not go, for Roger would not permit it, and he kept her there that night, and the next day took her to his favorite place of resort, — the rock under the pine, — and seat-ing her upon the mossy bank knelt beside her, and gave thanks anew to Heaven, who had heard and answered the prayer made so often under that tasselled pine, — that if it were right Magda should one day come to him as his. Then they went all over the farm and down to the mill, where some of the operatives who had lived in Belvidere and knew Magdalen came to speak with her, thus raising themselves in the estimation of the less favored ones, who gazed admiringly at the beautiful young girl, rightly guessing the relation she held to Mr. Irving, and feeling glad for him.

No repairs were needed at Millbank, and but few changes; so that the house was ready any time for its new proprietors, but Magdalen would not consent to going there as its mistress until September, for she wanted the atmosphere thoroughly cleared from the taint of Mrs. Walter Scott's presence, and it would take more than a few weeks for that. She liked Bell and she pitied Frank; but Mrs. Walter Scott was her special aversion, and so long as she remained at Millbank, Magdalen could not endure even to cross its threshold. Still it seemed necessary that she should do so before her return to Beechwood, and on the morning following the peaceful Sunday spent at Schodick she returned to Belvidere, which by this time was rife with the conjectures that Roger was coming back to Millbank and Magdalen was coming with him.

CHAPTER LV.

MILLBANK IS CLEAR OF ITS OLD TENANTS.

HAT afternoon Magdalen went with Guy over the house, where she was met by Frank, and welcomed as the new mistress. Appropriating her at once to himself, Frank led her from room to room, seeming pleased at her commendations of the taste which had been displayed in the selection of furniture and the care which had evidently been given to everything.

"It was Bell," Frank said. "She is a good housekeeper, and after the split with mother she attended to things. They had separate apartments, you know, at the last; — didn't speak a word, which I liked better than a confounded quarrel. I tell you, Magdalen, I've seen sights of trouble since you found that will, and I am happier to-day, knowing I've got out of the scrape, than I've been before in years."

He seemed disposed to be very communicative, and was going on to speak of his domestic troubles ; but Magdalen quietly checked him, and then asked where his mother was intending to go.

"The mills of the gods grind slowly, but *fine*, exceedingly fine," Frank said ; and then he told of his mother's fears for her money deposited in the bank of——. There was a rumor that the bank had failed, but as it was only a rumor he still hoped for the best.

"At the first alarm, mother went to bed," he said, "and she is there still ; so you must excuse her not seeing you."

Magdalen had no desire to see her, and when on her way to Beechwood she read in the paper of the total failure of the bank where Frank had told her his mother's money was deposited, she did not greatly sympathize with the artful, designing woman, who almost gnashed her teeth when she, too, heard of her loss. She was all ready for removal to "Rose Cottage," for which a friend was negotiating, and her trunks and boxes were packed with every conceivable valuable which could by any means be crowded into them ; oil paintings, chromos, steel engravings, costly vases, exquisite shells, knives, forks, spoons, china, cut glass, table linen, bed linen, and even carpets formed a part of her spoil, intended for that cottage, which now was not within her reach. There was still her *oil stock* left, and with that she might manage to live respectably, she thought, and resolving that no one should exult over her disappointment from any change they saw in her, she tried to appear natural, and when an attempt was made at sympathy, answered indifferently "that she was sorry, of course, as she could have done so much good with the money ; but the Lord knew what was best, and she must bear patiently what was sent upon her." This was what she said to her clergyman, who came to sympathize with her ; but when he was gone, she looked the house over again, to see if there was anything more which she could take, and in case of necessity turn into money. Some one in Belvidere wrote to Roger that the house at Millbank was being *robbed*, and advised strongly that means be taken to prevent further depredations ; and a few days after Mrs. Walter Scott was met in the hall by a stern-looking man, who said he came, at Mr. Irving's request, to take an inventory of all the articles of furniture in the house, and also to remain there and see that nothing was harmed or *removed*.

He laid great stress on the last word, and the lady grew hot and red, and felt that she was suspected and looked upon as a thief, and resented it accordingly ; but after that there was no more hiding of articles under lock and key, for the stranger always seemed to be present, and she knew that she was watched ; and when he inquired for a small and expensive oil painting which Roger had bought in Rome, and an exquisite French chromo, and certain pieces of silver and cut glass which he had on his list as forming a part of the household goods he was appointed to care for, she *found* them and gave them, one by one, into his hands. And so her stock of goods diminished and she hastened to get away before everything was taken from her; and one morning in August finally departed for a boarding-house in New York, where she intended staying until something better offered.

As soon as she was gone, a bevy of servants came out from Beechwood, and Roger came from Schodick to superintend them, and old Hester came to oversee *him*, and the renovating process went rapidly on, while crowds of the villagers flocked to the house, curious to see the costly articles of furniture which, during the last few years, had been constantly arriving, and of which the house was full to overflowing.

The mill was Roger's now, as well as the site of the old shoe-shop. He had bought them both on the day of their sale, and the operatives of the mill had hurrahed with might and main for their new master, never heeding the old one, who still remained in town, and who, whatever he might have felt, put a good face on the matter, and seemed as glad and as interested as the foremost of them. Only once did he manifest the slightest feeling, and that was when with Roger he entered Bell's sleeping-room, where the silken curtains were hanging and the many expensive articles of the toilet were still lying as Bell had left them. Then sitting down by the window, he cried; and, when Roger looked at him questioningly, he told of his little boy born in that room, and dead before it was born.

"Bell was glad, he said, — she does not like children; but I was so sorry, for if that boy had lived I should have been a better man; but it died, and Bell has left me, and mother's gone, and my money's gone, and I am a used-up dog generally," he added bitterly; and then with a sudden dashing away of his tears he brightened into his former self, and said, laughingly, "But what's the use of fretting? I shall get along some way. I always have, you know."

In his heart he knew Roger would not let him suffer, and when Roger said as much by way of comforting him, he took it as a matter of course, and secretly hoped "the governor would give him something handsome, and let him keep a horse!"

CHAPTER LVI.

THE BRIDAL.

MILLBANK was ready at last for its new mistress. But few changes had been made, and these in the library and the suite of rooms set apart for the bride. Her tastes were simpler than Bell's, and some of the gorgeous trappings had been removed and soberer ones put in their place. The house at Schodick had been despoiled of a portion of its furniture, which now formed a part of Millbank; Jessie's picture and the candle-box cradle were both brought back, and Hester had the little quilt safe in her trunk, and had bought a new gray satin dress for the wedding party to be given at Millbank, September 15th, the day after the bridal. The idea of gray satin Hester had gotten from Mrs. Penelope Seymour, who came to Millbank to see that everything was as it should be for the reception of her niece. She had stayed three days and nights, and Hester had admired her greatly and copied her dress, and had it made in Springfield, and fitted over hoops and cotton, and then tried to fix up Aleck into something a little more modern. But Aleck was incorrigible, and would wear his short pants and cowhide shoes tied with leather strings, and so she gave him up, and comforted herself with the fact that he stayed mostly in his room, and would not run much risk of being laughed at by the "grandees" expected with the bridal party from New York.

Roger had already gone to Beechwood, where Magdalen was waiting for him. It was his first visit there, and there were

strange thoughts crowding upon his mind as he rode up
the mountain side toward the house which had been built
for his mother, and whither she once hoped to come as a
bride. Now she was dead, her grave the ocean bed, her shroud
the ocean grass, and he, her son, was going for his bride, the
daughter of Arthur Grey. "Surely the ways of Providence are
inscrutable ; who can know them?" he said, just as a turn in
the road brought the house and grounds fully into view, together
with Magdalen, who, in her evening dress of white, was standing
on the piazza, her face glowing with health and beauty and
eager expectation. Very joyfully she received him, and leading
him into the house presented him to Alice and her aunt, and
then went for her little nephew, whom she brought to his
"Uncle Roger."

They were a very merry party at Beechwood that night, and
not a shadow rested on the hearts of any one. It was better
that Laura should be gone, better for her, better for them all ;
and when Magdalen saw how white Roger turned at the sight
of her father's picture, she felt that it was well perhaps that he,
too, was dead, for the two men could not have been wholly congenial to each other. The bridal was the next day but one, and
Magdalen in her plain travelling dress was very beautiful, as
she pledged herself to the man whose face wore a look of perfect peace and thankfulness as he clasped her hand and knew
it was his forever. He made no demonstrations before the
people, but when for a moment they were alone, as she went
up for her hat and shawl, he opened his arms to her, and clasping her tightly to his bosom, showered his kisses upon her face
and hands and hair, and called her his precious wife, his
darling, won at last after many years of sorrow.

They went to New York that night, and the next day arrived
at Millbank, with Mrs. Seymour, Guy, and Alice, and a few
friends, the Dagons and Draggons, whose quiet, unostentatious
elegance of manner created quite as great a sensation as Mrs
Walter Scott's more showy guests had done when her son was

the groom and Bell Burleigh the bride. Roger had given his
men a holiday, and had ordered a dinner for them upon the
Millbank grounds, but he had not hinted at a demonstration
or bonfire, and was surprised when the New York train came
round the bend in the meadow to see the crowds and crowds
of people assembled before the depot, some on the fence, some
on the woodpile, some on the platform, and all glad and excited
and eager to see him. The Belvidere Band was there also, and
preceded the carriage up to the house, which had never seemed
so pleasant and desirable to Roger as now, when he came back
to it with Magdalen, and felt that both were his beyond a possibility of doubt. Old Hester received them, and no one but
herself was allowed to remove the bride's wrappings, or conduct
her to her room. Hester was in her element, and Mrs. Walter
Scott never bore herself more proudly than did the old lady on
that eventful day, when she seemed suddenly to have grown
young again, and to be in every place at once, her cap-strings
flying behind her, and her black silk pinned about her waist.
The gray was reserved for the evening, when, instead of a
party proper, to which a few were bidden, a general reception
was held, which all were welcome to attend. There was a great
crowd, for rich and poor, old and young, plebeian and aristocrat,
came to pay their respects to the newly married pair; but not
a rude thing was done, or a rough word spoken by any one.
Roger, himself, did not know them all, and Magdalen only a
few; but her greeting was just as cordial to one as to another.
Her travelling-dress had been very plain, but this evening she
was radiant in white satin and lace and pearls, with the bridal
veil floating back from her head, and the orange wreath crown-
ing her shining hair; and those who had never seen such dress
and style before held their breath in wonder, and for months
after talked with pride of the night when all the town was permitted to see and shake hands with the sweet lady of Millbank,
Mrs. Roger Irving. Roger had forbidden a bonfire, but there
were lanterns hung in the trees all over the grounds, and the

17*

young people danced there upon the floor which had been tem-
porarily laid down, until midnight was passed, and the moon was
so high in the horizon that the glare of lamps was no longer
needed to light up the festal scene.

Mrs. Franklin Irving had been invited to be present, but
she wisely declined, and sent instead a most exquisite ring to
Magdalen, who let Frank put it upon her finger and kiss her hand
as he did so, a privilege he claimed because the ring was said
to be *his* gift and Bell's. His wife had conceded so much to him,
though Frank had known nothing of the ring until he saw it in its
velvet box on his wife's bureau. Unlike her, he had no feelings
of delicacy to prevent his being present at Roger's bridal party.
With no business on his hands, and nothing to expect from his
wife besides his board, he was quite as willing to stay at Millbank as in Boston, and seemed to take it for granted that he
was welcome there. And nobody cared much about his movements except Hester, who wondered " Why the lazy lout didn't
go to work and earn his own vittles, instead of hangin' on to
Roger. She vummed if she'd stan' it much longer. She'd set
him to work if Roger didn't."

And so as time went on and Frank still lingered about the
place, Hester gradually impressed him into her service, and
made him do some of the things which Aleck once had done
and which he was unable to do now. Sometimes he brought
water for her, or split her kindlings, or went to the village on
an errand, and did it willingly, too, though he always wore his
gloves, and generally carried his cane and eye-glass, which last
article he had of late adopted. It was Magdalen who finally
interfered and stood between Hester and Frank, and said he
was welcome to remain at Millbank as long as he chose, and
that if Hester had not servants enough another should be pro-
cured at once. This was the first and only time that Magdalen
asserted her right as mistress in opposition to old Hester, who
submitted without a word and ever after left Frank in peace.

September passed quickly, and in the late October days,
when the New England woods were gorgeous with crimson

and gold, and Millbank was still beautiful with its autumn flowers, Mrs. Franklin Irving came up to visit Mr. and Mrs. Roger, and was received by them with all the cordiality due so near a relative. Not by a word or look did she betray the slightest regret for the past, when she had been mistress where she was now only a guest. Millbank was to her as any stranger's house, and she bore herself naturally and pleasantly, and made herself very agreeable to Roger, and devoted herself to Magdalen, whom she liked so much, and was civil and almost kind to her husband, who was still there, and as Hester said, "just as shiftless as ever."

Bell saw the state of affairs, and while she despised her husband more than ever for his indolence and lack of sensibility, she resolved to give Magdalen a rest, and leave her alone with Roger for a time; so when in November she returned to Boston, she invited Frank to go with her, and secured him a place as book-keeper in a merchant's counting-house, and stimulated perhaps by the perfect happiness and confidence she had seen existing between Roger and Magdalen, tried by being kind and even deferential to him to mould him into something of which she would not be so terribly ashamed as she was now of the careless, shambling, listless, lazy man, whom everybody knew as Mrs. Franklin Irving's husband.

CHAPTER LVII.

CHRISTMAS-TIDE.

IT was the second Christmas after Magdalen's bridal, and fires were kindled in all the rooms at Millbank, and pantries and closets groaned with their loads and loads of eatables; and Hester Floyd bustled about, important as ever, ordering everybody except the nurse who had come with Mrs. Guy Seymour and her baby, the little four-months-old girl, whose name was Laura Magdalen, and who, with her warm milk and cold milk, and numerous paraphernalia of baby-hood, kept the kitchen a good deal stirred up, and made Hester chafe a little inwardly. But, then, she said " she s'posed she must get used to these things," and her face cleared up, and her manner was very soft and gentle every time she thought of the crib in Magdalen's room, where, under the identical quilt the poor heathen would never receive, slumbered another baby girl, Magdalen's and Roger's, which had come to Millbank about six weeks before, and over whose birth great rejoicings were made. *Jessie Morton* was its name, and Guy and Alice had stood for it the Sunday before, and with Aunt Pen were to remain at Millbank through the holidays, and help Magdalen to entertain the few friends invited to pass the week under Roger's hospitable roof.

The world had gone well with Roger since he came back to Millbank. Everything had prospered with which he had any-thing to do. The shoe-shop had been rebuilt, and the mill was never more prosperous, and Roger bade fair soon to be as rich a man as he had supposed himself to be before the will was found. On his domestic horizon no cloud, however small, had ever rested. Magdalen was his all-in-all, his choicest treasure, for which he daily thanked Heaven more fervently than for all his other blessings combined. And, amid his prosperity, Roger did not forget to render back to Heaven a generous portion of his gifts, and many and many a sad heart was made glad, and many a poor church and clergyman were helped, quietly, unos-tentatiously, and oftentimes so secretly that they knew not whence came the aid, but for which they might have given up in utter despair and hopelessness.

Magdalen approved and assisted in all her husband's char-ities, and her heart went out after the sad, sorrowful ones, with a yearning desire to make them as happy as herself. Especially was this the case that Christmas time, when to all her other blessings a baby had been added, and she made it a season for extra gifts to the poor and needy who, through all the long winter, would be more comfortable because of her generous remembrance.

When the list of guests to be invited for the holidays was being made out, she sat for a moment by Roger's side, with her eyes fixed musingly on the bright fire in the grate. Mr. and Mrs. Franklin Irving's names were on the list, with that of Grace and the young clergyman to whom she was engaged, and Roger waited for Magdalen to say if there was any one else whom she would have.

"Yes, Roger, there is. Perhaps you won't approve, but I should like to ask Mrs. Walter Scott, if you don't object too much. She has a dreary time at best, and this will be a change. She may not come, it's true; but she will be pleased to know we remember her."

Roger had entertained the same thought, but refrained from giving expression to it from a fear lest Magdalen would not like it, and so that day a cordial invitation to pass the holidays at Millbank was forwarded to the boarding-house in New York which Mrs. Walter Scott was actually keeping as a means of support. Her *oil* had *failed*, as well as the bank which held her money. "There might be something for her some time, perhaps, but there was nothing now," was the report of the lawyer employed to investigate the matter, and then she began to realize how utterly destitute she was. Frank could not help her, and as she was too proud to ask help of Roger, she finally did what so many poor, discouraged women do, opened a boarding-house in a part of the city where she would not be likely to meet any of her former friends, and there, in dull, dingy rooms, with forlorn, half-worn furniture and faded drapery, all relics like herself of former splendors, she tried to earn her living. The goods which she managed to smuggle away from Millbank served her a good turn now, and pawnbrokers and buyers of old silver and pictures soon made the acquaintance of the tall lady with light hair and traces of great beauty, who came so often to their shops, and seemed so sad and desolate. Roger and Magdalen had been to see her once, and Frank had been many times ; but Bell never deigned to notice her, though she was frequently in New York, and once drove past the boarding-house in a stylish carriage with her velvets and ermine around her. Mrs. Walter Scott did not see her, and so that pang was spared her. She had finished her *book*, but the publishers one and all showed a strange obtuseness with regard to its worth, and it was put away in her trunk, where others thing pertaining to the past were buried.

The invitation from Millbank took her by surprise and made her cry a little, but she hastened to accept it, and was there before her daughter-in-law, and an occupant of her former room. She was old and broken, and faded, and poor, and seemed very quiet, and very fond of Magdalen's baby, which she kept a great deal in her room, calling herself its grandma, and thinking, perhaps, of another little one whose loss no one had regretted save Frank, the father. He came at last with Bell, who was very polite and gracious to her mother-in-law, whom she had not expected to meet.

"Of course I am sorry for her," she said to Magdalen, who was one day talking of her, and wishing something might be done to better her condition. "But what can I do. She refuses to receive *money* from me, and as for having her in my house no power on earth could induce me to do that."

Alas ! for Bell. Man proposes, but God disposes, and the thing which no power on earth could induce her to do was to be forced upon her whether she would have it or not.

The Christmas dinner was a sumptuous one, and after it was over the guests repaired to the parlors, where music and a little dance formed a part of the evening's entertainment. Mrs. Walter Scott was playing for the dance. Her fingers had not yet forgotten their skill, and she had good-naturedly offered to take the place of Grace Burleigh, who gave up the more willingly because of the young clergyman looking over a book of engravings and casting wistful glances toward her. Whether it was the dinner, or the excitement, or a combination of both, none could tell, but there was suddenly a cessation of the music, a crash among the keys, and Mrs. Walter Scott turned toward the astonished dancers a face which frightened them, it was so white, so strange, and so distorted. Paralysis of one entire side was the verdict of the physician who was summoned immediately and did all he could for the stricken woman, from one-half of whose body the sense of feeling was gone, and who lay in her room as helpless as a child. Gradually her face began to look more natural, her speech came back again, thick and stammering, but tolerably intelligible, and her limp right hand moved feebly, showing that she was in part recovering. For three weeks they nursed her with the utmost care, and Bell stayed by and shrank from the future which she saw before her, and from which she wished so much to escape. In her womanly pity and sympathy Magdalen would have kept the paralytic woman at Millbank, but Roger was not willing that her young life should be burdened in this way, and he said to Frank and Bell:

"Your mother's place is with her children. If you are not able to take care of her, I am willing to help; but I cannot suffer Magdalen to take that load of care."

So it was settled, and Bell went home to Boston and prepared an upper room, which overlooked the Common, and then came back to Millbank, where they made the invalid ready for the journey. Her face was very white and there was a look of dreary despair and dread in her eyes, but she uttered no word of protest against the plan, and thanked Roger for his kindness, and kissed the little Jessie and cried softly over her, and whispered to Magdalen: "Come and see me often. It is the only pleasant thing I can look forward too."

And then Frank and Roger carried her out to the carriage which took her to the cars, and that night she heard the winter wind howl around the windows of the room to which she felt that she was doomed for life, and which, taking that view of it seemed to her like a prison.

"The Lord is sure to remember first or last," old Hester said, as she watched the carriage moving slowly down the avenue, "and though I can't say I would have given her the shakin' palsy if I'd of been the Lord, I know it's right and just, and a warnin' to all liars and deceitful, snoopin' critters."

Still Hester was sorry for the woman, and went to see her almost as often as Magdalen herself, and once stayed three whole weeks, and took care of her when Mrs. Franklin was away. Bell did not trouble herself very much about her mother-in-law, or spend much time with her. She gave orders that she should be well cared for and have everything she wished for, and she saw that her orders were obeyed. She also went once a day to see her and ask if she was comfortable; but after that she felt that nothing further was incumbent upon her. And so for all Mrs. Walter Scott knew of the outer world and the life she had once enjoyed so much, she was indebted to Grace, who before her marriage passed many hours with the invalid, telling her of things which she thought would interest her, and sometimes reading to her until she fell asleep. But after Grace was gone Mrs. Walter Scott's days passed in dreary loneliness and wretched discontent. She had no pleasure in recalling the past, and nothing to look forward to in the future. The remainder of her wretched life she knew must be passed where she was not wanted, and where her son came but once a day to see her and that in the evening just after dinner, when he usually fell asleep while she was trying to talk to him.

Bell would *not* suffer Frank to go into the city evenings unless she accompanied him, for she had no fancy for having him brought to her in a state of intoxication, as was once the case. And Frank, who was a good deal afraid of her, remained obediently at home, and, preferring his mother's society to that of his wife, stayed in the sick room a portion of every evening; then, when wholly wearied there, went to his own apartment and smoked in dreary solitude until midnight.

Such was Frank's life and such the life of his mother, until there came to her a change in the form of a second shock, which rendered one hand and foot entirely helpless, and distorted her features so badly that she insisted that the blinds should be kept closed and the curtains down, so that those who came into her room could not see how disfigured she was. And so in darkness and solitude her days pass drearily, with impatient longings for the night, and when the night comes she moans and weeps, and wishes it was morning. Poor woman! She is a burden to herself and a terrible skeleton to her fashionable daughter-in-law, who in the gayest scenes in which she mingles never long forgets the paralytic at home, sinking so fast into utter imbecility, and as she becomes more and more childish and helpless, requiring more and more care and attention.

The curse of wrong-doing is resting on Bell as well as on her husband and his mother, and though she is proud and haughty and reserved as ever, she is far from being happy, and her friends say to each other that she is growing old and losing her brilliant beauty. Frank often tells her of it when he has been drinking wine. He is not afraid of her then, and after he found that it annoyed her he delighted to tease her about her fading beauty, and to ask why she could not keep as young and fresh and handsome as Magdalen. There was not a wrinkle in her face, he said, and she looked younger and handsomer than when he first came home from Europe and saw her at the Exhibition.

And well might Magdalen retain her girlish beauty, for if ever the fountain of youth existed anywhere it was in her home at Millbank. Exceedingly popular with the villagers, idolized by her husband, perfectly happy in her baby, surrounded by every luxury which wealth can furnish and every care lifted from her by old Hester's thoughtfulness, there has as yet been no shadow, however small, upon her married life, and her face is as fair and beautiful, and her voice as full of glee as when she sat with Roger by the river side and felt the first awakenings of the love which has since grown to be her life.

And now we say farewell to Millbank, knowing that when sorrow comes to its inmates, as it must some day come, it will not be such a sorrow as enshrouds that gloomy house in Boston, for there is perfect love and faith between the husband and the wife, with no sad, dreary retrospects of wrong to make the present unendurable.

NEW BOOKS

Recently Published by

G. W. CARLETON & CO., New York,

Madison Square, Fifth Avenue and Broadway.

Marion Harland.

ALONE.—	A novel.	12mo. cloth,	$1 50
HIDDEN PATH.—.	do.	do.	$1 50
MOSS SIDE.—	do.	do.	$1 50
NEMESIS.—	do.	do.	$1 50
MIRIAM.—	do.	do.	$1 50
AT LAST.—	do. *Just Published.*	do.	$1.50
HELEN GARDNER.—	do.	do.	$1.50
SUNNYBANK.—	do.	do.	$1.50
HUSBANDS AND HOMES.—	do.	do.	$1.50
RUBY'S HUSBAND.—	do.	do.	$1 50
PHEMIE'S TEMPTATION.—	do.	do.	$1 50
THE EMPTY HEART.—	do.	do.	$1 50
TRUE AS STEEL.—	do. *Just Published.*	do.	$1 50

Miss Muloch.

JOHN HALIFAX.—A novel. With illustration. 12mo. cloth, $1 75
A LIFE FOR A LIFE.— . . do. . do. $1 75

Charlotte Bronte (Currer Bell).

JANE EYRE.—A novel. With illustration. 12mo. cloth, $1.75
THE PROFESSOR.—do. . do. . do. $1.75
SHIRLEY.— . do. . do. . do. $1.75
VILLETTE.— . do. . do. . do. $1.75

Hand-Books of Society.

THE HABITS OF GOOD SOCIETY; nice points of taste, good manners, and the art of making oneself agreeable. 12mo. $1.75
THE ART OF CONVERSATION.—A sensible work, for every one who wishes to be an agreeable talker or listener. 12mo. $1.50
ARTS OF WRITING, READING, AND SPEAKING.—An excellent book for self-instruction and improvement. 12mo. clo., $1.50
A NEW DIAMOND EDITION of the above three popular books.—
Small size, elegantly bound, and put in a box. - $3.00

Mrs. A. P. Hill.

MRS. HILL'S NEW COOKERY BOOK, and receipts. 12mo. cloth, $2.00

Mary J. Holmes.

LENA RIVERS.— . . .	A novel. 12mo. cloth,	$1 5c
DARKNESS AND DAYLIGHT.— .	do. . do. .	$1.50
TEMPEST AND SUNSHINE.— .	do. . do. .	$1 50
MARIAN GREY.— . . .	do. . do.	$1 50
MEADOW BROOK. — . .	do. . do.	$1 50
ENGLISH ORPHANS.— .	do. . do.	$1 50
DORA DEANE.— . .	do. . do.	$1 50
COUSIN MAUDE.— . .	do. . do .	$1.50
HOMESTEAD ON THE HILLSIDE.—	do. . do.	$1 5c
HUGH WORTHINGTON. — .	do. . do. .	$1.50
THE CAMERON PRIDE.— . .	do. . do.	$1.50
ROSE MATHER.— . . .	do. . do.	$1 50
ETHELYN'S MISTAKE.— . .	do. . do. .	$1.50
MILLBANK.— . . .	do. . do. .	$1.50
EDNA BROWNING.— .	*Just Published.* do. .	$1.50

Augusta J. Evans.

BEULAH.—	A novel. 12mo. cloth,	$1.75
MACARIA.—	do. . do. .	$1.75
ST. ELMO.—	do. . do. .	$2.00
VASHTI.— *Just Published.*	do. . do. .	$2.00
INEZ.—	do. . do. .	$1.75

Louisa M. Alcott.

MORNING GLORIES.—By the Author of "Little Women," etc. **$1.5**

The Crusoe Library.

ROBINSON CRUSOE.—A handsome illus. edition.	12mo.	$1.5c
SWISS FAMILY ROBINSON.— do. . . .	do.	$1.50
THE ARABIAN NIGHTS.— do. . . .	do.	$1.50

Captain Mayne Reid.—Illustrated.

THE SCALP HUNTERS.—	⎫	12mo. clo.,	$1.50
THE WAR TRAIL.— .	⎬ Far West Series	do.	$1.50
THE HUNTER'S FEAST.— .		do.	$1.50
THE TIGER HUNTER.— .	⎭	do.	$1.50
OSCEOLA, THE SEMINOLE.—	⎫	do.	$1.50
THE QUADROON.— .	⎬ Prairie Series	do.	$1.50
RANGERS AND REGULATORS.—		do.	$1.50
THE WHITE GAUNTLET.—	⎭	do.	$1.50
WILD LIFE.— . .	⎫	do.	$1.50
THE HEADLESS HORSEMAN.—	⎬ Pioneer Series	do.	$1.50
LOST LENORE.— . .		do.	$1.50
THE WOOD RANGERS.— .	⎭	do.	$1.50
THE WHITE CHIEF.—	⎫	do.	$1.50
THE WILD HUNTRESS.— .	⎬ Wild Forest Series	do.	$1.50
THE MAROON.— . .		do.	$1.50
THE RIFLE RANGERS.— .	⎭	do.	$1.5e

Comic Books—Illustrated.

ARTEMUS WARD, His Book.—Letters, etc.		12mo. cl.,	$1.50
DO.	His Travels—Mormons, etc.	do.	$1.50
DO.	In London.—Punch Letters.	do.	$1.50
DO.	His Panorama and Lecture.	do.	$1.50
DO.	Sandwiches for Railroad. . .		.25
JOSH BILLINGS ON ICE, and other things.—		do.	$1.50
DO.	His Book of Proverbs, etc.	do.	$1.50
DO.	Farmer's Allmanax. .	.	.25
FANNY FERN.—Folly as it Flies. . . .		do.	$1.50
DO.	Gingersnaps . . .	do.	$1.50
VERDANT GREEN.—A racy English college story.		do.	$1.30
MILES O'REILLY.—His Book of Adventures.		do.	$1.50
ORPHEUS C. KERR.—Kerr Papers, 4 vols. in one.		do.	$2.00
DO.	Avery Glibun. A novel. .	. .	$2.00
DO.	The Cloven Foot. do.	do.	$1.50
BALLAD OF LORD BATEMAN.—Illustrated by Cruikshank.			.25

A. S. Roe's Works.

A LONG LOOK AHEAD.—	A novel. .	12mo. cloth,	$1.50
TO LOVE AND TO BE LOVED.—	do. . .	do.	$1.50
TIME AND TIDE.—	do. . .	do.	$1.50
I'VE BEEN THINKING.—	do. . .	do.	$1.50
THE STAR AND THE CLOUD.—	do. . .	do.	$1.50
TRUE TO THE LAST.—	do. . .	do.	$1.50
HOW COULD HE HELP IT?—	do. . .	do.	$1.50
LIKE AND UNLIKE.—	do. . .	do.	$1.50
LOOKING AROUND.—	do. . .	do.	$1.50
WOMAN OUR ANGEL.—	do. . .	do.	$1.50
THE CLOUD ON THE HEART.—	do. . .	do.	$1.50
RESOLUTION.—	*Just Published.*	do.	$1.50

Joseph Rodman Drake.

THE CULPRIT FAY.—A faery poem, with 100 illustrations.		$2.00
DO.	Superbly bound in turkey morocco	$5.00

"Brick" Pomeroy.

SENSE.—An illustrated vol. of fireside musings.		12mo. cl.	$1.50
NONSENSE.— do. do. comic sketches.		do.	$1.50
OUR SATURDAY NIGHTS. do. pathos and sentiment.			$1.50
BRICK DUST.—Comic sketches		.	$1.50
GOLD DUST.—Fireside musings.		.	$1.50

John Esten Cooke.

FAIRFAX.— A brilliant new novel. .		12mo. cloth.	$1.50
HILT TO HILT.—	do. . . .	do.	$1.50
HAMMER AND RAPIER.—	do. . . .	do.	$1.50
OUT OF THE FOAM.—	do. *Just published.*	do.	$1.50

Victor Hugo.

LES MISERABLES.—The celebrated novel, 8vo. cloth. $2.50
  "   Two vol. edition, fine paper, do. - 5.00
  "   In the Spanish language, do. - 5.00

Algernon Charles Swinburne.

LAUS VENERIS, AND OTHER POEMS.—Elegant new ed. - $1.50
FRENCH LOVE-SONGS.—By the best French Authors. - 1.50

Author "New Gospel of Peace."

THE CHRONICLES OF GOTHAM.—A rich modern satire. - $ .25
THE FALL OF MAN.—A satire on the Darwin Theory. - .50

Julie P. Smith.

WIDOW GOLDSMITH'S DAUGHTER.—A novel. 12mo. cloth. $1.75
CHRIS AND OTHO.—   do. do. - 1.75
THE WIDOWER.—   do. do. - 1.75
THE MARRIED BELLE.—   do. (in press). - 1.75

Mansfield T. Walworth.

WARWICK.—A new novel. - - - 12mo. cloth. $1.75
LULU.— do. - - - do. - 1.75
HOTSPUR.— do. - - - do. - 1 75
STORMCLIFF.— do. - - - do. - 1.75
DELAPLAINE.— do. - - - do. - 1.75
BEVERLY.— do. *Just Published.* do. - 1.75

Richard B. Kimball.

WAS HE SUCCESSFUL?— A novel. - 12mo. cloth. $1 75
UNDERCURRENTS.— do. - do. - 1.75
SAINT LEGER.—   do. - do. - 1.75
ROMANCE OF STUDENT LIFE. do. - do. - 1 75
IN THE TROPICS.— do. - do. - 1.75
HENRY POWERS, Banker.— do. - do. - 1.75
TO-DAY.—   do. - do. - 1.75

M. Michelet's Remarkable Works.

LOVE (L'AMOUR).—Translated from the French. 12mo. cl. $1.50
WOMAN (LA FEMME).— do. - do. - 1.50

Ernest Renan.

THE LIFE OF JESUS.—Trans'ted from the French. 12mo. cl. $1.75
LIVES OF THE APOSTLES.— do. do. - 1.75
THE LIFE OF SAINT PAUL— do. do. - 1.75
THE BIBLE IN INDIA— do. of Jaccoliot. 2.00

Popular Italian Novels.

DOCTOR ANTONIO.—A love story. By Ruffini. 12mo. cl $1.75
BEATRICE CENCI.—By Guerrazzi, with Portrait. do. - 1.75

Geo. W. Carleton.

OUR ARTIST IN CUBA.—With 50 comic illustrations. - $1 50
OUR ARTIST IN PERU.— do. do. - 1 50
OUR ARTIST IN AFRICA.—(In press). do. - 1 50

Miscellaneous Works.

THE DEBATABLE LAND.—By Robert Dale Owen. 12mo.	$2.00
RUTLEDGE.—A novel of remarkable interest and power.	1.50
THE SUTHERLANDS.— do. Author of Rutledge.	1.50
FRANK WARRINGTON.— do. do.	1.50
SAINT PHILIP'S.- do do.	1.50
LOUIE.— do. do.	1.50
FERNANDO DE LEMOS.—A novel. By Charles Gayaree. -	2.00
MAURICE.—A novel from the French of F. Bechard. -	1.50
MOTHER GOOSE.—Set to music, and with illustrations. -	2.00
BRAZEN GATES.—A new child's book, illustrated. -	1.50
THE ART OF AMUSING.—Book of home amusements. - ·	1.50
STOLEN WATERS.—A fascinating novel. Celia Gardner.	1.50
HEART HUNGRY.—A novel. By Maria J. Westmoreland.	1.75
THE SEVENTH VIAL.—A new work. Dr. John Cumming.	2.00
THE GREAT TRIBULATION.—new ed. do.	2.00
THE GREAT PREPARATION.— do. do.	2.00
THE GREAT CONSUMMATION.—do. do.	2.00
THE LAST WARNING CRY.— do. do.	1.50
ANTIDOTE TO "THE GATES AJAR."— - - -	25
HOUSES NOT MADE WITH HANDS.—Hoppin's Illus. -	1.00
BEAUTY IS POWER.—An admirable book for ladies. -	1.50
ITALIAN LIFE AND LEGENDS.—By Anna Cora Ritchie. -	1.50
LIFE AND DEATH.—A new American novel. - -	1.50
HOW TO MAKE MONEY; AND HOW TO KEEP IT.—Davies.	1.50
THE CLOISTER AND THE HEARTH.—By Charles Reade.	1.50
TALES FROM THE OPERAS.—The Plots of all the Operas.	1.50
ADVENTURES OF A HONEYMOON.—A love-story.	1.50
AMONG THE PINES.—Down South. By Edmund Kirke.	1.50
MY SOUTHERN FRIENDS.— do. do. -	1.50
DOWN IN TENNESSEE.— do. do. -	1.50
ADRIFT IN DIXIE.— do. do. -	1.50
AMONG THE GUERILLAS.— do. do. -	1.50
A BOOK ABOUT LAWYERS.—Bright and interesting. -	2.00
A BOOK ABOUT DOCTORS.— do. do. - -	2.00
WOMAN, LOVE, AND MARRIAGE.—By Fred. Saunders. -	1.50
PRISON LIFE OF JEFFERSON DAVIS.—By J. J. Craven.	1.50
POEMS, BY L. G. THOMAS.— - - - -	1.50
PASTIMES WITH MY LITTLE FRIENDS.—Mrs. Bennett. -	1.50
THE SQUIBOB PAPERS.—A comic book. John Phoenix. -	1.50
COUSIN PAUL.—A new American novel. - -	1.75
JARGAL.—A novel from the French of Victor Hugo. -	1.75
CLAUDE GUEUX.— do. do. do. -	1.50
LIFE OF VICTOR HUGO.— do do. -	2.00
CHRISTMAS HOLLY.—By Marion Harland, Illustrated. -	1.50
THE RUSSIAN BALL.—An illustrated satirical Poem. -	.25
THE SNOBLACE BALL.— do. do. -	.25
THE PRINCE OF KASHNA.—Edited by R. B. Kimball. -	1.75

Miscellaneous Works.

A LOST LIFE.—A novel by Emily H. Moore	$1.50
CROWN JEWELS.— do. Mrs. Emma L. Moffett.	$1.75
ADRIFT WITH A VENGEANCE.— Kinahan Cornwallis. .	$1.50
THE FRANCO-PRUSSIAN WAR IN 1870.—By M. D. Landon.	$2.00
DREAM MUSIC.—Poems by Frederic Rowland Marvin. .	$1.50
RAMBLES IN CUBA.—By an American Lady. . .	$1.50
BEHIND THE SCENES, in the White House.—Keckley. .	$2.00
YACHTMAN'S PRIMER.—For Amateur Sailors.—Warren.	50
RURAL ARCHITECTURE.—By M. Field. With illustrations.	$2.00
TREATISE ON DEAFNESS.—By Dr. E. B. Lighthill. .	$1.50
WOMEN AND THEATRES.—A new book, by Olive Logan.	$1.50
WARWICK.—A new novel by Mansfield Tracy Walworth.	$1.75
SIBYL HUNTINGTON.—A novel by Mrs. J. C. R. Dorr. .	$1.75
LIVING WRITERS OF THE SOUTH.—By Prof. Davidson. .	$2.00
STRANGE VISITORS.—A book from the Spirit World. .	$1.50
UP BROADWAY, and its Sequel.—A story by Eleanor Kirk.	$1.50
MILITARY RECORD, of Appointments in the U. S. Army.	$5.00
HONOR BRIGHT.—A new American novel. . . .	$1.50
MALBROOK.— do. do. do. . . .	$1.50
GUILTY OR NOT GUILTY.— do. do. . .	$1.75
ROBERT GREATHOUSE.—A new novel by John F. Swift .	$2.00
THE GOLDEN CROSS, and poems by Irving Van Wart, jr.	$1.50
ATHALIAH.—A new novel by Joseph H. Greene, jr. .	$1.75
REGINA, and other poems.—By Eliza Cruger. .	$1.50
THE WICKEDEST WOMAN IN NEW YORK.—By C. H. Webb.	50
MONTALBAN.—A new American novel. . .	$1.75
MADEMOISELLE MERQUEM.—A novel by George Sand. .	$1.75
THE IMPENDING CRISIS OF THE SOUTH.—By H. R. Helper.	$2.00
NOJOQUE—A Question for a Continent.— do. .	$2.00
PARIS IN 1867.—By Henry Morford. . . .	$1.75
THE BISHOP'S SON.—A novel by Alice Cary. .	$1.75
CRUISE OF THE ALABAMA AND SUMTER.—By Capt. Semmes.	$1.50
HELEN COURTENAY.—A novel, author. "Vernon Grove."	$1.75
SOUVENIRS OF TRAVEL.—By Madame Octavia W. LeVert.	$2.00
VANQUISHED.—A novel by Agnes Leonard. . ' .	$1.75
WILL-O'-THE-WISP.—A child's book, from the German .	$1.50
FOUR OAKS.—A novel by Kamba Thorpe. . .	$1.75
THE CHRISTMAS FONT.—A child's book, by M. J. Holmes.	$1 00
POEMS, BY SARAH T. BOLTON. . . .	$1.50
MARY BRANDEGEE—A novel by Cuyler Pine. . .	$1.75
RENSHAWE.— do. do. . .	$1.75
MOUNT CALVARY.—By Matthew Hale Smith. . .	$2.00
PROMETHEUS IN ATLANTIS.—A prophecy. . .	$2 00
TITAN AGONISTES.—An American novel. . .	$2 00